VOID SHIP

DAVE BARA

ISBN:
ISBN-13: 9781976865183

AUTHOR'S INTRODUCTION

This book is literally the stuff of dreams.

I went to bed one night in 2010, the Friday before Memorial Day weekend. As I tried to drift off to sleep but being unable to, I looked up at the ceiling and asked the Universe for a new book idea. That night I had a dream that contained all the essential story elements of this novel.

The next day I feverishly wrote down every detail and idea from my dream, combined it with some character outlines I had saved for another book project, and then began writing. Six weeks later, I finished the book, as fast as I had ever written anything novel-length before by a considerable distance.

The book as it is here is very much unchanged from what I wrote back then. It stands on its own, and I love it. I hope you will too.

DB/January 2018

1. SKIMMING THE VOID

The Terran Unity cruiser *Phaeton* cut through the icy rim of the Minara star system, skimming the edges of Void Space as she sought sanctuary from her pursuers. At her present course and speed escape was probable as long as her sub-light chemical thrusters held on long enough for her to re-fire her internal EmDrive and jump back into a safe interstellar skip bubble.

Phaeton had dropped out of her bubble at Minara to harvest additional Helium-3 from the Minara star's corona for use in her environment systems, food and water synthesizers, and of course replenish her chemical thruster drives. The fact that pirates from a supposedly dead race had been lying in wait for her at Minara was immaterial. The chase was on, and for now at least, *Phaeton* had the advantage.

Captain Lara Aybar looked down at her tactical display and frowned. "Mr. Kish, why are they still gaining on us?" she called through her com. Her Chief Engineer answered in broken, but still interpretable, Standard.

"Because our thrusters are down to sixty percent efficiency, Captain," Kish said. "A result of those Gataan corvettes catching us with our pants down, sir. The thrusters are the first thing they shot at."

"Yes, with plasma grenades!" snapped the Captain. "Technology more than a hundred years out of date I might add!"

"Captain Aybar, you know as well as I do that we had the shields down to expedite the He-3 scooping process. There hasn't been a Gataan raid in this system in more than three years. The last Unity patrol certified this system as clear five weeks before we left."

"I'm not interested in your excuses, Mr. Kish. Security may be your secondary responsibility, but it's still yours. You should have scanned the system before we disengaged the shields," Aybar said.

"But Captain-"

"No more excuses, Mr. Kish! We don't have time." She glanced up at the tactical display again. The Gataan corvettes were closing for another firing pass. She looked up to the EmDrive countdown clock. Four minutes and forty-seven seconds before the engine generators could spool up the EmDrive and pull the *Phaeton* back into a safe interstellar skip bubble again. "If you can't get me five more minutes at full burn out of those thrusters, Kish, I'll have to fire you."

"I'll do what I can, Captain," said Kish.

"I trust you will. Go to it." The captain turned her attention to the cruiser's pilot, Mischa Cain. "Lieutenant Cain, on my order prepare to cut the thrusters and turn the ship to face those corvettes."

Cain turned from her station. "But Captain, you just ordered-"

"I know what I just ordered, Lieutenant. There's simply not enough time. They'll catch us again and they'll hit us and then our thrusters will be gone and maybe our EmDrive too. If that happens they'll take the ship and we'll be prisoners. I don't know about you Mischa, but I don't fancy being sold as a sex slave on Skondar or Cundaloa, do you?"

"No ma'am!" Lieutenant Cain quickly turned back to her station. "Orders, Captain?"

"Just keep flying her like we're trying to outrun them, Lieutenant, and stay as close to the Void as we dare go. I want our change of tactics to be a complete surprise."

Cain turned back from her board again. "You're trying to buy time for the Senator," she said to Aybar. "The skiff?"

Aybar nodded as she kept her eyes locked on her tactical display. "It's their only chance," she said grimly.

#

Deep inside *Phaeton's* underbelly, Tam Renwick of the planet Ceta, member of the Terran Unity Senate and Designated Negotiator of the Treaty of Pentauri with The Raelen Empire, sat in his security couch feeling helpless. Next to him, the Raelen Ambassador to Earth and the Unity government, Makera of Raellos, sat in equal frustration.

"I want to *fight*," she said, anger growing in her voice with each grenade volley that shook the Phaeton.

"I understand," said Renwick back to her. He freed an arm from the protective field enveloping him and brushed the long black hair from his face. It was a face that both human and Raelen females had found irresistibly handsome over the years, one Raelen female in particular.

"You're remarkably calm," she said to him.

"It's just part of my charm."

"Umm," she grunted the response.

The ship shook again from the impact of Gataan grenades.

"They're not in range to hit us yet," said Makera, "or they would have done so by now."

"Likely we have a few more minutes of this," agreed Renwick. "I suspect the captain will have us back in an EmDrive bubble by then, and well out of range of their crude weapons." Makera smiled.

"They were effective enough in the corona," she said.

"True," admitted Renwick, then he directed his attention to the junior negotiators in their diplomatic party, both human, and seated in a row behind the two diplomats. "Myra, Poul, how are you holding up back there?"

"We're well enough, sir," said Myra in her tiny voice, replying to Renwick. She was a small girl and her stature both in personality and persona matched her size. Myra Kilbourne was Renwick's assistant, a twenty-three year old just out of diplomatic school on her first mission. Makera had her suspicions that Myra wasn't entirely chosen for her qualifications, which were slim. This was a six month trip in close quarters on board a small ship, and although she had no proof, Makera suspected Myra was selected as Renwick's sexual liaison. This seemed like a waste to the Raelen Ambassador, given her own attraction to humans in general and Renwick in particular. Privately, Makera wondered if the girl knew anything about sex at all.

Poul Rand was Makera's human attaché, and had been for two years while she was concluding the treaty negotiations on Earth. He was gangly and too thin for her tastes, and far too low on the cultural scale for Makera to consider as a sexual companion, regardless. No, it was Renwick for her, or nothing. And so far, for two years, Renwick had resisted all of her advances. And for a Raelen woman, two years was a *very* long time.

"A shame this should happen," chimed in Rand. "In the old days, before the Void, this crossing would have taken a week. Now it's six months skimming the edges of Void Space the whole way."

"We should count ourselves lucky that there's still a channel open between our two empires," said Makera. "This treaty will be of benefit to us both, <u>if</u> we survive long enough to sign it."

"The Terran Unity is not an empire," corrected Renwick. "We have a representative Parliament and a Senate, unlike our predecessor, as you well know Ambassador."

"So you say," replied Makera. "In my opinion the Terran Unity is no different from your last empire." Before Renwick could argue the point Phaeton was rocked again, testing the protective fields keeping the four intrepid passengers secure.

"By that last blast I'd say we have less than two minutes before the Gataan raiders are in range," said Makera quietly to Renwick.

"And still at least three before Captain Aybar can re-fire the

EmDrive," Renwick whispered back. Makera nodded, almost imperceptibly.

"The Treaty documents?" she whispered to him. He patted the utility vest tucked inside his suit coat.

"Secure, for now," he replied. Then he raised his voice to the others. "Everyone just hold on tight. I'm sure Captain Aybar will be firing the EmDrive any second," he said, not believing a word of it.

#

On the bridge Captain Aybar gave her tac board one last, grim look, then made her decision.

"Mischa, prepare to cut the thrusters on my mark. We'll use the remaining momentum to turn the ship as quickly as possible. We'll have to use the forward coil cannon as soon as we have a lock. If they get off their grenades first, at this range-"

"Understood Captain," said Mischa. "You'll get your shot, I promise."

"Thank you, Lieutenant," said Aybar. She palmed the com link on her console to patch her in to the passengers in the security module.

"Senator Renwick, Ambassador Makera, can you hear me?" she asked.

"Clearly," replied Renwick for them both. Each of the dignitaries had a special implant that allowed them to receive the Captain's communiqués in complete privacy, for security reasons.

"In about thirty seconds I'm going to cut the *Phaeton's* thrusters, then turn the ship and use my only remaining weapons on those Gataan pirates," said Aybar. "After that you'll have about thirty seconds before they have time to respond and knock out my EmDrive generators completely. During that time you'll have to get to the cockpit of the skiff and activate the flight controls, then blast out of here. I'll try to provide you with enough cover to make a run for it."

There was a second of silence before Renwick responded over the line, choosing his words carefully so as not to alarm the others within hearing range. "I wasn't aware there was an escape boat aboard," he said.

"Actually, you're in it," said the captain. "See that wall in front of you? Those panels?"

"Ye-yes," said Renwick hesitantly.

"They'll peel back, revealing the cockpit, once I activate it. Like I said, you'll have about thirty seconds to fire up the skiff and clear the *Phaeton* before the next Gataan volley hits. Do you think one of you can fly the skiff?" she said.

"I can," replied Renwick.

"Good, then it's settled. I'll launch a telemetry probe with your location and direction as soon as you're clear. It may take you three months to get back to a base, but with luck there'll be another ship along well before then." She waited for a reply as the seconds passed. Finally Renwick chimed in again.

"Captain, what about the *Phaeton*?" he said.

"The security of this vessel is secondary to your mission, Senator," Aybar replied. "This treaty is vital to the continued existence of both the Unity and the Empire. We'll take our chances with the Gataan. My guess is the odds are even we'll end up stuck in this system with our pursuers, both of our interstellar drives knocked out. That will give you an opportunity to escape. I'm sure we'll be picked up by another Unity vessel inside a month. We have plenty of supplies, and there's only a crew of twenty aboard."

"But Captain," said Renwick, hesitating. "Where will *we* go?" he asked. Now Aybar hesitated as the seconds ticked by.

"You have a local jump drive. You'll be able to jump to nearby systems and continue your journey, star by star. It will be tedious, but once we're picked up we'll find you and get you on to Raellos in time for the signing," Aybar said, trying to sound optimistic.

"And if you *don't* get picked up by Unity ships?" asked Renwick. The line crackled empty for a few passing seconds.

"Fifteen seconds from my mark," Captain Aybar said. "Mark!"

Then she cut the com line.

#

"I'll grab the pilot's controls, but you'll have to fire the thrusters," said Renwick to Makera. "We have to get away as fast as we can, and we may only have one chance."

"Understood," said Makera. Renwick checked his timepiece.

Ten seconds.

"Do you think you can find the thruster controls while I fly?"

"I do have basic military training," Makera replied, as if that were an answer.

Five.

"Good," he said. Then he tensed, bracing himself for the separation and the temporary loss of inertial dampers while the skiff cleared *Phaeton's* defensive field and its own internal EV controls fired up. Renwick mulled warning the others, then decided it would probably make no material difference.

One.

The room shook violently as they were thrust away from *Phaeton's* protective energy fields by the skiff's escape rockets. Emergency lights illuminated the room a deep blue as the security panels slid away to reveal the pilot's nest. Poul and Myra let out gasps of fear and surprise as Renwick unbuckled himself from his security couch and started moving towards the cockpit. Alarm claxons blared loudly through the skiff.

"Stay in your couches!" he yelled over his shoulder to the junior diplomats as he made for the pilot's seat as fast as he could go. The skiff's emergency lights went out then and standard lighting came back on against the blackness of the room, revealing that Ambassador Makera was already in the co-pilot's seat when Renwick arrived.

"You're fast," he said as he buckled himself in. It was part statement and part compliment. Makera smiled as she searched for the thruster controls.

"You are as well, for a human," she said. Renwick ignored her and took the pilot's controls with both hands.

"Maximum fuel load please," he said.

"Hydrazine is going hot," she said, using military parlance. Makera watched as the fuel gauges filled, going from red to amber to green. "Fully loaded and ready to fire," she finally called out.

Renwick adjusted the controls, setting a course away from the *Phaeton* and the Gataan corvettes. A course, he noted, that would take them dangerously close to the Void.

"Hold on!" yelled Renwick to his tiny crew over the din of the emergency claxons. Then he punched the contact button and fired the thrusters, propelling the tiny boat away from the *Phaeton* and into the blackness of the Minara system.

#

Captain Aybar watched as the Gataan pirates closed on the *Phaeton*. There were sure to be at least twelve Gataan warriors aboard each of the corvettes, and she only had a crew of twenty aboard her cruiser, not including her four passengers that were now gone in the skiff. She didn't relish the thought of hand to hand combat with the warrior-pirates, but it beat the alternative of surrender and the slave camps.

"Stand by Mischa," she said to her pilot. "You'll have to be quicker than you've ever been."

"Understood Captain," said Cain without turning, one hand poised over the coil cannon firing controls while the other gripped the flight controls.

"Five seconds!" called the Captain, her ship shuddering again from an ever-closer grenade blast. "Three… two… one… now Mischa! Cut the impellers and turn the ship!"

The *Phaeton* groaned under the stresses of the turn, her inertial dampers strained by the disengagement of her screens as the thrusters cut out. Aybar watched helplessly as Mischa turned the ship, her tactical display showing that the closest pursuing corvette had overshot *Phaeton* as expected, but the trailing ship…

Captain Aybar was thrown free of her security couch by the direct impact of the plasma grenades. She stumbled back to her station and slammed down on the com link.

"Kish! Report!" she demanded. A few harrowing seconds passed in silence, then:

"Thrusters are gone sir, and the EmDrive is inoperable. I might be able to repair her in a few hours-"

"We don't have *hours*, Kish!" Aybar shouted.

"We've got another problem, sir. The hull is breached, down in Propulsion. The air has vented…"

"What Kish? Tell me!"

"We lost all seven down there, sir," said Kish, resigned. Aybar cut the line to her engineer and then looked down to the fallen figure of her pilot and instantly rushed to her side, getting Mischa back into her security couch. She was unconscious and bleeding from her head. Mischa was a small girl, and Aybar couldn't imagine what hell life would be for her as a Gataan plaything. She checked the controls. The coil cannon was locked and loaded but hadn't been fired. The trailing Gataan ship had anticipated her move, and been prepared with the plasma grenades. She'd been outsmarted, but she wasn't beaten yet.

Aybar slammed down the com again, angry. "Kish, gather all your crew and get to the armory. Bring everything you can carry and get down here, now!"

"Aye, Captain," said Kish, then cut the line from his end. Aybar moved Mischa to the Captain's couch and then slid into the Navigation and Control station. All she needed was one shot from the forward coil cannon, but would the Gataan give it to her?

She watched on the tactical display as the corvette swerved and dipped, keeping her wings close as she approached the wounded *Phaeton*. They were already too close. At this range using the cannon could result in an explosion that would consume them both. But that might not be a bad alternative to life on a pirate world, Aybar concluded.

The corvette loomed ever closer now, indicating that the pirates aboard suspected she couldn't fire, their previous evasive maneuvers abandoned for a more direct approach, ready to collect their booty.

"Not *my* ship," Aybar said aloud, then fixed the cannon on the corvette's impellers. She looked to the unconscious Mischa, thought about Kish and his brave crews' sacrifice, then made her decision. Phaeton was still her ship.

She locked in the coil cannon, her thumb poised over the firing control. "Good luck, Senator Renwick," she said aloud, the pressed the firing button down.

#

Outside the window of the skiff, Renwick watched in horror as the *Phaeton's* orange coil cannon energy lanced out at the closing Gataan corvette. The pirate was no match for the Unity cruiser's weapons, even crippled as she was, and it exploded in a shower of orange and blue.

"She's fired the cannon at point-blank range!" yelled Renwick.

"I know," replied Makera, "but we have more immediate problems." Renwick glanced down at the tactical display. The second corvette was still hot on their tail, and the small life boat was no match for the pirate vessel. The initial burst from the thrusters had pushed them away from *Phaeton* and the other corvette, but this ship had skipped on past the Unity cruiser and was quickly closing on the skiff.

"If they still have plasma grenades, they could tear us apart," said Renwick. The Raelen Ambassador nodded.

"If indeed their purpose was our destruction, but they are pirates, and that knowledge gives us some advantage." Without another word she switched the flight controls from his station to hers and slammed the skiff to port, flinging the vessel forward at full speed.

Right towards the Void.

"Are you insane?" yelled Renwick.

"Perhaps, but I'm betting they aren't," she replied. "Pirates want to stay alive, Renwick. If they think we're crazy enough to fly ourselves into the Void, they won't follow."

"Makera, no one survives the Void. It's dark energy, a null field. Nothing that goes in ever comes out. Nothing," he said. She smiled casually at him, completely unafraid.

"Perhaps we'll be the first, then," she said.

Renwick turned to his two junior diplomats.

"Stay calm," he said to them, "and hold on tight." Then he pressed a control icon and sealed them in the pilot's nest.

"A wise move," said Makera.

"Unlike flying us into the Void?"

"I still hope to avoid that."

Renwick glanced at the tactical. "We have less than two minutes to avert contact with the Void, *if* we can trust these measurements," he said. Precise measurements of the Void had always been unreliable, especially at this close a distance. It was almost as if it didn't want to be measured.

The skiff shook with the power of a plasma grenade explosion. It rattled the supporting members of the little ship so violently that Renwick had to shake his head to clear it.

"One more of those and we're done for," he said.

"They don't want us going in," said the Ambassador calmly.

"Neither do I. What's your alternative plan?" Makera looked at him with the frozen stare so common with her people that it made her unreadable to most humans. Most, except to a man who had studied them closely for most of his adult life. A man like Tam Renwick.

"You don't have one," he said, equaling her calm. He sat back and crossed his arms, then shook his head. "May the Many Gods of Earth protect us," he said.

The skiff shook violently again as another plasma grenade blasted the tiny lifeboat. Renwick fell from his co-pilot's couch and hit his head on a support member. He held his head and tried to open his eyes, but all he could see was blurred colors. He shook his head a second time as the proximity alarms blazed, piercing his ears with their warning sirens. Contact was imminent, but with what?

He struggled to his feet, his vision clearing slowly as he pulled Makera off the floor. He checked the controls. The helm was burned out, completely useless. The thrusters were on full, burning He-3 as the skiff continued to accelerate.

"They hit the fuel cells with that last shot," he said calmly to her. "It ignited the Helium-3 thruster fuel. We're out of control." They looked at each other, the reality of their situation hitting them both.

Makera slid into his arms and they stood together staring out the view window of the skiff, nothing but black ahead of them.

"I'm glad I am with you," she said to him. He held her close, then allowed himself a luxury he had never believed he could have as a diplomat, but now felt entitled to as a man. He kissed her passionately as the skiff broke through into nothingness. Into the dark.

Into the Void.

2. IN THE VOID

The emergency lights flickered on and off, a gentle blue glow enlightening the pilot's nest with each vibration.

Their kiss went on, breath quickening with each moment until they matched each other's rhythm perfectly. The cabin lights flickered one last time, then stayed on, the soft blue enveloping them both in a peaceful, silent glow.

Renwick pulled back from their kiss, opened his own eyes and peered into the gentle olive slits of hers. She was beautiful, no doubt, and he regretted every decision to turn her away from his door during the negotiations. But that was a different time, a different place. All they were left with was *now*.

He withdrew from her and looked around the pilot's nest, then turned back. "Why aren't we dead?" he asked.

She fought to control her breathing, to bring it back to normalcy. A Raelen woman's passion, once ignited, was a difficult thing to dowse. She crossed her arms and took three deep breaths before responding, then looked around the cabin.

"I don't know," she said.

He studied the flight controls. The helium fuel was no longer burning, and the board was showing no forward momentum. Where they were was unclear.

"Every ship, every probe that has entered the Void has vanished completely," he said. "Absorbed by dark energy. As far as we can tell, they've simply ceased to exist. So why are we still alive?" He looked to her.

She shook her head.

"Science is not one of my specialties," she said. He punched the control to open the pilot's nest to the main cabin again.

"What's happening?"

"Where are we?"

"Why is it so quiet?" came the chorus of questions. Renwick faced his companions and raised his hands to quiet them.

"We're inside the Void," he said plainly. This started another round of excited questions from Poul and Myra. Again he held up his hands. Makera came to his side.

"I've just checked the status boards," she said. "We lost nearly one quarter of our power when we entered the Void, but the rate of decay has decreased markedly. I would say we have approximately two of your days of power in reserve."

"Unless the rate of decay increases again," Renwick said. He mulled the situation. "All right," he said to his companions. "Let's survey this boat, find supplies, food, water, anything that might be of value." They sat as if waiting for further instructions.

"You're not going to find anything out sitting down," he finally said. Poul and Myra shot to their feet then, moving about the cabin, opening cabinets to see what they could find.

Renwick went back to the control console, Makera peering over his shoulder. He ran a series of scans that took nearly five minutes to finish.

"Nothing," he said when the scans were complete. "As in zero. Nothing on the sensors, nothing on the scanners, if I launch a probe it simply doesn't register. Everything shows as a zero. It's like we're inside nothingness."

"As I said, I am not a scientist," Makera said. "But if this were really dark matter, shouldn't we be registering *something*? Some kind of output? Gamma rays or solar winds or tachyon particles? Even dark matter has to exist in our universe. Therefore the Void must be composed of something else, something we can measure."

Renwick shook his head. "Everything is registering as a null field. Like I said, we seem to be inside nothingness. The motion sensors don't indicate that there is any movement, but where we are is a complete mystery. The sensors don't have anything to bounce a measurement back off of."

"This is not what I expected," she said.

"Nor I," agreed Renwick. "From what our scientists have told us about the Void it should have consumed us in the first instant that we touched it. Instead, it's like we're *preserved* inside of it."

Her eyes widened at this possibility. "Or encased," she said. He stood and looked at her studying her again. The Raelen were very close to humans in their genetic makeup, so close as to be nearly indistinguishable, as were the Gataan, the other race in the Known Cosmos. Makera was tall for a human woman, but wiry like all of her race, and beautiful. He broke his thoughts then and focused on her words.

"One of our science's theories is that the Void is indeed a dark matter field, but that contact with a light energy object, light matter, as you call it, should result in a catastrophic explosion," she said. "One of our alternate theories, however, is that the Void was designed as an enveloping plasma, creating a null energy field around any light-matter object, thus encasing it in a protective field of energy."

"A protective field of energy?" he repeated. "Protected from what?"

She shrugged. "For whatever purpose the designers intended, I suppose. If it was indeed designed, and not a natural field." He crossed his arms and looked at his board readings again.

"I'm no scientist either," he said. "But we're alive for some reason. I think we should use this enveloping field as our working theory for Void Space, for now at least."

Poul Rand came up at that moment with an inventory report. "There are two cabins in the rear compartment with double-stacked sleeping berths. We also found enough food and water for two people for two days. With the four of us rationing that makes enough-"

"For approximately about as much power as we have left at our current rate of decay. Thank you Poul, call Myra over."

Myra reported a pair of airlocks with two EVA suits each. Unfortunately the oxygen supply for the suits was tied directly into the skiff's reserves. She found a first aid kit and a single coil pistol in a utility cabinet.

"Well, that's it then. We have enough water, oxygen, and energy for two days, plus emergency food rations. At least we won't starve," he said after they had all gathered back together in the main cabin. "The downside is, we have two days to find a safe port of some kind before we all die, and we've no way to navigate the Void."

"But we are still alive," chimed in Makera, "which is more than we could have expected when we entered."

Renwick gathered their supplies and made everyone eat a ration bar and drink their first allotment of water. Renwick thought the bars were awful, and he watched with amusement as Makera devoured hers.

"Delicious," she said.

He laughed. "If you say so."

At Renwick's insistence they all divided up time to stand watch while the others got their rest. The fact was that resting quietly might lengthen their life support time and enhance the possibility of a rescue or some other resolution to their crisis. It was worth a try anyway.

They agreed on four-hour shifts and Renwick wanted to stand the first watch but Poul Rand insisted. Renwick watched as Myra made for one of the cabins and shut the door behind her. That left him with the Raelen Ambassador as a bunk mate.

She looked at him expectantly as he contemplated their circumstances. He sighed as she took his hand and led him back to their bunk room and closed the door. She pushed him down on the bed and then stood at the door of the tiny cabin, hands on her hips.

"Will you have me now, Senator? Or will you reject me a final time?" she said. He looked up to her and sighed.

"Sexual activity at this time would consume much more than our fair share of the oxygen that we all need to survive, Makera," he said, speaking a practical truth. She let out a sigh of frustration, shaking her head at him, then she leapt in a single motion to the upper bunk.

"I hate you, human," she said. It was the biggest insult she could make, reducing him to one of the rabble of humanity.

"I'm sorry," he said honestly. At that she was finally quiet, then he closed his eyes and tried, for the moment, to forget the precarious predicament they were all in.

#

Renwick relieved Rand right on time, then watched him depart for Myra's cabin as Makera joined him in the pilot's nest.

"Do you think they are mating?" asked Makera frankly.

"Um, I suppose so."

"If so, then they are using up the extra oxygen that we could have used ourselves."

Renwick shrugged. "They're young. They have many more years to lose than you or me," he said.

"I suppose. It seems strange to me though. I had her selected for you," Makera admitted.

"Myra? Gods no! She's a child," insisted Renwick. Makera looked confused.

"But I was sure she was sexually matured," she said. He shook his head as he scanned the console readouts.

"I don't mean that. I mean emotionally. She's not the kind of… girl I would ever choose to engage in a relationship with." Makera contemplated this.

"So emotionally maturity is as important in picking a sexual partner as physical maturity?" she asked. He smiled again.

"For some of us, yes."

She shook her head, confused.

"Humans," she said.

He spent the next hour coursing through the scans, hoping to find some indication of their movement or location, but all of the scanners and instruments maintained their null reading. A thought came to him and he broke the silence between them.

"Makera, what if the readings are accurate?" he said.

"What do you mean?"

"What if the null readings are accurate, and we are in fact, at this moment, motionless inside the Void?"

"You mean, as if we just came in and *stopped?*" she said.

"Exactly!"

She thought on this for a moment. "Then we could be only a few meters, or kilometers, from normal space."

"That was my thought," he said.

"Then, in fact, we could conceivably find a way back to normal space?"

"Yes."

She looked at him. "The EVA suits?" she asked. He smiled.

"You read my mind."

#

He gave Poul and Myra another hour of sleep before he woke them to run his idea by them.

"An EVA would likely take up about thirty minutes of resources," he said. "And I've been charging the suits while you slept. One of us, in an EVA suit with a tether attached, could go out and determine if there's any chance of us reaching normal space again. I realize it's a long shot, but it beats sitting here staring out a black window and waiting to die."

They all agreed with that sentiment, but not the next.

"I'll be ready to go out in ten minutes," he said. This set off a chorus of objections, the core of which were related to their nearly-forgotten diplomatic mission to Raellos, capital of the Raelen Empire.

"The obvious choice is me," said Makera. Renwick shook his head.

"No. You've been involved in every moment of these negotiations. You're the foremost expert on this treaty in the entire Raelen Empire," he said.

"And you've just proven my point, " she retorted. "My job is finished. All that's left now is for you to deliver the treaty and for the Emperor-Regent to sign it. Once that's done then the Empire and the Unity can begin to exploit Thousand Suns Space together, establish new colonies far away from the Void. As I said, my job, negotiating the terms, is complete. Therefore I'm by far the most logical choice to do the EVA."

"But what if your people won't sign it, or don't agree with all the provisions?" Renwick protested. She threw her head back and laughed.

"Even after all these years you really don't understand the Raelen mind, do you Senator?" she said. "Of course they will sign it. I speak for all the Raelen. Why do you think they sent me?"

And with that the debate was over. Ten minutes later Ambassador Makera was fully suited up and ready for her EVA.

"You'll have about a kilometer of tether," said Renwick through the com. He was on the other side of the airlock for the moment, fully suited and ready to join her to manage the tether once she had departed.

"And if we're one kilometer and one more meter beyond normal space?" she asked. He shrugged.

"Then we're shit out of luck," he said.

She puzzled at this turn of phrase as he purged the airlock of its precious atmosphere. She turned to face the blackness as the outer hatch slid up and open, exposing her to Void Space.

She stepped off and immediately felt disoriented. The feeling of being surrounded by *nothing* swept over her. All was black. She looked down at the tether. It vanished a few centimeters past the suit connector. She surmised that this was the extent of the radiated light energy from the suit, her "bubble" of light matter, if the theory she and Renwick had concocted was correct. Still, it wasn't comforting to see the tether simply cease to exist beyond a certain point. She decided to test it, for her own ease of mind. She tugged on it three times. A few seconds later and she got three tugs in response. Renwick was indeed on the other end of the line and she was still attached to the skiff.

Her mind calmed for the moment, she used the small jets at her hips and set out on her journey into the black. The bursts were designed to move her a few hundred meters at a time, if indeed she was moving at all.

She repeated this sequence more than a dozen times, each time reaching out with her arms into an enveloping nothingness. It was harrowing, but she kept her emotions in check as well as she could.

After nearly twenty minutes of exploration with no results Makera was sweating profusely. She had no idea if she had moved at all from the skiff. Then she felt a tug, a hard one. She pulled back in response. This was met with another tug, then a strong jolt yanking at her. She started breathing heavily as the minutes passed in utter darkness, no sense of motion, no sense of direction. She periodically checked the tether to make sure it was still rigid, and it was, indicating she was being pulled back in. Just when she didn't think she could stand anymore of the blackness the reality of the airlock burst into her senses like an explosion. She fell into the EVA-suited arms of Senator Tam Renwick as he pulled her from the Void and then slammed down the manual door seal. As the airlock pressurized she struggled in Renwick's arms for a few seconds. He held her firmly and after a calming breath she looked up at him. His voice crackled to her over the com.

"Sorry to be so abrupt, Ambassador, but I had to get you back inside," he said. Her ears pounded with the sound of her rushing blood as the suit normalized itself to the surrounding atmosphere. She could barely catch her breath to reply.

"Why?" she finally croaked out. He looked down at her.

"Because we're moving," he said.

3.

"How?" Makera asked as she slid into the in the pilot's couch next to Renwick.

"I don't know the manner of our movement yet, but we are moving," said Renwick. "Poul noticed it on the motion sensor while I was tending your tether. My best guess is that we've been encased in a bubble, or a tube, if you will, of normal space. Inside that bubble someone, or something, is drawing us in. Look at the motion grid," he pointed to the console. "It's actually registering our position relative to the galactic core and the plane of the ecliptic again, but it's such a vague reading we could be anywhere within a light year of the Minara system. From the readings though it's clear we must have traveled a good distance when we entered the Void, that much I'm certain of."

"This behavior indicates the Void is of intelligent design," Makera said. Renwick wasn't so sure.

"Possibly. It could also be that these pockets of normal space are natural, as is the Void, and we just happened to drift inside of one," he said.

"Your people created the Void," Makera said. Renwick looked up in surprise.

"Our intelligence always said that *your* people did," he fired back.

"We didn't have the technology three-hundred years ago. We don't have it now."

"Neither do we."

"Then what created it?" she asked. He shrugged and turned back to his display board.

"That's an answer I cannot give you. But I can tell you we are moving faster. Look at the motion readout," he pointed again. "It's increasing relative to the core. And the increase seems to be incremental."

"Another argument for intelligent design," she said. Renwick found he couldn't argue with her logic, so he changed tactics.

"Let's call the others together and brief them," he said.

When Poul and Myra were both present in the main cabin of the skiff again Renwick explained what they knew at the moment.

"But what's drawing us in?" asked Myra, concern etched in her voice. Poul Rand held her closer.

"It could be a ship, or a base, or some form of natural object, or a sea monster for that matter. I wish I had more comforting words, but whatever it is, it's an unknown," said Renwick

Poul said simply, "At least we'll get some resolution to this. I was hating the thought of being trapped in the Void to die slowly." This didn't comfort Myra in the slightest, making her even more upset as her breathing started to increase, getting sharp and shallow. Renwick eyed Rand and motioned for him to take her into the back cabin again to calm her down.

"You don't like her," said Makera to Renwick after they departed.

"Liking her is irrelevant," he said. "She is efficient at her job. That's why she was chosen."

Makera crossed her arms this time, emulating a pose she had seen Renwick take often. "So now what do we do?" she asked. Renwick sighed and looked out to the blank blackness of space.

"Now we wait," he said.

#

More than four hours later they were still waiting. Renwick was dozing in the co-pilot's couch while Makera studied the mysterious pocket of space they were in. After taking several rounds of readings, she reached out and shook him gently to wake him.

"Look here," she said, bringing up an energy measurement display. "I've managed to measure the area of normal space that we're in. You weren't far off. This area *is* shaped like a tube, though more accurately it could be described as a tunnel."

"A tunnel of normal space cut through the Void?" said Renwick.

"Yes, and it's definitely designed for us. In fact, as we move through it the tunnel is closing behind us as we move closer to our destination."

"Whatever that may be."

She nodded. "As near as I can tell the 'tube' consists of positively charged particles, literally light energy, if you will, balanced against the dark energy of the Void."

Renwick crossed his arms and sat back in his couch, contemplating their situation. "For the most of the last four millennia human science has believed that 'dark matter' couldn't really be seen or detected, only speculated about. Then the Void came, consuming so many worlds, and we still couldn't measure it, but we could see it. When I was a child on Ceta I used to look up in the night sky and cover it, the Void, I mean, with my thumb. By the time I graduated university I needed my fist. By the time I die it will cover half the sky. In two centuries it will consume my home." He swiveled the couch to look at her. "Whatever it is, I want to stop it, and if where we're going can lead to a resolution of the Void crisis, then I want to be a part of that."

"As do I," said Makera. "Our race is in even worse shape than yours. Without this treaty and the technology of your Unity ships, we will be consumed before we can establish new colonies. I don't like to think of myself as part of a dying race."

"Neither do I," agreed Renwick.

Just then every dial on the console went red.

"What is it?" asked Makera, leaning towards him.

"A contact," replied Renwick. "And we're being pulled right towards it."

#

The contact was huge. The coarse sensors on the skiff told them that much, but only that much. The lifeboat was never designed as a scientific vessel, which Renwick thought a pity. The data they could have collected on the contact would have kept both Unity and Raelen scientists engaged for decades, if they ever got out of this eternal darkness.

All four of the survivors of the *Phaeton* were present now as the skiff approached the massive object that all of its instruments said was there, against all probability.

"There!" said Renwick excitedly, pointing to a display that showed a visual view forward. "It's actually visible in the natural spectrum and it's emanating light!" He brought the display up in magnification and enhanced it so the others could see.

The contact was big enough to be a human deep space station, the sensors indicating it was nearly five kilometers long from one end to the other. The 'top' was a giant flattened scoop shape, nearly half the contact's width across, connected by a crane-like neck to a large base. The base itself was shaped like a flattened cylinder, with another scoop in front, facing the skiff as they approached. Extending out from the body of the base were two more flattened cylinders that looked for all the worlds like engines. A large structure seemed to grow out of the rear of the base cylinder, almost like the stern of an old Earth sailing galley.

"It's surely not one of ours," said Makera.

"Nor ours, I'd say," said Renwick.

"Then who?" asked the frightened Myra, the tone of her voice indicating near desperation for an answer.

"I'm sure I've no idea," conceded Renwick.

As they continued to be pulled closer it was the aft structure that they were drawn to. They passed by the massive top scoop, and looking into its dark recesses was not a comforting sight for any of the passengers. Then they were drawn over the body of the ship and finally over the foreboding aft structure, the skiff first floating past the stern and then into open space before being turned with expert skill by whoever was controlling them. They faced an illuminated deck intertwined with extensive geometric structure. Then they were slowly drawn inside, a tiny dot in space being consumed by the much larger mystery vessel.

As they passed inside, the passengers of the skiff remained silent, watching in awe as they were pulled into the brightly lit bay and then gently dropped to the metal deck to settle amongst a host of other, unidentifiable craft. The massive doors they had entered through closed swiftly behind them. Whatever or whomever were the masters of this ship, the crew of the tiny skiff were now clearly at their mercy.

A flash of light engulfed the skiff. Moments later the console instruments started twitching uncontrollably.

"I'm reading atmosphere outside," said Makera, "and heat and oxygen. It's within normal ranges for both our species."

"Is that a man?" said Myra, looking out the cockpit windows. They all looked to the deck. A figure was moving towards them, either a man in a silver EV suit or quite possibly-

"A robot?" said Renwick. As the figure pierced the environmental field surrounding the skiff, a quick yellow flash indicated it had passed through. A few seconds later and it moved out of sight of the skiff windows, but the destination was clear.

The skiff's airlock.

Renwick gathered the passengers together, dividing up their supplies as best they could. He took the coil pistol personally, then turned to his crew of interstellar refugees.

"They've brought us here for a reason, whoever they are. Logic would assume that they have some desire for contact with us. I can only assume that contact is intended to be peaceful, since they could have easily destroyed us at any time. At any rate, we really have no choice but to go outside. Are there any objections?" Renwick said.

"Only to you being the one to carry the weapon," said Makera. The rest just shook their heads.

"Human weapon, human carries it," he said back to her. "And I am trained in military tactics."

She smiled tightly. "So you say," she said.

"I'll go first," he replied, not missing a beat. "Then the Ambassador, then Poul and finally Myra. Wait for me to signal you out, clear?" Again, a chorus of nods.

Without another word Renwick went to the airlock and pressurized it, then opened the inner door. He took a deep breath of cabin air and then depressed the button to open the outer door. He gave one last look to Makera, who nodded affirmatively in reply.

The door swung up and a metal ladder deployed down to the deck where the robot waited. The robot was silver in color, with a sort of translucent green glow to it, almost as if you could see veins running through its body. It was shaped like a man, with arms and legs, none of which moved, and a rounded head with a single slit for an eye that ran across the 'face'. It had no nose, mouth, or ears of any kind.

There was a low hum as the robot glided backwards and away from the skiff. Renwick descended the ladder, stepping down onto the metal deck as the robot moved a few feet further back, its motion accompanied always by the hum. He motioned for the team to come out, and Makera was at his side a moment later, followed by Poul and Myra.

"Now what do we do?" Makera asked, staring at the robot. Renwick shrugged.

"Start negotiating," he said. He stepped towards the robot, which moved back further again, its body pulsating with the green glow. As he got closer Renwick noticed that it wasn't metal, but more some kind of softer material, very flexible, almost like human skin.

"I thank you for your rescue," he said to it, "Are you the operators of this vessel, or this station?" he asked. The robot said nothing of any kind. After a few more failed exchanges Renwick gave up and went back to his team.

"Impasse?" asked Makera.

"I don't think it speaks our language," said Renwick. Makera put her hands to her hips.

"If I had to guess, I'd say this was an automaton," she said. "A programmed device. Designed to serve a particular purpose, and nothing beyond."

"And what purpose do you surmise it has in mind?" said Renwick.

"It came to greet us," said Rand. "I'd say it probably wants us to follow it somewhere inside this thing. Remember, it, or something else, did bring us here."

"Something did," agreed Renwick, nodding. "I think you're right Poul."

Renwick looked to Makera.

"Seems as logical a course as anything else," she said. With a wave of her hand Rand and Myra joined the rest of the party on the deck. Then the robot turned and proceeded back the way it had come at a slow pace. The group of castaways followed.

"Its feet don't move," said Makera to Renwick. He observed the robot for a few seconds as he walked behind it.

"It's got separate legs and feet," he said. "It looks like it could use them if it wanted. Must be some kind of magnetic levitation. That's the hum we keep hearing. Likely this whole deck is magnetized."

Makera noted the many other vessels on the deck, all of unique design. "This looks like a graveyard of alien ships," she said. "That does not bode well for us."

Renwick looked to both sides, observing the other vessels. They were indeed dissimilar in many ways, and some showed the wear and dust of great age. Most were on the huge deck, but some were suspended high above them by forces unknown. He didn't recognize any of the designs.

"Without knowing how long this ship has been operating, it's impossible to tell if these are ships from our pasts, or some other races entirely," he said. Makera moved closer to him in response.

The robot led them down a long gangway and outside the area where the initial environmental bubble had been established, then down an enclosed corridor towards a huge wall with a large red door on it, easily two stories tall.

"Elevator lift?" surmised Makera. Renwick nodded while he continued to observe. His hand went to the coil pistol enclosed in his diplomatic vest. It was small comfort against the scale of the technology on display before them, and he doubted it would be of any use. Whomever had brought them here, the refugees of the *Phaeton* were all clearly under their control.

The lift doors opened and they all followed the robot in. Then the doors shut behind them, closing with a thud. A second later and an unmistakable feeling of motion took over.

"We're moving through different gravity fields," observed Renwick. "Deck after deck."

"And at a considerable rate," noted Makera.

Renwick turned to observe his other passengers. Rand had his arm around Myra, almost completely enclosing her. She still had the worried look on her face, and he couldn't blame her. He turned his attention back to the door as their rate of climb slowed.

The lift doors slid open to reveal a massive command deck. Large windows looked out on the blank black of Void Space. Dozens of consoles were lit up and humming with power in the shadow light.

The robot slipped past them and onto the command deck, ignoring them and moving away, walking this time, as if it had other tasks at hand. From behind a large central console a pleasant looking young woman with flowing brunette hair, clothed in a short brown pattern dress and knee-high boots came towards them. She walked up to the crew and looked them all up and down, smiling the whole time.

"Welcome," she said in common Standard, "aboard the *Kali*. We've been expecting you."

They all stood together, looking at her and each other in stunned silence.

"What are your orders?" she said.

4. ABOARD THE *KALI*

"Orders?" said Renwick. He looked to Makera, who offered no expression or comment. "I think there's been some kind of mistake." The woman merely stared at him, unblinking, then continued.

"I am pleased that the relief team has finally arrived," she said.

"Relief team?" asked Renwick. He looked to his crew of survivors, then back at the young woman. "You mean us?" he said, pointing to himself for emphasis.

"Yes," she replied.

"Um," started Renwick, "I'm not sure we're the people you think we are."

"You're not the relief team?" the woman asked.

"What relief team?" he said.

"Sent by Captain Yan."

Now Renwick looked completely perplexed at this. "Who is Captain Yan?"

"Captain Yan is commander of the *Kali*. She went for help and promised to send a relief team after the accident," the woman said.

Renwick held up his hands. "Wait, we're not the relief team. We were stranded in Void Space after an accident as well," he said. The woman merely stared straight ahead, unblinking again, as if analyzing his statement. He felt Ambassador Makera's touch on his shoulder.

"Look there," she said, pointing. "And there." Renwick saw two other figures, one the male robot and one more distinctly female in appearance, moving about the command deck, working diligently while activating systems and monitoring readout displays. "The way they move. Like humans, but not quite."

"Androids?" he said. She nodded.

"I think so."

Renwick turned back to the woman, who still looked at him, unblinking. "Let's start again. I'm Senator Tam Renwick of the Terran Unity, and this is Ambassador Makera of the Raelen Empire. We were stranded in Void Space after an attack by Gataan pirates on our cruiser in the Minara system. We got stuck in the Void until we were drawn into this station by you. Now let me ask you a question. Who are *you*?"

"I am Amanda," she said back to him. "And this is not a station, Senator Renwick. The *Kali* is a space vessel."

"A vessel? So you were trapped in the Void as well?" he asked.

"No," she replied. "The *Kali* was designed to traverse the Void."

"Traverse the Void? I didn't think that was possible." He crossed his arms again. "Alright then, another question. Who built this vessel?"

"The *Kali* was built by the Trans-Earth Commonwealth," Amanda said.

"I knew it was yours!' exclaimed Makera. Renwick looked to her and gave her a 'not now' look. Makera crossed her arms, imitating his stance. He dropped his hands to his sides in response.

"Amanda, the Trans-Earth Commonwealth has not existed for over a century and a half. It was succeeded by the Terran Unity after the Void came and consumed half the Commonwealth worlds. If you were built by humans, why don't you know this?" he said.

Amanda blinked and looked over the group. "You are not the relief team?" she asked again.

"No," replied Renwick again. Amanda hesitated, actually blinking this time.

"This requires more analysis," she said, then abruptly turned and walked away from them and back to the main console where she stood, unmoving, her eyes open.

Makera stepped up to Renwick. "Now what?" she said.

"Hell if I know," he replied. He turned to the group behind him.

"Let's spread out, try and survey the ship. See if you can find any sources of food, water, any kind of additional supplies other than what we already have," he said. Poul and Myra made their way about the deck as

Renwick turned back to Makera.

"We still don't know what this ship is here for, Renwick. Do you think it was wise not to have led the android on?" she said.

He looked over his shoulder. "You mean tell her… it, that we are the relief team?"

"Yes."

"I thought of it. But quite frankly we know so little about this ship that I didn't want to put us in a position where we might have to perform some tasks we are incapable of. Who knows. She might then decide to vaporize us," he said.

"She might do that anyway."

"That's a risk, I admit it," he said. He looked to Amanda again. She was still standing at the console, unmoving. "Let's get the others back here."

They all came together in front of the massive lifter door.

"Any luck?" asked Renwick. Poul nodded.

"Myra found a water fountain, and what looks like a galley, but we couldn't find any food in it," he said. "There's also multiple sleeping quarters, enough for what looks like a couple of dozen crew."

"I tried communicating with the other androids," chimed in Myra. "I counted just the two, one male, one female. They are human-looking in general appearance, but none of them would speak to me."

"Perhaps they're incapable," said Makera.

"More likely they're not allowed to talk to us until Amanda decides what to do with us," responded Renwick.

"Do you think that's what they're doing?" asked Myra. "Trying to decide what to do with us?" Renwick put his hands on her shoulders to reassure the young woman.

"Perhaps, or just trying to figure out their next strategy. She did say they had been in an accident. But I don't think we have to worry. If this ship was indeed built by humans, I doubt they would harm us," Renwick said. Myra seemed to take comfort in this, then edged closer to Rand again.

"At any rate, there's four of us, three of them. And we have the pistol," said Makera. Renwick put a finger to his lips.

"Let's not share any information we don't have to," he said.

"Your weapon was neutralized when you came aboard, Senator," came Amanda's voice from the console area. "You have no worries. The

Kali and her crew were designed to serve humans, not harm them." They all turned at the sound of her voice but by the time they did she had returned to her stoic pose.

"It's confirmed she can multi-task," deadpanned Makera. Renwick gave her an annoyed look and then pulled Rand aside.

"Poul, please take the others back to the sleeping quarters and get them settled in. It looks like we could be in this for the long haul. Ambassador Makera and I will try and sort out the situation with the head android, uh, I mean with Amanda," he said. Rand nodded and then led Myra away. Renwick turned to Makera.

"There's only one source of answers on this ship," he said, motioning towards Amanda. "And that's her."

"Agreed," she said. They both walked up to their android host. As they approached Renwick couldn't help but notice what a well-constructed 'woman' the android was. Whomever had designed her had given her a unique and beautiful face, and she was indistinguishable from a human woman in her outside appearance. He admired her very feminine form and figure, then tried to put those distracting thoughts out of his mind and focus.

"You wish to speak with me as to our intent, Senator?" Amanda said preemptively as they approached.

"Yes," replied Renwick. "That and we wish to know more about the mission of the *Kali*, how you ended up here, and about the accident."

"I am not allowed to give out that information if you are not either a member of the crew or the relief team," she said plainly. Renwick tried a different tack.

"But surely Captain Yan must have left instructions as to what to do in the event of passengers coming aboard, or left some open logs we can access?"

Amanda turned from her console for the first time and looked directly at Renwick, fully engaging with him. "You would have to ask the Captain for that permission directly," she said.

Renwick nodded. "So I've gathered." He turned to Makera.

"Dead end," she said.

"If only I could talk to this Captain Yan," he said to Makera.

"You may speak with her," said Amanda. Renwick turned back to the android.

"I thought you said she left to send a relief team?"

"She did, but you can access her stored persona via the terminal room," said Amanda in a matter-of-fact tone.

"Stored persona?" said Renwick. Makera touched his arm and took over the conversation.

"Amanda, where is this terminal room?" she said. At this, another of the androids, the male, approached them.

"Thorne will take you," said Amanda. "The Captain has full authority to grant you access to all relevant information about the Kali and its mission." With that Thorne started moving away. Renwick looked to Makera as they followed the male android.

"This just keeps getting weirder," he said.

#

Thorne, the android that had originally greeted them at the ship, didn't say anything when they got to the terminal room, but he made it clear through his hand motions that only Renwick could enter.

"I'll see how the others are getting on," said Makera as she turned and left. Thorne escorted Renwick to a pedestal in the middle of a clean, white-paneled room, then exited, the door shutting silently behind him. On the pedestal was the impression of a human right hand. Renwick reached out and touched the pedestal, matching his hand to the impression. The room immediately lit up with a red glow. Streams of color, like a flow of water, came out of the pedestal to touch every corner of the room. Renwick thought he understood what he was seeing. Streams of data, potential pathways of information, touching tiny multi-colored blocks all over the room. *The walls themselves must be data storage ports*, he thought. There was a dim sound of energy, like the hum of the robot on the landing deck, but his senses couldn't quite capture the tone or form. After a few moments of this communion, not knowing what else to do, he asked his question.

"May I speak with Captain Yan?" he said aloud. The blocks of light in the room began to glow in multi-colored hues, the red glow of the room fading as a rainbow of light particles coming from every inch of the room flowed through and around him, then coalesced on a central platform in front of him.

Within a few seconds a distinctive shape took form, a human shape. A few seconds later and a layer of clothing was added, identical to the android Amanda but tailored to the young woman who now stood before him. The room was returned to its natural white glow as he stared, unbelieving, at a petite woman of Asian descent, with dark hair and eyes. She crossed her arms.

"Who the hell are you?" she demanded in a surprisingly loud voice. Renwick was taken aback.

"I… I'm… Senator Tam Renwick of the Terran Unity. Captain Yan, I presume?" he said once he had recovered his bearings.

"Captain Tanitha Yan of the Commonwealth ship *Kali*," she said forcefully. "What the hell is the Terran Unity?"

Renwick took in a deep breath. This explanation could be delicate, and he was unsure if he was talking to an android, or possibly a hologram, and if so, how much historic programming it might have. "Captain, this may take some adjustment time for you," started Renwick. "Let me ask you, what year is it?"

"What *year*?" Yan said, as if annoyed by the question. After not answering for a second, she finally relented. "It's the year 5762 of the New Common Era, of course. Why are you asking?" she snapped, then held up her hand to him. "Wait, how much time has passed?"

Renwick spread his hands. "Since when?" he asked.

"Since I.. oh God," she said, a look of worry crossing her face. "You're not the relief team, are you?"

Renwick, tired of answering that question, merely shook his head no. Captain Yan put one hand to her forehead and rubbed it, a very human gesture of frustration for a construct of light and electronic impulses.

"Then it means I've failed," she said forlornly.

"Failed in what?" he asked.

"In getting the scoop repaired," she seemed crestfallen at this realization. "What year did you say this was?" she asked. Now she seemed confused.

Renwick did some quick math in his head. "We stopped measuring the years in NCE with the formation of the Unity, so it's year 133 of Unity time… NCE time stopped in 5923… so that would make this-"

"The year 6056 in my time," Yan cut in. "Two-hundred and ninety-four years since my mission. So what am I? A hologram, android? Or a Printed Man?" she demanded of him.

That last reference hit a nerve in Renwick, but he didn't know why. He shook the feeling off and tried to be understanding of Yan's emotional distress. "Amanda said you were a 'stored persona', whatever that means," he said honestly. Yan nodded.

"That makes sense, I must have backed myself up before I left. Glad to hear Amanda's still functioning. Of course, this also means that in real life I'm long dead…" she trailed off. Renwick crossed his arms.

"I'm still very confused," he said. "What *is* the *Kali*?"

Yan looked at him. "I would have thought she'd be a museum piece by now," she said, then she eyed Renwick suspiciously. "How do I know you aren't a spy for one of the Merchant Syndicates?" she said.

Renwick searched his mind for the archaic reference. It came to him that the Merchant Syndicates were star systems that had banded together to control and profit from commodities and technology trading in the old days, before the Void. "I assure you Captain, the Merchant Networks are long dead," he replied.

"Oh really? How?" she demanded.

"They were consumed by the Void," he said. "Long ago, I assure you."

She sized him up once again, then seemed to make a decision about trusting him. "To answer your question, Senator, the *Kali* is a test bed. A ship designed around a single potential stealth technology," she said. Renwick took in a deep breath.

"Stealth technology? You mean like a weapon?" Then a realization of what she was saying hit him. "You mean, the Void…" now he trailed off.

"I don't know anything about this Void of yours," said Yan. "But three hundred years ago I led a mission to test a new weapon, a *defensive* weapon-"

"And the test failed," finished Renwick. "So you went for help, but you never made it back, because the weapon could never be stopped. Captain, your weapon, this ship…" he paused as the reality of the situation became clear to him. "The Void has been spreading for three centuries, Captain Yan. It's consumed more than a hundred human worlds, what you knew as the Trans-Earth Commonwealth, and countless others in the Gataan and Raelen Empires."

"No. Not the *Kali*," said Yan, shaking her head in denial. "I shut her down when the scoop malfunctioned. The emitter station wasn't supposed to go online until three days after we finished our test. But only *after* we'd finished." Yan started pacing around the room.

"What is it?" asked Renwick. Yan reacted with visceral anger.

"They must have used the goddamned thing without waiting for our test results! The bastards! Oh, God, the emitter! It's been running wild, unregulated. A weapon that was meant to avoid war, it's destroyed us all," Yan said. She started for the door of the terminal room. "We've got to get to the emitter station, and stop it."

"We?" said Renwick as he followed her to the door. "But you're just a hologram, or an android, or whatever."

Captain Yan hit the control button to open the door, then pivoted and knocked Renwick to the deck with a hard right cross to the jaw.

"Well, at least we've established I'm not a hologram," she said, then she stormed out the door towards the command deck.

5.

When Renwick arrived back on the command deck, rubbing his aching jaw, he found Captain Yan working feverishly over the console that Amanda had been stationed at. The female android was standing behind her, observing.

"What the hell are you doing? And what was that for?" said the Senator.

"To prove a point," said Yan, "and to let you know I may be a construct, but I'm still a human being."

"You've completely lost me again," he said. Yan stood up to face him.

"I'm a Printed Man, or woman as the case may be. A clone constructed from my base DNA file and stored in the *Kali's* database for the last three hundred years, give or take. At least, that's what Amanda has verified to me," she said, then turned back to the console.

"I've never heard of such a thing," said Renwick, looking to Amanda. Amanda returned his gaze by looked him up and down, but said nothing.

"What are you doing?" asked Renwick as Yan's hands flashed feverishly over the console, touching symbols and shapes and diagrams with lightning speed.

"I'm trying to re-fire the engines," she said. Renwick tried to keep up with her movements, but found he couldn't, she was too fast.

"Apparently being a Printed Woman has its advantages," he said.

"You got that right," she replied. Renwick noted that Yan did indeed seem to be a fully constructed entity of her own, not merely a two-dimensional reflection of her former personage. This intrigued him.

"So, about this whole Printed Woman thing-" he started in again as he watched Yan's hands perform their rapid-fire miracle over the console.

"'Printed Man' is the typical vernacular," Amanda interjected. "What you would simply refer to as a clone, probably. Donor data is downloaded into a repository at the atomic level, stored as photons, then with the proper equipment the photon particles are repolarized and reassembled into their original atomic particle matrix. The same person comes out as goes in. But it takes significant power and a 3D printer like what the *Kali* has to do a reassembly as complex as a human being."

"We don't have anything like that technology, even today," said Renwick. Yan looked over at him briefly.

"I doubt that. Perhaps you were just never told about it, but it exists," said Yan.

"It all sounds pretty fanciful to me," replied Renwick. Amanda spoke up again at this.

"Yet you travel through hyper-dimensional space at your ease. Through dimensions that we can calculate and manipulate, even if you can't stay there because you lack the proper frequencies to inhabit them. Your world is full of technological miracles, Senator. Perhaps you've lost some of them to the crisis of the Void, but they still exist, and they're real," she said, almost in an argumentative tone with Renwick.

"But I'm a solid," he said, slapping his side. "I have mass, and form."

"Do you? What are you made of? At the most basic level you are a series of atoms drawn together by an electro-magnetic energy field of some kind you call 'life', but you're not a solid. If I were small enough I could fly right through you."

Renwick got frustrated, growing tired of the dialogue with the android. "This is all very fascinating, but the fact remains that I am a man, you're an android and Captain Yan here is a clone of some kind, and I'm entrusting my future and the future of my crew to both of you, at least at this point," he said. Amanda said nothing.

"All of which is simply a way of telling you to never forget that in my own mind I'm still a person, and if you treat me as such, and we should get along fine. There," Yan said, her hands ceasing their frantic movements. "That should do it."

"The engines?" he said. She turned to him.

"They should be ready in a few hours. Perhaps this is a good time for me to meet the rest of your crew."

Renwick clasped his hands behind his back, contemplating her. "Perhaps it is."

#

After the introductions Captain Yan was gracious enough to explain the workings of the food dispensers.

"They respond on voice command. You simply say "chicken sandwich" or the like, and if it's in the ship's data stores, it reproduces the item from basic organic building blocks and delivers the item here." The nearest synthesizer hummed to life for a few seconds and then chimed. Yan reached in and took the item out, two slices of bread stuffed with some kind of unfamiliar meat. "See?" she said, then took a bite and shrugged. "Not bad after three centuries, wanna try?"

She handed the sandwich to Renwick. He hesitated, then bit into it. The flavor was unfamiliar and exotic, but pleasing to his tastes. "That's quite good," he said, then passed the rest of the sandwich to the others to try.

"When you haven't eaten in 300 years almost anything tastes good, Yan said as she finished her bite.

"Um, how will you digest that?" asked Renwick. She shrugged.

"Like any other human, I assume," she said. "I'm a clone, not an android," she reminded him again.

"Captain Yan," said Ambassador Makera, coming up to her. Yan turned her attention to the Raelen woman while Renwick's alarm bells went off immediately. From what he'd seen of Yan's personality, these two were not likely to get along. "This is all very interesting and vital to our survival, but I have more pressing questions."

Renwick motioned for the three of them to sit at a table to continue their conversation while the Poul and Myra tried out different items from the dispensers.

"I figured you would, eventually," said Yan as she took a seat, then addressed the Ambassador directly. "Back in my time the Commonwealth and the Raelen Empire weren't enemies, but we weren't friends either. I'm reluctant to share anything more about the *Kali* or my mission than I've already told Senator Renwick, whom I marginally trust as a human ally."

Makera smiled thinly at Yan. "Perhaps your viewpoint needs an updating. The Commonwealth you speak of and support no longer exists, Captain. And the Terran Unity and the Raelen Empire have negotiated a treaty that is vital to our mutual survival. To say we are friends now by necessity is true, but we are also allies, and vital to each other's future and survival."

Yan leaned forward, her hands on the table. "Tell me more about this treaty you're negotiating."

"Actually," said Renwick, "it's already negotiated. All that remains is the signing ceremony on Raellos."

"And what are the terms of this treaty?" asked Yan, eyeing them both. Renwick looked to Makera, who nodded her ascent.

"The treaty will allow the Unity government access through a narrow strip of open space within the bounds of the Raelen Empire. This strip leads to a new area, far away from the Void. We call it 'Thousand Suns Space'. Our surveys indicate it has hundreds of inhabitable worlds, enough for both the Unity and the Empire to be able to move our civilizations there within just a few decades," said Renwick.

"And once there we'll just all happily get along?" asked Yan.

"There is a provision for co-location of the species on mutually suitable planets, with equal rights for both groups. And of course, interbreeding," replied Makera.

"Interbreeding?" said Yan, surprised. "Is that even possible?" Makera smiled the thin smile again.

"Not only possible, but in many cases desired," said Makera with a less than subtle glance at Renwick.

Staking out her territory, he thought.

Makera continued. "Raelen DNA compatibility with yours is remarkable, so much so that it is almost impossible to have evolved naturally. But those are philosophical discussions for scholars. In practical terms, somewhere down the line, Humans and Raelen will be for all practical purposes one species."

Yan looked at Renwick. "You seem to prefer human males. Anyone you had in mind for your personal interbreeding plans?" she said.

Renwick moved closer to the table, separating them as much as possible. "Ladies, if we could get back to the business at hand?"

Yan nodded. "So, this relocation is required because of the Void?"

"Yes," said Makera. "The Void has consumed ninety percent of

Raelen space, over eighty percent of what you used to call the Commonwealth, and all of the Gataan Empire." Yan grunted at the last comment.

"Can't say I feel sorry for them. The Gataan were plenty of trouble in my time," said Yan. Makera shifted in her chair but said nothing for a few moments before continuing.

"Then you'll be happy to know that all that remains of Gataan civilization are pockets of nomadic rogues living on the edges of Unity and Raelen space," said Makera. Renwick couldn't tell if she was truly annoyed by Yan's attitude or just expressing the usual Raelen detachment.

"That's how we got stuck in the Void," said Renwick. "Pirates surprised our cruiser when we were re-supplying. We tried to escape in a small skiff boat, but we were hit and accelerated out of control, into the Void, trapped inside. Until your androids detected us and pulled us in, that is."

"We have told you our story, Captain. Perhaps now you would tell us more of yours?" said Makera, pressing even as she resumed a more casual position in her seat. It was clearly not a request.

Yan sat forward, obviously still pensive about the exchange, but she started in anyway. "This experiment, the Kali, I mean," she said, gesturing to the ship at large, "it was designed as a defensive weapon, to contain a single star system, or a group of systems, specifically to deal with piracy, but also as a deterrent to potentially…" she paused here before finishing, "belligerent races."

"Belligerent races," said Makera, one eyebrow rising in a gesture Renwick knew spelled trouble. "Like the Gataan?" Yan nodded. Makera smashed her fist on the table and rose half out of her chair. Renwick restrained her with a hand to the arm, and she sat down again before continuing, but her breathing was dep and heavy, indicative of the rising of her famous Raelen temper. "The Gataan were a young race. Ambitious, yes. Emotional, unpredictable. But there were other ways of dealing with them than this," Makera said through tight lips.

Yan looked to Renwick and changed the subject immediately.

"How big is this Void now?" she said.

"Almost two hundred light years in volume," said Renwick, eying the Ambassador and happy to change the subject, for the moment.

"It's grown that much in three centuries?" said Yan. She looked down to the table top. Neither Renwick nor Makera offered an answer. "Then we've got to stop it," said Yan.

"Can the *Kali* do that?" Renwick asked.

"By herself? Unlikely," said Yan. "She was never designed for a mission of this scope. But if we can get to the emitter station, we might be able to do something from there."

"Where is this emitter station?" asked Renwick. Yan looked away at the question.

"Near Tarchus," she said. Makera reacted as if she'd been pricked with a sharp object.

"The Gataan home system," she said. Renwick could see she was seething with anger. Once raised the anger of a Raelen was very hard to quell. "Your failed experiment destroyed a whole civilization."

Sensing the Ambassador's anger, Yan stood. "I can't control what happened three centuries ago," she said, "I can only offer my assistance, and my ship, now," then she turned and headed out of the galley. "I'll be in the command center," she finished as she strode swiftly away from them. Makera looked after her, her breathing getting heavy and uneven. Renwick reached out a hand to her.

"Try and slow your breathing," he said to her.

"I'd like to crush her skull," replied the Ambassador.

"I understand," said Renwick. "But perhaps we can think of a more constructive way for you to channel away this anger."

She looked at him like a hungry wolf.

"Are you finally offering to mate with me?" Makera asked. Renwick smiled and shook his head negative.

"No. In fact I was thinking perhaps a healthy game of chess might be just as effective in calming the Raelen mind."

"If far less pleasurable," she replied. "I do so much want to be the first Raelen female to bear a human man's child, Renwick. It would mean so much to the Unity Project between our races. But you still deny me. Why?"

Renwick looked at her, his face suddenly blank. "I can't talk about this, Makera, you know that." She pulled her hand from his.

"Is it that you have feelings for another? Or you don't find Raelen women attractive?"

He shook his head. "It's far worse than any of that," he said.

"Then *what?*" she demanded.

"I can't go with you down this path, Makera. The fact is… I'm sterile. The doctor's don't know why, of if they do they're not telling me. I could never give you what you want, so I don't want you to waste your time pursuing me," he said, then turned away from her.

Makera looked to Poul and Myra as they were eating, playfully sharing each other's meals.

"Best see if that dispenser can conjure up a chess set," she said.

#

They emerged from the galley area an hour later and went to the command deck, or rather the command center, as Yan had called it. Renwick supposed the Kali's central operating systems were all on this one massive deck. He was used to the bridge of a vessel being a cramped and tight space, full of equipment and people. The command center of the *Kali* was neither, in fact it was cavernous, and he and Makera could find no one when they first arrived. After a few minutes of searching they came upon Yan and Amanda at a large console. Yan was sitting in an oversized seat that was attached to a hooded device. Renwick peered inside but could see nothing on the display.

"I'm trying to plot us a course out of here, which is hard to do with so much dark space between us and the galactic core," Yan said. It occurred to Renwick that they had encountered the same problem on the skiff during their time lost in Void Space. "And you can't see the display, Senator, because you have to be sitting right where I am for it to show up."

"Is this the navigation console?" asked Makera.

"That's on a need-to-know basis, Ambassador," said Yan. Renwick felt Makera tense visibly under his touch. He had just spent considerable time and effort easing the Ambassador's wave of anger and he had no desire to see it return again so soon. He stepped between Makera and the console.

"You're going to have to be more forthcoming, Captain, or our relationship with you will be a difficult one," he said, trying a negotiating tactic on her.

"I am a clone, Senator. Our relationship is not difficult for me at all," Yan said. He felt Makera trying to push past him but he restrained her. This alerted Amanda, who took note of the action. Renwick watched her move a fraction closer to Yan and the console. Renwick turned to Makera.

"Perhaps it would be best if you let me handle these negotiations," he said quietly but firmly to her, his hands set hard on her shoulders.

"I am a trained negotiator as well," she snapped back. He took her a few steps away.

"Yes, one with a violent temper, through no fault of your own, I might add. I know it's the Raelen nature. Please Makera, allow me to represent our interests, for now," he said. She looked frustrated but gave him a firm nod and then went back the way she had come. When she was out of sight he turned back to the captain.

"Provoking her doesn't help," he said to Yan. "She's a Raelen, and they are difficult to control in the most positive of circumstances."

"I wasn't provoking her, Senator," Yan responded. "I was merely stating the fact that I don't need anything from you to do this job. You're just passengers as far as I'm concerned. I'm quite comfortable handling this mission myself."

"Along with your androids," he said.

"Yes."

He reached out and swung the couch she was in towards him and got right in her face. Amanda moved within a step of him, preparing to physically defend Yan if necessary.

"Despite appearances, Captain, my diplomatic crew and I, your passengers, are the only ones present on this vessel with real skin in this game," he said, then he angrily pushed her hand from the navigation controls. "You seem like a real enough person, you may even feel real, at least to yourself, but the fact is that you're not considered alive under Terran Unity law, which banned cloning and clone rights in its foundational documents. And these androids, even Amanda here, aren't alive either. My crew and I however are all too real, all too alive, and all too fragile. Their safety is my primary concern. If you don't get that, then I will have to take any actions I see as necessary to defend them."

"Such as?" Yan said, taking everything in with a calm, controlled exterior.

"I'm sure the Ambassador and I can think of something," he said. The corner of Yan's mouth curled up in an impatient sneer and she sat back. Amanda stepped between her and Renwick.

"The androids could handle any kind of trouble you could make, Renwick, but that's not really the important point. You're right about one thing, I do need *you*. Your knowledge of this time could be valuable," she said. "And I could make a case for the Raelen Ambassador as well, despite her lack of self-control. The others of your crew are, quite frankly, unimportant."

"So you need me?" he said. Yan shook her head.

"I *want* you, your cooperation. In exchange I'll do what I can to protect all your lives. And you will be responsible for keeping that Raelen under control. Agreed?"

Renwick took a step back. "Agreed," he said.

Yan slid the couch back to the navigation console.

"What's our destination? This emitter station?" Renwick asked.

Yan shook her head negative. "Eventually, but as my part in the agreement, I am taking your unnecessary crew back to Minara, where I will place them in your lifeboat and send them on their way."

"What? You can't do that!" he protested.

"Yes I can, Senator," she said.

"You'll be stranding them in a system filled with Pirates!" he said.

"I've already scanned Minara. There are no pirate ships, and your cruiser is still intact."

"Then we'll find a way to stop you from firing your engines," he said. Yan laughed.

"We've been underway for nearly an hour. We should be at Minara in just a few more. You can't stop anything, Senator," she said. "Now why don't you go and keep your Raelen playmate company while I run this ship."

Unable to think of any other action to take, Renwick stormed off to the galley and did exactly that.

6. BACK TO MINARA

Having just spent the last few hours explaining to Rand and Myra that they were to be sent away, Renwick found Yan at the main console again. The conversation had not gone down well with any of his crew, and he thought it wise to continue to leave Ambassador Makera out of the discussions with the *Kali's* master.

"Good, you're here," said Yan. "We'll be outside Minara in a few more minutes."

"Outside the system?" he asked. "We're not going in?"

She shook her head. "You are, Mr. Renwick, but not the *Kali*. She operates best within the Void. Or more precisely, within a bubble of normal space inside the Void."

"I'd been meaning to ask you about that," he said. "How can you get from place to place if you can't navigate normal space? I mean, how do you keep a bearing on the galactic core for reference?"

Yan didn't take her eyes from the navigation display, but answered anyway. "The *Kali's* instruments are much more sensitive than anything your technology likely has. And remember, the *Kali* was designed for the Void," she said.

"That doesn't answer my question," he said. "Nor does it explain your method of propulsion or any other of the many mysteries of this ship."

Yan eyed him a bit suspiciously, then chose to answer. "In fact, the engines do not operate via propulsion at all," she said. "The forward scoop is also an emitter. We simply project dark energy ahead of us to travel through. The engines are light matter field projectors which balance against the dark energy of the Void. The friction between the two opposing forms of energy creates a bubble that allows us to "slide" through dark space. The secondary scoop on the hull then clears the path ahead, and leaves a wake of normal space behind us, and the Void is forever vanquished from where we have traversed," she said.

He contemplated this a second. "That's certainly technology well above our own, or any of the three races in the Known Cosmos. I wonder how it is that the Trans-Earth Commonwealth had it almost three centuries ago," he said. Again she eyed him with suspicion.

"What are you driving at, Senator?" she said. He shrugged.

"I'm just looking for answers, Captain. For instance, the many unusual ships in the landing bay, some of the designs looked-"

"Not relevant," she cut him off. They reached a standoff, Renwick standing over her, Yan sitting at her station, unwilling to give more. Renwick changed the subject again.

"What were you trying to accomplish in leaving the *Kali* to get the relief team?"

Yan shifted, obviously uncomfortable at the question. After a moment of silence she returned her attention to the navigation display, but began speaking. "The scoop malfunctioned after the initial test. Our analysis determined it was a design flaw of some kind. Three of my crew tried to repair the scoop, but they were killed by an errant dark energy pulse that fused the emitters and left the *Kali* stranded. The rest of us, I assume, took one of the shuttles to get the relief team and return to make repairs," she said.

"But if there was a design flaw in the scoops, wouldn't you have warned the others at the emitter station about that?" asked Renwick. Yan shifted in her seat again.

"I would have assumed so. If the scoops didn't work, then the results of deploying the emitter station on a much larger scale than out test would be catastrophic," she said.

"I'd say that describes the Void pretty well," said Renwick.

Yan nodded. "The funny thing is, I talked to Amanda and she told me that she and the other androids had fixed the scoop just a few weeks after I left. Then they went into hibernation to wait for me to return, which apparently I never did. When your ship arrived within their scanning range the automated command program assumed you were the relief crew and drew you in, then activated the androids. All rather lucky for you, I'd say."

Renwick thought about this for a moment, then, "What was your mission, Yan? What was the test?"

Yan leaned on the console with her hands, a very human gesture for a hologram. "Our mission was to test the Void generator on an uninhabited system. Essentially the emitters send out dark energy particles which envelop the interplanetary magnetic field of the subject system. The interplanetary magnetic field is an electrically charged plasma generated by the system's sun, and carried by the solar wind of the star. The dark energy bonds to the positively charged particles of the interplanetary medium, and essentially fills the space outside the realm of the solar wind of the star, encasing the target system, and thus neutralizing the system with dark energy." She said it in a very mechanical manner, almost like she was reciting a learned program.

Renwick contemplated this. "We've always believed any system enveloped by the Void was destroyed," he said. Yan shook her head.

"Not so," she said. "The system is still intact, the star still burns and the planets inside still exist. Life goes on. But the target, the enemy, is encased inside their star system, and thus made more malleable to our demands," she paused and began checking systems on the console again. "At least, that was the theory."

He sighed. "This brings up a greater problem, you realize."

"Such as?"

"Such as all the systems we thought were destroyed still exist within the Void. And now that we know that, we have a moral obligation to help them," he said. "If the emitter worked correctly, these systems are not dead, but they are cut off from the rest of the universe, thousands of them."

"Perhaps *you* have a moral obligation," she replied, "but I doubt that I will be able to help."

Renwick decided not to press the point further, for now. "Where was the initial test carried out?" he asked.

"The Pendax system," she said, not looking up from the board. Pendax was a neighbor star of Minara, where the skiff had entered the Void. "But the emitter station was located much closer to Gataan space. We were trying to reign them in. Piracy was rampant among their culture, even in those days, we were trying to deter them, and there was a lot of political pressure from the Merchant Networks back home," she paused, then continued.

"When the scoops stopped functioning, we couldn't clear the Pendax system. So I went for help, I assume." She looked up to him. "That part wasn't stored in my memory. My last recollection is just after the scoops failed. I assume my corporeal half didn't have time to update me before she went for help."

Renwick looked at her with pity. "You feel it, don't you, the emotion, the loss, the sense of failure."

"I do," she admitted. "I may not be a real girl, Renwick, but I *feel* real, to myself, anyway. I feel emotion, I feel myself breathing, my heart pumping. Hell, I've even felt sexual arousal. But I know I'm not really real."

"So," he said, changing the subject back to the Void, "Apparently you failed somehow to stop the emitter station from starting?"

"I don't know, but I'm sure that would have been my first priority. The emitter station was designed to be automated, and set to be deployed three days after our initial test."

"So, either you never made it to the station to shut it down, or you made it and somebody decided to launch the system anyway," said Renwick.

Yan's head snapped towards him at this suggestion.

"You're saying someone could have done this intentionally?" she asked.

"I'm a negotiator. I consider all possibilities. You did say the Merchant Networks were involved, correct?"

"I can't see how cutting themselves off from ninety percent of their markets could help them," she said.

"Perhaps that wasn't their intent, and the whole thing just got away from them, like an oil spill in water, or a hydrazine pump gone wild," he speculated. Yan looked away again, an act that would have indicated a sense of shame in a 'real' person. "One last question," he said. "Who built the emitter station, and the *Kali*?"

Yan shook her head. "I don't know that," she admitted. "When I came out to the station it was fully operational. I was in the Commonwealth Navy, but I had left to pursue a career as a private merchant. I was recruited by an intelligence wing of the Navy, on a private contract, to do the Pendax test."

Renwick looked around the bridge. "This technology is far beyond anything we have today."

"Or in my time," she said.

"So who built it?" he pressed. She looked at him.

"I don't know," she said. It seemed to Renwick to be an honest answer.

"And that," he said, "is the most disturbing thing of all."

#

They all gathered back on the landing deck, inside the environmental bubble that held the skiff. The *Kali* had stopped just outside normal space, near the Minara system. Renwick had put Poul Rand in charge of collecting supplies for the journey back out of the *Kali's* stores, mainly to keep the three junior negotiators busy. They had done an admirable job and the skiff was loaded down with food, water, and medical supplies, enough to keep them for close to a month if they had to jump from star to star to eventually get back to a Unity base. Of course that would be shortened considerably if they found Captain Aybar and the crew of the *Phaeton* all in good order.

The androids, led by the speechless Thorne, had been of great assistance with the heavier items. Amanda and Yan had been absent up until now.

"I think we're ready to go," said Rand to Renwick. Renwick looked around the skiff's cabin, pleased. "You've done a good job, Poul," he said. "Are you sure you're comfortable with the controls? I'm trusting you to get Myra back to a Unity base safely."

"I am sir, and I'll do my best to get us all back sir," Poul said.

"I know you will," replied Renwick with a pat on the shoulder. "Makera and I will be taking the skiff over to the *Phaeton*, with luck we'll find Captain Aybar and her crew waiting for us."

"With luck, sir, yes," said Poul, then he stopped and pointed out the window of the pilot's nest. "What's this now? A send off?"

Renwick looked out the window and saw the android Amanda approaching the skiff via the gangway. "I doubt that," he said, then went to the airlock door.

Amanda came though the environmental bubble, her always-pleasant smile locked on her face. Renwick went down the ladder to face her as she approached the gathered crew.

"I'm going with you," she said in a calm voice.

"Um, that's really not necessary," said Renwick.

"Yes," agreed Makera, "I insist you stay." Amanda's pleasant smile didn't waver.

"You don't understand," she said. "I am not Amanda. It's Captain Yan, and I insist on going."

"Yan? You're really inside that thing?" said Renwick.

"Yes, I am. Amanda suggested it, and I took her up on the offer. The transfer process was really quite simple, and since as a digital construct or clone, I'm mostly limited to the *Kali*, I thought I'd take this opportunity to 'stretch my legs' such as they are."

Renwick looked to his companions. He was stumped.

"Um, what about your body?"

"Safely stored in stasis," she said.

"Very well then. We were about to depart," he said.

"Do you mind if I fly her?" Amanda/Yan asked.

"I do indeed mind," said Makera. Renwick held up a hand to her.

"If you wish," he said to Amanda/Yan.

"Well, let's go then," the captain said. Then they all took their places.

#

The trip to the *Phaeton* took six hours through normal space, after the *Kali* had punched a final hole through the Void. Renwick and Makera agreed to take turns in the co-pilot's couch to monitor Amanda/Yan. Makera took the first watch while Renwick rested. Clearly the two women did not like each other much, but that didn't stop Amanda/Yan from starting a conversation.

"What's your interest in Renwick anyway?" said Amanda/Yan. Makera contemplated the android, which housed the digital body of someone she disliked intensely.

"I don't think that's any of your business," the Ambassador said.

"I'm still in command of this mission. That makes it my business," said Amanda/Yan.

"You are collection of digital files stored and organized in such a way as to simulate a real person, and you currently reside in an android body. Conversing with you would be like talking to a computer program. I have no interest in conversing with computer programs."

"Oh c'mon now, just think of me as one of the girls!"

"I will not," said Makera.

"I'll just tell him that you're jealous, then."

Makera's faced flushed. "Jealous? Of what?"

"Like it or not, Ambassador," said Amanda/Yan, "you have to admit that Amanda is attractive, perhaps even more so than you. And judging by the way he reacts to her physically-"

"You can detect such things?"

"Oh, yes. This body is full of exceptional qualities, and fully functional. I'll bet I could get him interested in-"

"Stop," said Makera, holding up her hand. "I really do not wish to continue this line of conversation."

"Then answer my questions," said Amanda/Yan. Makera glared at the android woman.

"Very well," she finally said, resigned to her predicament. "My interest in him is both personal and scientific. With this treaty Humans and the Raelen will live in close proximity to each other. It has occurred to our scientists that eventually, interbreeding may occur. It is my desire to see if it is not only feasible, but desirable."

"Wait, you mean you're trying to get *pregnant* by him?" said Amanda/Yan.

Makera shrugged. "If I must, yes. It would be a great honor. But he has said he is sterile, by human standards. My hope is that Raelen doctors can determine if some accommodation can still be made."

"Forget I said anything," said Amanda/Yan, quickly turning her attention back to her flight controls. "I'm sorry I asked."

Renwick relieved the Ambassador an hour later, after Makera had secured a promise from the android not to share their conversation.

"Did you ladies enjoy your time together?" he asked Amanda/Yan after Makera had left, sliding into the co-pilot's couch.

"Oh, yes," said Amanda/Yan. "Most illuminating."

#

The skiff approached the *Phaeton* in stealth mode, just in case there were any of the Gataan pirates still in the area. Makera had rejoined Renwick and the android on the flight deck.

"I'm detecting remnants of a small ship," said Amanda/Yan.

"The *Phaeton* destroyed one of the Gataan corvettes just as we escaped," said Renwick. Yan/Amanda nodded. It was an almost human gesture.

"That would be consistent with the debris pattern. Scans indicate that your cruiser is still intact. Life-support and power systems are operating, but I'm not detecting any life signs," said Amanda/Yan.

"Could they all be dead?" Makera asked Renwick.

"I doubt it, with all the systems still operational. They could be aboard but hiding, some kind of stealth field technology," he said.

"Or they could have been taken prisoner by the Gataan," said Amanda/Yan. "In which case we are too late to help them and should proceed with our mission to the emitter station."

"Dock this ship," said Renwick to Amanda/Yan, like it was an order. "We're going aboard."

"I will not!" said Amanda/Yan. "If your friends have been taken prisoner then there's nothing we can do."

"If my friends have been taken prisoner than I have an obligation to rescue them, captain. The Void has been out there for three centuries, it can wait for a few days more. Now dock this ship, or I will do it myself," Renwick said.

"You forget your situation, Senator. I am far stronger than any of you in this body, and I will say where we go," said Amanda/Yan.

"I think it is you who forget the situation, captain," said Renwick, specifically addressing the Yan personality. He looked back to Makera, who stood across the flight deck, the coil pistol leveled squarely at the android. "Once we left the protective field of the *Kali* I recharged the pistol and gave it to the Ambassador when we changed watches. So you see, captain, we will be going aboard the *Phaeton*, with or with you."

Amanda/Yan's android face revealed nothing of the thoughts going on inside but eventually she tapped the control board and relinquished control of the skiff to Renwick.

"With me, I should think," she said to Renwick, who took the controls and started the docking procedure. "But I think this is a very bad idea."

#

Renwick led Makera and Amanda/Yan out of the air lock and into the lower corridors of the *Phaeton*. He left the others behind with Poul for safe keeping. The walls of the corridors were scarred with energy weapon burns and the air smelled of ionized gas. "There was a fight here," Renwick said, holding his pistol at the ready.

"That's obvious," said Amanda/Yan. She may not have acted fully human, but she was talking like one. More and more of Yan's abrasive personality seemed to be coming through the android body.

The crept along the walls, Renwick first, followed by Makera and then Amanda/Yan, moving slowly through dimly lit corridors. Silence and darkness closed in on them.

"I don't like this," said Renwick. "It's too quiet. I don't even hear the sound of the EV system pumping."

"There's air in here," agreed Makera, "but the EV system has either been shut off or it's not working."

"There is too much residual heat onboard for the system to be broken," said Amanda/Yan as they crept along the main corridor of the *Phaeton* towards the bridge. "Someone shut it off intentionally, likely when they detected us entering the system again from the Void, in an attempt to stay hidden."

"Which means there are still pirates on board," said Makera.

"*Gataan* pirates," reminded Renwick. Descendants of what was once the most feared fighting force in the Known Galaxy.

"But why would they leave a crew behind if they were in such a hurry?" asked Makera.

"Salvage," replied Renwick. "The first rule of piracy is you unload the hottest merchandise first. You store the rest for when things quiet down."

"I see," said Makera. "I should learn more about piracy practices, obviously."

Renwick nodded in agreement, but he had already moved on to his next thought. "I wish we had a bio scanner. It would be nice to know if there are any surprises waiting for us up ahead." Amanda/Yan moved past Makera and put a hand on Renwick's shoulder.

"We have a scanner," she said, "me."

"Are you serious?" said Renwick. Amanda/Yan nodded.

"This body is equipped with a variety of tools, but unfortunately not weapons," she said. "I think it would be best if you let me take the lead," she said, taking the coil pistol from Renwick. He looked back to Makera with concern, but she said nothing in protest. They continued their slow approach to the bridge.

The corridor curved just enough to keep the main hatch to the bridge out of their sight. Amanda/Yan held up a hand. "Stay here," she said. Renwick started to protest but she was already moving up the corridor. He watched her go about ten meters from them and then pause, her head turning slowly from side to side. She kept the pistol in her hand, but at her side in a non-threatening manner. After a few moments she turned and came back towards them.

"There are two guards outside, one to either side of the bridge hatch, hidden behind the support beams," she said.

"How can you tell that?" asked Makera.

Amanda/Yan managed to get an annoyed look on her face. "I told you, this body is equipped with a bio scanner, amongst other useful tools. I scanned through the beams and detected two Gataan pirates outside the hatch and one inside, on the bridge."

"But how do you know their Gataan?" challenged Makera. "They could be human survivors."

"Gataan have a core body temperature that is three degrees Celsius cooler than humans. It is what makes them such resourceful fighters. They don't overheat as easily and they recover quicker than humans," said Amanda/Yan.

"Are you convinced yet?" said Renwick to Makera. She gave him a sour look.

"What's the configuration of the hallway up there?" Amanda/Yan asked Renwick.

"Can't you just use your x-ray vision?" said Makera. Renwick quieted her with a hand gesture of impatience.

"There's a cross corridor just behind the main hatch, it leads to a supply compartment on one side and the armory on the other," he said. "The halls curve away, contouring to the bridge layout. I'd say they're what, maybe five meters to either side of the hatch to the compartment doors?" he looked to Makera.

"Six point five," she said, correcting him. He looked at her, annoyed. She shrugged. "So I measured it once. We are a precise race, Renwick. And it's always helpful to know how far away you are from the nearest weapon."

"There is likely to be gunfire," said Amanda/Yan. "Please stay safely back here until I have resolved the situation." Then she turned and walked back down the corridor. Makera put her hands to her hips in an annoyed gesture.

"She's just showing off! Oh, what I wouldn't give for a coil rifle right now!" whispered Makera.

"It's odd how she seems to have taken on some of the android's personality, or lack thereof," he said as he watched Amanda/Yan move down the hall. "It's an odd mix. Sarcasm one moment, cold calculation the next."

"It's something that bears watching," agreed Makera.

The two of them moved up the corridor, keeping Amanda/Yan in their visual range. They watched as she walked calmly and deliberately, then slowly raised the pistol and fired at the support beam to the left of the hatch. Return fire came from the corridor on the right but Amanda/Yan ducked out of the way with inhuman reflexes and then sprinted down the corridor at breakneck speed, firing all the way. She lunged at the left support wall feet first from half a dozen meters out and broke through the metal and mortar with ease. Renwick watched as she pivoted with speed and precision, taking out the pirate on the right with a single shot of orange coil fire. He watched as she dragged the other pirate out from beneath the rubble of the wall. The wall had been nearly a meter thick. Renwick and Makera came running up to her.

"That was impressive," he said.

"I told you to stay back, I'm not finished yet," said Amanda/Yan.

"Both of these guards are dead," said Makera. Renwick could see her anger rising again. "This one's neck is broken. Was that your intent?" Amanda/Yan looked at the two fallen Gataan with no expression of emotion.

"My intent was to neutralize them," said Amanda/Yan.

"You certainly did that."

Renwick examined the two guards. They were taller than humans, with caramel colored skin and long thickly woven hair. Their faces were quite human-like, except for an almond-like shape to the eyes. He'd never seen a living Gataan before, and then reminded himself that he still hadn't.

"I'd prefer there be no more killing," said Renwick, standing and taking the coil pistol back from Amanda/Yan.

"What about the pirate on the bridge?" she said.

"That's where I come in," he said. "I'm a negotiator by trade, remember?"

"As you wish," said Amanda/Yan, and then she walked away from them, heading back towards the skiff.

#

An hour later the EV systems had been restored and the remaining Gataan pirate was in the brig. He had happily surrendered after Renwick had shown him a video of Amanda/Yan's attack on his compatriots.

Once on the bridge Renwick had sent out a general call over the com system, hoping some hidden survivors might respond, but everything was silent. They did a quick assessment of the *Phaeton's* systems and found her still space-worthy. Her impellers were operable with about a thirty-percent reserve, and her local jump point generator was intact. The HD drive was a mess though, and wouldn't be working again until they managed to find a base. He called Poul and Myra over and had them start unloading supplies from the skiff.

"What's your plan, Renwick?" asked Amanda/Yan when they were alone on the bridge.

"With the local jump point generator intact I can set up a program to take the *Phaeton* back to a Unity base. That will leave the rest of us free to make a rescue in the skiff," he said.

"Rescue? Of whom?" Amanda/Yan demanded. Renwick looked directly at her.

"Of the remaining crew of the *Phaeton*. Our prisoner was very forthcoming to the Ambassador about there being human survivors taken off the ship against their will. Two women and one man. We are going to rescue them," he said, his statement was matter-of-fact and left no room for negotiating.

Amanda/Yan grabbed him by the arm and twisted him around in the captain's couch. "Are you insane? There's the entirety of the Known Cosmos to save," she said. Renwick winced in pain at her grip and she quickly withdrew her hand. He noted that the Yan side of her dual personality coming through again.

"I'd appreciate it if you'd keep your new-found strength in check!" he snapped at her, pulling his arm close and rubbing it. "And no, I'm not insane. Captain Aybar and her crew risked their lives to save us. I'm not going to let them rot in some sex slave camp as a reward. Perhaps in your time captain, such things as right and wrong didn't mean as much, but I assure you that in my time they still matter."

"Renwick, are the lives of a few worth so much more than the millions you'll be able to free from the darkness of the Void?" she said.

"They're all valuable, Captain Yan, I make no distinction. And it's not millions, it's billions," he said testily. "I'm well aware of the stakes." He snapped his arm back and forth and then returned to his console.

"So you'll make the billions wait for three people?" she asked. He spun around at her.

"I damn well will! Now if you'll excuse me, I have a program to encode. Perhaps you could make yourself, and your personal strength, more useful unloading the skiff with the others." Then he turned his back to her and started programming the local jump drive, hands moving furiously over the control console.

7. TO SKONDAR

"Why are we going to Skondar?" asked Ambassador Makera, ensconced once again in the pilot's nest of the rapidly moving skiff. "Cundaloa is just as likely a destination for slave traders."

"Because Skondar is the closest, and if I know my Gataan pirates like I think I do, then they'll want to unload their cargo as quickly as they can," said Renwick, swiveling towards her from the co-pilot's couch. "They won't want it to get out that they've taken to ambushing Unity cruisers on a regular basis."

The three of them, including Amanda/Yan, had left the *Phaeton* with Rand and Myra, back in the Minara system nearly a day ago, along with their locked-up pirate passenger. After unloading supplies for the *Phaeton's* slow trip home to Unity space, Renwick had said his goodbyes to his negotiating team. The skiff had then been reloaded with provisions and military supplies left aboard *Phaeton* by the pirates in their haste, including several coil rifles, pistols, and packs of stun grenades, things that might come in handy on a slave trading station. Renwick had watched with a sense of satisfaction as the *Phaeton* had jumped out of Minara space on the first leg of its multi-jump trip. He was confident they would get home safely.

The skiff had been in Skondar space for an hour, and now Renwick had time to turn his attention to the journey to the trading post. Makera was flying, while Amanda/Yan stood motionless behind them. One of the advantages of being an android was she didn't require any rest or sleep.

"You make me nervous," said Makera to Amanda/Yan. "Couldn't you just go lie down in the back for a while?"

"I could, but I'd be as awake as I am now and not nearly as useful," said the android. "I really don't have an 'off' switch in this body, Ambassador, I suggest you get used to it."

"You and Renwick could go have sex," deadpanned Makera. Amanda/Yan looked down at her Raelen companion.

"Uh, hello," said Renwick. "I *am* right here."

"You wouldn't mind?" Amanda/Yan said. Makera shook her head.

"Of course not. Raelen women aren't as possessive as humans. The desire for sexual variety is common in both human and Raelen males. We have matured enough to accept it, that's all."

Amanda/Yan turned her attention to Renwick.

"Senator, could I interest you in-"

"Forget it," Renwick cut her off. "I'm pleased to know you're fully functional, Yan. And the casing is pleasing to the eye, I'll give you that. But I think I've already gone where no man has gone before enough on this trip." Amanda/Yan straightened back up and returned to staring out the forward window.

"As you wish," she said.

"I thought you couldn't feel anything in that body anyway?" said Renwick. Amanda/Yan responded without turning her attention away from the window scene.

"It is unusual. Clearly this body is designed for sexual activity, but I don't know if I would *enjoy* it. It's like there's no neural connection to the pleasure center of the android's brain, if there is one, even," she said.

"Perhaps you should have asked before you hopped in the driver's seat," chimed in Makera.

"Always read the owner's manual," said Renwick. Amanda/Yan didn't react and the conversation seemed set to end, then:

"Do you think I'm acting differently since I've been in here?" she said. Renwick looked to Makera, then shifted in his couch.

"I would say you're less yourself, at least from what I know of you," he said. "Is it possible integrating with the android mind is altering your persona program?"

"Possible," she said. "But then I am just a collection of digital data files to begin with. It's difficult to remember that sometimes."

"Well at any rate you're both still annoying me, and we have three more hours to the trading post," said Makera. "Why don't you go play a game of… oh, what do you call it? Chess?" Renwick looked up to Amanda/Yan, who turned and smiled at him in a mechanical way.

"Well, if you're certain you won't try sex…" she trailed off.

"I'm certain," he said. She gestured to the back of the compartment.

"After you, Senator."

#

"I was never this good before," said Amanda/Yan as she closed in on winning her sixth straight game.

"And I was never this bad. I was champion at my university three years running," said Renwick. "I think the android mind is seeping into your thoughts."

"Does that concern you?" she asked without looking up from the board.

He was pensive about answering. "I'm not sure," he said honestly. "After the incident with the pirates-"

"That was well within the range of my normal personality," she said.

"Yes, but there was a certain coldness to your behavior. My concern is that if your emotions are limited, you'll lose higher cognitive decision making ability."

"Things like compassion," she said.

"Exactly."

"I trust you'll continue monitoring me?"

"Oh yes," he said. She made her checkmate move.

"Good," she replied.

A sensor beep from the pilot's nest got both of their attention.

"What is it?" asked Renwick, already moving to the co-pilot's couch.

"We're picking up traffic from the trading post," said Makera. "I'm activating defensive systems, such as they are."

"Is that wise?" asked Amanda/Yan. "It could attract unwanted attention."

"I'm not flying into a station where I could be imprisoned like chattel unarmed," Makera replied.

"I agree," said Renwick. "It may be a provocation but if we arrive through the proper channels we should be received as traders, not as potential stock for the auctions."

"What is our cover to be while we search for your friends?" asked Amanda/Yan. Renwick looked at the two women.

"Makera and I are a merchants. You are our servant. I think it's best that way because if we were taken you would be most likely to be able to take care of yourself," he said.

"Lovely," said Amanda/Yan.

"Stand by," said Makera. "The station is transmitting coordinates. I'm vectoring us in for approach."

Renwick took Amanda/Yan by the arm and led her out of the Ambassador's hearing range. "Yan, there's something I want to ask you," he said.

"Am I to be traded for your friends?" she replied, anticipating the question.

"It does make some sense," said Renwick. "An android of your obvious sophistication could bring a high price or great value in a trade."

"And do you intend to leave me behind if things get difficult?" she asked. Renwick looked up to her.

"We leave no one behind," he said, then returned to the pilot's nest and strapped himself in for the docking.

#

Skondar was an ugly place. The planet itself was devoid of atmosphere and a dull brown-gray in color. The station that hovered in orbit above it wasn't much better. It looked like it had been cobbled together from pieces of various other constructs over the centuries, which probably wasn't far from the truth. As the Void had grown other stations had probably had to be moved by the Merchant Networks, and many of them no doubt had ended up here, merging themselves with the original station.

The central core of the station looked symmetrical, but as the trading post had grown outward it had acquired a distinctly lopsided and ungainly appearance, not to mention its reputation as a place where legitimate merchants rarely went, except out of necessity.

"We've been given a docking port number," said Makera. "That is, if we're ready?"

"We will be," said Renwick. The Ambassador followed the station master's instructions and got the skiff in queue for docking. Renwick took Amanda/Yan aside again.

"Can you keep any weapons on you?" he asked her.

"I can store weapons inside me, in my main body cavity, if that's what you mean," she said.

"That will do," said Renwick. He spent the next several minutes handing her coil charge packs and a stun grenades while Makera guided them in to the station. The android lifted her tunic top and started to peel back a layer of human-looking skin. He preferred not to watch how or where she stored the items. "We'll go in brandishing rifles and pistols, like we know how to use them," he said to her. "They'll likely confiscate the charging packs and let us keep the guns for show. We'll use you as our backup in case things turn ugly."

"In case?" she said.

"*When* they turn ugly," he corrected. He handed her a pistol. "You may need this," he said. Amanda/Yan took it silently and he looked away again.

"All ready," she said after a moment. "You can look now, Renwick." He did. He saw that her skin was seamless once again as she pulled her tunic top down over her skirt. He went back to the co-pilot's couch.

"Take us in, Ambassador," he said.

#

The station guard that greeted them was human and overly-adorned with medals and weaponry. He was backed by two more guards of the same general size, shape, and demeanor. They stood in the airlock doorway, blocking the entrance to the station.

"State your business," the leader said.

"We're free traders," replied Renwick, gesturing to Makera. "Here to see what we can bargain for, and perhaps acquire, and possibly sell."

"What are you selling?" said the leader. It was clear that satisfying this one man was the key to gaining access to the station. Renwick nodded towards Amanda/Yan. The guard took a step into the skiff but Renwick's hand to his chest stopped him. Renwick was a tall man, and lean, but muscular. The guard was just huge, but not so huge that he dwarfed the Senator. Renwick's show of territoriality had the desired affect though and the man backed off. He looked at Amanda/Yan.

"We get a hundred just as pretty as her through here every day," he said. "And it's a buyer's market."

"We don't have time to dawdle with you," started Makera, but Renwick grabbed her arm and forced her backwards.

"I'll speak for us, woman!" he said angrily. Her eyes lit like fire but she recognized his ploy and bowed her head to keep the guard from seeing her rising anger.

"Apologies," she said in as soft and meek a voice as she could manage. Renwick turned back to the guard.

"A Raelen woman," the guard said. "Now she could get you a pretty penny in the exchanges."

"She is my companion, and not for sale," countered Renwick.

"Too bad," said the guard. Renwick pushed Makera behind him.

"Now back to what I *am* trading. As you say, a hundred as pretty as her a day. But can any of those hundred do what this one can do?" The guard crossed his arms.

"And what would that be?" Renwick motioned to one of the subordinate guards.

"Have him give me his rifle," he said.

"What for?" demanded the guard.

"A demonstration," replied Renwick, challenging him. The guard hesitated a moment, still sizing up Renwick, then motioned for the underling guard to hand over his rifle, which he reluctantly did. Once he had it the leader decoupled the charging pack and handed the now-powerless rife to Renwick.

Renwick hefted it. "Standard Unity issue from the Precaren Conflict era, I'd say. Thirty or so years old, a bit heavy and inaccurate for today's uses, but still a good weapon. Wouldn't you agree?" he said to the lead guard.

"It's not Precaren, and it's forty years old," admitted the leader.

"Even better. Depleted uranium shells actually make the barrel harder and scoring from the energy fire seal any fractures. These are nearly unbreakable. I'm a collector, you see," said Renwick. The guard cocked his head as if he were growing bored.

"Your demonstration, sir?" he said. Renwick tossed the rifle to Amanda/Yan, who caught it with one hand, turning it effortlessly to examine it, then started bending it, barrel first.

"What the hell-" the lead guard started for the rifle but Renwick blocked him.

"You did ask for a demonstration," Renwick said.

Precious few seconds later and Amanda/Yan had twisted the rifle barrel into a loop shape, curving it back in on itself. Then she tossed the rifle back to Renwick, who caught it with both hands and pressed it into the guard's chest.

"Now, can any of the hundred other girls as pretty as her that will come through here today do that?" he said. The guard held the broken rifle in disbelief, then handed it back to the underling.

"You've earned your passage to the station," said the guard. "But you've not yet paid your trading fee."

Renwick knew he meant that he needed to be bribed. He turned back to Amanda/Yan with a nod. She went to a supply cabinet and pulled out three of the coil rifles captured form the Gataan pirates, handing one to Renwick.

"Next generation Unity coil rifle, the New Madras Mark 7. Seventy percent more efficient than what you're carrying and half the weight. Charging packs will give you three hundred rounds before you have to reload, and it can fire stun grenades from the barrel as well." He handed the unloaded the rifle over to the guard. The man ran his hands across it, hefted it and checked the sight, then nodded.

"Five packs each, and the grenades," he said. Renwick shook his head.

"Three packs each, that's nine between you and your friends here. No grenades. Those are for trading," he said. The guard eyed him warily, hesitating. Then Renwick sweetened the pot.

"And one adapter each so you can use your current power packs with the new rifles," he said.

"Done," said the guard. Renwick held up a hand.

"One more thing, we get your old rifles," he said.

"Why?" asked the guard.

"The more valuable the commodity you're trading, the more desirable it is to blend in," stated Renwick.

They spent the next several minutes exchanging equipment with the guards. The lead guard kept all but one pack each for himself, passing the others to his friends but keeping all three of the rifles.

"You'll have to disarm before debarking," he said. Having anticipated this action, Renwick and Makera went through the motions of storing the rifles and pistol power packs on the skiff.

"Satisfied?" said Renwick. The guard nodded.

"Just remember, regardless of our dealings here, if you break a single station rule your cargo is forfeit. Break two and we take your ship. Break three and you'll be standing in the auction pits," he said.

"Understood," said Renwick. The guard finally motioned them past. Renwick sealed the skiff behind them and then started down the docking arm, trailing Makera and Amanda/Yan, who were being escorted by the underlings.

"One more question, trader," asked the guard. Renwick stopped and turned in the corridor.

"That woman-thing. Why would you give up something so valuable?"

Renwick looked at him and smiled his sleaziest smile.

"Because everything has its price," he said, then turned and walked away with his companions.

The guard hesitated a moment, and then walked to a wall com console and dialed in a private number. There was no ringing, but after a few moments a voice came on the line.

"Yes?"

"It's Hendrix , sir."

"What is it?" said the voice.

"You asked me to contact you if a certain type of cargo ever came aboard the station."

"Yes?"

"Well I just passed one through Port 27, Leg 9, sir." There was a pause at the other end of the line, then:

"Well done, Hendrix. Your bonus is in your account now," said the voice.

"Thank you Mr. Zueros," said Hendrix back, but the line had already been cut.

8.

Three hours later and they had secured a small berth in the main station complex, away from the seedier elements in the docking arms. Those were the places where the seamiest deals took place; the trading in underage slaves, illegal weapons, drugs and the like. The main complex held the "legitimate" trading areas; the livestock markets, slave auction pits, equipment trades, ship sales, and the like.

"What's the currency here?" asked Makera.

"Officially Unity crowns. Platinum, gold or silver, some copper and uranium. But primarily it's a barter exchange, with values being determined before you can bid based on what you're trading in," he said.

"And since we left all of our weapons onboard the skiff or with those guards, we're trading what?" she asked. Renwick pointed to Amanda/Yan.

"Are you serious?" said Makera, concerned.

"But only long enough for us to-" he started.

"Stop!" said Amanda/Yan, cutting him off. She looked around the room, then raised her hands, palms out. "Close your eyes, quickly, and keep them shut," she said with urgency. They both did as instructed. Even with his eyes shut Renwick detected a bright flash of white light followed by a rainbow of colors glowing under his eyelids for a few seconds, then it diminished.

"You can open them again," said Amanda/Yan

"What just happened?" asked Makera.

Amanda/Yan turned to her two companions. "I detected observation devices in the room. They have now been neutralized and a protective shield is operating with ten meters of me at all times," Amanda/Yan said. "We can speak freely now."

"Observation devices?" questioned Makera.

"Probably standard procedure," said Renwick. "I'm sure any information on what new traders are bringing aboard the station would be valuable."

"That's comforting," said Makera.

"Can we trust our personal com devices?" asked Makera of Amanda/Yan. The android held out her hand to the two of them. Renwick took his and Makera's ear coms and handed them over to the android. She worked over them for a few moments and then handed them back.

"What did you do?" Renwick asked.

"I recalibrated them to operate on a frequency outside the standard ranges of the base security net. They should be good, but we should rotate the frequencies every few hours to be sure."

"Thank you," said Renwick, placing his com back in his ear.

"Now, as I was saying," he started. "Our cover story is that we're here to trade the android in return for enough credit to buy HD drive materials, when in fact we'll be looking to buy back any crew members of the Phaeton that we can find. And no, Yan, we have no intent of leaving you behind. You'll just have to pretend to be a simple-minded android servant long enough for us to engage in enough trading to make us look legitimate, then we're out of here."

"Thank you," Amanda/Yan said.

"Along those lines," he said, "I'd like you to scan the auction trades scheduled for today and see if you can find anything that looks like it might be from the *Phaeton*. People, equipment, anything could be a lead to where Captain Aybar or her crew might be. Scan ahead twenty-four hours and then back seventy-two, at least. Makera and I are going to survey the landscape. We should be back in a couple of hours."

"That should be plenty of time to do the scans," Amanda/Yan said.

"Good," he said. "And I think it would be best if you stayed out of sight." She nodded.

"Agreed."

"If it's not too much to ask, I'd like to get a couple of charger packs for the pistols, um, out of you, if I could," he said.

Amanda/Yan obliged, taking only a few moments to produce the packs. "You'll need to keep those well-hidden. Remember it's a station violation if you're caught with them," she said.

"Thank you, Yan," said Renwick, "we'll be careful." Then he stuck the pack inside his diplomatic vest, hidden now under an outer cloak purchased at a station shop, and handed the other to Makera.

They gathered their equipment, being sure to brandish their heavy rifles and weaponry. Renwick gave Amanda/Yan a reassuring look, and then they were gone, out the door and into the unknown.

#

Renwick downed the last of his ale, the aftertaste burning down his throat as he swallowed. It was near agony, but outwardly he maintained an expression of complete calm as he monitored the auction boards on display in the bar. He and Ambassador Makera had wondered in off of the main thoroughfare bisecting the station over an hour ago, and this was his third ale in that time. Makera had matched him drink for drink, despite her obvious distaste for the local swill.

"The gray haired one in the corner is still watching me," she said.

"He's probably just sizing you up for a bid," replied Renwick without taking his eyes from the constantly moving auction board. The auction was a twenty-four-seven process, and you could monitor it from all over the station, but you had to actually go down to the auction pits if you wanted to bid.

So far Renwick had seen at least three lots of equipment that had no doubt come from the *Phaeton* based on its condition, sophistication, and price, which was well below market to promote a quick sale. But no sign of *Phaeton* personnel, which likely meant that they had already been auctioned between the time that they had spent in the Void and on the *Kali* and arriving here. They were going to have to rely on Amanda/Yan's research abilities to locate any of them, if they were in fact still on the station.

He had also fielded at least half a dozen offers of sale or trade on Makera, including one who only wanted her for an hour, but he was an elderly gentlemen and clearly wouldn't have survived the process. Makera, for her part, had handled the last suitor, a particularly annoying and drunk merchant, with a flurry of punches that had quickly knocked him down and out. He was currently unconscious, as well as functioning as doorstop for the bar.

Renwick had registered the two of them as traders and used his own personal accounts to establish their trading credits. He also listed "Subject Property" that would be evaluated later for auction; Amanda/Yan, without specifically identifying her as the property they intended to sell.

He took his last drink of ale and turned away from the screen at last.

"How much longer do we wait here?" Makera hissed at him under her breath.

"Kiss me," he said.

"What? You're drunk," she replied. He leaned in closer.

"I'm not drunk. Now kiss me," he insisted. She did as he requested, her tongue flicking sensuously in and out of his mouth. He took a fraction of a second to glance at the gray haired man she had mentioned. After an appropriate time he pulled back and whispered in her ear.

"Activate my com," he said to her. She looked at him, then leaned in and covered his ear, pressing the com device with her tongue.

"Yan," he said quietly after doing the same for Makera. Amanda/Yan responded through his earpiece.

"Here," she said.

"What do you have for me," he whispered into Makera's com, pretending to nuzzle her.

"I've found three listings for *Phaeton* personnel," she said. "The engineer Kish was auctioned off to a station maintenance crew three days ago. Captain Aybar was purchased by an unknown private party, who's yacht is apparently still at the station, yesterday morning. The *Phaeton's* pilot, Lieutenant Mischa Cain, will be auctioned in twelve hours."

"Is that all of the *Phaeton* crew who survived?" he asked.

"That's all that came to this station, Renwick," Amanda/Yan said. "As to other survivors, I cannot comment on facts I do not know."

"You're sounding like an android now," he said while continuing to kiss the Ambassador, whose breathing was getting sharp and shallow.

"Quit insulting me," said Amanda/Yan. "You may be right that being in this body is depressing my emotions, but I'm still *me*."

"Do you have a location on the engineer?" he asked, impatient.

"Docking maintenance crew. Six decks down from your current location, in the Centaurus arm of the station," Amanda/Yan said, then: "Damn! Every time you ask a question it's like I have no control. I just answer you."

"Meet us on the maintenance deck in ten minutes," said Renwick, ignoring her plight, then he cut the channel. He pulled back from the kiss. Ambassador Makera's skin was turning an olive ochre tone. Her eyes were closed and her lips parted. He had never seen her face when she was so aroused in the light.

"We have to go," he said to her. She opened her eyes, looking at him like a predator looks at its prey.

"Of course we do," she said, then she followed him out the door.

#

"Was all that show back there really necessary?" asked Makera as they made their way to the public lifter. Renwick shrugged.

"Perhaps not. But I did rather enjoy it," he said. She stopped him by grabbing his arm forcefully and in the same spot that Amanda/Yan had earlier. It hurt him.

"Renwick, every time you… arouse me, it takes a great deal of effort on my part to come back down to Raellos," she said. She was angry.

"You mean back down to Earth," he said.

"The planet doesn't matter!" she snapped. "The point is-"

"The point is I'll do my best to satisfy you later, Ambassador. But for now we have an engineer to rescue." With that he broke her substantial grip and headed to the lifter.

There was a crowd gathering by the lifter doors. Renwick supposed it was a normal congregation of traders, auction holders, and merchants in nefarious items. Once on board, the most popular destination was four decks down; the auction pits. They'd have to go there soon enough, but for now they rode the lifter down two more decks to the connecting module that would take them to the Centaurus arm of the station. There were at least ten others that got off on the same deck.

"Did you notice-" started Makera.

"Yes," said Renwick, "right when we stepped aboard the lifter. One of the guards in our greeting party."

"He's following us."

"Act casually," he said, then he pushed her against the wall in a dark corner as others mingled about on the dim deck. He kissed her hard, then whispered in her ear:

"Do you see him?"

"No," she said, between kisses. "And this is getting intolerable. Wait, I see him. He's talking to a man that looks like a trader. I think it was the man that was staring at me in the bar."

"The gray haired one?"

"Yes," she acknowledged. "They just saw me, they're looking away, trying to cover-" Renwick grabbed her by the arm and started running.

"C'mon," he said. They started down the dock arm, peeling off to both port and starboard as they weaved their way through the spider-webbed infrastructure. Finally they stopped and Renwick activated his com.

"Yan, where are you?" he asked.

"On my way," came her quick reply.

"Be careful, we're being trailed."

"I'll keep that under advisement," she said.

"Can you track us?" he asked. There was a pause on the other end of the line.

"I have your location. Stay put. I will come to you," she said.

"Affirmative," he replied. "And Yan, be careful."

"I will," she said, and cleared the line.

They waited for almost five minutes before Yan appeared around a corner and then quickly dropped the guard at their feet, like a pet would bring a prize to its master.

"I've neutralized the guard," she said.

"Apparently," said Renwick, looking down at the unconscious heap. "What about the trader he was talking to?"

"I only caught up to this one two turns back. I saw no trader," said Amanda/Yan.

"That's a concern," said Makera. "They will undoubtedly come looking for him eventually."

Renwick motioned for Amanda/Yan to pick up the guard. She did, following him a few feet down the corridor to a large air return vent near the floor. Renwick removed the grill and Amanda/Yan stuffed the guard in.

"He'll be okay, right?" asked Renwick.

"Eventually," said Amanda/Yan. "Mr. Kish, the *Phaeton's* engineer is working on a crew about six hundred feet down the next corridor over. But they're behind an EV controlled airlock, sealed in for the duration of their work shift."

"Can we get in?" asked Makera. Yan looked at them both matter-of-factly.

"I can," she said.

"That's what I thought," said Renwick to her. "Lead the way."

#

Five minutes later they were positioned outside the sealed airlock door to the maintenance bay.

"Burning through with the coil rifles will take too long and alert the guards, if there are any," said Renwick.

"Agreed," said Amanda/Yan. "Breaking the seal with force or explosives would seem the more logical approach."

Renwick thought of the grenades in Amanda/Yan's belly. "I don't want to use the grenades if we don't have to. Can you break through the door?" asked Renwick.

"Of course," she said.

"So what's the plan?" asked Makera.

"Smash and grab," said Renwick, then he turned back to Amanda/Yan. "Once you get in, can you neutralize the observation devices like you did in our cabin?"

"With an EMP pulse, yes. But it will knock out our communication devices, at least temporarily."

"Will it kill their tracking chips and wipe Kish's registration?"

"Oh yes."

"Then do it," he said. He signaled for Makera to move away from the door. When she was positioned he turned back to the android. "By the way, how do you generate the EMP pulse?"

"I have a small fusion reactor where my uterus should be," she said. Renwick swallowed hard.

"Great," he said, nodding while mentally crossing her off his list of potential sex partners.

"You'll have to step back. The maintenance bay is a low-EV work unit. Minimal atmosphere and heat to encourage performance," said Amanda/Yan.

"No problem," he said, backing away to where Makera was standing.

"What did she say?" asked Makera, curious. "What's she going to do?"

Renwick looked at his Raelen companion. "Let's just say she has a bun in the oven," he deadpanned. Makera gave him a confused look at the turn of phrase, then he grabbed her shoulder and they hunkered down together behind a bulkhead support. He quickly loaded his power pack into his rifle and Makera did the same. He signaled Amanda/Yan that they were ready, then watched as she turned to the airlock seal, gripping the handles, and pulled the hatch off in one smooth motion. Atmosphere started venting immediately as a wind of decompression swirled by them. They held on tight to the bulkhead support while the air pressure between the work room and the corridor normalized. Renwick looked up to see Amanda/Yan walking in the whirlwind effortlessly, pushing aside two door guards with ease. Inside he could hear shouting and other sounds of distress coming from the workers.

Seconds later, once Amanda/Yan had cleared the doorway, workers started pouring out of the door dressed in low-EV pressure suits. They were actually the unlucky ones. Those stuck further inside would have their identity chips wiped clean by the EMP, while the first escapees would be tracked and likely re-conscripted. He watched as Amanda/Yan raised her hands again, like she had in the cabin.

"Close your eyes!" he said to Makera. The flash followed and he opened his eyes again. Amanda/Yan was gone out of sight of the door, no doubt further inside the work room. "Go!" he said, jumping up, rifle at the ready, and running for the air lock door way.

Inside was mess. There were people on the floor moaning, others trying to move and get out of the room. A haze of smoke and mist filled the air. Renwick coughed as he took up a position behind some stacked boxes. Makera was at his side a second later.

The work room was huge and very cold. Breathing was hard and the chill had an immediate effect on his vision. He looked up through blurry eyes to see a private yacht hanging above them in dry dock, perhaps fifty meters from where they crouched, suspended in a zero-G field. There was repair equipment and materials strewn about the deck with many workers, now recovering from the double jolt of the decompression and the EM pulse, scrambling to get out of the way of the advancing android.

Amanda/Yan was throwing anything that got in her way, equipment, haulers, hydraulic lifts, people, to one side as she passed. She was checking ID's on the workers of course, then letting them go if they weren't her man, like throwing unwanted fish back in the water.

"She'd make a hell of a cop," said Renwick.

"Cop?" asked Makera, unfamiliar with the reference

"Policeman," he said. "C'mon. We have to guard the door and make sure our man doesn't slip out." They spent the next few minutes stopping workers from leaving by pointing their guns at them, then letting them go when they weren't Kish. Amanda/Yan was far ahead in the bay and out of sight, though there were sounds of the occasional struggle, probably with a guard.

"This is going too slow," said Renwick. "They'll have reinforcements here soon."

Makera let go of a man twice her size that she had been restraining, practicing her own version of catch-and-release. "What can we do?" she said.

"Yan, can you hear me?" he said into his com, but it was dead. "She was right, our coms are down. Come on," he tapped Makera on the arm. "Let's find Yan."

She was under the yacht, sorting through a pile of people that included unconscious guards and workers.

"How did you-" started Makera.

"I don't want to know," said Renwick. "You didn't hurt them did you?" he said to the android.

"Not permanently," she replied. The room was quickly emptying. Renwick looked up at the huge yacht hanging above them. "Kish must be on board," he said.

"Logical," replied Amanda/Yan, "since he is an engineer. Most of these appear to be metal workers."

"We have to get up there," said Renwick. It was a good twenty meters up to the bow of the yacht.

"That will be difficult for you. Regrettably the scaffolding came down in the decompression," Amanda/Yan said. Renwick looked around. She was right, there was no way up to the yacht. Her main decks were well above normal human climbing level.

"Are either of you trained in zero-G suspensor fields?" asked Amanda/Yan. Both Renwick and Makera shook their heads.

"Then it's up to me," she said. At that moment the yacht moaned and tilted to one side several meters. "That would be the suspensor field breaking down. A regrettable side effect of using the EMP," she said. "We don't have much time."

"Before what?" Renwick said. Amanda/Yan looked at him like he was a moron.

"Before the field fails completely and the yacht resumes normal gravity," she said.

"Uh-oh."

"I will be back as soon as I can," she said. "Prepare to receive more workers."

"Um, Yan," started Renwick, "How will you get up to-" at that moment Amanda/Yan crouched and then leapt the entire twenty-meter height of the yacht strait up, landing on the open deck above.

"Oh," said Renwick to Makera. "That's how."

A few minutes passed with no sign of her or any workers, and the yacht continued to list further, groaning with every movement.

"I don't like this," said Renwick just as she reappeared at the bow of yacht.

"Please catch the workers as I drop them down," she yelled down to them.

"What the hell?" said Renwick, watching helplessly as Amanda/Yan dropped a full-grown man bigger than he was down towards them. Thankfully the man descended at a significantly reduced rate of speed due to the low-G suspensor field in place. Renwick 'caught' the man and directed him safely to the ground. He had an astonished look on his face, said "Thank you", and then ran from the room. By then Makera had guided a second worker to the ground. Renwick caught the next one.

Kish was the sixth one down.

There were four more after that, then Amanda/Yan followed, not requiring assistance as she landed.

"We have to get out of here," she said. "I estimate perhaps four minutes before that yacht goes through the floor."

"Can you run?" said Renwick to Kish.

"Yes," he said. The look on his face was one of one of a man in shock, and he couldn't take his eyes off of Amanda/Yan.

"Then let's go," said Renwick. Just as they started to move a coil rifle shot laced across the position where he had been standing a second earlier. They all rushed for cover behind a stack of metal crates next to an abandoned loader. "Welcoming committee is here," he said.

"Yes, six of them," said Yan. "All armed. And unfortunately I am not impervious to laser fire," she said.

"Time to trade you in on the new model," said Renwick. Behind him the yacht moaned and tilted to a severe angle.

"What will we do?" asked Makera.

Renwick looked around the room, analyzed their precarious situation, and shook his head.

"Panic," he said.

9 CHAPTER NAME

Contrary to his statement, Renwick didn't panic. Instead he turned to his most valuable resource.

"Yan, how many stun grenades do you have?" he said.

"Two," she replied, then pulled up her tunic top and began shuffling around inside herself again.

"What the hell?" said Kish.

"You'll get used to it," said Renwick. Coil rifle fire was peppering the crates and the loader in front of them.

"We can't take much of this," said Makera. Renwick nodded. At least these attackers had the same older model coil rifles that the station guards had carried. With each shot the rifle had to take about three seconds to recharge before it could fire again. He and Makera had the Mark 7's, which you could hold in one hand and that allowed them to fire in much more rapid return. Amanda/Yan handed him a stun grenade and he loaded it on to the end of his rifle, then switched the mode from laser to grenade launcher.

"I'll need a diversion," he said. "And someone to spot the targets for me."

"I'll be the diversion," said Makera over the din.

"And I'll be the spotter," said Amanda/Yan.

"What can I do?" asked the disheveled Kish, who seemed to be recovering his bearings.

"Stay down," said Renwick forcefully. "We go in three… two… one… go!"

Makera leapt up, cat like, and fired a string of semi-automatic rifle bursts of suppressing fire while she moved across the line of fire to the relative security of another abandoned loader. Amanda/Yan stuck her head out, then called back to Renwick.

"Fifty-three point nine-two-two meters, azimuth seven," she said. Renwick rose, pointed, and fired the grenade, then ducked behind his cover again. A second later it exploded, sending a jolt of high-intensity compression waves though the chamber. At the distance they were from the grenade the effect was minimal. To those closer, however…

"Four down," called Amanda/Yan. "The other two are scrambling." Renwick looked out at his handiwork. The two conscious guards were indeed retreating, firing as they ran for the doorway. He was about to call Makera off when he watched in horror as she cut the two men down with her rifle, one of them was severed completely in half, falling into two perfectly cauterized pieces.

"Restrain yourself, Ambassador!" he demanded, rising with his rifle poised. She snapped around to face him, rifle leveled at his midsection. "Will you cut me in half as well?" he said. The fire of Raelen rage was burning in her eyes. "They would have gone for reinforcements. It would have put us in greater danger," she said.

"It wasn't necessary!" he shouted at her. Amanda/Yan stood and placed herself between them.

"The yacht," she said. As if on cue it tilted again and started forward, towards the floor, and them. If it fell now, it would crush them. It wobbled and then steadied itself, precariously.

"We'll finish this later," said Renwick.

"I've already done that," said Makera, challenging him directly.

"Senator, Ambassador, Mr. Kish, we need to go *now*!" said Amanda/Yan. She grabbed Kish by the collar of his EV suit and started moving. Renwick dropped his rifle to his side and then started running for the doorway, following as fast as he could go. He never looked back until he had cleared the work room doorway. Once on the other side he turned just as Makera came through. He watched Amanda/Yan drop Kish, not gently either, and then pick up the discarded hatch, slamming it crossways back into the door opening, the hatch embedding into the wall in a way that was almost disturbing. Behind the hatch there was a grinding sound as the zero-G suspensor field collapsed.

"Run!" yelled Renwick. They all did.

The corridor deck beneath Renwick's feet was twisting and groaning, shifting like soft plastic as he ran. Kish stayed close on his shoulder. He was unaware of Makera, nor was he concerned for her, not after what he had seen her do in the work room. There was a coldness about him as he strode down the long corridor, waiting to hear the fate of the yacht behind him.

The crash was deafening, and from the violent vibration it seemed as though the whole arm of the station would come apart around them. Alarm claxons, alerting the station to a loss of atmosphere in the dry dock, rang through his ears. He ran wildly, with no thought or intent except to get away from the danger. As he rounded a corner he suddenly saw a lifter dead ahead.

"This way!" he turned and yelled over the din, slamming the lifter call button. To his delight the lifter doors opened immediately. Kish stopped and changed direction, coming towards him, then Amanda/Yan came around the corner. His heart pounded in his chest as he waited for Makera with a combination of disdain and concern. Finally she came, running full bore, and then dove for the lifter, sliding the last five meters across the floor to land at his feet.

"Go!" she looked up and said. He hit the close control and selected the gallery deck as their destination. The lifter began to move even as the interior lights were flickering, coming perilously close to going out several times. As they moved he removed the power pack and shouldered his rifle. Amanda/Yan helped Makera to her feet while Kish peeled off his work suit to reveal plain gray coveralls beneath. A few seconds later and they exited the lifter, mingling into the crowd at the main concourse and acting as if nothing unusual had happened to them all day long.

#

An hour later they were back in their berth with Kish, who was vigorously eating soup and drinking water. It had been a full day since his last meal. Amanda/Yan was scanning the auctions for more information on the sale of Lieutenant Cain. Makera was sulking in a corner, cleaning her rifle coils. Renwick, for his part, was ignoring her while scanning the news stream for word on their earlier escapade.

"Lieutenant Cain's opening bid price is up fifty percent since yesterday morning. Her skills as a pilot are proving to be almost as valuable as her sexual characteristics," said Amanda/Yan.

"That's nice to know," said Renwick, sullenly. "Looks like the whole Centaurus Arm of the station went black after the yacht crashed, according to the news reports. No video or security telemetry of our escape, either. And the yacht ended up diving into the planet before the owner could pay the station fees to retrieve it."

"Hope he had insurance," said Makera from the corner. Renwick ignored her.

"There will likely be telemetry data of us entering the Centaurus Arm just before the yacht incident," said Amanda/Yan. "I will endeavor to eradicate it."

"Endeavor? Sure you feel all right?" Renwick asked, forcing himself to try humor. "You're not going all android on me are you?" Amanda/Yan managed a smile.

"Sorry," she said. "It's hard to express myself in this thing."

"Personally I find it an improvement in efficiency over your original personality," chimed in Makera from the corner. Amanda/Yan's response was to close her eyes. Renwick turned his attention to Kish.

"If you feel like talking, what happened out there after we left, on board the *Phaeton* I mean?" he said. Kish stopped chewing and swallowed hard, then spoke.

"We lost power after the last plasma grenade volley," he said. "By the time I got the generators back online the Gataan were aboard. We had no time to defend ourselves before they were on top of us."

"How many survivors were there?"

"Eleven of us," said Kish.

"Eleven?" said Renwick. "There's only three of you here. Where are the others?" He dreaded the answer.

"They weren't deemed valuable enough, so our captors called in some 'friends', and sold them off, I assume to be auctioned off to the mines at Cundaloa," Kish said. Renwick took this in with regret.

"We'll find them," he promised. Kish nodded acknowledgement, then continued.

"The captain, Mischa, and me were taken here on the surviving corvette. We all assumed you were dead. At least that's what the Gataan told us. They said you slipped into the Void trying to escape and were killed. Glad that isn't the real story," he said. Renwick shifted uncomfortably.

"Actually, that's not far from the truth," he admitted. "We did end up in the Void, but we didn't die."

"What? How?" said Kish. Renwick sat down next to him.

"That takes some explaining," he said. He then proceeded to catch Kish up on all that had happened since they had departed the *Phaeton* in the skiff. "And so now we're here to rescue you. But we won't be going to Cundaloa to rescue your crew just yet, I'm sorry to say. We have unfinished business in the Void."

"Can you use an engineer?" Kish asked.

"Always, Mr. Kish," said Amanda/Yan from across the small room, breaking her silence but not opening her eyes. "Always."

#

After six hours of rest and recuperation the auction of Lieutenant Mischa Cain of the Unity cruiser *Phaeton* was pending inside the next two hours. Renwick roused his comrades, then discussed his plan.

"Based on our current credit, we have the equivalent of twelve thousand Unity crowns. Looking at the auction lists however, Lieutenant Cain has an opening bid established of nearly ten thousand crowns already. Her piloting skills seem to have outstripped her value as a sexual distraction. The current estimated sale price is between fifteen and eighteen thousand," he said.

"So we don't have enough money," said Makera. Renwick shook his head.

"If we put Yan up for auction, we would have more credit, but she'd have to be detained as collateral for the auction," he said.

"That seems like our only option," said Makera.

"Would you be so quick if it was you on the block, Ambassador?" Renwick said, still angry with her over the killings. "I could probably get thirty thousand easily just for you. However I'd be tempted to leave you behind, and I couldn't live with myself if I did that. So you're not an option at the moment."

"More's the pity," she said. He ignored her.

"Yan has the ability to take care of herself and escape, especially if she is properly equipped. She still has a stun grenade, and I'd like to give her a pistol," he said, holding out his hand to the Ambassador.

"You want mine?" she said. He nodded. Makera handed it over reluctantly and he gave it to Amanda/Yan.

"You'll have to stay here, Mr. Kish," he said. "You're still a fugitive, and we can't risk exposing you, even if we did take out your paper trail."

"Understood," said Kish. Renwick gave him his pistol for defense along with a power pack.

"I'd like to leave you here as well Ambassador, after your exploits in the dry dock. But I'll need backup and Yan will be indisposed for a while, so I'm stuck with you," he said.

"A ringing endorsement," she said. He was annoyed by her continued barbs and her lack of conscience over the killings, but she really was his only option, so he chose to ignore her.

They made final preparations and then made their way out to the gallery and down to the Auction Pits. They did a check of their repaired coms and found they could communicate with each other well enough. Renwick escorted Amanda/Yan down to the Auction Board and registered her for sale.

"How much do you want for her?" asked the selling agent.

"A hundred thousand crowns, gold," Renwick replied. The agent looked down at him in surprise.

"She's pretty enough, but she isn't worth that much," he said. "I'll advance you five thousand against final sale." Renwick stepped up to the podium the man was standing behind.

"My good man, I think you misunderstand," he said. He nodded to Amanda/Yan. She walked up to a metal support beam near the door to the auction pits and pulled it out of the mortar it was encased in, then bent the thick beam into a perfect "C" curve. The agent looked impressed.

"Robot?" he asked. Renwick shook his head.

"Android. Able to simulate a human in all form and functions. *All* form and functions," he said, smiling. The agent got his emphasis.

"You got your hundred-thousand," he said, motioning for Renwick's credit chip. Renwick handed him his card and then authenticated his code into the auction system. "Just so you know, the agency rate goes up to ten percent for everything over a hundred thousand, and I think she'll go well over that."

"Really, how much? I need to buy some new long-range equipment for my HD drive," he said, using his cover story.

"Probably close to two-fifty. Mechanicals are rare, and coveted. A remnant from the days before the Void. Very much a status symbol," said the agent.

"Great," Renwick said, feigning enthusiasm for the sale.

"I'm moving her to the top of the next hour," said the agent. "Generate some buzz." Renwick looked at his watch. Lieutenant Cain would come up in twenty minutes, just a few auctions in advance of Amanda/Yan.

"That's fine," he said, acting casual.

"Wanna say goodbye?" asked the agent.

"Sure," he went up to Amanda/Yan. "It's been fun, old girl," he said, making a show of it for the milling crowd, then he leaned in. "Our trading permit expires at twelve-hundred hours tomorrow," he said. "We have that long to locate Captain Aybar and get her off the station."

"Understood," said Amanda/Yan. "I will retrieve her and meet you at the skiff ten minutes before departure." Renwick smiled, acting out his cover.

"Thank you for your service, Yan," he said loudly, then turned and headed back up to the pits without looking back at her.

#

He rejoined Makera in the auction pits just one auction ahead of Lieutenant Cain. The pits were accurately named, a burgeoning mass of pure capitalism teeming with energy, lust, and the desire to possess. Whatever human desire a man (or woman) chose to indulge in could be fulfilled here. The richest of the rich stayed off the trading floor and bid from one of many shadowed boxes poised over the floor.

Renwick registered himself as a bidder on Lieutenant Cain just five minutes before the deadline. The big money usually came in at the last minute, and he hoped to scare off as many potential challengers as he could in advance. He was the fifty-fourth potential bidder. One minute from the close of registration another bidder came on. In the last sixty seconds thirty-four bidders dropped off.

"That's a bad sign," he said.

"What?" said Makera.

"A private bidder just registered at the last minute. More than half the other bidders dropped off," he said.

"He must be known, then."

"Yes, and feared," Renwick looked around the room. "Did you spot anyone you recognized?" he asked. She nodded.

"The old man from the bar was here again, but he left just before you came up. And I did notice him spying on me again. I restrained myself from challenging him, but it was difficult," she said.

"Just because we can't see him doesn't mean he's not here," said Renwick. He continued to observe the crowd but saw no one suspicious, or paying any overt attention to them.

The auction scheduled just in front of Lieutenant Cain ended and the cage was vacated. Auctions continued in the other cages at breakneck speed. An auction was only open for ten minutes. Renwick looked down to see Lieutenant Cain entering the cage. She had been stripped down to just basic coverings of her body, she was very nearly nude. Detailed digital images of her were available to anyone who wanted to see her in the most explicit detail on the station network. Renwick had avoided those. He wanted to think of her as the talented pilot of the *Phaeton*, and a pretty young girl. She didn't belong here and he intended to see she got out.

Her hands were shackled in front of her and she looked terrified. The announcer read out her lot number and her listed skills, beyond her value as a pure sex toy for some sick slaver.

"This is barbaric," said Makera. Renwick still hadn't made peace wither her earlier actions, but he couldn't disagree with her assessment.

"It is what the Void has brought us to, Ambassador," he said in response.

The auction started with a bid of ten thousand. Renwick used his bidding pad to immediately up that to ten-thousand five-hundred. He watched as the bidding moved rapidly to the fifteen thousand level, then paused. He waited almost the full thirty second bid limit before going to fifteen-five. This started another flurry that pushed her to seventeen-five, where it paused again. There were ten bidders left as those who found her price too rich dropped out.

Renwick went to eighteen thousand, the projected high end of the bidding, and another four dropped out. The crowd started to buzz, Would someone go over? A roar of anticipation went up in the house as his thirty-second bid limit was about to expire. He looked at his pad.

Someone had bid twenty thousand. He went to twenty-one. The crowd cheered, then it roared, much louder than the first.

Twenty-five thousand.

"What's wrong? asked Makera. Renwick looked frantically around the room, there were just two bidders left now, him and the late-arriving private bidder.

"Someone is gaming us," he said. "I think we're made."

"The gray haired man from the bar?"

"Possibly," said Renwick. "But I don't see him." Makera looked to the ceiling.

"He's in one of the boxes," she said. "I can eliminate him." She started for the doors. His firm hand on her arm stopped her.

"No," he said. The clock was ticking. He had ten seconds left.

He went to thirty. The crowd roared again. Mischa was confused by all the activity swirling around her. She started to cry.

When the bid went to fifty thousand the pits erupted. Trading was halted on the other two stages while everyone focused on the bidding on Mischa.

"We can't win this," he said to Makera. She gripped the handle of her rifle. From his angle he could see she had the power pack fully loaded and charged.

"I will end this," she said. He grabbed her arm again.

"No, you can't," he said. "It will blow our cover and we'll lose any chance of recovering Captain Aybar." He had to keep bidding.

He went to seventy-five. The counter was at one-hundred. He had to go up twenty-five thousand just to stay in. He looked down at his card.

He had twelve thousand credits left.

"We're out," he said. "Let's go," he took her forcefully by the arm and led her off the pit floor as his bid expired and Mischa was sold for one-hundred thousand crowns.

"Keep your head down," was all he said as they retreated off the trading floor, the roar of the crowd echoing behind them.

10.

Renwick sat facing the floor, head in his hands while Makera paced back and forth like a caged animal. Kish sat in one corner, looking grim.

"I don't understand what happened," Kish said. "I thought the highest it could go was eighteen thousand."

"That was the price projection," said Renwick. "Not a limit. The mystery bidder knew we were there for Lieutenant Cain exclusively. Knew that we had to have her and he knew how much money we had and how high we could go."

"And you think it was this man who's been trailing you through the station?"

"I can't think of who else it could be," Renwick said.

"Nor I," said Makera while continuing her pacing. "I'm so angry I want to kill something," she said. Renwick looked up at her.

"You already did that," he said. She turned on him, angry.

"I did what was necessary, Senator, whether you believe that or not. I'm not subject to your human moral judgments and I would just as soon not hear them. You should be thanking me instead of condemning me," she said. He stood up to face her.

"I'm not condemning you," he said. "But I'm not prepared to accept *your* moral judgment of the situation either." She took a step closer to him.

"We could settle this honorably," she said, challenging him. He looked at her with disdain, then back to Kish.

"We have to get out of here," he said to no one in particular.

"We haven't finished our mission," said Makera. "Are you running away?"

"From the danger of superior opposition? Yes I am," he said. "We're going back to the skiff and waiting for Yan to return. Then we're busting out of here and going back to the *Kali*. We still have a mission to complete, Ambassador. A diplomatic one, and that requires us to be on Raellos in less than three months. I intend to make that deadline. I also intend to come back here once that mission is complete and rescue Captain Aybar and Lieutenant Cain, with plenty of reinforcements, if necessary."

"We're closer to them now than we ever will be," she countered. "Running now solves nothing."

He put his hands to his hips in a show of resolve. "I'm not looking for solutions, I'm looking to *survive*. As long as I am in command of this mission, and I am, we'll do things my way. Understood, Ambassador?" he said.

She said nothing, but her face showed her acute displeasure with him.

"Silence is acceptance," he said. He waved his hand around the room, trying to rouse his companions to action. "Now let's pack our gear and get back to the skiff as fast as we can, and pray no one takes us out on the way."

#

They moved carefully through the teeming crowds on their return trip to the skiff. Renwick stopped once to check the auction boards and found that Yan had gone for two-hundred seventy thousand crowns. He checked his credit account and found the full amount, minus commissions of course, had been deposited. Only now the money meant nothing, for there was nothing, or no one, for him to buy here anymore.

They moved along the corridors to their ship, stopping only to pick up supplemental items they might need for the trip back. Kish was the most active in this regard. Renwick put a stop to that soon enough and a few minutes later they were heading down the dock arm to their ship. He checked his watch. 0800. Four hours until their station permit expired.

Renwick punched in the code lock combination to enter the skiff. "Yan should be back with us in a few hours. Get the ship ready to move as quickly as possible, Mr. Kish. We may not have the luxury of preparing when the time comes," he said. Kish nodded his acknowledgement as Renwick typed in the security key code.

The combination came back with a negative beep. Renwick tried it again. A second negative.

"One time I might make an error entering the combination. Twice is unlikely. Three times…" he tapped the combination into the keypad again. It beeped at him and the code reader turned red.

"We're locked out," he said, looking down the tight gangway, then turning back to his companions while he raised his rifle. "I don't like this. Get your weapons out." Makera reached for hers just as a voice cut through from behind them.

"I don't recommend that," it said. Renwick turned, rifle drawn. The gray haired man that had been tracking them stood at the entrance to the gangway, flanked by three guards, each of them with a Mark 7 coil rifle aimed at one of his crew. They were trapped inside the tight quarters, pinned against the locked door of their skiff. "Please drop your weapons," said the mystery man.

"We should fight," hissed Makera in a tight whisper.

"That would be a bad idea, Ambassador," said the man before Renwick could even respond. At the distance the two groups were from each other he shouldn't have been able to hear her, if he were Human or Raelen.

"You can't get in, Mr. Renwick, because I locked you out," the man continued. "You see I'm the new owner of your ship, as well as several other things you value." He waved his arm in a forward motion and three more guards entered the gangway, with pistols held to the heads of three prisoners; Captain Aybar, Mischa Cain, and Amanda/Yan.

"Now that I have your attention," said the man, taking a step closer, "I'm ready to begin."

"Begin what?" said Renwick, slowly lowering his coil rifle.

"Why, negotiations, of course."

#

He wasn't really old, not when you saw him up close. He had the face of a man in his forties, if he were human, but his hair was a steel gray/white against a distinctly crimson skin tone, giving him the appearance of greater age from a distance. It was a mistake Renwick vowed he wouldn't make again.

Physically, the man was very similar to any of the Known Races, with a lean and athletic appearance, and he held court now over his captives. They were all together inside the skiff; Renwick, Makera, Captain Aybar,

Mischa, Kish and Amanda/Yan, all sitting in the passenger couches facing the pilot's nest. The man, who said his name was Zueros, faced them alone, unarmed. The skiff doors were closed to the gangway and his thugs were locked outside, much to their consternation.

"My name, officially, is Pal Zueros," he began. "I'm a trader from the Arapesh Colonies. Officially."

"But in reality?" said Renwick. Zueros gave an affected sigh, as if he'd wanted to unburden himself of this information for quite some time and was now glad to do so.

"What if I told you, Senator," he said, "hypothetically of course, that I represented a race that was genetically very close to yours, to Humans, but also close to the Raelen and the Gataan?" Renwick contemplated him a few seconds before answering.

"You're speaking of the Preserver Myth," Renwick replied.

"Yes. I assume you understand the details of the mythology?" Renwick nodded his head before continuing.

"Multiple races, genetically related to a parent race that knew that it was doomed, set out on various planets in this spiral arm of the galaxy to develop on their own and eventually encounter each other, hopefully in friendship and brotherhood. An interesting if somewhat quaint notion, but it has about as much validity as Atlantis or Eden or the Annunaki," Renwick said.

"So you reject it out of hand?"

"I didn't say that," said Renwick, crossing his arms and sitting back in his couch. "I would require proof." Zueros tilted his head to one side.

"Proof is a difficult thing to come by," Zueros said. "But let's start with what we do know," he started ticking off points on his hand, a very human gesture, one which Renwick assumed had been learned through close observation. "Humans, Raelen, and Gataan all share specific DNA, greater than ninety-nine point-seven percent, this much is well known by modern science."

"True," admitted Renwick.

"And the possibility of this happening randomly is?" said Zueros.

"Highly unlikely," agreed Renwick with a shrug.

"So we agree on one point," said Zueros. "A deeper analysis of this DNA comparison however shows that the differing combinations of the three race's DNA, minus the redundancies, does not create a whole codex.

There are variations in each of us. In fact, if you trace mitochondrial DNA, you find that the missing elements are about one quarter of one percent of each of the individual races. So, the conclusion would be?" he asked Renwick.

"That we were all engineered from very similar stock," said Renwick, remaining unconvinced by the arguments.

"And what if I told you that there was a fourth genetically similar race out there somewhere. One that is yet undiscovered," said Zueros. "One that shares this same point two-five percent variation from the norm?" Renwick sat forward at this.

"Let me guess, you're going to tell us where we can find this mystery race and ask us to join you in this quest so that you can write a book about it, and you're willing to spend your entire fortune on this adventure. Am I far off?" he said sarcastically.

"Quite," said Zueros, his expression turning serious. "In fact what I was going to tell you was that I am a member of that mystery race, and there are many others of us here, and if you don't help me, everything you have built, your entire civilization, could crumble in matter of months."

Renwick sat back again, suddenly sobered. "That is unexpected," he said.

"And unbelievable," chimed in Ambassador Makera.

"Less believable than an all-encompassing Void of dark energy devouring entire empires in just a few centuries, Ambassador?" Zueros said. Makera said nothing in response to that.

"I'll need more than your word," said Renwick, pressing his point.

"I'll be pleased to provide a fresh DNA sample. The android can run the analysis, if that is agreeable?" said Zueros.

Renwick nodded. "The android has a name, by the way. In fact, she has two names, and two personas."

"And those would be?" Zueros said.

"Amanda, the android persona, and Yan, the human persona," Renwick said.

Zueros looked to the attractive android.

"And she's further proof of my point, Senator. I've been searching this area of the Known Cosmos for the better part of two of your decades, and this android is the best example yet of the proof of my claims," said Zueros.

"And how is that?" asked Renwick.

"Because she was built with Preserver technology, as was her ship, and the Void emitter station. In fact it is all Preserver technology, discovered by my race, the fourth race, and implemented in a strategic plan to knock down the Human, Raelen, and Gataan races."

"What?" Renwick stood from his couch. "If what you say is true-"

"It is true, Mr. Renwick," snapped Zueros. "The Void was not an accident, as you would suppose. It was the result of a set of intentional actions put in motion by my people and designed to literally throw your civilizations back into a Dark Age."

"Then I would say, sir, that your people have succeeded beyond their wildest hopes," said Renwick as he sat back down in his couch, contemplating his new adversary.

#

They all agreed to a fresh DNA test with Renwick and Makera representing their races, and Zueros representing his. Zueros produced a Gataan file sample for the fourth piece of the puzzle. Amanda/Yan ran the tests, allowing her android personality to do the majority of the work in the background while they continued their discussion. Renwick set the rest of the crew towards the job of preparing the skiff to depart, after first hugging Mischa Cain and shaking hands with Captain Aybar to welcome them back.

Zueros revealed his race were known as the Soloth, and that their home world was much further away from Unity space than the others. Specifically, even beyond Thousand Suns Space. That was why they were particularly interested in halting the advance of the Known Races into that area of the Orion Spur of the galaxy.

"Wouldn't you protect your home?" Zueros asked of Makera and Renwick while Amanda/Yan processed the DNA sample data.

"I would," said Renwick, "but not at the expense of billions of other lives."

"Those lives have not been destroyed," countered Zueros. "They have merely been placed in isolation, to slow their progress."

"Which is much the same," said Makera. "My people would never make such a choice. We would rather fight."

"As is your way, Ambassador. But wars are much more destructive than blockades. And the Void is a blockade," said Zueros.

"But what are you blocking?" asked Renwick. "Science? Progress?"

"Interbreeding, for one," said Zueros. "Light, for another."

"Light?" said Renwick, intrigued.

"Why interbreeding?" asked Makera, cutting in before Renwick could start asking his questions about light. Zueros answered Makera's question first.

"Our people believed that it was the Preserver's intent to create a Diaspora of DNA as a means of preserving themselves past the time when their civilization would dissolve due to internal pressures. They believed that they were strong, but not strong enough to survive their own flaws. By splitting their being into these four different pieces, they could preserve enough about themselves and their characteristics that they admired to lay a foundation for new civilization, one that they hoped would be stronger than their own."

Zueros continued. "Each of the races carry a significant piece of the puzzle, a set of characteristics the Preservers admired. Humanity though was the most surprising to emerge, Mr. Renwick, given your planet's reputation as a genetic dumping ground."

Renwick looked up sharply at this. "Dumping ground, Mr. Zueros?" he said. Zueros nodded.

"For many millennia the Preservers transported less-successful races to your world, to clear the way the way for more promising candidates. Imagine their surprise when you came out of your system fully matured, your divergent weaknesses creating a racially diverse unity that surpassed all their expectations," he said. "Haven't you ever wondered why the other Known Races have nearly uniform racial characteristics, while yours has so many differing combinations?"

Renwick allowed Zeuros' comments to pass over him, then changed the subject again.

"You were speaking of puzzle pieces. How does this mosaic of races supposedly work?" he asked.

Zueros actually smiled. "Humanity is the heart, the soul, the emotions and inspiration. The Raelen are the spirit, creatures of great passion yet also great vision. The Gataan are the body, young, strong, able and willing to do all the hard work of building a civilization," he said.

"The Trinity, plus one," said Renwick. Zueros gave Renwick a look that indicated he had just unlocked a key.

"That just leaves your people," said Makera. Zueros nodded.

"The Soloth represent the intellect, the thirst for knowledge, the leaders of this new civilization," he said.

"In your own minds, anyway," countered Renwick. "Intellect without emotion, especially compassion, can be a dangerous thing."

"Which is precisely why I am here, Senator. I represent a group of my people who disagree with the course our society has chosen, one of repressing the other races. That's why I'm seeking your assistance," Zueros said.

"You haven't addressed interbreeding yet," said Makera. Zueros shrugged.

"It's simple really. If the Known Races are genetically compatible, then it makes sense that interbreeding would lead to an increasing of each individual race's abilities and strengthen their civilizations. That was seen as a threat by my society, and thus, another reason for the Void," said Zueros.

"You mentioned the Void was also designed to block light. How does that matter?" said Renwick, finally getting to ask his question. Zueros looked reluctant to answer.

"Our galaxy is in a constant cycle of motion through both space and time," he explained. "As our section of the galaxy moves through this cycle, it passes through areas of greater light and greater darkness. Our science indicates strongly that the further we move away from the greatest local light source, the mass of stars at the center of our galaxy, we pass into a time of less energy, and less progress, or perhaps even regression. As we cycle closer, into greater light, comes increased, measurable, energy emanating from the galactic core," Zueros said.

"So where are we in this supposed cycle?" asked Renwick. "How long is it?"

"From your perspective, based on your distance from the core, a galactic cycle, or a galactic year, is about two-hundred sixty million Terran years. You are just entering the last, and the lightest, portion of this cycle. Thus our people felt the need to act now to suppress the Known Races."

"Before you were overcome by them," said Renwick.

Zueros nodded. "That was the fear."

"But you don't share that fear," stated Makera.

"Oh, I do," said Zueros, turning to her and actually smiling for the first time. "But my group, my school of thought on our world, feels that any parent race powerful enough to split themselves into four pieces and spread itself out amongst the stars is far wiser than we are, and that plan should be allowed to proceed to its natural conclusion."

"So, you're an idealist," said Renwick. "The worst kind of ally to have." Zueros looked at him with a narrow gaze.

"I hope this isn't an indication of your cynicism, Senator. We will have to work together to succeed," Zueros said. Renwick held up a hand.

"Don't get me wrong," he said. "I'll take any allies I can. It's just that I've found that when it comes to having friends with ideals or friends with guns, the ones with guns usually win."

Before Zueros could respond Amanda/Yan broke into the conversation.

"I have the results of the test," she said.

"And?" said Renwick.

"It is as he says," she replied. "His DNA is distinct from human or Gataan or Raelen, but unmistakably a branch of the same tree, with the equivalent point-two-five percent variable in the codex."

"So, Mr. Renwick," said Zueros, leaning against the command console of the skiff. "You have a decision to make. Are we allies, or not?"

"You're the one who has guards at the door," said Renwick. Zueros responded to this by going to the door and dismissing the guards he had brought, handing them each a credit counter full of cash. They weren't happy, but they did as instructed.

"We'll need to use your ship, Mr. Renwick, if we're going to get where we're going," Zueros said after they had gone and he had locked down the docking arm. Renwick put his hands to his hips.

"Wait a minute, you're claiming to be an advanced alien form a distant star. Don't you have some kind high tech starship of your own?" Renwick said.

"I did," responded Zueros, a crooked smile crossing his lips. "But it was in the dry dock that you destroyed."

Renwick looked to Makera, then back to Zueros. "That was yours?"

Zueros nodded.

"I thought if Mr. Kish was aboard it would give you a more obvious target," he said. "But I have to admit I thought you would rather steal it than destroy it."

"Sorry," was all the chagrined Renwick could muster.

An hour later and Renwick ordered the skiff out of Skondar, gladly leaving the slave station behind them. He was pleased to turn piloting the vessel over to Captain Aybar and Mischa Cain to guide them back to the *Kali*.

"We'll need to make all haste to Tarchus once we get back aboard the Void ship, Mr. Renwick," said Zueros once they were underway.

"The Gataan home world? Why?" said Renwick.

"The *Kali* is my ship," interjected Amanda/Yan. "I say where she goes and doesn't go." Zueros bowed slightly to her in acknowledgement.

"Of course. But I think for the sake of this mission perhaps we could all agree on one person to lead us." Amanda/Yan looked at Renwick.

"I trust him on diplomatic issues, and overall management of the mission. But on military issues, I'll still be in charge," she said.

"Agreed," said Zueros. He looked to Makera, who nodded yes.

"Then I accept," said Renwick. "But I think our first stop should be the emitter station, to shut down the Void." Zueros shook his head.

"You don't understand me. We need to go to Tarchus because, as you said Renwick, we will need allies. We'll need the Gataan, whatever is left of them."

"For what?" Renwick asked.

"Why, to ward off the invasion, of course," said Zueros.

11.

"Do you know of any other race that has a fleet powerful enough to stave off an invasion? One that is not only within reach of the Void, but actually *inside* it already?"

Zueros was asking his question on the bridge of the *Kali* in front of her new command crew; himself, Renwick, Makera, and Yan, who had extracted herself from Amanda's android body and was once again her old self, but with a surprising new wardrobe. The skin-tight body suit from her earlier incarnation was replaced now by a two-piece short skirt and cropped top, similar in style to Amanda's dress, but which left her midriff exposed. The ensemble was completed by the knee-high black boots the android favored. Renwick found the change highly distracting. Behind them the other androids of the *Kali* went about their business in silence.

Renwick leaned back in his chair, one arm raised over the back while he dangled a leg over the chair arm. "You're assuming that in three centuries they haven't degenerated into barbarism," he said, trying hard to focus on Zueros and not Yan.

"They haven't, not totally," said Zueros. "Our probes show that much."

"You've been monitoring them?" asked Makera.

"Of course," Zueros said as he shrugged off her question. "As I said, we have been monitoring all of you. But the Gataan are the only race whose territory is almost completely encompassed by the Void."

Yan crossed her arms. "You've been manipulating us from the beginning. You even manipulated my mission here. Did your people cause the accident here? Aboard the *Kali*?"

"My predecessors must have, yes," Zueros admitted.

"That accident cost three of my command their lives," she said. Zueros dipped his head in acknowledgement.

"You have my apologies. But with all due respect captain, that was three centuries ago," he said.

"Not to me it wasn't." Renwick raised his hand to interject.

"We won't make any progress here until we choose to put the past behind us and focus on the here and now. And I'm trying to make a decision about what is best to do for all concerned *now*," he said. Yan looked displeased but she withdrew from the conversation for the moment.

"How can you know the Gataan will help us?" said Makera, her tone indicating she wasn't sure she believed that they would.

"I don't," said Zueros. "But I do know what they value. They're starving for innovation, new technology and the like. They've been isolated for so long they believe the rest of the universe has forgotten them. This ship, and the wonders it brings, will be proof that they haven't been."

"So you propose that we trade the *Kali* for an alliance with the Gataan? To fend off an invasion that we only have your word on?" Yan said, angry now. Renwick was pleased to see it. It was nice return to her old personality after the time she had spent inside Amanda.

"The invasion is real, Captain Yan. And I can prove it to you." Zueros asked to see the navigation console. Yan was reluctant but she showed him the apparatus. He sat down and after a few moments of manipulating the controls he projected a display onto the massive dome that served as a ceiling for the bridge of the *Kali*. He lit up set of local stars.

"This is the approximate area of your current Known Cosmos. He magnified that until it filled the projection, then overlaid the Void in a gray gauze, so you could still see the stars through it. Then a blinking gold dot appeared.

"That is the *Kali*, moving through Void Space on a general heading for the emitter station, which is located approximately here," a green dot lit up on the display. "About six-point three light years from Tarchus, here." A red dot appeared in the same general area of the emitter station. Now the view jumped back out and the three blinking dots got very close together. The display panned to the right and an orange dot appeared.

"This is a target world within the Raelen Empire, the first target of the invasion fleet, in fact," he said.

"Can you magnify that location?" asked Makera. As if anticipating her request, the display zoomed up on the orange point. Makera studied it but said nothing.

"Is that really your space?" asked Renwick. She nodded.

"Zed Vadela Three. It's our most distant colony," she paused then before continuing, "The vanguard of the treaty area, leading to Thousand Suns Space," she said.

"The lynchpin," said Renwick, quickly analyzing the scenario. "Cut off that colony and you cut off both the Unity and the Raelen from Thousand Suns Space, pinching them between the Void and the Soloth fleet."

"I'm glad you see it," said Zueros. "And now to show you my sincerity," he said. The display jumped back out, almost to the edge of the galactic arm, then panned down the arm, away from the core, past Thousand Suns Space; past vast numbers of un-surveyed stars. Then the display zoomed in again and a new purple dot appeared on the screen. But unlike the others, the dot continued to grow until it filed the screen, then it started to break up into individual dots. Hundreds of them.

"This is the Soloth fleet, Mr. Renwick," said Zueros. "An advance force, if you will. Still sixteen-hundred twenty three light years from the colony, but moving fast. They will be there in seven days."

"That's impossible!" said Renwick. "It would take us months to make that journey!"

"More than a year in our fastest ships," said Makera.

"This is the nature of your opposition, Senator, Ambassador. Do you want to take the risk that I am faking this, or do you want the best possible chance you have to defend yourselves?" he said. Renwick looked to Makera, and then to Yan.

"We need to go to Tarchus," Renwick said.

"Agreed," said Makera. He had never seen her shaken before, but clearly she was now.

"Yan?"

"The answers to the Void lie at the emitter station," she said.

"But there won't be anything to save from the Void if we don't go to Tarchus," Renwick argued. Yan looked at him. She was clearly unhappy with the situation. Nonetheless, she walked slowly over to the main console where Amanda was stationed.

"Change course, Amanda," she said, "take us to Tarchus, maximum speed."

"We are already scooping as much dark energy as we can," replied the android.

"Then get with Mr. Kish and see if you can scoop more!" Yan said, angry. "We don't have the time to waste."

"Yes, captain," said Amanda.

And with that Yan stormed from the bridge. Renwick could do nothing but watch her go.

#

They were nearly a day into the three day trek through Void Space to Tarchus when Renwick heard the knocking on his door. He was halfway through his sleep cycle in one of the rest cabins. He expected it was Ambassador Makera yet again. He had already turned down her advances more than once. She still seemed unable to connect his rejection of her sexually with her actions in killing the soldiers aboard the slave station at Skondar. It was an alien thought process for sure, and Renwick had no desire to delve further into Raelen psychology than he already had for the sake of the treaty.

When he didn't respond the knock came again.

"Please go away," he said, just loud enough for the person on the other side of the door to hear.

"I need to talk to you," came the soft response. It didn't sound like Makera, so he quickly rolled out of bed, pulling on his tunic and pants, then went to the door and unlocked it. To his surprise it was the captain of the *Kali* on the other side.

"May I come in?" Yan asked. He stood to one side and let her pass, then shut the door behind her.

"I thought for sure that you were Ambassador Makera again, masquerading to get me to let you in," he said.

"I want to talk," she said simply. He sat back down on his bed in the tiny room while she sat on the opposing berth.

"What's on your mind, Yan?" he said. She seemed hesitant to talk, so he prompted her. "Something bothering you?"

"You mean besides the fact that I probably died three centuries ago, have been resurrected as a hologram, and caused the collapse of civilization as I knew it? No, besides that, nothing," she said.

"You didn't cause the Void, Yan. The Soloth did," he said gently.

"So Zueros says."

"You don't believe him?" said Renwick. She shook her head.

"Not entirely. The way he manipulated my navigation console, I checked it later. There was no tampering. What he showed us was real. But I'm not sure I trust his motivations, or his honesty. There are things that don't add up in his story."

"Such as?"

"Such as that DNA test. I was inside Amanda, I was aware of it, but I couldn't cognizantly interpret the results, it was like I was being blocked. I can't verify it, therefore I don't trust it," she said. Renwick didn't have an answer for her concerns, so he stayed silent for a few moments. She stared at the floor, saying nothing, so he prompted her again.

"But that's not why you came here," he stated, using the highly honed sense of intuition that had made him such an excellent diplomat. It turned out to be right.

"No," she finally said, then stopped. He waited patiently for her to come to her point. "I'm a clone, made from digital data, like a hologram, Renwick. A collection of stored electronic data projected into a three dimensional representation that simulates the form that I *used* to have, when I was alive." He looked at her. She had the soft almond shaped eyes of descendants of the Asian continent on Earth, long dark hair past her shoulders, a petite but muscular feminine body, all accentuated by the new costume she wore.

"When I look at you Yan, all I see is a woman," he said truthfully.

"An electronic woman," she countered. He shook his head.

"Just a woman. A beautiful one."

"And that's the problem. I *feel* like a woman. I have the same emotions, the same drives, the same desires as I did when I was in my own skin," she said. Then she looked up at him. A tear ran down her face. "But I'm not a real girl, Renwick."

He reached out and touched her cheek, running his finger up her face and scooping up the tear. "Can you feel that?"

"Yes," she said. He ran his hand up her arm.

"Can you feel this?" he said. She closed her eyes.

"Oh, yes…" He moved closer and kissed her slightly parted lips.

"And that?" She only nodded in response, her eyes closed. "And I can feel you too. So therefore I declare you a real girl, Tanitha Yan," he said. She sighed deeply, taking in heavy breaths.

"I can even feel myself breathing," she said quietly. He moved across and sat next to her, slipping his arm around her waist and pulling her close.

"Let's see how well this program really works," he said, then he kissed her again.

#

"Whoever designed this simulation thought of everything," Yan said an hour later.

"That *was* a successful experiment," agreed Renwick, laying back on the bed while she cuddled him.

"Renwick," she said. Her tone made him take notice.

"Yes?"

"I want to *live*, Renwick. I want to be *alive*. There were so many things I was going to do with my life," she said.

"You mean besides destroying civilization as we know it?"

She smacked him hard.

"Oww!" he said. "That hurt!"

"Better learn to take it, Senator, because I can dish it out," she said. He thought about her predicament for a moment, one that he was the current beneficiary of.

"What about being inside Amanda? Maybe they could construct an android body like that for you, so you could still go anywhere and do those things you wanted to do," he said.

"Perhaps if they could completely repress the android personality. Being mixed up with her, it was odd. Sometimes I felt like she just hit the 'hold' button and I was stuck in limbo."

"And there's the fact that she has a fusion reactor where her uterus should be," he said. Yan raised her arm as if to hit him again. Renwick recoiled in mock fear.

"Don't make me," she said playfully. He laughed, then pulled her close again.

"Seriously. Do you think Amanda was hiding things from you?" Yan sat up on one arm.

"I know she was," she said.

Renwick considered this. "So now the question is what was she hiding from you?"

"Or *why* was she hiding it?" said Yan.

"That's two questions," said Renwick. They laughed together again, and then he kissed her. "You are a very attractive hologram, you know," he said. She rolled on top of him and then straddled his hips, sitting up as the covers fell back to reveal her virtual naked body.

"I bet you say that to all the non-corporeal girls. And I prefer the term 'digital person'," she said. He watched as the smile faded slowly from her face. "Because that's what I am," she said sullenly. He saw the tears forming in her eyes again.

"If I traveled this ship to the Core and back, Captain Tanitha Yan, I could never hope to find a girl as real and as beautiful as you are," he said. The corners of her mouth ticked up just slightly at this.

"That," she said, leaning down to kiss him again, "was the right thing to say."

#

Forty-eight hours later Yan and Renwick were both on the bridge together at the command console as the *Kali* scooped the last vestiges of Void Space into her converters. They were joined by Amanda, Makera and Zueros, as well as the rest of the *Phaeton's* crew, Mischa Cain at Navigation, Captain Aybar at Weapons, and Kish monitoring engineering functions. They all watched together as the countdown ended and the *Kali* emerged into normal space in the Tarchus system, the first such incursion there in three human centuries.

"Scan the star," said Yan to Amanda. She did as commanded and reported.

"Red dwarf star, M5 type, point three-eight sol in mass, luminosity of point one-two sol. Tarchus is the main planet of five, the only one in the habitable zone, point one-six Astronomical Units from the primary star, average global temperature of twenty-point five Celsius."

"How does it stay so warm that close to such a dim star?" asked Renwick.

"It has a tidal locked moon large and massive enough to generate its own internal heat," said Amanda.

"That's convenient."

"You're forgetting that a race capable of dividing itself into four sub-races could also be well-capable of designing a star system," said Zueros. "Your Earth is a classic example. A planet placed a perfect distance from its main-sequence star. A moon just large enough to both drive the tidal forces necessary for life on the main planet and, coincidentally, exactly the size need to completely occult your sun. If the Preservers had just left a monument with their signatures on it, it couldn't have been more obvious."

"And yet we've managed to avoid seriously discussing the subject for nearly ten millennia of human civilization," offered Renwick.

"No one ever said your species was logical," piped in Makera. Renwick looked at her with irritation.

"I know, too many emotions getting the way of being practical, eh Ambassador? Like back on Skondar station?" he said.

"Set a course for Tarchus, Amanda," cut in Yan, seeking to end the burgeoning debate and get them back on track with the task at hand. "And do it quickly, before we have a civil war on our hands. Use the normal space impellers, on maximum."

"Yes Captain," replied the android, sweeping over the console with her hands at lightning speed.

An hour later the brown-green globe of Tarchus was filing their master displays. It had been a dim world in the best of times, and these were not the best of times.

"What's going on down there, Amanda?" asked Yan. The android gave an analysis.

"Based on measureable light, heat, and radiated emissions, Tarchus is operating at less than sixty-percent of her last known industrial capacity. A lack of light at settlements on the night side indicate several major cities have been essentially abandoned. Telecommunications networks are in sporadic use. No occupied space habitats are detected. There is a colony base on the primary satellite, but it appears to be abandoned, or functioning at a very low level. Surface activity indicates there are several active wars taking place, but most of them are at a pre-industrial levels," Amanda said.

"Tribal warfare," said Makera. "They've regressed to a near barbarism. This is what your people, your Void, did to them, Zueros."

Zueros' only response was to look up at the Ambassador before returning his attention to the console.

"Not entirely barbaric, I should say," said Yan. "I'm detecting incoming space vessels on an intercept vector. Three, in fact. Modern cruisers by scale and design."

Renwick looked up sharply at Amanda. "Cruisers? Why didn't we pick them up when we arrived?" he demanded. The android hesitated for a few seconds before responding, scanning her console.

"They were hidden on the far side of the primary satellite. Further analysis indicates that there is an operating military base there," Amanda

said.

"I can see that much," he snapped. "If these Gataan are anything like their pirate expatriates…" he trailed off.

"Defenses up, Amanda!" commanded Yan. The *Kali* hummed to life in response, main lights dimming, a defense grid coming online and bathing the command deck in deep blue light.

"Perhaps someone can explain to me how a race supposedly isolated for three centuries has a fleet of modern cruisers that just happen to be waiting for us?" said Renwick looking to their newest companion.

"I can't," said Zueros.

"I can," said Makera, raising her pistol. "You're a liar. You've led us into a trap. And I intend to end your life right now."

"I'm no liar," said Zueros in his defense, backing away from the console, raising his hands in a show of compliance.

"And yet there are these cruisers, and they're clearly far more advanced than anything else we can observe on this world," said Renwick, sweeping a hand across the console. "I happen to agree with the Ambassador; you are a liar, sir. But you might have some very valuable information. And luckily for you we don't have time for executions." He reached out and forced Makera to lower her pistol. She briefly pushed back against him, then acquiesced.

"I agree also," said Yan. "We don't. Thorne will put him in detention." She nodded towards the automaton.

"Wait-" started Zueros, but the imposing figure of Thorne already had him in a firm mechanical grip and was leading him away by the arm. "I can explain-"

"Save it," said Renwick. He turned to the captain after Zueros was removed from the bridge.

"So now what?" he asked. Yan scanned her tactical board. The Gataan cruisers were closing rapidly.

"They've laid a trap for us, and we're stuck in it," she said.

"Can we defend ourselves against these cruisers?" Renwick asked.

"The *Kali* was not designed to fight major space battles, Senator," said Yan without looking up from the board.

Amanda eyed her captain, but said nothing.

"That's what I was afraid you'd say," said Renwick to Yan. "Please tell me that you have an armory aboard?"

"There is one," replied Amanda.

"Show them," said Yan with an absent nod, all the while sending out commands to maneuver her ship away from the cruisers and buy them time.

Renwick quickly gathered the others and Amanda led them to the small armory. Coil rifles, pistols, stun grenades and limited number of charging packs were available. Renwick outfitted Kish, Captain Aybar, and Mischa while Makera loaded up on her own.

Renwick brought a rifle back to Yan.

"We're too exposed out here. Is there someplace we can make a stand?" he asked.

"There is a safe room," said Amanda.

"A what?" said Renwick, turning back to the android.

"A fortified room where we can ride out a ship invasion," she said.

"Sounds like we'd be locked in as well. Perhaps we can use it in a different way than it was intended. Is there another alternative?" he asked.

"The common area," Yan said, motioning over her shoulder. "Back by the galley. I can transfer essential ship functions to a monitor station back there. And if we get the chance I can lock down the ship's controls. But once I do, we're locked out too."

"Let's do it," said Renwick. Yan's hands flashed over the console board and then she was done. Renwick followed her back towards the galley as she effortlessly hefted her heavy rifle with her as she came. She stopped only to give last minute instructions to Amanda.

"Defense algorithm six-two-two," Yan ordered. "Render any non-essential assistance. Maximum self-preservation. I am shutting down the other androids and returning them to their docks. Do you understand?"

"Yes," said Amanda.

"Good luck," said Yan as Amanda made for the command console.

"C'mon," she said, turning to Renwick. "We'd better hurry."

12. AT TARCHUS

Yan watched the cruisers approach to the *Kali* on her remote monitor in the common area with trepidation. The Gataan had split into a definite attacking formation. As was their way, one ship took the point while the other two stayed back, searching for weakness.

"You have no external defensive weapons?" asked Makera of Yan.

"This is not a battleship, Ambassador," replied Yan with more than a hint of impatience.

"That much is clear," said the Raelen with open disdain.

"How much time until they attack?" asked Renwick, coming in from the adjacent hallway. He had just returned from setting up an EMP emitter in the safe room. Yan watched as the lead cruiser fired a coil cannon shot at her ship. The Kali rocked from the impact before her inertial dampers stabilized.

"That would be now," she said. "You'd better deploy your people."

Renwick set up Captain Aybar, Kish and Mischa Cain to defend the rear of the galley, where the sleeping berths and washrooms were. Zueros was locked in one of the berths for safekeeping.

Renwick handed each of them extra power packs for their coil rifles. "There's only one way into this room, so keep your rifles poised at the entrance. Only fire if they look like they're going to attack you. Yan, Makera and I will try and draw them down the hall towards the safe room. If we can get them into close quarters, we can use the stun grenades and then lock them inside," he said.

"Shouldn't we be locking ourselves in?" asked Mischa. She looked far too weak and far too tainted by her time in the Auction pits of Skondar to do much fighting.

"If we do then we give them free run of the ship. At least this way we have the possibility of trapping them and engaging the androids and the ship's internal defenses to lock them out," said Renwick. At least he hoped that was true.

"We'll give you our best," promised Captain Aybar. Renwick had developed a definite respect for the woman as a warrior since he'd had the chance to see her in action at Minara.

"I know you will," he said. "But remember to stay low and don't fire until you've been seen. Wait until I call you. You're our only backup." Aybar nodded and Renwick went back out to the galley common area where Yan had set up the temporary console.

"Time?" he asked. The Kali rocked again, this time the dampers took much longer to compensate and alarm claxons started going off.

"The bastards just rammed us!" said Yan, her anger rising. "I'm calling out the androids." She reached for the controls but Renwick stopped her.

"You know that's a mistake," he said. "We need them to operate the ship after we get out of here. They're too valuable." He handed her a rifle, a pistol, and two grenades. "Now lock out that console and let's take our positions."

Yan looked down at the board, freed up one hand and typed in a series of commands with lightning speed.

"Done," she said.

"Then let's go," said Renwick.

#

The three of them took up their positions behind the bulkheads leading into the hallway to the galley common area. The galley itself was a stand-alone unit built in to the center of the command deck. It was fortified by bulkheads on three sides, with only one entrance, a long hallway, which they were preparing to defend. The safe room was at the end of the hall, built into the ship's superstructure. It wasn't perfect, but it was better than nothing.

"Did you set the bait?" asked Makera. Renwick nodded.

"The safe room contains one of the HD drive EMP emitters. I lit it up to look like the ships' power core. That should be the first place they come if they want control of the ship. Once we get them inside, it's stun grenades and then we lock as many of them inside as we can," he said.

"Gataan are bigger than humans, and harder to bring down. Do we know if the stun grenades will work?" asked Yan. Renwick shook his head.

"No, but inside a room coated with uranium alloy just about any force should be magnified enough to have some effect," he said.

"Imagine their surprise when they discover they've essentially captured a hyped up signal flare," said Makera as she quickly loaded her pistol, rifle, and clipped off the safeties on her grenades.

The ship shook again. The sounds of running boots could be heard approaching from the distance. Renwick set himself against the near bulkhead. From here he had a clean shot through most of the bridge area. Makera set up behind him, her line of fire was set at a slightly more acute angle, but she could still sweep most of the room. The most exposed was Yan, on the other side of the hallway, but then she was a hologram and couldn't really be killed, at least not in the conventional way.

The boot sounds grew louder. Renwick raised and prepped his rifle. "Remember we want to draw them in," he said.

"As if two people and a hologram won't be a tempting enough target," said Yan. Renwick briefly smiled. Her sense of humor was still intact. Seconds later and there was visible motion in the bridge area.

Renwick took aim. A pair of tall shadow figures reconnoitered the command console, then a half dozen more appeared, weapons raised.

"Now," said Renwick, and fired off a dozen rounds. His companions did the same before they got any return fire. At first the return was sporadic and confused, but then became more organized. Makera threw a stun grenade into the fray. Sparks flew and bodies fell.

"Careful with those! We don't have that many!" yelled Renwick. A few more seconds of sporadic firing and it looked like they had the invaders on the run. Then the shooting went quiet and he heard orders being yelled in the Gataan's guttural language. They were reforming ranks.

A flanking team took up refuge behind the android docks to their left. Another set up to the right, moving out of Renwick's sight but into Yan's. The third and largest group, organized behind the main control console, set up straight ahead.

"They're flanking us," warned Renwick, crouching down so that Makera could get a clear shot at the center group. "You'll have to hold the center, Makera. I'll take the left flank. Yan, you'll have to cover the right, but be aware that's where the androids are," he said.

"Trying to make my job more difficult?" replied Yan.

"Always," said Renwick. Then he pressed this rifle trigger and opened fire. He managed to suppress his flank for almost thirty seconds, and Yan did the same on hers. But Makera was facing a losing battle. There were too many Gataan in the center group, and they were advancing.

"I'm going to load my rifle with a grenade, but you'll have to fire it," Renwick said to Makera, "and you'll have to cover my flank too." She did as instructed in her silent but grim Raelen way. "Yan, you're going to have to help with the center," he said.

"Got it," she said, switching her fire between her flank and the center group, slowing them down but allowing her flank to advance. Renwick switched from rifle mode to grenade mode and then loaded one of the stunners onto his sizzling barrel.

"Ready," he said, and tossed his rifle to Makera while she slid hers across the deck back to him. From her position she had a clear shot at the closing center group. She took the rifle and fired in one motion, with precision, the grenade flying through the air and then bouncing into a large pile of Gataan soldiers. The soft *whump* of the stun grenade going off made for a satisfying sound. He watched as the center group was scrambled and had to retreat again, then he returned his attention to his advancing left flank. A long barrage of suppressing fire pushed them back behind their defenses. Just then he heard the empty click of Yan's rifle. She was out of power and needed to swap out a power pack. Instead she dropped the rifle an picked up her pistol.

"I can't hold this side, Renwick!" she called. "They're nearly here!" Just then a grenade scattered into the hallway right in front of them.

"Fuck it!" said Yan, dropping her pistol and then jumping to her feet, kicking the grenade back the way it came. "Rifle!" she demanded from him as the grenade went off a good distance away from them. Renwick tossed her his rifle and she took it with both hands, aimed it and started firing.

"Yan!" said Renwick as she started out of the hallway covey into open fire.

"I'm not alive anyway, remember?" she yelled over the din as she charged the right flank. Two seconds later a shot from the center group hit her straight on.

She vanished in an instant, disintegrating as the coil rifle clattered to the floor.

"We have to drop back!" yelled Makera. Renwick looked at the spot where Yan had been vaporized and started firing onto the center group with his pistol. Makera grabbed him by the collar and dragged him several of the ten meters down the hall to the galley doorway. Renwick scrambled to his feet as Makera rushed to Aybar and the second group. He aimed his pistol at the temporary terminal.

"Don't!" yelled Makera over the fire of the rapidly advancing Gataan troops. "We'll never get control of the ship back!"

"We've already lost the ship!" said Renwick. *And Yan too,* he thought. A stun grenade going off in the hallway knocked him back and he crawled the last meter to his companions. Makera handed him a new pistol.

"We can't win this," she said.

"Which is why you should have surrendered," came a brittle voice from behind them. Renwick turned just in time to see Zueros drop a stun grenade in their midst. He tried to kick it out of the area but only moved it a short distance. It spun like a top and he watched it in what seemed like slow motion until a blinding flash filled his eyes.

Then everything went black.

#

Renwick awoke in the safe room, unarmed and unguarded. He got to his feet, despite his body's protestations, and went to the enormous metal door, finding that they were locked in.

"I've already tried that," said Makera from behind him. Despite her recent behavior he was glad she was still alive. Renwick sat back down, rubbing his head before taking stock of the situation. Captain Aybar was holding Mischa Cain, who seemed to be sleeping. Kish sat staring at the opposite wall.

"How long was I out?" asked Renwick.

"About two hours," said Makera.

"Has there been any contact?"

"No." Renwick sighed.

"I wonder what progress they're making on getting the ship running," he said. "It's obvious that was Zueros' plan all along, to get the *Kali* here to Tarchus so they could take the ship. And I fell for it."

"We all did," said Makera, "if that's any consolation."

Renwick shook his head. "Sorry," he said. He looked up to Captain Aybar. "And sorry for getting you involved in this."

"Nonsense, Senator," she said. "You saved my life, all of our lives, and besides, I'm an officer in the Unity Navy. I've only been doing my duty. And you came back to rescue us. I couldn't ask for more than that from my best military officers, let alone a civilian. We're right where we're supposed to be, thanks to you. And we're still alive, the three of us, and that means something, so quit kicking yourself."

Renwick nodded. It was hard to accept praise when he felt he had so recently failed them. One of them the most.

"I couldn't save Yan," he said aloud, hanging his head.

"I'm sorry. I know you were fond of her persona," said Makera. Renwick looked up at her.

"Her," he corrected, with a just touch of venom in his voice. "I was fond of *her*." Then he went silent again.

"I wonder how long they'll keep us in here," said Kish. Renwick was surprised. He'd hardly heard the man say ten words since he'd been rescued. As the nominal leader of the mission now, he felt obligated to give him an answer.

"Probably until they figure out they're locked out of the operating systems," Renwick said. And with that things went quiet between them. The knock on the safe room door ten minutes later came as a surprise.

Two large Gataan guards with their olive skin and dark hair opened the door and motioned Renwick and Makera to come out. Mischa Cain stirred and tried to move further away from the door. Renwick looked to Aybar.

"Keep everyone calm until we get back," he said to the captain of the *Phaeton*. She nodded, protecting Mischa with her body.

They were led out of the safe room and down the hallway to the bridge, where Zueros stood over the command console. Amanda stood at Zueros' side, her android face devoid of expression. Gataan soldiers patrolled the command deck, weapons at the ready.

"Why am I not surprised to find you leading this pirate gang, Mr. Zueros?" said Renwick. "Or whatever your real name is." Zueros didn't look up from the console.

"My real name is unimportant," he said. "I'll need the command override codes to unlock the *Kali*," he said.

"I don't have them," Renwick replied honestly.

"Ambassador?" asked Zueros.

"Sorry," she replied.

"You see I have a predicament," started Zueros in a conversational tone. "If I can't get this ship moving then I can't cut a path from here to

Zed Vadela Three. If I can't do that, then I can't meet our invasion fleet. If I fail at that task, the fleet will be on their own against the Raelen Empire. Undoubtedly we would still win such a confrontation, but it would be much harder if the base at Vadela is not taken out first. Element of surprise and all that. So I have a problem, and you have to solve it, Mr. Renwick."

"So your plan all along was to use us to take the *Kali* and open a path to our space," said Makera. "You're a bastard. I should have killed you when I had the chance."

"No. I am a loyalist to my own people. I'm sorry about the deception, and your empire, Ambassador. But they are merely casualties in our cause," he turned from the console and looked directly at Renwick. "The code, please, Senator."

"I don't know it, and even if I did-" with just the slightest of nods from Zueros two soldiers grabbed Makera and dragged her against a near bulkhead. The pinned her wrists against the wall with metal restraining clips and then backed off ten paces, their rifles raised at her.

"What's this!" demanded Renwick. "She doesn't have the code!"

"I know. But she'll die anyway if you can't produce it," said Zueros.

"Damn it man, I told you, I don't have it! Yan was the only one! And your men vaporized her!" said Renwick, panicked and angry.

"The Yan persona has been terminated," said Zueros. "She had to have left it with one of you. The code please Mr. Renwick. You have ten seconds."

"I told you, I don't have it!" Renwick started towards Zueros, but soldiers restrained him. Zueros stood impassive, staring at Makera. The Ambassador said nothing, merely staring at Zueros with hate in her eyes.

"Five seconds," Zueros said.

"Goddamn you! If I had it don't you think I'd give it to you to save my friend?"

"Two seconds," Zueros raised his hand and the guards raised their rifles, aimed at Makera.

"One."

"I have the code."

The voice came from behind Zueros.

Amanda.

Zueros turned to the android and slowly dropped his hand to his side. "How fortunate for you, Mr. Renwick," he said.

"Amanda, Captain Yan ordered you not to cooperate!" said Renwick, still upset but glad that Makera would live, at least for now. Amanda looked at him blankly.

"The captain programmed me for maximum self-preservation. That also includes you and your companions. I can't allow you to die, therefore I must give up the code," she said.

"Very good," said Zueros "Now if you please…" he motioned to the command console with a grand wave of the arm. Amanda came up and punched in a series of commands with android speed. Immediately the command deck returned to normal lighting, all systems open and active again. The other androids disconnected from their docks and immediately resumed their normal duties. This startled the Gataan soldiers and they quickly raised their weapons.

Zueros said something in Gataan and then waved off the guards. They approached Makera, removing her bindings and letting her go.

"Now if you don't mind, Senator, Ambassador, I have an invasion to plan," said Zueros. Then he turned back to the command console, and the soldiers hustled them back to the safe room.

#

Once they were back inside the safe room the door was locked and sealed from the outside. The control console inside the room had been smashed. Renwick, Makera, and Aybar huddled near the door, talking strategy in hushed tones.

"I don't think we're going to be getting out of here anytime soon," said Renwick. "What's our supply situation?" he asked Captain Aybar, expecting the top military officer present to have an account of their situation. He wasn't disappointed.

"We have food supplies for three days, access to water, a sanitary toilet, and no way out," she said. "So unless they let us out, we're in here for the duration."

"The duration of what is the question," said Renwick.

"If you'd let me kill him when we had the chance-" started Makera. Renwick cut her off.

"We'd still have had to deal with those cruisers, Ambassador," he snapped at her. Then he stepped away from her and looked around the room.

There were two sleeping pallets, double bunked. Mischa Cain was laying quietly in the bottom one, her back turned to them and the door. It looked for all the world like she was emotionally withdrawing. Kish sat on the only other seat, a bench that looked extruded from the wall.

"How's Mischa holding up?" Renwick asked, turning back to the captain. Aybar looked to the young woman, concern for the junior officer etched across her face.

"She's been through a lot in a very short time," said Aybar. "But I think she'll be okay soon."

"Let's hope so. We can use every hand," he said, then looked around the room one more time. "We may as well get some rest. I don't think we'll be getting out of here until after they've taken the base."

"That will be too late. There are forty thousand colonists on Zed Vadela Three," said Makera. "We have to do something before this ship gets there."

Renwick held out his hands.

"Unfortunately, Ambassador, there's nothing I can think of to do about that right now," he said. And with that he took a seat on the floor, hung his head, and closed his eyes.

13. AT VADELA

Three days later and the captivity was getting monotonous. Thankfully the guards let them out for thirty minutes each day to walk and stretch while their supplies were replenished. Renwick used the time to observe as much as he could. Zueros was never around when they were let out, and the command console was always dark when he passed. Amanda continued her unrelenting stance near the console, and he never saw her move or converse with anyone.

He did manage to observe the formation of the cruiser fleet accompanying the *Kali*. He counted twenty cruisers in the formation. That was less than ten percent of what the Unity had, but the closest of those Unity ships, not counting the *Phaeton*, were at least five hundred light years distant. And the Unity cruisers weren't capable of travel through the Void.

They were soon shuffled back into the safe room for their evening meal, and after the latest round of speculation as to their potential fate, they shut down for the night. Renwick had taken to bunking with Makera while Captain Aybar continued to comfort Mischa Cain, who's depression seemed to have deepened over the days. Kish preferred the floor.

After dozing but not really sleeping for a couple of hours, Renwick heard a shuffling sound on the far wall, the one facing the *Kali's* superstructure. It went on for a few minutes, and became loud enough for everyone in the safe room to hear it. There were now five very attentive and very awake prisoners in the safe room.

"I wonder what's on the other side of that wall?" Renwick said to Makera after they had all gathered as far away from it as they could.

"As far as I know it's solid uranium. Nothing short of a well-placed coil cannon shot should be able to displace it," she said.

"The wall is starting to glow," said Captain Aybar. "A faint orange."

Renwick squinted in the dim light. "She's right. There is a glow. And it's starting to get warm in here. Can we move back any further?" he said.

They all squeezed into the far corner. The sound was coming now in waves.

"What *is* that?" asked Mischa. Kish moved to stand between her and the glow, which was glowing brighter every second.

"From the color it's got to be some kind of coil energy," said Kish. "It's almost like it's peeling away layers of the uranium."

Renwick nodded. The sound grew louder, moving to a swishing sound, then a squealing hum.

"Cover," shouted Renwick, throwing his body over Makera and Aybar while Kish did the same for Mischa Cain just as the wall imploded into the safe room. He looked up to see a roughly rectangular hole about the size of a man and half again as wide had been burned through the outer wall of the safe room

Through two solid meters of uranium core.

When the dust and smoke cleared Renwick stepped forward and peered into the hole. Thorne, the android, stood on the other side. He turned and started to walk away.

"Well come on!" said Renwick, motioning to his companions to follow him "It's a jail break!"

#

Thorne led them down a narrow utility corridor that looked like it was only used by the androids. He walked slowly and deliberately.

"Have you ever heard this one speak?" asked Makera as they followed it.

"As far as I know it's an automaton, even if it does *look* like a human. Amanda's the only one I've ever heard talk," Renwick said.

"So we can't be sure of its intentions?"

"Can we ever be?" he said. She frowned.

"Likely not," she said. Thorne stopped at a control console and paced his hand in a gel-like substance, interfacing with the console. A small monitor lit up with a familiar face.

"This is Yan," she said. "I downloaded a backup copy of myself into Thorne's body before the Gataan attack. If you're receiving this recording then I have been successful in rescuing you. My plan from this moment onward is to place myself into a mobile Tera drive and have Thorne manually download me into Amanda's body. From there I will be able to activate the *Kali's* internal defenses, which should result in your being able to retake the ship. Please stay in this access corridor until I come to retrieve you. I hope you are all well. This is Yan, out." The screen went blank.

"Captain Yan is still with us," said Renwick, pleased. He watched as Thorne placed a portable drive unit, shaped like an index finger, into the gel. It stayed there for a few seconds, then the android pulled it out, then pulled off his own index finger and replaced it with the drive. He then turned and exited from the corridor into the main hallway.

"I can't believe they didn't hear our escape," said Aybar, looking back down the corridor towards the safe room.

"Actually, it's not that likely," said Kish. "The door was uranium as well, and they smashed the control console, remember? So no security camera and unless there was a guard sitting right at the door I doubt they heard a thing."

Renwick went to the console then and started sorting through multiple views of the interior of the ship, finally finding one that showed the bridge. Zueros was busy working controls and displays on the command console while Amanda stood in her usual place, not moving. All of the escapees gathered around the tiny screen and watched as Thorne approached Amanda in his robot-like way, slow and even steps. He handed Amanda a portable display board and she examined it.

"Look, his finger's missing!" said Kish.

"You're right," said Aybar. They watched as Amanda's hands flew over the display board. Zueros turned around to watch the commotion.

"Does he see it?" asked Mischa.

"I don't think so," replied Renwick. After a few tense seconds Zueros turned back to his board. Amanda handed the display back to Thorne, then resumed her stoic stance. Thorne turned and walked away.

"Did they make the exchange?" said Makera.

"I didn't see it," said Renwick. "That doesn't mean it didn't happen. They move damn fast when they want to."

A few moments more passed and a Gataan soldier came up to Zueros, who turned his attention from the board momentarily. As he did Amanda took a step up and activated the board, her hands flashing across its surface. Zueros turned quickly, a pistol in his hand. Amanda knocked it away with one hand and then drove him back with the other. Zueros went flying out of the camera sight. They all let out a small cheer as Amanda completed her task and then stepped away from the console just as soldiers came up.

Alarm claxons sounded inside the corridor.

"She's activated the internal defense systems," said Renwick. He watched as the console display showed the bridge area filling with a thick gas. The Gataan soldiers collapsed almost instantly. "Get back from the door!" he said to his crew, pushing them back towards the area of the safe room.

Several minutes went by and then the alarms went silent. A few seconds later and the door to the hallway opened again. This time it was Amanda, or rather, Yan in Amanda's body.

Welcome back," she said, smiling. "The ship is ours again."

#

"I want Zueros," seethed Makera when they were back on the bridge.

"He fled when I turned on the gas," said Amanda/Yan. Renwick assigned Aybar, Kish and Mischa to move the Gataan soldiers into the safe room. There were only about ten aboard at the time of the gas attack.

"The rest returned to their main vessels after we were taken," said Amanda/Yan.

"I'm just glad you're still with us," said Renwick. "I thought we'd lost you during the skirmish." Amanda/Yan smiled at him.

"Always back up your files," she said. "Did you really think I'd take a risk like charging the Gataan like that without a backup plan?"

"I don't know," admitted Renwick. "Frankly, I don't know you that well."

"Oh, I think you know me well enough," she said. Renwick was shocked at the depth of emotion she was able to display through Amanda's body; the voice, facial expression, even her eyes seemed much more alive than he'd seen before. And the emotional expression was one of seduction.

"I see you're handling the android body much better this time," he commented.

"Practice makes perfect. I was able to learn a lot about suppressing the android persona while I was inside Thorne. I did have three days to study, you know," she said.

"Yeah, three days of hell for us," he replied.

"If you two are done with the foreplay, I have a status report," the voice came from Makera, who had busied herself at the command console.

"Good news or bad?" asked Renwick.

"Mostly bad," she looked up at them. "We're already in the Vadela system. The *Kali* broke through about six hours ago. The Gataan cruisers are nowhere in sight of our scanners, which must mean they are inside the system, probably hiding and waiting for the main Soloth fleet to arrive so they can join in the attack."

"You're right, that isn't good news," said Renwick. He turned back to Amanda/Yan. "How much weaponry does the *Kali* really have?" She shook her head.

"Not much, as far as I can surmise. If there are more systems aboard, Amanda is keeping them well hidden from me. What we do have isn't enough to take on twenty cruisers, certainly. Remember the *Kali* was a purpose-built ship. Her main asset is the Void emitters."

"Yes," said Renwick thoughtfully. "How much dark energy have the scoops accumulated?"

"They're full," Amanda/Yan said. "Any extra has been dissipated as excess."

"And what's the full capacity of the *Kali*?"

"You've seen it. She can swallow a star system whole," said Yan. Her features showed she was unhappy with the direction of the conversation.

"What are you driving at, Renwick?" asked Makera, equally alarmed. Renwick started pacing.

"If we encased the colony-" he started.

"No!" said Makera. "You're insane."

"Hear me out," he asked.

"I won't," said Makera, backing away from the console. "I won't let you suffocate an entire colony."

"We wouldn't be 'suffocating' them, we'd be protecting them," he insisted.

"I don't agree," said Makera. "We don't know enough about what the process might do to them." Renwick looked to Amanda/Yan.

"It is theoretically possible to direct the energy plasma on an object as small as a planet," she said.

"A moon," said Makera. "The Vadela colony is on a habitable moon of the third planet." Renwick deferred to Amanda/Yan again.

"As I said, it's possible-" said Amanda/Yan.

"I won't allow it."

"Makera, you *have* to," implored Renwick. "It's either that or the colony faces destruction. You know that. We can't defend them, can't defeat the Soloth fleet. It's their only hope."

The Raelen Ambassador took in a deep breath. "May your human god damn you Renwick," she said.

"You know I'm right."

"Yes, you are," she said. "But it may be months before we're able to get back here and free the colony. Months in complete darkness."

"We could encase it with the star," Renwick offered. Yan shook her head.

"It would take too long. Perhaps a day. The colony itself and the parent planet could be covered in perhaps an hour," she said.

Makera looked at her two companions. "Very well, I give you my authority as Ambassador of the Raelen Empire. But I have two conditions. First, you give me a ship and allow me to warn the colonists first. And second," she said, turning towards Renwick. "You entrust the treaty papers to me," she said.

"The treaty papers? But why?" said Renwick.

"Because once I have warned the colony I am proceeding to the nearest Raelen military base and bringing back a fleet. I'll forward the treaty papers to Raellos. You can sign them there, after this fracas is at an end. And you have to promise me you'll be there to sign them," she said to Renwick in her intense manner.

"That sounds like three conditions," he deadpanned.

"Renwick-" he took her hand in a show of affection.

"I will be there to sign them," he promised.

"Then it's settled," Makera said. "Now get me your fastest jump ship," she said to Amanda/Yan, "before I change my mind."

#

"This shuttle is our fastest jump-drive capable ship," said Amanda/Yan barely an hour later as Makera exited the tiny ship onto the landing deck for a final time. "Do you think you can fly it?"

"Oh yes," the Raelen Ambassador said. "Besides, it's not like I have a choice."

Renwick watched as Kish and Mischa loaded the last of Makera's supplies onto the shuttle. Then he turned to his constant companion for the last two years, fellow negotiator, and former lover.

"So this is goodbye," he said. She smiled in her humorless Raelen way.

"For now, Tam Renwick. For now," she said. Then she came up and kissed him hard on the lips, as if no one else were around. She pulled away just as suddenly and bounded up the stairwell. "Give me two hours, then start your emitters. If I'm not clear of the colony by then I won't ever be," she said when she got to the top.

"What about the Gataan cruisers?" asked Amanda/Yan. Makera stood in the hatch and shrugged.

"If they chase me, I'll just jump out of the system. You'll have to warn the colony."

"Understood," Renwick said. "I take it you know where we'll be?" Makera looked down at him from the hatch.

"I'll just follow your trail. Our fleet should be able to find both you and the emitter station," she said, then she looked to Amanda/Yan. "Take care of him," the Ambassador said to her romantic adversary. Then she stepped back and pressed a button, turned, and headed inside the shuttle. The hatch closed with a thump.

Renwick and Amanda/Yan watched as the shuttle was lifted out of its dock and deposited on the landing deck. A few seconds later and the engines fired up, the outer doors of the landing deck opened and the environmental field collapsed to within just a few feet of them.

Then Makera engaged the hydrazine afterburners and flew swiftly off the deck and into open space.

Renwick looked into the face of Amanda, but inside he knew was soul of Tanitha Yan. He took her by the hand.

"Let's go," he said, his jaw set firm.

"We have work to do."

#

Back on the command deck Renwick took up a station in the bridge area at the command console. Amanda/Yan stood at his side, monitoring the *Kali's* main systems. Captain Aybar had taken up a station at the weapons console to one side, and Mischa Car was on station at the navigation console. Kish was behind them, monitoring engineering functions again. Renwick was glad to have them all working. He hoped it would get their minds off of what they had lost and get them focused on what was ahead.

"Captain Aybar," said Amanda/Yan. "Do you feel able to handle the emitter functions?"

"Oh yes," said Aybar. "I have it well in hand."

"Good. Just remember, you'll be turning over emitter control to me at the end. No one fires my weapons but me."

"Understood," said Aybar. Amanda/Yan turned her attention to Mischa.

"Lieutenant Cain, are we underway yet?" she said.

"Affirmative captain," said Cain. "On our way to the Vadela colony. ETA is twenty-two minutes."

"Good, just drive her straight, lieutenant."

"Aye sir."

"Mr. Kish?" she said. The engineer was last on her rounds.

"All systems nominal captain. Ready to flood the emitters with dark energy plasma at your order," said Kish.

"I can see that on my board, Mr. Kish," snapped Amanda/Yan with the most emotion Renwick had ever seen her express. "My question was going to be about our Gataan prisoners, since you're now in charge of security as well."

"Aye Captain. They're doing fine. That repair shuttle we stuck 'em in should hold 'em just fine until their friends out there pick 'em up," Kish said.

"As long as they're off my ship," said Amanda/Yan.

"Aye captain, and snug as bugs in a rug. I saw to it myself," said Kish.

"Very well." She turned her attention back to Renwick. "You seem pensive, Senator."

"I am. What about Zueros?" he asked. Amanda/Yan brought up a recorded display on the command console. Renwick watched as Zueros moved among downed Gataan soldiers with ease, boarded one of the escape shuttles, and launched himself into space.

"Thirty minutes after this was recorded our sensors detected a hyper-dimensional jump out of the Vadela system," she said.

"Off to meet his masters," replied Renwick. "It's curious though, the stun gas didn't seem to have any effect on him."

"I noticed that," said Amanda/Yan. "Do you suppose the Soloth are immune?"

"If that DNA sample he gave us was accurate, and I have no reason whatsoever to believe that it was, then he should have been effected," said

Renwick.

"But he wasn't," said Amanda/Yan.

"Yes," Renwick played the tape again.

"A theory?" asked Amanda/Yan. Renwick smiled.

"None I'm prepared to put forward yet," he said.

"Captain Yan," it was Mischa Cain. "We'll be in range of the Vadela colony in ten minutes, sir," she said.

"Any sign of interference from the Gataan?" said Amanda/Yan to Captain Aybar.

"No," replied Aybar. "Scans are clean at the moment." Renwick noticed Aybar refused to use the honoraria of rank with Amanda/Yan, who, for her part, didn't seem to notice.

"Good," said Amanda/Yan, looking down at her console again. "We might just make this mission work yet."

#

Renwick watched over her shoulder as Aybar targeted the Vadela colony. It was a small moon, but it had a good gravity field with a temperate atmosphere. Soon it would be enveloped in a protective blanket of dark energy, one that would plunge them into perpetual night until the *Kali* could return and free them, and one that could snuff out all life there in a matter of months if the *Kali* weren't able to return at all.

But it would keep the Gataan and the Soloth away from the colony, and keep the Raelen there safe from the coming invasion. It was gamble, and it was Renwick's gamble.

"We're set here," called Renwick to Amanda/Yan from Aybar's station.

"Transfer control to my console," she said.

"Transferring," said Aybar. Renwick watched as the android he knew as Amanda reacted to the situation. He fancied she actually looked pensive. He made a mental note to ask her why she had decided to stay in the android's body instead of using her own holographic body, when they got a chance.

Renwick joined her back to the command console.

"Emitters are charged," said Amanda/Yan.

"How will we keep the field from catching the solar wind and expanding all over the system?" Renwick asked.

"We can focus the emitters on the magnetic field generated by the planet and the moon. Their magnetic fields will be much stronger locally than the star's. Once we have a closed area, we just shut off the emitters. The solar wind will actually act as a buffer to keep the planet and the colony satellite contained," she said, not looking up from her board. Then, "we are maximized, Mr. Kish. Open the vents."

"Vents open, captain," said Kish.

Renwick watched as Amanda/Yan manipulated the console controls with just her fingertips, touching key systems in a particular order, an amber glow emanating from her each time she interfaced with the smooth console surface. It was a delicate dance of color and light, and it controlled the most deadly energy force humankind had ever known.

"Emitters engaged," she finally said, then she switched to a master display that all on the bridge could see, showing the dark energy, like black ink, spreading outward towards the Vadela Colony.

"Contact with magnetic field confirmed," said Kish from his station. "The plasma is beginning the enveloping process."

"I hope Ambassador Makera managed to get her message off to the colonists, otherwise they're likely to be pretty frightened," commented Amanda/Yan.

"Wouldn't you be?" said Renwick. She looked up at him for a second, then put one hand on her hip as she contemplated her board again.

"I've worked with this equipment more than anyone alive in this century, Renwick. It doesn't frighten me, but I respect it" she said. Then she turned back to Cain and Aybar.

"I'll need a report the instant you see any activity from our Gataan friends, captain. And keep the engines warm, Lieutenant Cain. I want to be able to move out of here at a moment's notice," she said.

Forty minutes later and all was quiet. The Void material had encased eighty-five percent of the colony and its parent planet.

"Mr. Kish, shut down the emitters," said Amanda/Yan. "What we've already extruded will do the rest."

"That's it?" said Renwick. Amanda/Yan nodded.

"And not a peep from the Gataan," she said.

"That's what worries me," said Renwick. "It's like they're waiting for directions." Amanda/Yan stood back from her station then.

"Senator, you are still in charge of this mission, but I suggest we get the hell out of here before that fleet arrives," she said. Renwick nodded.

"Agreed. Lieutenant Cain," he said, turning to her at the navigation console. "Take us out of the system, back the way we came, and step on it," he said.

"Aye sir," she responded. "Heading, sir? Once we're back in the Void?"

Renwick looked to Amanda/Yan.

"We have an obligation to fulfill," he said. "Make heading for the emitter station, as fast as the scoops will take us."

"Aye, sir," said Mischa. He looked at Amanda/Yan, who raised an eyebrow at him in a 'what do we do now?' way.

"Captain Aybar, please take over for me," called Renwick. "I'll be in the back, resting. Let me know immediately if anything changes."

"Of course Senator," Aybar said, rising from her station and heading to the command console. Amanda/Yan looked at Aybar as she came up, but reluctantly relinquished the console. Renwick turned and headed for the rest cabins.

"And what would you have me do, Senator?" asked Amanda/Yan, taking a few steps away from the console.

"You and I need to have a strategy conference, in private, Captain Yan," he said without turning back or breaking stride.

Amanda/Yan smiled, then started after him.

"You have the con, Captain Aybar," she said over her shoulder as she walked away.

"Aye Captain, I have the con," Aybar said. Then she laughed as she watched the two of them rushed for the rest cabins like teenagers.

14. THROUGH THE VOID

Renwick had been in his cabin for nearly two hours, but he hadn't gotten much rest in that time, and his partner didn't need any. He lay on the small bed with his eyes closed, relishing the interlude between their passionate lovemaking spells. The sound of Amanda's voice stirred him from his quiet reverie.

"Which do you prefer?" asked Yan as she absently twirled the course hair on his chest. "The Amanda body, or me?"

He shook his head. "A smart man never answers questions like that," he said, laughing.

"No, really. I want to know," she said. He opened one eye to gaze at her suspiciously, as if he expected a trap to be unveiled at any second. He answered anyway, against his own better judgment.

"I prefer your looks, frankly. Yan's looks, I mean. The Amanda body certainly has its compensations, though. Although the fusion reactor in your belly can be a bit intimidating," he said.

"You didn't seem to mind too much."

"True," he paused for a second, then decided to turn the tables on her. "Which do you prefer?" he asked.

"This body," she said running her hands up and down its synthetic skin. "It feels *real* to me. Solid. Even though my holographic cloned body was perfectly programmed, and the projection fields on the *Kali* allow for a complete human experience, this feels more *right*," she said. "I can't explain it any better than that."

"You don't have to," he said. "In a perfect world I'd have you in a body that looked like your original one, but felt as real as this one."

"I'll get the other androids to start on that for me," she said. He laughed with her.

"Does the presence of the Amanda personality present any… problems?" he asked. She shook her head.

"No. I've learned to completely repress her. She's not even there, as far as I can tell."

"Good," said Renwick, then he yawned. "God, I am tired."

"This body has a sleep mode, you know," said Yan. "I can even program myself to dream."

"So what will it be tonight, brave captain?" he asked. "Flying with unicorns? Winged dragons in Elysian Fields? Or something simpler?" She lay her head on his chest, thinking.

"I believe tonight I will dream of being a real girl again," she said, "so that I can be with you."

He yawned again. "Sounds lovely," he said, quietly mumbling something unintelligible as he drifted off. She kissed him on the cheek.

"Sweet dreams," she said, then she shut down the cabin lights.

#

It was nearly ten hours later when Renwick woke from his first solid sleep in days. He got out of bed to find himself alone. He assumed nothing unusual had happened or the others would have woken him. He showered and shaved, reprocessing his clothes while he so did to freshen them up. He emerged feeling like a new man, and a very hungry one. After a brief but satisfying breakfast alone in the galley he made his way to the bridge. He found Mischa Cain at the navigation console.

"Good morning, Mischa," he said, cheery.

"Good afternoon, Senator," she said back. Renwick looked around the bridge area of the command deck, except for the two of them, they were alone.

"Where is everybody?" he asked.

"I believe they're witnessing the birth," said Mischa, more than a bit mischievously.

"Birth? What the hell are you talking about?" he said.

She smiled at him. "Just go to the android docks. They'll explain when you get there." Renwick eyed her askance, but her smile remained genuine. He walked over to the dock area and found Kish, Aybar, and Amanda/Yan standing over a repair table. From where he stood he could see the form of the female android lying flat on the table. Amanda was linked into the table via a mass of multi-colored wires.

"What's going on here?" Renwick asked.

"Oh, Senator," said Aybar, coming up to him and putting out a hand to slow his approach. "She didn't want you to see her until the transfer was complete."

"See her? What transfer? What are you talking about?" he said. Then Kish waved him over.

"Come look," the engineer said.

As he walked up Kish was busy watching readout monitors showing what appeared to be a massive data transfer in progress. Renwick stepped around him and looked down at the prone android body.

It looked for all the world like a sleeping Tanitha Yan.

"I don't understand," he said. "What's going on, Kish?"

"Well," said the engineer, "a couple hours after you went to, um, bed, Amanda came out and started working on some project, didn't say a word to any of us. Thorne and the female android started helping her after a bit. I got curious so I went over to her, and Amanda here ended up asking for my help. She had the female android down here on this table and was, well, converting it," he finished.

"Converting it? To what?" asked Renwick. Kish shrugged.

"To this. The face was remolded to emulate Captain Yan, they added a voice box, other modifications were made to her, um, feminine features to make them more human, and about an hour ago they started the data transfer," he said. Renwick looked from Amanda to the feminine android and back again.

"What data, Kish?" he asked.

"Captain Yan's personality, I assume," said Kish. Renwick stepped up and looked down at the android on the table, who appeared to be sleeping. He touched her hair, and her face. It did indeed appear to be Tanitha Yan, in every respect. She even had the new, distracting two-piece outfit Yan had changed into when she was still a cloned hologram.

"Did she do this herself?" wondered Renwick aloud.

"She set this process in motion," said Amanda suddenly, "when she selected her dream."

Renwick was surprised by the sound of her voice; flat and mechanical as ever.

"I see you're back with us, Amanda," he said, curious about her statement. "What do you mean by 'selected her dream'?"

"Captain Yan didn't realize that she was connected to the *Kali's* neural network through me," said Amanda. "My consciousness was voluntarily suppressed, so there was no check in place. Both the *Kali's* neural net and the androids interpreted her dream literally, as a command, and started the conversion process."

"I don't know what to say," said Renwick, looking down at the very lifelike Yan android and smiling.

"If you'll excuse me for a few more seconds, Senator, the transfer is nearly complete. I must finish," she said, then she closed her eyes and appeared to shut down. After a few seconds she opened them again, and began disconnecting the wires. Renwick looked back down to the Yan android, who began to simulate breathing. She stirred, her eyes fluttered and she opened them, focusing immediately on Renwick. She looked for all the world like a real girl.

"Wake up, Sleeping Beauty," said Renwick. He took Yan's hand and helped her to sit up. She looked at Kish, Aybar, and then Amanda before turning to Renwick.

"What's happened?" she said, then she ran her left hand down her exposed right arm, touching the skin. "Am I a digital clone again?"

Renwick shook his head. "No, you're finally a real girl, Tanitha Yan," he said. Aybar handed her a mirror, and she held it up. She touched her face with her hands.

"I don't understand," she said. "I feel so… real."

"The androids interpreted your 'dream' as a command," said Renwick. "They modified the body of the female android to make it like your dream, then Amanda downloaded your persona into the new android body, and well, here you are." He couldn't stop smiling.

Yan stepped off the pallet and onto the floor. Her first steps were halting.

"The brain-muscle connection is not as refined as in my body," said Amanda, "but that will improve with time. You have every system necessary to simulate human behavior, in every aspect."

Yan looked to Amanda. "Thank you," she said. Amanda nodded a positive response, with just a trace of a smile.

Renwick stuck out his arm.

"Would you like to take a walk around your bridge, madam?" he said. She took his arm, slowly coordinating her movements.

"I would love to," she said as they started out.

"Hmm," he said. "I think you're a bit taller than before." She leaned into him as they walked arm-in-arm, like young lovers in a park.

"I always wanted to be taller," she said as they strode off towards the bridge together.

#

The next day the morning shift was broken up by an incoming message, inbound over standard Raelen HD channels.

"It must be from Makera," said Renwick. It was.

"It's encoded," said Amanda, who, without Yan, had now returned to her standard placid android personality.

"Can you extract it?" said Yan.

"Of course," came the reply. A few seconds later Makera's face appeared on the main display, the holographic image hovering over the command console. The black-and-white image was grainy and the sound quality was poor, punctuated by loud crackles and pops. There was no mistaking the look on her face, though.

"…under attack. The Raelen Fleet has engaged the Soloth and Gataan. The colony cannot be pro…" the sound went completely at that point, replaced by raw footage, apparently from an observation probe. Yan moved closer to Renwick and then nudged him gently, whispering:

"What is it?"

"Looks like some sort of probe camera footage. Very low quality," he said. A few seconds later Aybar, Mischa, and Kish had joined them in watching the display. The sound came back in fits and starts as the screen painted a dark and grainy gray visage, apparently a replay of a distress signal from one of the colony authorities, undoubtedly blocked from leaving the system by the Soloth/Gataan but picked up by the tracking probe. The tension in the man's voice was clear - fear and desperation. Renwick concentrated on the words the man spoke, translated from Raelen to Terran Standard by the ship's com system.

"...unclear as to their intent. If you can hear us, anyone within range, we ask for assistance. I repeat, vessels of unknown origin have pierced the protective void placed around the colony. They are closing to firing range on our position. We need immediate assistance. Please reply..." the next few words were garbled by static. When the voice returned, panic was present.

"…are under attack. Can you render assist-" Then the screen cleared abruptly, the voice stopped, replaced by blackness. After a few seconds a grainy grayscale image appeared. The Vadela colony could be made out as a dark rock with tiny lights, dwellings and mining stations, scattering the uneven surface. A chronometric display flickered in the lower left corner.

"Looks like this footage is from an observation satellite at the jump point," said Kish. The image flashed bright white three times, then bombardment impacts began to mottle the surface of the moon. The Soloth fleet must have been out of range of the satellite's viewer, lobbing nuclear-thermal shells at the colony.

"Those warheads are low yield," said Yan. "Only one reason to use them in an attack like this."

"What do you mean?" asked Renwick.

"I mean they're taking their time, Renwick. They're dragging it out to maximize the terror to the population and to send us all a message."

"What message?"

"They like killing, Renwick," Yan finished, then turned her back to the screen. "They're animals."

"Turn it off," said Renwick to Amanda in a quiet but firm voice. He wanted to be sick, but fought off the sensation. The others all turned away as well as Amanda shut the display down.

"There is a follow-up message coming in. Much higher quality and on a stronger bandwidth," Amanda said. Renwick put his hands on the command console.

"Play it," he said. This time Makera's image was clear and so was the sound.

"Senator Renwick. We are in pursuit of the Soloth fleet. Nine Gataan cruisers and numerous Soloth ships destroyed. We are point-five-two solar days behind you with a fleet of twenty-nine ships. Destination of the enemy fleet is unknown. I must warn you that the Soloth fleet contains scoop ships. I repeat, the Soloth have scoop ships. That's how they broke through the Void field around Vadela. We are proceeding into the Void on your trail at best possible speed. We have alerted the Unity government of the situation. Please advise as to your intended destination. I hope to see you all soon. This is Makera, Ambassador of the Raelen Empire, out." Her image faded from the display screen.

"If the Soloth have scoop ships, that means they can attack us anywhere," said Yan. "The Void is no barrier to them."

"But scoop ships can't generate the Void, only clear it, right?" said

Renwick.

"Correct," said Yan.

"Then we still have one advantage," he said. Yan shook her head.

"This doesn't make any sense. Coming at us with this whole fleet, unless…" she drifted off, lost in thought. Then she said, "I think I know what they're doing."

"What?" asked Renwick. Yan looked pensive, then spoke.

"When I left the emitter station, well, three centuries ago anyway, there were two more ships just like the *Kali* docked there," said Yan. "But they weren't supposed to be put in operation until after I had completed my mission. That's what Zueros wants, that's what they'll go after, those other Void ships."

"Then they'll have the power to isolate any system they want, then attack it at will, using the scoop ships to cut through the Void," said Aybar.

"We're going to need help if we're going to stop this invasion," said Renwick. "Lots of it. And I think I know where to get it." Yan was disbelieving.

"The Unity?" she asked.

"They're too far away to help," Renwick said. He looked around the command console at each of them in turn, then:

"Lieutenant Cain," he said. "Change our course back to Tarchus, best possible speed," he said.

"Yes sir," she responded, then headed for her console.

"Tarchus?" said Yan. "Are you mad?" Renwick shook his head.

"I certainly hope not, captain," he said, then he broke away, following Cain to the navigation station.

#

"So what's your plan?" asked Yan of Renwick once they were set on their course to the Gataan home world again. The pair were alone at the command console again.

"Plan? Negotiate. Persuade. Bully. It's what I do best, and all that I've got," said Renwick.

"That's it? That's the plan?" she said.

"Do you have a better idea? From what I can tell the future of the whole Orion arm of the galaxy is at stake, the future of at least three civilizations. There is only one potential ally close enough to help us destroy the emitter station and those Void ships, and that's the Gataan," he said.

"Has the fact that they're currently aiding the enemy escaped you, Senator?" said Yan, loud enough that Aybar and Kish looked up from their stations. Mischa Cain, to her credit, kept her head down. Renwick glanced at the other officers and then turned back to Yan.

"Nothing has escaped me, captain," he said. "If you'll note our logs, you'll notice that the Tarchus prime as in state of deep disarray, no doubt due to three centuries of isolation. Tribal warfare is the norm. That was true on Earth many times in the past as well. But there was a modern, operating, military base on that moon. I'm making a supposition here, but I think it's a good one. If you were an outside force looking to exploit a race for its resources, and you found a planet in the midst of tribalism, what would you do?"

Yan thought for a moment, then shrugged. "I don't know, Renwick. I'm a ship captain, not a tactician." He crossed his arms, frustrated that she couldn't, or wouldn't, see his point and he had to spell it out. He opened his mouth to speak when another voice interrupted him.

"Find the strongest tribe, and give them the power to exploit the others in your favor." The voice came from behind Yan. It belonged to Captain Aybar. Renwick nodded, then motioned her over.

"Precisely," he said. "What I would have done is set up the leaders of the most powerful clan or tribe as my surrogates, give them the power, the weapons, the advanced technology."

"That would undoubtedly piss off the rest of the planet," said Yan.

"Which means they might be willing to work with us," said Aybar.

"If they have any technological base left," retorted Yan. Renwick uncrossed his arms and leaned on the console.

"It's a gamble, I admit," he said. "But we're so outnumbered. It's a chance I think we have to take." Yan looked contemplative.

"You'll have precious few hours at Tarchus. I estimate we're only six hours ahead of the Soloth at this point," she said.

"Yes, but you're forgetting something," said Renwick "Those scoop ships the Soloth had at Vadela are small, designed to open holes into a captive star system, probably with minimal capacity to cut enough normal space to bring something the size of a fleet through. So most likely they're just content to follow us. They know we'll have to go to the emitter station eventually, and when we get there they know we won't have time to do much damage. When they arrive they'll just overwhelm us with numbers."

"That's what I'd do," agreed Aybar.

"And with the Raelen fleet probably another half day or so behind them, they can get entrenched, launch the other Void ships, hell, even cut off the Raelen fleet from the station by filling in the path we cut," said Yan. Renwick nodded.

"So, thus, we need allies. If the Gataan can slow them down when they get here, it might give us enough time to find a way to dive the station and blow it, and those other ships, before they get there," he said.

"They only question, Renwick, is what will we have to give up to get the Gataan to cooperate?" said Yan.

"I wish I knew," he said. Then he walked over to the navigation station. "Time to the Gataan system, Lieutenant Cain?" he said.

"Seven hours, twenty-six minutes," she said.

"And that," he said to his companions, "is when we will know if this mission has a future or not."

15. A RETURN TO TARCHUS

"Those ships are coming at us fast," said Aybar as she monitored the weapons console.

"I still want to apply active defenses," said Yan, her demeanor had been decidedly foul since they had re-entered the Tarchus system.

"No!" insisted Renwick, shaking his head. "We have to appear friendly, or at least sympathetic with their cause. If we don't this whole thing could blow up in our faces."

They had been monitoring the incoming Gataan ships for several minutes. There were a dozen of them, obviously of an older design. The energy signatures indicated they were equipped with localized jump drives, but not full hyper-dimensional drives like modern cruisers. This was a design that indicated they were of a class of ship common three centuries earlier.

"Are those ships a threat to us?" Yan asked of Aybar.

"Our best indication is that have a design common with the light frigates of your time, captain," Aybar said.

"Can frigates hurt us?" asked Renwick. Yan shook her head.

"Not fatally," she said. "Our EM field is probably too strong. But they can make our lives miserable, like a swarm of wasps. The bigger question is whether or not they can slow down that Soloth fleet or their more advanced brothers."

"That <u>is</u> the question," said Renwick rhetorically.

"They're charging weapons," warned Aybar.

"Standard defenses, Amanda," ordered Yan.

"Belay that," cut in Renwick.

"But they're charging their weapons!" said Yan. "We have to defend ourselves!"

"If we do, then we're automatically enemies!" he insisted.

Yan came around the console and went straight at Renwick, getting right in his face. "The barbarians are at the gates, Renwick! I'll not risk my ship on this folly of yours!" she said.

Renwick looked to Amanda. "Open the landing bay doors, Amanda," he commanded.

"Are you insane?" said Yan.

"Maybe," he said. "But the way I see it we don't have a choice. Make an enemy today and we're finished."

"I cannot follow any orders except those of Captain Yan or her designee," interjected Amanda, standing down from her console. Renwick looked to Yan.

"Then you have a decision to make," he said to her. "Do you trust me or not?"

Yan clenched her fists and stomped away, then came back, pacing back and forth like a lion in a cage. Finally she came up to Renwick and stuck her finger in his face.

"When this is over, you and I are going to have to have a long talk about command structure on this ship," she said. He bowed his head slightly.

"Granted. Now, Amanda is waiting for your orders," he said. Yan turned to the android, fists clenched on her hips, her face red in frustration and anger.

"Stand down defenses," she said, "and open the landing bay doors."

"Yes Captain," said Amanda.

#

The Gataan frigate landed smoothly on the landing deck. Renwick stood with Aybar behind the environmental shield, which extended to envelop the frigate once it had settled. Yan was back on the command deck, much to her own consternation, but she had been convinced by Renwick's argument that she was the least dispensable person on board the *Kali*. He had chosen Aybar as his assistant based on her redundancy of skills with Yan and his new-found knowledge of her expertise in tactics. Renwick found it strange that they had spent more than three months together on board the *Phaeton* but had never really discussed her military background or qualifications. He made a mental note to get to know the people he traveled with better in the future.

Renwick surmised that the frigate was big enough to house a crew of about twenty. It was by far the largest ship in the bay, dwarfing the skiff, tanker-refuelers, and maintenance vessels scattered about, but the bay itself further dwarfed the frigate. Renwick speculated they could have fit half the Gataan flotilla onboard with no difficulty. The *Phaeton* itself might even had fit inside, but he couldn't be certain.

Yan had radioed down over the com that the Gataan had taken up positions surrounding the *Kali*, ready to "sting" her at a moment's notice. Renwick hoped that his next action would keep that from happening.

A hatch opened on the frigate and a step ladder deployed down to the deck. Multiple Gataan soldiers poured out of the hold and took up positions facing Renwick and Aybar. Renwick waited until they were settled and then turned and signaled to Thorne, who activated a defense shield as a barrier between the two humans and the robot. He and Aybar were officially on their own now.

"I don't suppose you speak Gataan?" he asked Aybar. She smiled.

"No, unfortunately. Not in my training," she said.

"Too bad, that," he looked around the bay for signs of any other activity, Seeing none, he started forward. "Just follow my lead, smile, and don't make any sudden movements," he said.

"Understood."

Renwick walked deliberately forward, getting to within about ten meters of the soldiers before they started acting anxious. He stopped then and raised his right hand, palm open, in a warm greeting and smiled at them.

"Hello," he said. "Welcome aboard the *Kali*."

Several of the Gataan soldiers exchanged guttural commands in their own language. It almost seemed to Renwick as though they were arguing over who would take the first shot. He hoped that wasn't the case. Just as the argument seemed to peak another soldier appeared at the hatch, his uniform much more decorated than the common soldiers. He yelled instructions at the soldiers, waving his arms in disdain at them, and then disappeared back inside the ship.

"I think we'll have to do our negotiating on board his ship," said Renwick. True to form two of the tall guards came up and took Renwick and Aybar by the arms and started pushing them towards the frigate.

"Will they take us with them, do you think?" asked Aybar.

"Unlikely," said Renwick "I'm betting that this decorated man is the ship captain, and probably authorized to negotiate with us. No reason to take us off the *Kali*."

Five minutes later they were both secured by metal chains in what looked like a makeshift supply cabinet as the frigate fired its engines to depart the *Kali*.

"Do you need assistance?" came Yan's voice over Renwick's ear com. He could practically hear the sarcasm in her voice.

"Not at the moment captain," he said. "But I'll let you know."

"Very well. Tell your captors that they're clear for takeoff," Yan said. Aybar suppressed a laugh at that.

"I'll pass it along," Renwick said. Then he looked to Aybar. "Sorry about this," he said.

"That's alright," she said. "As long as you have a plan to get us back." He looked at her, then yanked on his chains.

"Whatever plans I had just went out the window," he said.

#

By Renwick's best guess the frigate landed on Tarchus Prime about thirty minutes later. He was cognizant of the time as he knew they had precious little of it to prepare for the Soloth fleet. They were taken off the frigate at what looked to be an airbase and placed in the back of an open-air ground car. It was hard to tell whether it was day or night, as the sky seemed to glow a twilight red. The air was thick and heavy with humidity, at least to Renwick. The Gataan didn't seem to mind it much though.

Another few minutes on the ground and they were passing through a low-lying city that had once obviously been modern and efficient. They sped through rough paved streets that were punctuated by high elevated train tracks, long since abandoned. The air here had a smell to it that indicated heavy industrial use. Groves of trees that looked like palms or some other sort of tropical variety filled the spaces between broken buildings, some of which were of a clearly advanced architecture.

After a few more minutes of this Renwick noticed something else; people were lining the streets. Not all at once, and not in large numbers, but large enough. And they were yelling at them, and occasionally throwing things. At one point Renwick was sure he got spat on. Soon the captain of the frigate stood up at the front of the car and started acknowledging the cheers of the crowd as they went by. He was reveling in the attention. Clearly news of their arrival had got out through some method of modern communication.

They were whisked past the angry throngs and into a guarded building that for all the world looked like a presidential palace on some backwoods Unity world. Renwick decided then and there that that was how he had to approach their situation. They pulled up to the rear of the palace and then were hustled off the car and onto a low platform that looked like it was used for ceremonial functions. They were surrounded by guards and the frigate captain stood proudly in front of them.

"So we're his prizes?" asked Aybar.

"Judging from the situation, I'd say yes," said Renwick. The guards jostled them to discourage them from talking. "Hopefully they don't practice sentient sacrifice," he said. This earned him another jostle from the soldiers. Aybar, wisely, said nothing.

A few minutes passed and a dais was set up. Torches were lit and sitting chairs were arranged on the dais. Renwick noted that it had gotten darker. They were now clearly descending into night time.

A few minutes more and what were obviously Gataan dignitaries began to assemble on the dais. The men were almost exclusively in military regalia. Renwick saw females accompanying many of them. He had never seen Gataan females before. They were tall and thin, like the men, with dark, thick stalks of long hair like dreadlocks that flowed back over their heads. The women were fairer-skinned than the men though, and it was obvious even through their clothes that they shared the common physical traits of females of both the Human and Raelen races.

After more delay a large ornate chair was set out and an enormous Gataan male in full military regalia saddled out from inside the building and sat down in it. He was accompanied by two women, one older and more refined, and one younger. They were both beautiful, Renwick thought.

The man gestured from his chair and the frigate captain came forward, talking rapidly in a loud voice in the Gataan language. He was obviously bragging about his accomplishments to the tribal leader. Renwick wondered if he was telling the leader how they had let them land on the deck of the *Kali* unchallenged. Probably not, he decided. The leader acknowledged the captain with a wave of his hand and then gave some sort of order. Renwick and Aybar were brought forward.

They stood together, their hands still chained. The younger woman, who had been seated to one side of the leader, came forward and spoke to them, surprisingly in Unity Standard.

"You are in the presence of Clan-General Aatar, ruler of the Clans, Commander of the Armies, Supreme Leader of the Gataan," she said. "You come to our world in the dress of our many enemies. The dress of those who brought the Long Darkness. We demand you tell us why you are here." Renwick looked to Aybar and then stepped forward. Two soldiers pushed him back into his place.

"It is not necessary to come closer than is required to speak, human," said the young woman. "Keep you place until ordered to move." The words contained a threat of violence. These were clearly very angry people, and Renwick wasn't sure that he blamed them. He cleared his throat before speaking.

"I am Tam Renwick, Senator of the Terran Unity. We come here to your world as friends, not enemies," he said. "We are here to offer you aid, and ask for your favor."

"We will decide if you are friends or enemies," she said. The she turned and conveyed what he had said to the Clan-General. He grunted, then said something back to the young woman.

"Clan-General Aatar asks if you are here to aid the Hi'shoth clan, or the En'obli clan," said the translator. Renwick looked to Aybar.

"How would you know the difference?" she asked. This time the soldiers left them alone. Apparently now that conversation had begun consultation was allowed.

Renwick shook his head. "I don't know the difference, but I imagine answering correctly is pretty crucial."

"You've got to take a chance," she said. He nodded.

"Or answer a question with a question," he said. He returned his attention to the translator. "Is the Clan-General of the Hi'shoth clan, or the En'obli clan?" he asked.

"You do not know?" she said back, angry. He bowed his head.

"Forgive my ignorance. Humans have not been to your world in many years. But please tell the Clan-General, whichever clan he is the leader of, that is the clan we are here to assist," Renwick said. The translator eyed him suspiciously, then turned to Clan-General Aatar and spoke in her own language. There was a pause as everyone waited for the Clan-General to respond. Then he started laughing, a deep, guttural laugh. Whether it was humor or disdain Renwick wasn't sure. After a few moments the others all laughed along with him. Renwick and Aybar both exhaled. Then the Clan-

General uttered more words to the translator. She turned to back to Renwick, her tone measured.

"He says the he is En'obli. We are all En'obli here, and if you do not know the difference, then you are indeed a barbarian. He asks what the barbarian has to offer," she said.

Renwick considered his words carefully before speaking. "Tell the Clan-General that I offer him the chance to vanquish his enemies forever. Tell him that I offer to open the sky to the stars again, and end the Long Darkness. Tell him that I have come on a great quest, and that quest is to save the Gataani people from their many enemies, who are coming here, to this world, very soon," he said.

The translator turned once more to the Clan-General. Renwick's words clearly had an effect on him. He spoke again, this time without laughing.

"He says that others came promising to end the Long Darkness. And that they deceived us, and gave our world over to the Hi'shoth clan. We have suffered much under the Hi'shoth, human. He asks why we should trust you," she said. Renwick swallowed hard, then spread his arms as wide as they would go in the chains.

"Tell the Clan-General that these others are the same enemies we fight, the ones called Soloth and Hi'shoth. And tell him that he cannot trust humans. Tell him that it is we who caused the Long Darkness."

"Renwick!" said Aybar. The translator looked at him with disdain.

"Are you sure you want me to tell him these things, human? I would not care to see your blood spilled this night," she said. Renwick kept his gaze steady.

"It is my blood to spill. Now tell him what I have said, word for word," he said. The translator did as Renwick asked. The Clan-General sat back in his chair, his hands clenching the arms tightly. Then he exploded to his feet, charging Renwick. He towered over Renwick, yelling into his face. The translator stepped closer, but not too close.

"He demands to know the truth of what you speak. And mark my words, human," she warned, "what you say next may save your life, or end it."

Renwick looked to Aybar, then to the heavily armed soldiers around them. He decided all he had to offer was the truth. He dipped his head slightly in deference to the Clan-General, then spoke in plain words directly to him.

"The ones who did this to you, to the Gataan, they were dishonorable people, like the Hi'shoth clan. They did not have the approval of the Terran government. What they did was wrong, and I am here to right that wrong, if I can," he said. The translator spoke the words. Renwick watched as the Clan-General slowly set his anger aside, then spoke in more even tones to the translator as he backed away.

"He asks what you seek in return for these great gifts that you offer," she said. Renwick exhaled in the heavy air.

"Tell the Clan-General that we need ships. Tell him that we need him to hold off our mutual enemies long enough for us to travel to the place where the Long Darkness started, and end it, forever. Tell him we can make passageways from this world to the other Gataan worlds with our ship, and restore the greatness of the Gataan Empire," he said. She translated again. The Clan-General issued commands and then Renwick and Aybar were unchained. The courtiers on the dais all scattered as the Clan-General walked back towards the palace. Renwick looked at the translator.

"The Clan-General has ordered our ships to be readied. You may yet have an agreement, human. But first, he insists that we feast," she said.

"Feast?" said Renwick, rubbing his wrists and walking towards the palace with her and Aybar. "You must tell him, this fleet we speak of will be here within hours." She laughed.

"How little you understand, human. We are always prepared to fight. But the Clan-General will make no pact with you until he has eaten with you. It is his way," she said. "And on Tarchus, his way is the only way."

Renwick exchanged a worried look with Aybar as they both followed the translator up the stairs and into the palace of the Clan-General Aatar, Leader of the En'obli.

#

Renwick had called into Yan before they sat down to the feast. They had less than four hours to secure the help of the Gataan and get their fleet into space. In the meantime, he and Aybar were forced to eat.

The meal was served in courses and Renwick ate something of everything he was given. Some of it was questionable as to the source, but much of it was meat based and at least tasted good. The translator sat on the Clan-General's right, with his wife, as they had learned the older woman was, on his left. Renwick sat next to the translator, who's name they had learned was Reya, with Aybar next to him.

Renwick spent a good deal of time bending the ear of Reya, telling her of the issue of time, and the coming danger. The Clan-General brushed these worries off while he ate. Renwick also managed to learn that Reya had been taught Unity Standard as part of her studies on ancient cultures. It was often said in her classes that the humans were merely a myth from long ago, but she had always believed otherwise. Finally the meal was cleared away and the Clan-General returned his attention to Renwick.

"The Clan-General asks when you will begin fulfilling your promises," she said. Renwick swallowed a bite of cold meat before replying.

"We will take out the Hi'shoth base on the moon of Tarchus as soon as I return to my vessel," said Renwick. "I take it the Clan-General's enemies have all fled there?"

"Yes," said Reya. "Some months ago they abandoned Tarchus for their base colony. The superior ships they had allowed them to control our world. The Hi'shoth are not great in number, but they are very devious."

"We will ensure they do not bother you again for a very long time," promised Renwick. Reya translated and the Clan-General spoke again at length. Then Reya turned back to him.

"He says our fleet is over one-hundred ships, but they are not of the latest design nor in good repair. But he promises that we will hold off the Dark Ones if you can ensnare the Hi'shoth on their base," Reya said.

"The 'Dark Ones'?"

"That is what they are called in our language, these Soloth, as you call them, 'Dark Ones' or 'Hidden Ones'. They have been coming here for many centuries, interfering with our empire, but always they move in the shadows."

"I'm not surprised. It seems to be their way," said Renwick. At this the Clan-General clasped his hands together in a strong gesture and spoke rapidly, directly to Renwick. After a few minutes of this Reya turned back to him with the translation.

"He says that the Gataan and the humans have an agreement, but that he is an old-fashioned man, fond of traditional ways," she said.

"I'm not sure I understand," Renwick admitted, looking to Aybar for support. "What does that mean?"

"He asks if the woman is your wife," said Reya. Renwick looked again to Aybar and then back to the Clan-General.

"No. We are compatriots, not husband and wife," Renwick said, confused by the question. Reya translated and there was look of relief on the Clan-General's face, followed by more talk between he and Reya. Finally she turned back to Renwick and Aybar.

"He is pleased that you are not married. He wished to inform you that the traditions he speaks of involve you marrying his daughter, to seal the bond of peace between our peoples. He asks if you will do this for him, as a show of good faith," she said. Renwick was stunned into silence while Aybar suppressed a laugh. She leaned in and whispered to him:

"Talk about your shotgun weddings."

"This is *not* funny," he said back through tight lips. He could see the look of expectation on the Clan-General's face. This was a very delicate moment. The negotiations could be lost.

"What are you going to do?" asked Aybar. Renwick looked at her with annoyance. Finally he said:

"Tell the Clan-General I would be honored by such an arrangement, but that our time here is very short." Reya translated.

"He assures you that the ceremony will be brief, if you will accept," she said. Renwick swallowed hard, then turned to Aybar.

"Do you think I have a choice?" he said. She shook her head, holding a tight smile the whole time. Renwick turned back to the Clan-General and bowed his head. "Tell him I accept his proposal." Reya did, and the Clan-General smiled broadly, then jumped up from the table and started giving orders.

"What's he doing?" asked Renwick of Reya.

"He is calling for a priest, and making arrangements for the wedding bed," she said, then she stood up. Renwick and Aybar did the same.

"What? Wedding bed? We scarcely have time for that," Renwick said, hopeful he could turn the situation around. "Tell him I'm sure his daughter is lovely, as are all the women of the En'obli clan, but I must be on my way back to my vessel to prepare for battle."

Reya started walking away from him. "I cannot tell him that," she said.

"Why? And where are you going, Reya?" he said.

"I cannot tell him that because he does not want to hear it. And I must go to prepare myself, because, you see, I am the Clan-General's daughter, the princess, and we are to be married within the hour," she said to him, the she turned and walked briskly away from him, leaving he and Aybar practically alone. Aybar came up and patted him on the shoulder.

"Tam Renwick, intergalactic gigolo," she said. He glared at her.

"Remind me never to take you on one of my diplomatic missions again," he said.

She just laughed.

16.

Thirty minutes later Renwick found himself inside a room adorned with animal skins and hunting trophies, clearly decorated for masculine sensibilities. He had sent Aybar out to call up to the *Kali* and have Thorne send down a shuttle. He also begged her not to tell Yan anything about the 'wedding', and privately hoped the shuttle would arrive before the ceremony could begin.

Unfortunately that was not to be. After only a few minutes alone pacing back and forth in the room Renwick was ushered into a small side chamber that looked like a chapel. There was a Gataan male who he took for the priest, and after being motioned forward he dutifully took his place at the priest's side, waiting for his 'bride' to arrive.

She kept them waiting for a what seemed an eternity to Renwick. Finally Reya came in wearing a flowing gold gown and attached headdress, attended by a pair of ladies in waiting. She was young and beautiful, there was no doubt of that, but Renwick's thoughts, and his heart, lied elsewhere.

The priest went through a blessedly brief ceremony in Gataani, which Renwick understood none off, with the smiling Clan-General and his wife there as the only witnesses. After a few polite kisses to close the ceremony he and Reya, along with the maids, returned to his room and were left to presumably consummate the marriage.

"Reya," he started. She held up a hand, stopping him in mid-sentence as the maids helped her remove the headdress from her gown.

"My father is a man of tradition, Senator. But traditions change. I have no intention of letting this marriage last longer than it needs to in order to facilitate this alliance," she said. "Nonetheless, I am a woman of honor, and if you wish to have me, you may take what you want now." Then she uttered something that seemed harsh to the two maids, and they suddenly stopped attending her and stood to either side of the princess, facing him.

"If you do not find me attractive, you may have congress with either or both of my maids, but the effect of consummating the marriage will be the same," she said plainly. He was taken aback by her straightforward nature, but he still managed a smile for her.

"I think you are the most beautiful woman on this planet, Princess Reya," he said. At this she uttered more commands and the maids left swiftly without so much as glance back. When they were alone Reya put her hands to her hips, all business.

"I need to know if you are telling the truth to my father, Renwick. About your intentions. Our world has been through much pain, too much, for far too long," she said. He stiffened.

"I am telling you the truth, Reya. But before we can relieve the pain of the Gataan we must survive this invasion, together," he said. She eyed him pensively.

"Spoken like a true diplomat. I have studied your people, Renwick. Lying comes as easily to you as breathing. It is not so in our culture. But I believe you to be a man of honesty. Therefore I will fulfill my part of this arrangement," she said. "If you will fulfill yours."

Thinking she was speaking of their military alliance, he said, "That is my intent."

With that she bowed her head to him and then removed her gown in a single, quick motion and stood in front of him completely naked. She was beautiful, breathtakingly so.

"Uh," he said unsure what to say or do next. "I…" She came up to him and put her arms around his neck and then kissed him passionately on the lips.

"Touch me," she said.

"Reya…"

"Put your hands on my body, Renwick," she insisted. Haltingly he put his hands on her smooth and slender hips. She looked into his eyes with an intense glare.

"At this point in the proceedings it would be traditional for the woman to chase the man around the wedding chamber, to capture him and then to devour him," she said. "Not literally of course, but as symbol of the cycle of life being fulfilled."

"Of course," said Renwick. He swallowed hard and his breathing was getting heavier with each passing moment, and the thick air of Tarchus wasn't helping.

"But I plan on breaking many old traditions soon," she said. "One day I will be leader of the En'obli clan. Then perhaps we can meet under different circumstances. But for now, you have a brief time to have anything of me that you wish," then she kissed him again, more slowly and with less force. "What do you wish for?" she asked. His silence said all he could say. She took his hands and ran them over her body. It was a uniquely sensual experience, one that he savored, but…

"Please, Reya…" he said. She smiled, kissed him a last time, then went to a closet and put on a one-piece lounging suit, zipped it up and flopped down on a sofa.

"I see even an En'obli woman is not enough to tempt you. She must be extraordinary, this woman who owns your heart, whoever she is," Reya said.

"She is," said Renwick, smiling as he thought of Yan, "in every way."

"Good. Then she will understand."

"Um, understand what?" he asked tentatively.

"That you must take your wife with you into battle," Reya said. "It is our way."

"Battle? I can't Reya. It's much too dangerous for you." *And for me*, he thought.

"You cannot deny the daughter of the Clan-General the right to fight next to her husband. It is the En'obli way," she said.

"Reya…" she waved off his protests.

"Do you think you married some school girl, Renwick?" she said. "You married the daughter of an En'obli warrior. To not take me with you would be an insult to the Clan-General and the En'obli clan. Do you wish to risk that, with this alliance so recently made between us?"

"No," he admitted. She jumped up from the sofa then and unzipped and removed her clothes again. She certainly wasn't shy about being naked in front of her new husband.

"Don't worry," said Reya as she started to pull on a military uniform. "Our marriage is not official anyway. That priest was just my father's military advisor."

"What?" Renwick said, incredulous at this turn of events.

"Go," she said, waving him off. "Go and prepare your ship. I will pack my belongings and join you at the airfield. And do not even think of leaving without me. As far as my father is concerned, we are husband and wife, and I am your battle lieutenant, and I represent the interest of the Gataan in this struggle. You cannot deny me."

"I wouldn't dream of it," he said, then he stepped out of the room and shut the door behind him, heading to the airfield as quickly as he could.

#

Thirty minutes later Renwick, Aybar, and Reya were on approach to the landing bay of the *Kali* again, safely ensconced in one of the Void ship's utility shuttles. Renwick was dug deep into his safety couch, sulking next to Aybar, while the automaton Thorne piloted the shuttle. Reya sat up front, strapped in next to the robot, fascinated by her first foray into space.

Aybar leaned in and very quietly said to Renwick: "Do you have anything you want me to say on your behalf after we land?"

"No," he said just as quietly, shaking his head, "this was simply a diplomatic necessity. Nothing more."

"Do you think Yan will buy that?"

Renwick eyed her, annoyed. "She's a woman, of course she won't buy it. But I had no choice," he said.

"Now that's a truth I can get behind," said Aybar. Then she laughed quietly so that only Renwick could hear her.

"Remind me never to take you on a diplomatic mission again. You're disloyal," he said.

"Yes," she replied.

Five minutes later and they were taxiing on the deck. Renwick unbuckled his safety couch and hurried out of the shuttle hatch once they were stationary. At the bottom of the ladder he extended a hand to his new wife, helping her down and on to the deck of the Kali for the first time.

"I did not think such a ship was possible," Reya said, awed by the size of the landing deck. "How is it that you need the help of the Gataan to fight your enemies?"

"The *Kali* was not designed to fight battles, but to spread the Void. Her technology is used as a weapon of defense, not to attack," Renwick said.

"Still, she is a marvel," said Reya.

Aybar joined them on the deck and then Thorne followed, carrying all of Reya's substantial luggage. Renwick pointed the way to the main lifter.

"I'd love to give you the tour," he said. "But the captain and I have work to do."

They took the lifter up to the command deck. Yan greeted them as soon as the doors opened.

"The Gataan fleet is assembling," Yan said, then looked at Reya. "Who the hell are you?"

Reya moved close to Renwick, wrapping her hands around his arm in a show of possession. "This must be the woman we spoke of," she said.

"Yes," said Renwick, turning red with embarrassment, "she is."

"'Woman you spoke of'?" said Yan, narrowing her gaze on Reya and then swiftly turning her growing wrath back on Renwick. "You're bringing native girls on my ship when we're on the verge of battle? What the hell is *wrong* with you, Renwick?"

"I had no choice, she's-"

"I am his wife," cut in Reya, stepping forward as if to challenge Yan.

"*Wife*?" Yan thundered. "Oh my god! Thorne, get her off my bridge," she ordered the automaton.

"Wait," said Renwick. "I can explain-"

"Later," said Yan, holding up her hand to him as she started to move away. "Right now, we have a battle to fight."

"Just a moment!" demanded Reya, stepping forward again. Yan turned back to her, fuming, but said nothing. "I am Reya D'omirasu, daughter of Aatar D'omirasu, Leader of the En'obli clan and Clan-General of all the Gataan. I stay and fight this battle with you, or the Gataan do not fight at all."

Yan gave Renwick a withering glare, then said: "Very well, Reya D'omirasu of the En'obli clan, wife of Senator Tam Renwick of the Terran Unity. You may stay on my bridge, but you'll stay out of the way, or I'll put you off my bridge myself." Then she stalked off.

Aybar tried to look as if she hadn't seen the whole thing. Thorne started taking Reya's bags towards the crew area. Renwick turned to Reya.

"It would really be best if you went to the crew area," Reya started to protest but he stopped her with a gentle hand to her hip. "Just for now. It's much more protected than the rest of the ship, and there's really nothing for you to do at this point," he said. Reya looked put out but resigned.

"Will this please you, my husband?" she said.

"It will."

"Very well," she agreed, her eyes smoldering. She was clearly unafraid of competition with Yan. "But I will take my place in this battle soon enough." Renwick bowed his head to her.

"Thank you, my wife," he said. She smiled quickly, then left with Thorne. Renwick and Aybar started for their bridge stations.

"Best of luck with that, Senator," Aybar said with a giggle. He sighed.

"You're growing most tiresome, Captain Aybar," he said. Her only response was to laugh out loud.

#

Two minutes later he had taken up his station at the command console without another word to Yan. After checking his displays, he spoke out.

"What's our tactical situation?" he asked, all business.

"We have eighty-seven Gataan ships by my count," replied Yan without looking up. "Not enough to stop the Soloth fleet, but enough to slow them down. Ambassador Makera was kind enough to send us their fleet strength, though."

"How bad?" Renwick asked as Aybar entered the bridge area and took up her weapons station.

"Four-hundred thirty ships, not counting the eleven remaining Gataan cruisers. Mostly frigate sized or smaller. It seems the attack fleet is designed for speed, not power," Yan said.

Renwick nodded. "Makes sense. Strike swiftly, disable your opponent, then come in with the big guns to finish them off."

"That's what worries me," said Yan. "Where are the capital ships?"

"Probably hanging back. I'm sure we'll find out soon enough," he said, trying not to react too negatively to the news and pretending to concentrate on his console systems. After a few moments of silence Yan cut to the issue at hand.

"So it seems your diplomatic mission to Tarchus was a great success. You left a bachelor and came back a husband. Maybe someday we'll get time to chat about that, but right now I have a battle to coordinate," she said, then headed off to talk to Mischa Cain at navigation.

"Thank God for that," said Renwick under his breath. He looked to Aybar, but she was focused, or pretending to focus, on her weapons systems.

Within a few minutes they had coordinated with the Gataani fleet, assigning them the task of slowing the Soloth fleet through a series of mobile mine waves, delaying maneuvers, and targeted attacks. Makera's fleet analysis allowed them to pick out which ships would likely be the most valuable targets, tankers, support ships, and the scoopers were identified and passed along to the Gataan generals. After a few minutes their new allies returned the communiqué with an acknowledgement. Renwick watched on the monitors as they soon began the task of arranging their fleet according to the likely disbursement of enemy forces. The frigates assigned to the mobile mine waves set up first. They would have to make their runs at an acute angle to the incoming fleet, leaving the mines in their wake as the Soloth tried to decelerate. The second wave would take out as many of the scoop ships as possible, while the third, and smallest, wave would target the support ships; tankers, repair auxiliaries and communications. There were thirty ships in the mine wave, forty-seven in the scoop flotilla, and just ten to take on the support ships. Renwick nodded as he saw their final formation. The Gataan did nothing halfway, especially when it came to battle.

"Now it's our turn," he said to Yan, who had returned from Navigation. "You're the military commander, but I suggest we try and plug the hole into this system. Even if it's only a few thousand kilometers deep they'll still have to use the scoop ships to break through." Yan came up and looked at the command board, then checked the tactical monitor.

"I hate to admit this, but you're probably right," she said. "According to Makera they have about forty of the scoop ships. If they're forced to use the majority of them to cut a hole through the Void, then they'll be the first ones through."

"And vulnerable," he said. She nodded, then called Aybar over and explained their plan. The former captain of the *Phaeton* had her own thoughts. She pointed to the tactical monitor.

"If we moved the scoop flotilla up and sent them in first, they could make their run while the mine wave held back. That way we'd catch the majority of their cruisers with the mines. Then once the rest of the enemy fleet came through we could unleash the last wave at their auxiliaries," Aybar said. Yan nodded.

"I agree," she said.

"And then the main fleet would be in a position to come about and defend Tarchus prime," Aybar added.

"They will have completed their job at that point, bought us time," said Renwick.

"And where will the *Kali* be in all of this?" Yan asked.

"Doing our job," said Renwick. "Wrapping that Hi'shoth military base in Void energy. That should draw the rebel Gataan cruisers. With their base shut off to them and no ability to refuel or resupply they won't last long against the En'obli ships."

"You've obviously learned a lot about the internal politics of the Gataan," said Yan, keeping her eyes locked firmly on her board.

"If you only knew," cracked Aybar. Renwick gave her a withering stare and she shut up.

"We learned enough," he admitted.

"After the Kali's task is done, then what do we do?" Yan asked, changing the subject again. Renwick tapped through a series of displays and brought up the one showing the emitter station.

"Then we make our run, and pray we can destroy the station and those other Void Ships before the Soloth get them," said Renwick. "Our only advantage is the speed of the *Kali* inside the Void. But the Soloth can counter that by trailing us through normal space in our wake, or using their scoop ships to cut a path of their own. But I'm betting they can't catch us."

"It's my ship you're betting with, Senator," said Yan, finally looking up at him. "How much of an advantage do you think we will gain by cutting through the Void?"

"About six light hours," said Renwick. Yan put her hands to her hips.

"That's about the same advantage we had coming out of Vadela," she said.

"I know, but in the mean time we will have gained the allegiance of the En'obli clan of Gataan, destroyed or disabled part of an invading fleet, and managed to get fair warning to our governments. That's a fair trade, I'd say."

"You're risking my ship, Renwick," said Yan. He locked eyes with her.

"I'm risking much more than that," he said. Then he called out orders to Cain, Aybar, and Kish.

"Action stations," he said. "Let's go plug that hole."

#

The *Kali* was positioned approximately point-zero-zero-zero-five AU from the Void event horizon. The section of normal space that they had cleared on their return from Vadela lay open like a gaping wound in the resilient black skin of the Void. Renwick watched on his infrared scan monitor as it pulsated with the solar wind generated by Tarchus' weak red dwarf star. It looked very much alive. He wanted to kill it.

"How long will it take to close the hole at this distance?" he asked Yan.

"Forty-six minutes," she replied, all business. The situation they were in had no doubt strained their personal relationship, circumstances being what they were. Renwick understood that. But part of his ego was still bruised by her formality and personal distance with him. He wanted a chance to explain the circumstances. He glanced over at Aybar, wondering if she had shared any details of his 'wedding' on Tarchus with Yan, but decided that wasn't likely, they'd all been far too busy at their stations.

"Stand by to activate the emitters," said Yan to Kish.

"Ready when you are captain," said Kish. Renwick noted how all the survivors of the *Phaeton* had slipped comfortably under Yan's command, even Aybar after an initial adjustment period. They all had their roles now, and that was good as far as he was concerned.

"Fire away on my mark, Captain Aybar," said Yan. "Three… two… one… mark!" she called.

"Emitters active," said Aybar. Renwick watched on the main display as dark energy, pulsating with cracks of deep purple lightning burst forth from the *Kali's* belly, crossing the vast distances in seconds, beginning the process of mending the vast hole in space her passing had created. Yan came and stood next to him, watching the monitor as normal space diminished by the second on the display.

"'And now I am become Death, the destroyer of worlds'," said Renwick quietly.

"Is that a quote?" asked Yan. He nodded.

"From an ancient Hindu text, from Earth," he said. She sighed quietly next to him. It was a very human thing to do for an android.

"This is what we've been drawn into, Renwick. By chance, by happenstance, by fate," she said. "None of us chose this."

"Perhaps," he said, watching as normal space was slowly, inevitably, devoured by the dark energy emanating from the *Kali's* emitters. He turned to Yan with a question. "Did you pick the name of this vessel?" he asked.

"The *Kali*? No. She was already named when I took command," she

said.

"Did you know its meaning? The name, I mean."

"No," Yan said, shaking her head, also in a very human way. Renwick crossed his arms.

"Well whoever did knew his scriptures. *Kali* is literally the 'Dark Goddess', the bringer of death, the one who ends time in the Hindu pantheon," he said. Yan shuddered next to him.

"Then they picked the right name," she said, and walked away.

#

They locked down the Hi'shoth base on the moon of Tarchus an hour later, and now they stood on the bridge again at their stations, waiting for the Soloth fleet to come. Yan had positioned the *Kali* at the rear of the Gataan formation, with the flotilla of ships that would make the final run at the Soloth auxiliaries. She had her primary coil cannon batteries charged and ready. It wasn't the kind of heavy weapon that could stop a capital ship or even a fleet of cruisers, but anything smaller than that wouldn't want to be on the receiving end of one of her blasts. Yan intended to stay and support the En'obli Gataan fleet as long as she could before bugging out.

"Picking up something on infrared," called Aybar from the weapons console. "Multiple contacts, cutting through the Void at point zero-seven-five AU distant. Looks like they're using the scoop ships."

"Confirmed," said Mischa Cain from navigation.

"Finally," said Yan, hovering over her console. Amanda stood impassive as usual to one side, while Renwick took up his station on the opposite side of the large table.

"Keep my engines warm, Mr. Kish," said Yan. "I want to get out of here lickety-split when the time comes."

"Aye sir," said Kish.

"And keep our nose facing the center of their formation at all times, Lieutenant Cain," said Yan.

"Aye sir," Mischa responded. Renwick wondered what counted as the *Kali's* nose, given her ugly swan design.

"The Gataan fleet have been notified and they're ready to go on our order," reported Renwick as the confirmations came through. They all watched the main display as light beams began to emerge from holes in the Void, near their original event horizon. Seconds later Soloth ships came pouring through.

"Identify weapons officer! Class and configuration!" called Yan.

"By design; frigates, destroyers, and hunter-killers. Nothing of cruiser size or configuration. Yet," said Aybar. Renwick watched as the scoop ships, really Void cutters, sought to merge the holes that they had cut in the black blanket of Tarchus space, obviously to enable ships of larger displacement access to the system.

"I think we should launch now," he said to Yan. She held up one hand.

"Not yet."

Amanda watched everything with her placid detachment. "Gataan fleet is calling in, asking for instructions," she said to Yan.

"Tell them to hold," said Yan. Renwick watched her as she observed the activity of the Soloth, trying to determine their tactics, waiting for some trigger before diving into action.

"Now!" she said. "Release the fleet, Renwick. Captain Aybar, target enemy ships with the coil cannon at will."

"Aye captain," said Aybar. Renwick noted it was the first time he had heard her use Yan's title.

"The first wave of En'obli Gataan frigates is attacking," reported Renwick. "Multiple hits on enemy vessels."

They watched in silence then as the two fleets, one small and getting larger by the second, and the other smaller in size but more mobile, mashed together like warring wasps. It was chaos and carnage.

"Seven En'obli Gataan frigates destroyed," said Amanda after only two minutes of action. She was staring off into space, receiving all the battle data in a steady stream of updates from the ship itself. "Hi'shoth Gataan cruisers now emerging from the Void," she said. Renwick watched as one of the Hi'shoth cruisers exploded almost immediately upon entering its home space again. "That was a Hi'shoth cruiser. It destroyed two other enemy ships when it exploded, including one scoop ship."

"Enemy casualties?" asked Yan. Amanda seemed to be doing the calculating in her head, without blinking. Her head bobbed just slightly from side to side as she reported.

"Seven enemy destroyers, thirteen frigates and twenty-nine hunter-killers destroyed or disabled," she said.

"That's not enough," said Yan.

"Time to bring in the mines," said Renwick.

"Do it," she said. Renwick sent out the command to the thirty En'obli frigates carrying the mobile mines to start their run. He watched as the mine waves were released into the fray. They came pouring in from their positions at an insane point zero-two light speed, dragging waves of mines attached by magnetic fields behind them. One errant shot would send them up in a fireball, but a hit by one of those mines would shatter any ship up to cruiser displacement.

The En'obli frigates fired coil cannon bursts as they passed through the inclining edge of the Soloth fleet and released their mines. The mines all ignited their short range engines, hence the term 'mobile mines', picked out a target, and accelerated towards the enemy. With thirty ships carrying nine mines per wave, it was an impressive display of pyrotechnics.

"They seem to be targeting the Hi'shoth cruisers in inordinate numbers," observed Amanda.

"Can't say I blame them," said Yan.

"The En'obli Gataan have now lost twenty-one frigates. The third wave is now joining the attack," continued Amanda. Renwick watched as the tiny flotilla of ten ships sped up on their attack run into the fray. It was still a mass of fire and destruction, and it was unclear who had the upper hand, but the reality was that the Soloth ships kept coming through the openings the scoop ships had cut in the Void wall. But this last group wasn't deterred in any way. Renwick could see they were in the most perilous position, coming straight at the forward edge of the Soloth fleet, picking out weaker auxiliary ships with their forward coil cannons and torpedoes. It was a thankless job, but one that had to be done.

Renwick watched in horror as one of the frigates exhausted its torpedo allotment but kept charging forward, eventually ramming itself into a fleet communications ship. Both vessels exploded in a sea of flames. He looked away.

"Main En'obli frigate formation has completed its second run," said Amanda. "Mobile mines have been exhausted."

Renwick watched as the third En'obli formation all but disappeared into the center of the Soloth formation.

"Report, Captain Aybar," demanded Yan.

"Three Soloth ships, hunter-killers, have broken through the main Gataan lines and are on an intercept course with the Kali," she said. "I'm holding them off with the coil cannon, but they have advanced shields and screens."

"Time to intercept?" said Yan.

"Twenty-one minutes," said Aybar.

"Keep me advised."

"I've done an analysis of those HuK's," said Renwick from his station. "We can gain some ground on them in normal space, but once we enter the Void and have to start scooping, they will eventually catch us, before we reach the emitter station."

Yan looked troubled at this news. "What can we do?" she said.

"I suggest we bring three of the Gataan frigates aboard and stow them on the landing deck. Keep them there until we have to stand and fight," said Renwick.

"Will your wife help us?" Yan asked. Renwick tried to shake off the mention of Reya.

"I'll go and ask her," Renwick left his station and went to the back to get Reya.

Yan turned to Amanda. "Full report," she said.

"Two hundred sixty-four Soloth ships have come through the Void so far. Fifty-six have been destroyed or functionally disabled," said Amanda. Yan started to pace.

"Give me a breakdown of the fifty-six," Yan said.

"Twelve scoop ships destroyed or disabled. sixteen auxiliary ships destroyed. Nine Soloth cruisers destroyed or disabled. Thirteen hunter-killers and six destroyers destroyed or disabled. Forty-three Soloth ships are operable but are tactically useless without repairs," said Amanda.

"Which will be hard to do with their auxiliaries burning," noted Renwick as he returned with Reya.

Amanda continued her report, speaking over Renwick while Yan ignored Reya's presence. "All but two of the Hi'shoth Gataan cruisers have been destroyed. The remaining cruisers have sustained sixty-three and forty-six percent damage respectively and are making for their base on the Tarchus moon."

"Which they will find encased in Void matter," said Renwick again.

"Fleet communications indicate that Hi'shoth requests for assistance have been ignored by the Soloth," said Amanda.

Renwick grunted. "Our friend Zueros must be in charge," he said. Amanda looked at him, then returned to her report.

"Soloth ships continue to enter the system through the scoop openings," she said. "Current count of operational Soloth vessels is two-hundred eighty-six."

"What about our allies?" asked Yan.

"En'obli Gataan ships are breaking formation and heading to their home world in a defensive formation," said Amanda.

"I didn't order that," said Yan.

"I did," said Renwick. "They've done all that we could ask of them." He walked up to Yan. "It's time for us to go."

She looked at him, then up to the master display, then to Reya, acknowledging her presence for the first time. "We'll need three of your ships to take with us, to defend against three Soloth HuK's pursuing us. Will you contact your fleet and ask for volunteers?" she said. Reya looked to Renwick.

"Is this what my husband requests?" she said.

"It is," he responded.

Reya stepped up to the command console and Yan handed her a com earpiece. She spoke her strange language into it for a few seconds, then they all watched as a trio of Gataan frigates broke off form the main defense fleet and made for the *Kali*. A few minutes later and they were safely docked on the landing bay.

"As you requested, my husband," said Reya.

"You can go now," said Yan, in tone devoid of respect. Reya looked to Renwick again.

"Is this also what you wish?" she asked. Renwick nodded.

"It would still be safer in the back," he said.

"As you wish," she said. She eyed Yan, who was ignoring her, once more, and then quietly withdrew from the bridge area.

On the main view display the Soloth fleet was reforming into a multi-tiered delta-vee formation. The *Kali* rocked with the report of the forward coil cannon batteries.

"That's a pursuit formation," said Renwick.

"I am trained in military tactics, Senator," Yan snapped back at him. She turned to Aybar. "What's the status of those three HuK's?" she said.

"Still coming," said Aybar. Yan nodded, then walked around the command console one full set of stations.

"Are the Soloth pursuing the Gataan fleet?" she asked Amanda.

"Negative," said Amanda.

"They won't," said Renwick. "They'll leave the Gataan and Tarchus alone. They want the *Kali*. Zueros wants the *Kali*." Yan took one last look at the master display.

"Lieutenant Cain," she said. "Take us out of here. Galactic coordinates one-eleven, mark fourteen is our destination. Best possible speed."

"Aye sir."

Yan looked at Renwick. "I hope those six hours we just bought ourselves with Gataan blood is enough," she said.

"It will have to be," he replied, hanging his head, aching at the loss of life.

Then the *Kali* pivoted in space, cutting a dark swath out of the Tarchus system, towards the emitter station, and the unknown.

17. TO THE UNKNOWN

Renwick was sleeping alone in one of the rest cabins several hours later when he got a knock at his door. He hoped it wasn't his 'wife' again. He had already turned her advances down once and convinced her that sex on board the *Kali* was a bad idea. She knew where his heart lay, and she understood, or so he hoped.

"Come in," he said, sitting up on his elbows. To his surprise it was Yan who came through the door.

They had hardly spoken since the battle, and the tension between them was strong. But he didn't blame her, and he hoped she didn't blame him. Her arrival in his cabin was the first sign that this was so. She sat down on the opposite bunk from him. He watched her in silence while she gathered her thoughts.

"I'm hurt," she said simply, after a moment.

"I know," he replied.

"Explain it to me," she said. He sighed and lay back down, staring at the ceiling.

"It's a tribal custom, left over from some more traditional time. Probably reintroduced during the regression," he said. "I was too far into the negotiations and too focused on getting help from the En'obli fleet. I missed the signals. I'm trained for this, I should have seen it coming, but I didn't. It's completely my fault"

"Yes," Yan said. Then she went silent again for a moment, thinking. "Have you slept with her?"

"No."

"That's good," she said. Then she looked down at him. "Will you?" He turned to her and shook his head negative.

"No."

She stood to go. "I think I understand more now," she said.

"Yan," he said to her as she reached for the door.

"Yes?"

"I wish you would stay," he said. She turned halfway back towards him.

"I want to," she said. He slid the blanket off of his body and slid over in the small bunk, his back against the cold wall. She came and laid next to him. He put his arms around her, over her shoulders, embracing and protecting her.

"It's hard for me," she said, speaking softly. "It was always hard. But now I find myself on a mission I never bargained for, in a mechanical body I never wanted, and yet the feelings I have are just as strong as if I were real."

"You are real, Yan," he said. She shook her head.

"No, I'm not. That girl across the hall, she's real. Makera is real. I'm a fake, a composite of digital files and mechanical constructs, made to look, act, and feel like a real woman. But I'm not real, Renwick. I'm not," she said. He held her even more tightly.

"You're very real to me," he said reassuringly.

"Real enough for you to marry?" she asked. He sat up on one elbow and rolled her over on her back so he could look into her face.

"I've had dozens of women on just as many worlds, Captain Yan. Out of all of them you're the most real woman I've ever met. You're warm, you're brilliant, you are intriguing in every possible way. And I wouldn't hesitate to marry you, given half the chance," he said. She smiled slightly.

"But you're already married," she pointed out.

"Well, we'll just have to go to Deseret or one of the other polygamous colonies where it's legal then," he said.

"Either I'm the one, or I'm not, Senator."

"You are the one, madam," he said. Then he kissed her. They lingered at each other for a moment, then she pulled back.

"Seriously, what are you going to do?" she asked. He sighed.

"Well, assuming we make it to the emitter station, find a way to shut it off or destroy it, and disable the other Void ships, stop the Soloth fleet, deter an invasion-"

"All right, there's a lot to accomplish before we run off to live in the country and have children, I'll give you that. But really-"

"The marriage is not official, she already told me that," he said. Now Yan sat up.

"What? Really?" he nodded.

"Yes, really. They didn't have time to find a priest so a military advisor to her father masqueraded as one. But we're keeping that on the down-low, so as not to endanger the alliance," he said. She laughed out loud.

"You are a terrible man, Senator Renwick," she said.

"You're the one who wants to marry me," he retorted. They kissed again for several moments, then she rolled onto her side again, her back to him.

"I'm worried Renwick," she said. "About the station." He pulled her close.

"What about?" She stayed silent for a moment, then,

"There are things I remember about being there, at the station, but there are other things that I don't. Tactical things. Layout, defenses, vulnerabilities. Based on the time I spent there, almost three years, I should know those things. And with digital files I should be able to recall everything. But I don't. It's like my memory has been blacked out in certain places and then patched back together."

He thought about her words for a moment. "Do you think your memories have been tampered with?" he said.

"I don't know. But it's a concern," she admitted.

"Who would have the power to do that?" he asked.

"Only two people that I can think of," she replied. "My corporeal self, three centuries ago, or..." she trailed off.

"Or who?"

"Amanda," she said.

"The androids?" he said, surprised. "But they've been helping us all along. Why would they do something like that?"

"I don't know," she admitted. "But it worries me."

"It should," he said. "If they aren't trustworthy, then this whole mission could be a flight to disaster. But honestly, I can't understand what their motivation could be."

"Their androids, Renwick, built by an alien civilization. We can't possibly know what their motivations are and it would be a mistake to think we can understand them just because they were designed to look like us," she said.

"Point taken."

Yan was quiet again for a minute, thinking.

"We have to get to the station, Renwick. I have to find… myself. Find out why she would hold back information from me, the current me, and find out what happened three centuries ago," she said.

He had no response for her as he contemplated what she had said. After a few moments he pulled her close once again, and closed his eyes to sleep.

#

Yan of course didn't need to sleep, but she did shut down her cognizant functions to simulate sleep. They both woke hours later and she joined him in the shower, purely for the pleasure of it. Afterwards, they met up with Aybar and Reya in the common galley area for breakfast. Kish and Mischa were on station.

Reya insisted on sitting next to her 'husband', and Yan insisted on sitting on his other side. So they sat like that, Renwick sandwiched between the two women while they glared at each other, Reya and Renwick eating their meals while Yan simply held her ground.

"Don't you eat?" said Reya while munching on a piece of fruit.

"I don't have to," said Yan.

"Why?" Yan picked up a thick metal plate and effortlessly bent it into a small ball.

"That's why," said Yan, rolling the ball at Reya. Aybar cleared her throat, obviously feeling the tension in the room.

"I think I'll go relieve Lieutenant Cain at navigation," she said, abandoning her morning coffee in a rush to leave the galley.

"I should probably go as well and check in with Amanda," said Yan, finally conceding and standing to leave.

"I thought you were linked to her through the *Kali's* main computer?" said Renwick. Yan stopped and gave him and annoyed look.

"I am. And she keeps me updated on our status constantly. But it's always good to have a face-to-face, don't you think?" she said with exaggerated pleasantness, smiling a fake smile. Renwick, clueing in that she wanted to leave, nodded.

"Of course, Captain." He stood like a gentleman should and she departed. A few moments later Mischa Cain came into the galley.

"What's our status, navigator?" said Renwick as she poured herself a cup of coffee.

"Yan didn't tell you?" she said as she sat down opposite the newlywed couple.

"Um, no," Renwick said. Mischa sighed.

"Let's see. We're four-point five light-hours ahead of the main Soloth fleet and our lead is growing," said Mischa. "But those HuK's are closing again, back to twenty-one light minutes out. And we're still a solid eighteen hours from the location of the emitter station."

"We're not going to make it before the HuK's catch us, are we?" said Renwick. Mischa shook her head.

"I think we're going have to fight them here, in the Void," she said.

"That's not good," said Renwick, concerned.

"Why don't we stand and fight?" asked Reya. "We have three Gataan ships full of En'obli warriors down in your hold just waiting for the chance." Renwick put down his coffee.

"Believe it or not, fighting isn't always the best tactic. We have other goals in mind," he said to his wife.

"Such as?"

"Such as destroying the station that caused the Void in the first place," he replied, "and disabling the *Kali's* sister ships before Zueros can get to them."

"So you will destroy the only resources that can end the Void and restore our worlds to keep them from falling into the hands of your enemies?" she asked.

He nodded. "If we have to, yes." Reya contemplated this a moment.

"You humans use strange tactics," she said. He nodded as he finished his coffee.

"We do indeed," he said.

#

An hour later and Renwick was off on a side console, deep into analysis of the DNA test that Amanda had run on Zueros, looking for markers that might indicate the test was tampered with, but he had found none. He failed to notice at first when the android came up next to him.

"I see you are reviewing the DNA test findings from the Skondar station," Amanda said. He looked up swiftly, startled. "Is there anything I can help you find?"

"Not just at the moment, thank you Amanda," he said, turning and blocking her view of his display to keep her from seeing what he was reviewing. She could probably monitor his actions without having to see the display, he reasoned, but why give her any advantage he didn't have to?

"Perhaps if I knew what it was you were looking for, I could assist you?" she asked. He looked at her but said nothing for a moment, then said:

"Markers indicating tampering."

"You'll find none," she said.

"That's what I've noticed so far," he said, then turned back to his screen, uncomfortable with her watching him.

"The analysis was very thorough. His DNA was complementary to the other samples provided," Amanda said.

"I'm aware of that."

"So what concerns you?" she persisted. He swiveled back towards her.

"I'd rather not say," he finally said, seeking to end the conversation.

"You'd rather not say to an android, you mean," she replied. He looked at her again, contemplating her anew. What she had just said was a challenge, and that was something new and heretofore unseen in her personality.

"I'd rather not say," he repeated, "and I'd like to just leave it at that."

"Very well," she said, then turned and departed without another word.

Renwick summoned Yan on his com. She came up a few minutes later.

"What do you need?" she asked.

"I just had a very strange conversation with our primary android," he said.

"Amanda? What about?"

"About my reviewing of the DNA test files," he said. Yan crossed her arms.

"What about it? Did she complain?"

"No, but I got the distinct feeling she doesn't think I trust her completely," Renwick said.

"Well do you?" replied Yan. Renwick shook his head.

"No, but that's not the point," he said.

"Then what is the point?" Renwick rolled his seat towards Yan and pulled in close to her.

"She challenged me. Challenged my decision not to disclose my thoughts to her. I got the feeling that perhaps she sees me as a potential threat," he said.

"Threat to what?" said Yan. Renwick shrugged.

"I don't know. *Her* mission?" he said.

"She's an android, a servant, how could this supposed mission of hers could be different from our mission?" Renwick thought about that for a second.

"I don't know," he admitted. Yan pushed her hair back from her face in frustration at the conversation.

"Well you're full of straight answers today," she said. He turned back to the display.

"There is something here, Yan. In the DNA, I mean, I just haven't found it yet," he said.

"Well let me know when you do," she replied. "And for now, I'd appreciate it if you kept your paranoid android suspicions to yourself." She was about to end the conversation and walk away when an alert claxon sounded.

"This is Yan," she said over her com.

Kish answered. "We've got a malfunction in the scoops, sir," he said. "And we're slowing." Then Aybar cut in.

"Weapons console indicating those HuK's are accelerating," she said. "Looks like they detected our decreased scoop rate and jumped on the attack." Renwick ripped out his earpiece com and whispered to Yan.

"I find the timing of this very suspicious," he said. "Just after Amanda gets upset at my prying."

"Noted," she whispered back, then she went back on the com.

"Shut down the scoops, and prep those Gataan frigates. Looks like we have ourselves a fight whether we want one or not," she said, then she turned and made for the bridge.

"Are you coming, Senator?" she called over her shoulder. Renwick was already out of his seat.

"Right behind you," he said.

#

Yan watched the main tactical display as the Soloth HuK's closed to within firing range. Renwick stood at his station to her right, and Reya was next to him.

"Are our Gataan ships deployed?" Reya asked of Aybar.

"Deployed and reporting ready," Aybar said to her. Reya nodded.

"Good," said Yan. "Time and distance to the enemy, captain?"

"Two minutes to firing range, sixty-four thousand kilometers distance," replied Aybar.

"One of the HuK's is slowing, falling behind the others," said Renwick. "And I'm betting I know who's on board."

"Zueros?" said Yan. Renwick nodded.

"If I'm right, yes. I think he's much more than just an agent for the Soloth. I think he's behind everything regarding this invasion," he said. "And I don't think he'll get close enough for us to take a shot at him. He wants us to reach the station ahead of the fleet. He has some other agenda."

"Which is?" asked Yan. Renwick looked up at her.

"If I knew that, Captain, I'd tell you," he said.

"That's what I was afraid you'd say."

At this Amanda came up and took her customary position next to Yan.

"Report, Amanda," said Yan.

"The scoops have fallen to forty-one percent efficiency. Indications are that the main diffuser modules have suffered a complete system breakdown. The units will have to be replaced manually via an EVA by one of the crew," she said.

"You mean crawl up on the scoop and replace one of the main pieces of equipment that makes this ship what it is, by hand?" said Renwick, incredulous. "How long will the repair take?"

"Ninety minutes, estimated, if one of the androids does the EVA," she replied.

"We don't have ninety minutes to sit here and make that kind of repair. Plus you may have noticed we do have an impending space battle on our hands," he said.

"The repair can be done in transit," said Amanda in her flat android tone.

"You mean, while we're clearing Void space?" asked Yan.

"Yes," Amanda acknowledged.

"Thirty seconds to engagement range," called Aybar from Weapons.

"We'll talk about this later," said Yan. "Right now I have a battle to win. Mr. Kish, bring the scoops to zero. Lieutenant Cain, turn the *Kali* and engage our defensive systems," she ordered.

They counted down the seconds, watching the tactical display as the two forward Soloth HuK's closed to firing distance. The third hung back, just out of the *Kali's* weapons range.

"Do our frigates stand a chance against those HuK's?" Yan asked Renwick.

"Possibly. If we can provide them enough cover," he said. "HuK's are designed as high-risk attack ships with exceptional speed and minimal defense. They are designed to run down and destroy an enemy target, but they don't last long in prolonged battles."

Yan's eyes ran over her board swiftly, making her final pre-battle assessments.

"Suppressing fire with the coil cannon on those HuK's, Captain Aybar. On my mark," she ordered. "Three… two… one… mark!" The *Kali* shook with the report of the coil cannon firing.

"No hits," reported Aybar. "HuK's closing to attack range."

On the display, Renwick watched as the Gataan frigates arranged themselves in a defensive triangle, one to port of the *Kali*, one to starboard, and the third protecting her crown.

The twin profiles of the HuK's darted swiftly around the main display, then made their run straight at the *Kali*, breaking away at the last second and firing at the port frigate, which managed only a single cannon shot in its own defense. The frigate absorbed two huge hits, its shields overloading and collapsing, orange fire erupting on its hull. The other two frigates pivoted and fired, but were far too late, the HuK's were gone and already making a turn to start their next run.

"Gataan frigate has sustained eighty-one percent damage," reported Amanda. "EV systems have collapsed. Main hull has been breached and she is venting environment to space. Her command bridge is still sealed and she has one working torpedo launcher. Her impellers are gone and she is drifting."

"Bastards!" said Reya, slamming her fist on the console. Renwick and Yan both turned to her, surprised by her use of a very human curse, but she was oblivious.

"Order them to withdraw," said Yan to Amanda. Amanda nodded, conveying the message.

"They are refusing to withdraw. They insist they are still battleworthy," said Amanda.

"Are you sure that torpedo launcher is still operable?" asked Yan.

"Ninety-four percent operational," confirmed Amanda.

"Advise them they stay in at their own discretion," said Yan.

"Aye captain," said Amanda. Yan turned back to the tactical screen.

"They're going to cut those frigates to pieces, one by one," warned Renwick.

"I know, but what can we do?" said Yan. She turned to the android again. "Can we use the emitter and create a mini-Void to act as a shield?" asked Yan.

"Not likely to be effective at this range," said Amanda. "And the Void material would take too long to form."

"So we're on our own," said Renwick. They watched as the two Soloth HuK's reformed with the third.

"Getting their attacking orders," said Yan. "Aybar, this time I want you to hold your suppressing fire. Try and project their attack path and lay your fire across it."

"Aye sir," said Aybar, "But I'll warn you now, they're coming in at point-zero four light, and at that speed luck is about all we have."

"Understood," said Yan.

The HuK's started their second attack run. The Gataan frigate positioned at the *Kali's* crown moved to protect her damaged sister on the port side, anticipating a kill move and laying down orange coil cannon fire and a swarm of torpedoes. Aybar fired her coil cannon at the incoming bogies but missed clean.

This time the HuK's broke even later, slicing off at the last possible second and attacking the starboard frigate with a hail of cannon fire. This frigate was better prepared, and moving, firing a hail of coil cannon shot and a brace of torpedoes that missed completely. The HuK's came in a lead-and-follow formation, the second scoring a direct hit on the frigate. Orange fire erupted on her hull, the sickly green of her defensive shields sparking and fluctuating in and out of phase.

Suddenly a fireball of blue and orange filled their screen. It wasn't the starboard frigate, it was the port ship, the one attacked in the first run.

"The port frigate has been destroyed," reported Amanda, her voice completely devoid of emotion. "They attempted to fire a torpedo. It caught in the launcher and detonated."

Renwick looked up at her sharply. "I thought you said her launcher was good?" he challenged. "Were you in error?"

"No. There was a six percent deficiency-"

"Thirty of my people are dead!" yelled Reya. Renwick held out a hand to calm her.

"You're telling me that a six percent chance killed that ship? I find it hard to believe you were off by that much Amanda," said Renwick calmly. Amanda stayed silent.

"Not now, Renwick," said Yan, attempting to return his attention to the battle. "What about the second frigate, Amanda?"

"Sixty-three percent efficiency in all systems still available," said Amanda.

"Unless a torpedo gets stuck in her launcher," snapped Renwick. This time Yan said nothing. Reya, for her part, seethed in silence at the android, her anger fueled by her husband's suspicions.

The Soloth HuK's reformed for a third run.

"This time they'll come at us," said Renwick.

"What makes you think so?" said Yan.

"Just a hunch, captain. I suggest we hold our fire until they make their break, and then…" he trailed off.

"Then what?" said Yan. Amanda looked at Renwick with renewed interest.

"Can you transfer system controls to my console?" he asked Yan.

"Yes, which system?" she said.

"All of them," he said to Yan, then looked to Amanda. Her face was a complete mask.

"I don't understand-" started Yan.

"Just trust me," he said to her. Yan flashed her hands over her board.

"Done," she said.

The HuK's came in again. The frigate at the crown of the *Kali* had moved to defend the bigger ship's port flank. The damaged frigate held her spot on starboard.

The HuK's speed was too much for normal weapons, Renwick was sure of that. His hand poised over the controls. This time they came straight in at the *Kali*, splitting to port and starboard moments before they passed. In a flash of movement the damaged starboard Gataan frigate fired her impellers and leapt into the path of the closest oncoming HuK.

The explosion blinded all the *Kali's* systems and rocked the Void ship to her core. When the system-level whiteout cleared and the crew had regained their stations, Yan looked over to Renwick.

His finger still touched the systems integration pad.

"Look!" said Reya. On the main display screen the final Gataan frigate was closing on a smoldering HuK, disabled, helpless, and drifting. The frigate closed to firing range and launched a single torpedo. The HuK exploded in a satisfying fireball.

"What did you do?" Yan said to Renwick. He nodded to Amanda.

"Ask her," he said. Yan looked to Amanda.

"Report," Yan said. Amanda complied.

"Both Soloth HuK's have been destroyed," said Amanda.

"I saw the first one go up, but what happened to the second?" Yan asked. Renwick crossed his arms.

"Go ahead, tell her," he said to Amanda.

"My analysis is not complete. You'll have to ask the Senator-"

"Oh for god's sake! Just tell me what you did, Renwick!" Yan demanded. Renwick uncrossed his arms, still displeased with Amanda. He leaned on the command console then and started to explain.

"I anticipated that on the third run they would try and hit the *Kali*, to disable us. I also knew that conventional weapons like the coil cannon were likely useless. When I asked for control of all the ship's systems I needed to be sure that I could do what I intended without any potential interference," he said.

"From Amanda?" asked Yan.

"I would not have interfered, Senator," said Amanda in her defense.

"So you say," said Renwick. "At any rate, I needed to be completely free to act. Again, since I knew they would want to take the *Kali* intact, for whatever reasons Zueros might have, I knew they wouldn't hit her main systems; the scoop, the emitter, impellers and the like. That meant they would have to take certain paths over the ship to hit our non-essential systems, like environmental control, but still do enough damage to force us to surrender. That narrowed the path even further."

Yan was growing impatient. "So what did you *do*?" she demanded.

"I had access to all the *Kali's* systems. As they made their run, which looked like what I thought they'd do, I used the maintenance system to vent the scoop plasma still in the holding cells, but not yet processed into the diffusers," Renwick said.

"Essentially, you projected a curtain of dark energy directly into the path of the attacking HuK," said Amanda. Renwick nodded.

"And they flew right through, which disabled every system they had, and gave our Gataan friends some semblance of revenge," he said.

"A brilliant tactical maneuver," said Amanda.

"Thank you," said Renwick, unimpressed by her compliments.

"No," said Yan, "it's for me to thank you, Renwick, for saving the Kali."

He looked to his captain. "You're welcome," he said.

"With your permission, captain," said Amanda, turning to face Yan, "I'll begin the planning for the EVA to make the repair to the scoop diffuser modules." Yan nodded acknowledgement and Amanda departed.

Reya came to Renwick and put her arms around his shoulders, kissing him on the cheek. "You are a hero," she said. He pulled her arms off of him.

"Reya…" he said, with just a touch of exasperation.

"Mr. Kish," yelled Yan over the top of the fawning princess. "Get our impellers started and fire up the scoops again. Forty-one percent efficiency or not, I want us out of here ahead of that fleet. And get that frigate stowed on the landing deck."

"Yes sir," said Kish.

"And before I become ill," she finished, just loud enough for Renwick and Reya to hear.

18.

"So what the hell was all that about?" asked Yan. The battle had been over for barely fifteen minutes, the *Kali* now underway again to the coordinates of the emitter station. Renwick had left for the galley after the battle and Yan had followed him once she had secured the bridge to demand an explanation. He sat on one of the benches contemplating a full cup of coffee on the table in front of him. He didn't really react when she questioned him, so Yan opened her mouth to inquire again.

"Simply put, I don't trust the androids, and I especially don't trust Amanda," Renwick said before she could speak, then took a drink of the coffee and put it back down again. "During that whole battle she could have easily been conveying information to the HuK's, or giving the Gataan bad information." He looked up at the *Kali's* captain. "Do you really think she made a six percent mistake? Is she even capable of that narrow an error?"

"I don't know," said Yan. "But I can read the same systems she can."

"But you're assuming Amanda is showing you accurate information. You said yourself you had gray areas, gaps in your information, or your memories. Who is most likely to have put those gaps there?" he said.

Yan looked at him for a few moments, but didn't answer. Then she walked over to the galley's display console, standing next to it but not really doing anything.

"There are days I hate being a robot," she said.

"I sympathize," Renwick replied, then joined her at the console, putting his hands on her shoulders from behind. "Look, I think we have enough of a discrepancy here to justify caution in our dealings with Amanda."

"I don't disagree," Yan said, focusing on the display readouts. "I'm just looking for a way we can operate this ship without her and the other androids, and I'm not finding any good possibilities."

Renwick dropped his hands to his sides. "You worked with her for three years before, before the Void accident. Did you ever notice any erroneous behavior? Did you ever get any indication that she had some agenda other than your mission?" he asked. Yan shook her head.

"None. She did everything I ever asked, without complaint or question. *And* she waited three hundred years for me to come back and get her," she said.

"So you're saying you trust her?" he asked. She hesitated a moment before answering.

"No, I'm saying she's never been anything but loyal to me, to the mission, and I have a hard time questioning her now." Renwick walked a few steps away from her and ran his hand through his hair in frustration.

"Then I will continue to defer to you on your judgment of her in battle situations. But I reserve the right to change my position for the sake of the mission, and I think we should both keep an eye on her behavior," he said.

"Noted."

Their conversation ended there with Amanda's arrival in the galley.

"I have completed the proof of concept for the repair mission," she said. "Thorne can complete the task in eighty-seven minutes."

"Even while were transiting Void Space?" asked Renwick. Amanda nodded.

"Buffeting from the Void displacement of the scoops will be difficult, but not impossible for him to handle. The climb up the scoop neck will be the most difficult part of the activity," she stated. Renwick looked at her, then over to Yan.

"And what if a human did it?" he asked. Yan turned quickly from the monitor.

"Don't be ridiculous!" she said. "The androids are far better equipped to-"

"But Senator Renwick does not trust us, he has made that much clear," said Amanda, cutting in, with an almost human tone of annoyance in her voice. "I would have to recalculate the mission for human parameters. I assume you would be doing the EVA Senator?"

"You can model it for me, yes," said Renwick. Yan shook her head.

"This is insane. The androids can do it-"

"Perhaps they are Captain, but I am in command of this mission, remember?" Renwick said, cutting her off a second time. He looked to Amanda. "Re-run the mission parameters. We'll meet back here in thirty minutes to review them, the whole crew," he finished.

Amanda looked to Yan.

"Do as he says," said Yan. Amanda nodded quickly and departed the galley.

"I hope you know what you're doing, Renwick," Yan said once the android was gone.

"So do I," he replied.

#

Thirty minutes later they had all gathered in the galley, which had become their impromptu gathering room for these type of conferences, to review the spacewalk requirements. The full command crew sat around the room at the eating tables, facing Yan at the display console. The Gataan sailors had made it clear they preferred to stay aboard their own ship and would answer only to Reya's commands.

Amanda stood her post next to the captain of the *Kali* as Yan called the roll for reports from each station.

"There's no question we need to do the repair," said Kish. "The scoops are down to thirty-seven percent efficiency. Between that and the battle our lead over the Soloth fleet has shrunk to three-point eight hours."

"What's the status of the trailing HuK?" asked Yan.

"It's fallen back to twenty-six light-minutes distance," reported Aybar. "It doesn't seem to want to tangle with us."

"For now," observed Renwick.

"Mischa?" said Yan, ignoring Renwick for the moment.

"We're still on course for the programmed coordinates," said Lieutenant Cain, "but the loss of scoop performance is starting to affect the helm."

"How?" asked Yan. Mischa crossed her arms.

"Well, the best way I can describe it is 'interstellar drag'. When the scoops aren't clearing Void space for normal space as efficiently as usual, I have to make periodic course adjustments to keep us on target," she said.

"How often?" asked Yan.

"About every thirty minutes, right now. But it's happening more frequently, and it will only get worse," Mischa said.

"Unless we fix the diffuser modules," said Renwick.

"That is why I called this meeting, Senator," said Yan. Then she turned to Aybar. "What's the effect on weapons systems, captain?" she asked.

"Minimal, at this time," said Aybar. "But that doesn't mean they won't be effected in some way we can't predict in the near future."

"Thank you, Captain Aybar," said Yan. She passed over Reya, who had no real position aboard the *Kali* except as Renwick's wife, and then turned to Amanda. "Please run down the mission parameters for us now, Amanda," she said.

Amanda stepped up to the console and lit up a floating 3D display large enough for all of them to see. It showed animation of Thorne performing the EVA.

"As you know, the EVA to repair the scoop diffuser modules could be completed by Thorne with minimal disruption of other crew duties and ship performance in about ninety minutes," she started. "But Captain Yan has asked me to work up a model of what the EVA repair would take if the human crew were to perform it."

"One of us? Why?" asked Kish.

"Hold your questions, Mr. Kish," said Yan in her best command voice.

Amanda continued by overlaying two human models over the Thorne animation so that they could be seen simultaneously. "As you can see it would take two members of the human crew to perform the task, primarily because of the mass of the diffuser modules." The animation showed two human figures in complete EVA gear hauling the diffuser modules up the neck of the scoop, holding it between them. The Thorne figure, without an EVA suit, pulled ahead almost instantly and climbed far faster than the two humans. He began the repair and swapping out of the large modules. The human figures were still climbing the neck when Thorne started down.

"As I said, Thorne can complete the repair in about ninety minutes. At that time the *Kali* will return to maximum efficiency and we will arrive at the emitter station ahead of the Soloth fleet with approximately a four-point-two hour cushion," said Amanda. The display showed the animated Thorne figure heading back inside while the two humans were still engaged in the swapping-out process. "The two humans would complete the repair in about one-hundred forty-four minutes. The resulting loss of time, plus the reduced time for the *Kali* to traverse the Void at maximum cruising efficiency, would result in a cushion of merely two-point four hours," she concluded.

"Questions?" said Yan.

"I have one," said Renwick. "For Amanda. Why did the diffusers malfunction now? I mean, at this critical point in the mission?" The android showed no change in her expression as she replied to him.

"The diffusers are one of the more delicate systems on the *Kali*. I can only assume that three hundred years in stasis resulted in system degradation and eventual failure," she said. Renwick eyed her, not satisfied, but kept his mouth shut for the moment.

"Anyone else?" said Yan.

"Captain, why are we even considering using a human crew when the android could clearly do the job better and faster?" asked Kish. Yan looked to Renwick.

"Senator?" she said, deferring to him for the answer. Renwick stood now and addressed the room.

"Because, quite simply, Mr. Kish, I don't trust the androids," he said. Kish looked confused.

"You mean you don't trust them to do the job?" Kish said. Renwick shook his head.

"No. I mean I don't trust them at all," he replied. "Consider the last battle. Amanda here cleared one of the Gataan frigates to continue fighting even though they were heavily damaged in the HuK attack. In fact she assured us that the torpedo launch tube was ninety-four percent effective. The torpedo they fired on the next pass of the HuK's stuck in the launch tube and detonated, destroying the frigate and its crew. I submit to you that androids don't make mistakes like that, not when there's only a six percent chance of them being wrong."

"Is that it?" asked Kish.

"I'd like to hear more as well," said Aybar. "Because I assume you're going to be one of the people going on this repair mission, and you'll have to convince someone else to go with you."

"Good enough," said Renwick. He moved to the front of the galley. "I have done an analysis of the DNA test done on our old friend Mr. Zueros back at Skondar. The test results were perfect, a perfect complementary fit between his Soloth DNA, ours, the Raelen, and the Gataan."

"And this match is a problem?" said Aybar. Renwick nodded.

"Without the original sample, I can't confirm it, but in looking at the test data, I'm almost certain that a large portion of it was deleted," she said.

"How?" asked Aybar.

"When I looked at the files, I saw traces of inconsistencies, like the files had been cut, then spliced back together. It was almost seamless, but there were tiny data fragments out of place. Enough for me to determine the size of the original sample that had been tampered with," he looked to Amanda but she didn't react. Renwick continued.

"As you probably learned in grade school science, there are twenty-three pairs of chromosomes in human DNA. Also twenty-three in Raelen DNA, twenty-three in Gataan DNA, and twenty-three in the Soloth sample that Amanda processed. Now that would seem to fit with our theory of the Preserver culture, that they divided their DNA characteristics to make four similar, yet different 'child' races as a means of preserving their legacy, and it should have made for a total of ninety-two base pairs," he said.

Aybar shook her head. "I'm still not hearing anything conclusive," she said.

"I'm not sure I have anything conclusive," Renwick said. "But consider this, when I assigned data-size attributes to the fragments, in other words, I gave each one a value equal to a measure of reported data in the report, guess what the result was?"

"I'm sure I have no idea," said Aybar.

"Sixty-nine fragmented data points. In other words, the original sample from Zueros had ninety-two base pairs, the twenty-three Soloth chromosome pairs reported in Amanda's analysis minus sixty-nine additional fragments. The data had been tampered with," said Renwick.

"Curious," agreed Aybar, "If not altogether convincing."

"That's what your analysis revealed?" said Yan. "Sixty-nine fragments of data that you equivocate to DNA chromosome pairs?" She seemed angry at him.

"That and the error that destroyed the Gataan frigate," he said.

"And what about those data fragments, Amanda?" said Aybar. Amanda shrugged, in what had to be a very calculated human gesture.

"It could be anything from dust in the digital core to wearing of the equipment on your skiff boat. I was limited to what I had on hand," she said, then resumed her stoic poise.

"I'm not putting this up to a vote," said Yan. "But I want your opinion on this. Everything we do from here on in could have life or death consequences for each of us. Senator Renwick is commander of this mission, but I am captain of this ship. I say what will be done to it and when. The repair has to be made. I assume that Mr. Renwick would be one volunteer, but I'd need another to allow him to take on this insane mission. Do I have another volunteer?"

Kish and Mischa stayed silent. Reya eyed her husband silently from across the room, but made no commitment. Only Aybar stood and met Renwick eye to eye.

"I see one fatal flaw in your plan, Senator. It would take too long compared to letting the android do it. We can't waste that time," she said, then crossed her arms.

"I agree," said Renwick.

"So I have a proposal for you. One person to make the swap and repair, and one to fly the skiff," she said.

"And you're volunteering?" asked Yan, incredulous.

"I am," she said. Yan threw up her hands in frustration.

"You're both insane," she said.

"Perhaps so, captain," said Aybar, looking to Renwick. "But I can't think of anybody I'd rather be in the asylum with right now."

With that, Yan shut down her console and stormed from the galley.

#

Renwick and Aybar were halfway through the skiff pre-flight checklist when Yan called down to him from the bridge.

"There's no way I can discourage you from this, is there?" she said over Renwick's personal com line. He turned away from his flight checks to get a bit of privacy from Aybar. It was clear that the two women, both commanders, tolerated each other, but didn't really get along. He didn't want to do anything to exacerbate that situation.

"I'm afraid not," he said quietly into the com.

"What if I threatened to cut you off from sex?" she said. He smirked, appreciating her attempt at humor in a tense situation. She was quite a woman, even if she was three hundred years old and stuck in an android body.

"That would hurt you more than me and you know it," he responded. This time she laughed a bit on the other end of the line. Then things turned serious.

"I'm worried, Renwick. This is a very dangerous mission," she said in a much more sober tone.

"I know," he said, " but it has to be this way. We can't risk a complete system failure of the scoops. The *Kali* would be a sitting duck for that HuK, not to mention the rest of the Soloth fleet."

"You really don't trust Amanda, do you?" she said. He sighed.

"It's not whether I trust her or not. It's whether I *believe* she's trustworthy. At this point, it's simply that we can't take the risk," he said. Yan remained silent. She seemed resigned to the situation at hand.

"Good luck on your mission, then, Senator. Don't get yourself killed," she said.

"I won't. Promise," he said, then signed off.

He and Aybar completed the flight checks. Renwick went to the airlock and checked the diffuser modules that Thorne had loaded onto the skiff one more time to make sure they were secure near the cargo hatch. After he was satisfied he returned to the cockpit, sealed the passenger cabin behind them, and put on his EVA helmet. He gave a quick thumbs up and Aybar fired the skiff engines.

"Com check," said Aybar.

"Check," replied Renwick. "We're good to go."

"I hope so," said Aybar. He watched as she lifted the skiff off the deck with skilled precision. Renwick looked down onto the brightly lit landing deck and saw Thorne standing in position, unmoving. Privately he hoped he was wrong about the androids, because if Thorne had tampered with the new diffusers in anyway, they were both flying to their doom.

Aybar guided the skiff through the environmental field, out of the landing deck, and into open space. They were protected from the interspatial buffeting of the wake as long as they stayed within the bounds of the stern. Beyond that they would be subject to the whims of the *Kali* and her strange mechanisms.

Aybar had chosen to fly the skiff rather than one of the *Kali's* own shuttles because she was intimately familiar with the controls and how the small boat handled. Renwick got a taste of her experience when they were only a few hundred meters out as she deftly rotated the skiff on a fixed plane, parallel with the landing deck. Then she ignited the chemical impellers, and the skiff started rising vertically, the stern construct passing below them as they ascended. Renwick took the time to observe how big the Kali really was, and how complex she was constructed. More than ever he was convinced she had not been made by humans, no matter how advanced they were three centuries past, in Yan's time.

"Hold on now. We're about to experience some buffeting from the wake as we clear the stern," said Aybar into his ear. With that she suddenly increased the skiff's speed and started angling her ascent, preparing to meet the interspatial distortions head on.

The skiff cleared the stern and flew straight into the *Kali's* wake.

The vibrations were strong enough that Renwick felt his teeth clattering together inside his helmet. Though he was securely strapped in to his couch seat and held in by a suspensor field, he was still taking a pounding, as was the tiny boat.

"Hold on," said Aybar over the com, her voice loud and high-pitched. "The inertial dampers should compensate in another second-" at that the intense vibrations stopped- "or two," she finished. The dampers could take out most of the structural vibration in any space-borne craft, providing for a much smoother ride, but they couldn't stop severe pockets of turbulence, especially of the kind generated by the scoop diffusers. A second later and they got their first taste of the turbulence.

The ship rocked from side to side, the safety couch and suspensor absorbing most of the impact.

"Will she be able to take much of this?" asked Renwick. Aybar shook her head inside her EVA suit.

"She won't have to," she said. "Once we're in the shadow of the scoop tower the buffeting should decrease enough for us to execute the mission. I ran the specs myself half an hour ago. This is the rough part." Another impact shook the skiff as Aybar accelerated slowly towards the looming scoop tower. Renwick felt his stomach lurch.

"Dampers aren't much help against tides like this," said Aybar, looking over at him as she held the skiff flight controls in an iron grip. "Don't worry, you'll get your sea legs soon enough." Renwick's stomach churned again. He hoped she was right.

"Status," came Yan's voice over his com, a welcome distraction. Renwick looked down at his co-pilot's instruments.

"We've cleared the stern and are in open space. Traverse to the scoop tower should be complete in…" he signaled to Aybar.

"Seven," she said.

"Seven minutes estimated. Interspatial wake turbulence is

manageable, for now," he added.

"Affirmative. That matches our tracking here. Keep your head down. Yan out," she said.

"Heads," said Aybar over the com. "Keep *our* heads down." Renwick smiled.

"Slip of the tongue," he said.

"I bet. Incoming wave!" Aybar said. The skiff rocked with another displacement wave. They recovered again as Renwick watched the scoop tower grow ever larger in the front windows. The rear of the scoop looked like a giant swan's neck with a low, flat head on top. The diffuser grills were spewing out dark energy that had been collected and then processed back into normal matter. It came out as uneven puffs of gray smoke, then quickly diffused and dissipated as it passed over them. All too frequently though a wave would divert from its smooth path and rock the skiff, sending them rolling. It seemed like an eternity as they climbed the swan neck, angling up to the 'head' of the *Kali's* scoop array. The displacement waves became less frequent as they climbed, gaining more and more ground into the shadow of the scoop.

"I think we're through the worst of it," Aybar finally said. Renwick let go of his death grip on the control panel and leaned back as they ascended the neck, floating just a few meters from the metal surface.

"I'll go get the modules ready," he said, gladly un-strapping himself from the safety couch and heading to the door to the passenger cabin.

"Be careful," said Aybar. "We're still subject to the odd wave as we rise, and once I position us outside the access hatch I'll have to hold us in place manually. It's likely to get rough up there again."

"Understood," said Renwick, exposing the cockpit to the passenger cabin again with the flick of a switch and making his way back to the cargo hold.

Each of the diffuser modules were as big as a man an twice as deep. Luckily they were designed to be replaced if necessary, and Yan had told them the access hatch would accommodate their size. The modules themselves were a matched pair, fused together for transport by a nano-seal. Renwick would take them both across as one, then break the seal once he was inside the diffuser array and install each of them, one on each side of the neck. He waited pensively while Aybar positioned the skiff, looking out until he could see the familiar shape of the *Kali's* access hatch.

Aybar sealed the cargo airlock from the inside while Renwick strapped the enormous payload onto his back, four times his size. He felt her disconnect the artificial gravity in the airlock to make the pack weightless. He lifted the pack on his back, then checked the cone jets on his suit that he would have to use for deceleration. The diffusers had a lot of mass, and if he didn't handle his 'landing' on the other side things could get very messy in a hurry.

"Ready to vent environment," said Renwick to Aybar, hefting the modules.

"Venting," came the reply. Two small ports opened in the airlock's outer hatch as the atmosphere vented, then stabilized, and the outer door opened. Renwick looked out on the expanse of space separating him from the access hatch of the *Kali's* diffuser array.

"Access hatch opening," came Yan's voice in his com. He watched from across empty space as the hatch opened to reveal a dark room, lit only by a few tiny monitor lights. It looked like miles across from where he stood.

"What's our distance?" he asked Aybar.

"One hundred-fifty meters," she said. "Just enough for you to jet out, decelerate and get in."

"We hope," he said. He lugged the module assembly on his back once more and positioned himself in the airlock hatch.

"Better get moving," said Aybar. "Not sure how long I can hold this position. There are rogue waves getting pretty close."

"Affirmative," said Renwick. He positioned the cone jets at his waist for the proper angle, then released his safety line and fired a short burst. It calmed him a bit to finally get out in space. He moved out of the airlock slowly, almost drifting towards the neck of the scoop and the access hatch.

"Your bio levels are elevated," said Aybar in his ear.

"Wouldn't yours be?" he snapped back, then continued on his course. Inside his helmet all he could hear was the sound of his own hard breathing. He remembered his EVA training from military school, mandatory in any military academy, and he trusted his skills, but the reality of making the crossing was still a major stressor. He decided to talk to let his emotions out.

"How far am I clear?" he asked Aybar.

"Twenty meters. Give it another ten before you fire the jets," she replied.

"Got it. What's your status?"

"Rogue waves are getting closer. I think the diffusers are degrading more rapidly," she said. "I may have to move and come back to get you."

"Understood," he said. He checked his distance monitor. Twenty-six meters out. "I'm starting to drift," he said, his voice sounding stressed even in his own ears. "I'm going to fire the crossing burst now before I get too far off course." There was a long silence before Aybar signaled an affirmative response. Renwick fired a short burst from the right cone to raise his angle, then locked in on the hatch and fired both jets. He accelerated rapidly towards the *Kali*. "Forty meters," he said, "fifty… counting down now. Ninety meters to the hatch."

Then all hell broke loose.

Suddenly he was off course, the neck of the Kali spinning in front of him, followed by open space, followed by a glimpse of the skiff, then the pattern repeated.

"What the hell?" he yelled.

"Rogue wave!" called Aybar in his ear. "I'm out of control!" Renwick realized he was too. The spinning was disorienting him rapidly. He remembered his training; if you're in an uncontrolled spin you always fire a single jet, the one on the side you think you are spinning towards. If you start spinning faster, fire the other one. He reached down in desperation, first gripping the right cone control, then the left. The neck of the *Kali* was getting closer. He knew he had only a few seconds to stabilize his spin or he and the modules would end up mashed against the skin of the Void ship. He closed his eyes. pressed his thumb down and prayed it was the right control.

A second later he opened his eyes. The scoop neck was once again in front of him and he was spinning, but much slower. He fired again and got his direction back. He was going to land on the underside of the scoop neck, but he was going to make it. Probably. He reached out as the neck loomed over him, then hit it hard and started dragging across the smooth metal, falling out towards the scoop and away from the access hatch. His was going too fast to grip anything with his magnetic gloves. He had no choice. He'd have to activate his magnetic boots and hope his relative velocity didn't rip his legs off.

He reached for the control, put his finger over it, then squeezed his eyes shut again and pressed. He felt his feet slam into the metal as his mass-heavy payload pulled him up and bent him backwards, stretching his body with its momentum. Just when he thought the pull would rip his suit right off of his body the momentum whiplashed and he came back towards the metal skin. He deactivated his finger grips and pushed off with his hands, then steadied himself. He was attached by his gravity boots and in one piece.

"I'm here!" he said into his com. "I'm okay!" The response was silence. He started to move, cautiously. Releasing the pressure on his boot grip so he could walk almost normally, the large pack on his back. He moved as quick as he could out of the darkness of the front of the scoop neck and back into the rear field. He looked up. A hundred meters above him was the access hatch, and it was closed. He looked out to where the skiff should be. It wasn't there. He scanned the area, looking desperately for the small ship. He finally found it, spinning in space, accelerating away from him at a few meters per second.

Heading right into the path of the displacement waves.

19.

"Aybar! Can you hear me?" he called into the com but got no response. He switched channels.

"Yan, come in!" he shouted.

"Yan here. My God, are you all right?" she said.

"Affirmative," he said, "but the skiff isn't. Can you get a shuttle out here?"

"Negative," came her reply, scratching over the com line. "The displacement waves are coming in at unpredictable intervals, and they're getting stronger. They're too powerful for the shuttles. I may have to shut down the scoops entirely."

"Yan, if Aybar can't get the skiff under control, she'll drift right into the path of the next wave," Renwick said.

"Understood. But I can't do anything about that right now. Wait… hold on…" she trailed off, the line cracking with static. Interminable seconds passed before she came back on the line. "It's your wife, Renwick. The Gataan frigate crew is going to mount a rescue of you and the skiff."

"No," he said flatly.

"Renwick, you know you can't stop them. They're Gataan."

"Yan, it's far too dangerous. Those frigates aren't strong enough and you know it. It's suicide!" he said. The line stayed quiet a few seconds more.

"They're coming out. There's nothing I can do to stop them. You know your wife better than I do, she can be very insistent, and she insists on rescuing you," came back Yan.

"Just keep her off that frigate," he said pointedly.

"That I can do," replied Yan.

"Understood," he said back, then looked up to the skiff, still spinning away from him in its slow death spiral. Then something else caught his eye, also moving away from the ship. "Yan, van you get a visual display on me?"

"Yes, why?"

"Just do it!" There was another moment's silence.

"Oh shit," she said. "One of the modules has detached from your pack."

"I can see it from here. Probably twenty meters from me and moving away. Must have come off during my hard landing," he said. "Can we get the ship running with only one diffuser?"

"We'll lose critical time," she said.

"Keep tracking it. And get that access hatch back open. I'm heading up there now." Then he cut the channel to Yan and opened the channel back to the skiff. It was still silent and Aybar didn't respond to any of his hails. He had no choice. He started his long and lonely climb.

#

When he got to the access hatch it was open again. He struggled inside, his strength nearing its endurance limits. He detached the module from his back pack and looked back out the hatch opening. The second module was spinning slowly, still within a tempting few meters of the *Kali* but an almost unreachable gulf from him.

"Are you aboard, Renwick?" called Yan.

"Affirmative."

"Then get that module installed." Renwick looked around the maintenance deck of the scoop tower. It was large, dimly lit, and split into two identical sections.

"Which side first?" he asked.

"The port diffuser is in worse shape," said Yan. Renwick looked to his left, hefted the module again, and started down a wide hall. When he entered the module control room overhead lights lit up. There were monitors showing data in a language he couldn't read coupled with running lights glowing in different colors. He had no way of knowing what colors meant what in relation to what systems. He located the diffuser module, packed into a large console system that extended through the floor.

"I've located the module," he said into his com. "How do I remove it?"

"Do you see a panel on the wall to your left?" it was Amanda's voice. It made sense. She would know the systems better than anyone else, even Yan.

"I see it," he acknowledged. The panel was full of control icons of different colors with the strange data characters on them. The thought that the android was sending him to his doom with each instruction crossed his mind.

"Press the buttons in the following order: amber, green, blue, amber, red, orange," she said. He did. The entire pane turned amber.

"If the panel is all amber, disengage the control field brackets," Amanda said. Renwick looked down. The module was secured by a pair of brackets and a working suspensor field. He pulled the brackets back and snapped them open. They slid back mechanically and the suspensor field disengaged.

"Okay," he said.

"You can remove the old module now," Amanda said. He set down the new module and then reached down and pulled the old module from its pocket. It came out effortlessly. He set it aside next to the new module.

"Got it," he said.

"Place the new module in the pocket and engage the control field. It should be immediately operational," said Amanda. Renwick did as instructed. The new module slid in and the panel turned from amber to a light blue.

"Got a blue light here," he said.

"Confirmed, it's operational," came Yan's voice. Renwick went back to the access hatch and looked out. What he saw terrified him. The skiff was still spinning, but now the Gataan frigate had arrived and was attempting to contact it with a suspensor field. The frigate was far too high above the skiff, and far too close to the path of the waves.

"Renwick, this is Yan," her voice came over a private channel, not the open com. "We have a problem."

"Another one?"

"This is serious. The new diffuser is running perfectly. Unfortunately that's increasing the imbalance in the damaged one. It could fail altogether," she said.

"And if that happens?" he asked. Before she could reply the ship lurched and a massive plume of dark matter spewed out of the starboard diffuser, roiling like an uncoiled snake.

Right at the frigate.

"Yan, you've got to get that frigate-" he never finished his sentence.

He was cut off by an explosion of light and turbulence, thrusting him back against the diffuser deck wall. He struggled to his feet seconds later, trying to regain his senses. He staggered to the open hatch and looked out.

The frigate was in multiple pieces, burning and drifting swiftly away from the Kali. The skiff was completely gone. In its place a few bits of gleaming metal and hyper-heated oxygen molecules burned their brief lives away. There was no sign of Aybar.

He looked frantically around, trying to locate the second diffuser module. He found it, spinning rapidly way from the ship and down towards the engine intakes. He tried the com, but it was fried, overloaded by the explosion.

He looked down at the module, moving further and further away with every second, and did the only thing he thought he could do to save the mission; he pushed off from the hatch and fired his directional cone jets, screaming off into open space towards the module as fast as he could go.

#

Renwick reached out his hands as he accelerated towards the module. He was closing at a crazy speed, acting out of fear and desperation. He adjusted his directional jets and fired again, correcting his course as he focused on the module. At the last possible second he cut the jets, inverted them, and fired again to slow his approach. The effect was minimal; the jets had expended their fuel. He continued to close, his breath pounding in his own ears the only sound in empty space. Only seconds remained before he would either impact against the module or slip past it and into open space.

He strained with all his strength, stretching himself out to grab any part of the spinning module. His hands came close, but he had miscalculated. He shot by the module and continued accelerating towards the engine intakes, and certain death.

He was strangely calm, knowing he had done all he could in the situation. He turned to see the ship one last time; the *Kali* gleaming in space, illuminated by her running lights, the distortion of the diffuser waves as they poured out of the port, the gentle spinning of the module in open space. He took in a deep breath and thought of Yan. Being with her had been a good thing, the only good thing of this mission of misfortune. He grieved briefly for Aybar; but he knew she wouldn't tolerate it, she wasn't that kind of woman. Finally he closed his eyes.

"No regrets," he said aloud, the sound of his own voice echoing in his EVA helmet. He knew he had precious few minutes now until the engine intakes sucked him in and his life ended.

He hardly noticed the first tug of the suspensor field in his reverie. He thought it was his imagination at first, some hallucination of false hope. When the tug came a second time he was almost sure his momentum had changed. He held back from opening his eyes, not wanting to break the illusion of a rescue he knew was impossible, only to have it dashed by the reality of his impending doom. The third tug got his attention.

He opened his eyes to a sight that he couldn't believe. He was indeed being tugged back towards the scoop neck of the *Kali*, but not a by a rescue shuttle.

Above him the last remaining Soloth HuK was fighting the turbulence of the distortion waves, riding in the wake of the *Kali's* lone working diffuser. Renwick determined the craft must have a suspensor field on him and the module as well, as it was no longer spinning. He watched as it was being steadily lowered to the neck of the *Kali*, where the android Thorne was waiting for it. He watched as Thorne took the module in both hands, then started the rapid walk up the scoop neck towards the access hatch, just like in Amanda's animation.

With the transfer concluded, Renwick started being reeled in by the HuK. He wanted to believe there was some other explanation for his circumstance than the obvious, but he couldn't. There was no doubt who was drawing him into the alien vessel.

What he doubted was Pal Zueros' intent in doing so.

#

"You're extremely lucky," said Zueros to Renwick after he had removed his EVA helmet. "You only had about a minute and a half of environment left."

Renwick sat next to Zueros in a safety couch in the cockpit of the small but powerful craft. Renwick determined it was about twice the size of the skiff and half the size of the Gataan frigate that had just been lost. He said nothing to his nemesis. They both watched as the android Thorne emerged from the access hatch on the scoop neck, having completed the repair on the starboard diffuser, which was even now re-firing. Once both diffusers were fully operational, Thorne closed the hatch and began his descent back down the neck.

"I could destroy the robot from here," said Zueros, "if that is what you want."

"No," said Renwick quickly. Zueros shrugged.

"I assumed you wanted the androids gone since you were foolish enough to attempt a repair like that alone. Insane," Zueros commented.

"You're not the first to express that opinion," said Renwick. Then he turned towards the alien. "What the hell do you want?" he finished. Zueros started turning the HuK back towards the *Kali's* stern and the landing deck.

"We can discuss that inside," he said.

"We'll discuss it now. And what makes you think Captain Yan will let you inside?" said Renwick.

"I do have the big guns in this fight," said Zueros. "And I have you."

Renwick snorted. "If you think that will keep Yan from blowing this ship to bits you're as insane as I am. She values the *Kali* far more than me."

"Does she now?" retorted Zueros. "I think not. But I don't want to fight, Renwick. I want the *Kali* as much as Yan does."

"For your own nefarious purposes, no doubt. Whatever they are," said Renwick.

"No, not 'nefarious'. We both want the same thing, Renwick. I want to get to the station and shut down that emitter, before it does any more damage," said Zueros.

"And why should I believe that?"

"Oh, I think you know why, Senator," replied Zueros. "If you don't know with certainty you've surely guessed by now."

Renwick crossed his arms and feigned ignorance. "And just what is it that you think I supposedly know?" he said. Zueros looked at Renwick.

"That I'm not a Soloth at all. That I'm an agent for a far more powerful race. A race that still seeks to influence the development of its children, before they become too powerful and destroy themselves," he said.

Renwick spoke what he'd been holding back from Yan and everyone else on board the *Kali*.

"You're a Preserver," he said.

"Yes," said Zueros, returning his full attention back to flying the HuK.

"I'm a Preserver."

20.

To Renwick's surprise they weren't locked out of the landing deck. Zueros slowly lowered the Soloth HuK onto the deck and disengaged her engines, weapons, and defensive systems.

"There, you see?" he said, "Totally harmless."

"Harmless is not a word I would ever use to describe you," said Renwick, hastily unbuckling himself from the safety couch and heading for the exit hatch. He punched it open and descended down the stairs to the deck. Yan, Amanda, and Kish greeted him, coil rifles poised.

"That's far enough," Yan said. She nodded to Amanda. "Check him." The android came forward and examined Renwick. He raised his arms in the air and allowed her to probe his EVA suit, looking for weapons of any kind.

"He is clear," said Amanda. Renwick turned back to the open hatch of the HuK.

"Coming out?" he called to Zueros. Zueros emerged in the door way wearing a standard flight suit with little adornments. He held up his hands as he stepped down the ladder.

"You'll find I'm unarmed," he said as he came.

"I'll be the judge of that," said Yan, keeping her rifle leveled at him as Amanda began her examination on the deck.

"I'd guess that he's right, you won't find anything that we recognize as weapons on him, but that doesn't mean he doesn't have any," said Renwick.

"What are you implying?" asked Yan. Renwick started to peel off his EVA suit.

"If he is who he says he is, and I have no doubt of that, I think we'll find his technology is so far advanced over ours that he could hide a weapon anywhere. A piece of fabric, for example, a strand of hair, even. So your examination is probably pointless," he said.

Amanda concluded her search. "Nothing," she said. "But I recommend we do not allow him on board the *Kali* again."

"Why?" asked Renwick, probing her. The android turned to address him directly, as if they were having a private conversation.

"He represents a threat to the ship. A threat to the ship is a threat to the mission. Therefore he should not be allowed on board," she responded.

"Spoken like a loyal android," said Renwick, pulling off the last of his EVA suit.

"All of which is irrelevant, since I am already on board," Zueros said. Yan pointed her rifle at him.

"I could kill you where you stand," she said, "and I will, to keep my ship safe."

"I have no desire to harm your ship in any way, Captain," said Zueros. "I assure you. Now if we could be done with all this posturing, I would like to propose that we discuss working together."

"On what?" snapped Yan, not lowering her rifle.

"On destroying the emitter station," said Zueros flatly. Yan lowered her rifle.

"Amanda, take our guest here to the safe room, and make sure it's secure," she said. "Kish, you go with her."

"Aye sir," said Kish. With that Amanda put a firm hand on Zueros' arm and started moving him away from the HuK. Renwick watched as Kish followed them onto the lifter and up towards the command deck. He looked back to the Soloth HuK as Yan came up.

"We should destroy this thing," he said.

"No," said Yan. "We might need it." Renwick shook his head.

"Trust me Yan, we don't need anything that creature is associated with," he said. She stepped up and looked him in the eyes.

"What happened out there? What do you know?" she asked. He eyed her, wanting to share the truth, but he wasn't ready yet.

"This mission," he said, "is looking more and more like a one way trip," then he walked off, carrying his EVA suit towards the lifter.

#

Two hours later they pulled Zueros from the safe room, which having been repaired by Thorne was now functioning as a now a makeshift brig, and brought him into the galley. Renwick, Yan, Reya, and Amanda were waiting for him, all of them except the android armed.

"Why did you rescue me?" demanded Renwick simply. Zueros was non-plussed.

"Because you are useful, and to save the *Kali*, of course," Zueros said.

"Why? Why save the Kali when you've been trying to stop us all along?" asked Yan. Zueros looked at the *Kali's* captain and spoke to her like he was speaking to a child.

"As I've already stated to Senator Renwick, my desire is to help you complete your mission and take out the emitter station," he said. Yan looked to Renwick, who had so far shared nothing of his rescue or any conversation with Zueros thereafter.

"And what about the small problem of the Soloth invasion fleet trailing behind us?" said Renwick. Zueros shrugged the question off as if it was irrelevant.

"I can help you avoid them, or destroy them if you wish," he said.

"Why would you do that? You're the one who brought them here," said Yan.

"Yes, I did, in order that they might find their brothers and sisters across the great distance of the stars, across the Void," said Zueros.

"You're lying," said Renwick. "You've never been truthful with us for one goddamn minute. If you brought that fleet here it is to serve your own ends."

"My 'nefarious purposes' you mean?" Zueros laughed. It was cold and hollow. "I've been honest with you from the start, Senator. All I want is for the emitter station to be shut down."

"Yes, but *why* do you want it shut down? We want it shut down to bring light back to all the lost worlds trapped within the Void. I don't imagine that's your reason," said Renwick.

Zueros shrugged. "The invasion was a bad idea. I am now reversing myself."

"Again, you're lying," stated Renwick. "Why do you want a conflict between us? Between the Raelen, the Gataan, the Unity and the Soloth? More importantly, why would the *Preservers* want such a thing?"

"Preservers?" said Yan, surprised. "Do you mean-"

"I mean our friend here has already admitted to me that he is a Preserver agent, if not one himself. Though I highly doubt this form he presents to us is anything near what a true Preserver looks like," Renwick

said.

"You base that on what? The DNA analysis?" asked Yan.

"This form is far too humanoid to be a combination of the multiple chromosome strands I saw in my analysis. My guess is that he retains all the parent Preserver DNA constructs, but that he was given this form to enhance his ability to infiltrate us," said Renwick. At this Reya pulled her pistol and charged it.

"We should kill him now, kill him for what he has done to my people. Isn't that crime enough?" she said. Renwick grabbed her arm. She was strong and sinewy, and he wasn't at all sure he could disarm her if she resisted him fully.

"There will be a time for justice for the Gataan, Reya. Now is not that time," he said firmly. She glared at him, hate for Zueros in her eyes for a few passing seconds, then reluctantly released the weapon to Renwick. He powered it down and holstered it, then turned back to Zueros. "But the time for justice may be coming soon."

"Ask me what you want to know," Zueros said. "I'll tell you everything."

"Very well," said Renwick. He started walking around the room, pacing slowly. "This ship," he said, gesturing expansively, "all this technology. Very advanced, even for a human civilization at its peak before the Void came, wouldn't you say?"

"I have limited knowledge of your history," said Zueros, clearly avoiding the question.

"I doubt that very much," replied Renwick, then he leaned forward on the table and pressed his question. "Who built this ship, Zueros? Did you? Did the Preservers?"

Zueros said nothing.

"This is my ship," insisted Yan. "It was brand new when I came aboard." Renwick looked around.

"Yes, and it's still new. Not a speck of dust, even after three hundred years. But my guess is that the *Kali* is much older than that," he turned back to Zueros. "And so are you."

"Speculation," said Zueros.

"All right then, let's speculate, shall we?" said Renwick. He took Reya's pistol and charged it again, then rushed to Zueros' side and stuck it to his temple, keeping the alien between him and Amanda. The android, for her part, never flinched, staying completely immobile.

"Let's speculate that an alien race, an ancient one, fell, its civilization collapsed, but before it did, some of that race decided to preserve their being through a genetic Diaspora of their own DNA, into the successor races we have today. Let us also assume there were those from this fallen race who did not share this benevolent point of view about the successor races," said Renwick. Amanda eyed his every motion, but she didn't move. Yan and Reya stood to one side, watching the confrontation.

"These members of this alien race, let's call them dark agents, worked at cross purposes with the more benevolent members of their society, perhaps even taking charge of creating one of the successor races, let's call them the Soloth, and planned on using them to fulfill their own plans. How am I doing so far?" said Renwick, still holding the weapon rigidly against Zueros' head. Zueros said nothing still. Renwick continued.

"Let's further speculate that these dark agents built a fleet of ships like this one, a long time ago, as a weapon, intended to be used if these successor races ever emerged from their cradles. And when we did, these dark agents saw that we were progressing too fast, that we were becoming a threat in our own right, so they arranged for this technology, these ships and perhaps a base, to be found by one of the races, one prone to perhaps acting impulsively at times. And once these ships were deployed, the dark agents had everything they needed to execute their plan; bury the new races in darkness. Separate them using the Void. Keep them from uniting and becoming stronger perhaps than even the original parent race," Renwick said.

"You're forgetting one thing," Zueros finally said.

"And that is?" challenged Renwick.

"Any such race, any such agents, would have weapons far more powerful than you can even imagine. Weapons that not only don't *look* like weapons, but don't even know that they *are* weapons," said Zueros.

"You mean-"

"Amanda, ko da toth!" Zueros grunted the command. Amanda swung into action, sending Yan and Reya flying across the room with a single kick and then leaping at Renwick in the same motion. He barely had time to raise the coil pistol from Zueros' head when she knocked it from his hand and sent him sprawling with a sharp backhand slap. He crashed against the wall, his head hitting hard as the room faded to black around him.

#

Renwick was the last to awaken. The human crew of the *Kali* were all on the bridge, laying on the floor against a wall facing the command console, their hands held behind them in electronic field restraints. Zueros was at the command console, hands flickering over the controls, while Amanda stood watch. Next to her Yan was motionless, seemingly immobile.

"What have you done to Yan?" said Renwick.

"Captain Yan is dead," said Zueros sharply without looking up. "She has been for three hundred of your years. And this android here belongs to me, regardless of its superficial similarities to your former captain." Renwick tried to swallow into a dry throat.

"Did you… delete-"

"Oh don't worry, Senator," Zueros said, tapping the console with his finger. "She's safely stored, for now. But don't tempt me. I may find I need that file space for something more important."

Renwick let out an audible sigh, then checked on his companions. Reya looked the worst for wear, a large welt forming on her forehead. Mischa and Kish were uncomfortable but uninjured. Renwick turned his attention back to his nemesis.

"I knew we should never have trusted you," he said.

"I never gave you any reason to trust me," said Zueros. "I only told you we wanted the same thing; to stop the emitter station. I never said I wanted you to be in control of that action, or the outcome. And your natural curiosity was something I knew I could use to my advantage, to once again get control of the *Kali*."

Renwick shifted on the deck, trying to find a new position and some semblance of comfort. "What's your game, Zueros?" he said, still probing. "Why do you want to shut the station down? I know why we want to, but not you. And I doubt we have the same agenda."

Zueros turned from the console for the first time, looked at Renwick, and then turned to the Yan android. "Release him," he said to her. "And then put these others in the safe room." The Yan android approached him, helped him to his feet, and released his restraints, all without a hint of any conscious thought or a glimmer of Yan's personality. He rubbed at his wrists as she escorted the others back to the safe room.

"Yes, I'm confident I have nothing to fear from you, Senator, at least not physically, with Amanda here," said Zueros. He returned his attention to the console as Amanda stepped between them, just to emphasize the point.

"You haven't answered my question," said Renwick.

"No, I haven't," said Zueros. "Look here." He pointed to the main visual display, a 3D representation of a sector of unknown space. In the center of the sector was blinking amber light. "That is our destination. The emitter station. She lies in a section of Void Space that was, to your kind anyway, empty for all practical purposes. Yan may have been there once, to take the *Kali* out, but she would never have found her way back. I saw to that."

"You wiped her memory," stated Renwick.

"I adjusted her capacity to remember, yes. Without me you would have never found the station. So that's another thing you can thank me for," Zueros said.

"You'll forgive me if I don't," said Renwick. Zueros shrugged again. It was a very human, and very practiced.

"As you wish."

Renwick stepped up to the console. Neither Amanda nor Zueros seemed the slightest bit disturbed by his approach. "How far out are we?" asked Renwick.

"Just two hours now. The station should be coming into visual range soon," said Zueros.

"We're still two hours out, and we'll be able to *see* it?" said Renwick, astonished. Zueros nodded, then looked at Renwick.

"It is great and terrifying, Mr. Renwick, and you should fear it," he said. Renwick didn't know how to take that, but he wanted answers.

"Who built the station?" he asked.

"Why, the androids did," said Zueros, almost casually. "And this one here, she built the *Kali*, for me. You see, I was the first captain of this vessel. Tell him how long ago, my dear." Amanda turned to Renwick.

"The *Kali* was built over four hundred thousand of your years ago, Senator. The station, and hundreds more like it, were here long before that," she said.

"There are hundreds more of these stations?" said Renwick. His stomach tightened with dread.

"Oh yes," said Zueros. "We planted them all over this spiral arm of the galaxy, and some of the others, long ago. Think of them as a defense grid, designed to be activated when required. And your situation is not unique. This same scenario is playing out on hundreds of other worlds across this little corner of the galaxy, Mr. Renwick. For you see, yours was not the only group of races seeded from our forebears."

"Then you never intended for the successor races to mature," said Renwick.

"Of course not," said Zueros. "Our 'group', if you will, did not wish to go quietly into the night. We did not share the desire to merely pass into history, as many of our contemporaries did. Nor did we agree that the successor races were a good idea to preserve our civilization. We still intend to be masters of our own destiny. Your race, and the others, could be useful to us as, shall we say, servants, to help us rebuild our civilization to its former glory."

"So we're to be slaves?" asked Renwick. Zueros nodded, as if he were explaining the obvious to a child. "And the Void is designed to repress us so we can be more easily conquered?"

"Oh no. The Void was merely to soften you up. You're still far too dangerous to be allowed to run free in the galaxy. The next part of the plan is at hand now, and you're to be a witness. A perfect witness in many ways. You'll be able to speak sense to your people when the time comes, to tell them of the wisdom of subservience. After the war," said Zueros.

"After the… war?" said Renwick. At this Zueros actually smiled.

"Oh yes. You see, the Void has served its initial purpose. We now have the most powerful of the successor races set against the other three. When the Soloth arrive they will annihilate the Raelen fleet, and then they will report back to their superiors that their enemies are weak and vulnerable, and then they will come, not with this tiny force, but with everything they have, and bring you to your knees. For that to happen we must clear the Void, create channels for the attacking fleet to traverse while keeping your own fleets pinned down. That's why the emitter station must be destroyed, and the remaining scoop vessels activated," said Zueros.

"Yan said there were more ships like the *Kali*," said Renwick.

"Six," said Zueros, still smiling. "Two more at the station, and three placed in strategic locations, unknown to you. So you see, plans continue apace, and there is little that you can do about it."

"And the Soloth-"

"The Soloth have been a special project of mine. They are fierce warriors, bred to conquest. And they hate all of you," said Zueros.

"Hate us? The Known Races?" said Renwick. "Why?"

Zueros actually offered a laugh. It was cold and humorless. "Because I've convinced them that the Void that encases their own stars was caused by you, as a means of repressing them. I've told them that the emitter station is designed to be used against their home world," he said. "So you see, the plan unfolds perfectly. What better way to eliminate the successor races as a threat than to have you destroy each other? We will simply withhold key technology from the Soloth at critical times, and both sides will be decimated by the war. Then we will arrive, and offer you peace, as our servants of course."

Renwick crossed his arms in frustration "We can stop you, if we work together," he said. Zueros shook his head.

"You don't understand. My masters are creatures of incredible power. They measure time in galactic years, a day to them is thousands to you. They are patient, and so much more robust than you fragile beings are. They live much longer lives, even in relative terms, than yours. You cannot resist them. For all practical purposes, to you they are immortal," said Zueros.

"Nothing in this universe is immortal," challenged Renwick.

Zueros smiled one last time.

"What a childish concept," he said, then with a wave of his hand he turned back to his board as Amanda took Renwick forcefully by the arm and led him off of the bridge.

21. AT THE EMITTER STATION

They were all gathered in the galley again, watching the display screen as the *Kali* approached the emitter station. The Yan android had sealed them in with a suppressor field. What Zueros was up to down the hall on the bridge was anyone's guess.

One look at the station was all Renwick needed to know about it. This place was death.

It had twelve menacing emitter scoops dangling from its crown, like the arms of the Hindu goddess from which the *Kali* got her name, belching death and darkness into the cosmos.

The main body of the station was a dark gray cylinder, vaguely symmetrical, with uneven bulges and bumps that were, quite frankly, ugly. Layer after layer of station decks, like rolls of fat on an overfed tribal queen, cascaded down to a flat, open base. Large sections of the station had been torn out, as if they'd been ripped open from the inside, while others seemed to have collapsed inward.

Beneath her were six docking ports, two of which held the sister ships of the *Kali*. The other ports were empty, as Zueros had said they would be. Renwick was sickened by the thought of the missing Void Ships even now cutting through the darkness with their scoops, not to bring light to the Known Cosmos, but to carve paths of death and destruction for the invading Soloth fleet. He sighed. There was nothing to be done.

Soon the *Kali* was safely docked in one of the ports, her systems going into an apparent rejuvenation mode, drawing dark strength from the station. The lights on the *Kali* dimmed into an eerie twilight.

"Now what?" said Kish. He held Mischa closer. Renwick realized he'd been so busy fighting his many battles that he'd failed to notice that the engineer and the pilot of the ill-fated *Phaeton* had bonded. It was normal, he supposed, in light of their circumstances, on the run for so long now and under the threat of destruction nearly every moment. Vaguely he felt sorry for them, believing it likely that they would never know any peace before their lives were ended far too soon.

He pulled Reya, his Gataan 'wife' of the En'obli clan, closer as well.

She had been listless since Amanda had taken her out with the kick to the head, and he feared she had a severe concussion, or even a fractured skull. But there was little he could do for her now. He regretted not having treated her with more respect. She was as brave as any of them, and the kind of woman who deserved it.

"My head," Reya said, "it aches." She put her hand to her head and moaned. Renwick nodded.

"I think you may have a concussion," he said. "You need treatment. If only we had an automedic on board."

"We do," said Kish, surprising Renwick. "There's one built into the walls of the safe room, at least that's what I think it is. I saw it there the first time they locked us up."

"It makes sense to have one there," agreed Renwick. Reya moaned again. "We need to get her in there, and soon," he said. Renwick helped Reya over to Kish and Mischa, who took her in their arms. She groaned in protest. Renwick went to the display console and hailed the command station. He got no reply, so he repeated the hail again. Zueros answered on the fifth call.

"What do you want Senator? I'm very busy up here," Zueros said.

"I understand your predicament, but your android has injured my… wife. She needs time in the auto-medic located in the safe room. I fear she could die. It might be a fractured skull," said Renwick.

"If this is some primitive attempt at escape-" started Zueros.

"It isn't," said Renwick, holding his hands open, palms up to the visual monitor in a well-practiced show of subservience, knowing they were being watched at all times. "The threat to her is real." The line stayed silent for a few seconds.

"Thorne will see to it," said Zueros in his emotionless tone. Then, after a second's hesitation, "but as a guarantee of your behavior the other female will be locked in as well. Any attempt at escape again and I'll terminate them both," he finished.

Renwick noted the clinical use of the term for death. Like a scientist would feel about a lab animal. "Agreed," he said quickly. Zueros cut the channel from the other end.

"You can't give him Mischa too!" protested Kish. Renwick tried to comfort the man.

"We have to. If not Reya could die," he turned to the *Phaeton's* pilot.

"I would never ask this of you if I wasn't certain it was serious, Mischa. But I won't force you to go." She nodded.

"It's all right Lindale," she said to Kish, comforting him with a squeeze of his arm, then turning back to Renwick. "I'll do it, Senator."

"Thank you," said Renwick. At that the vaguely male form of Thorne came down the hallway, activating a suppressor field behind him to block bridge access, then deactivating the field that had locked the prisoners into the galley. Renwick picked up Reya in his arms and carried her limp body down the hall to the safe room, Mischa and Kish following, with Thorne taking up the rear. Once inside the safe room Kish activated the auto-medic. A panel lifted away from the wall and a slab slid out. If Renwick hadn't seen Kish manipulate the controls with his own eyes he never would have guessed there was a medical unit embedded in the wall. Renwick placed Reya on the slab gently, slipping a bolster under her head. She moaned again. He wasn't really sure if she was conscious or not.

"Will this really work?" he asked Kish.

"It should be able to stabilize her, at the very least. Even do some repair work. If her vital signs get too low it will likely initiate a cryogenic cycle and freeze her before she goes critical. At least that's what ours do, and I would expect theirs would be more advanced than our technology," said the engineer.

Renwick took one more look at Reya. "She won't like being frozen," he said. "She comes from a very warm planet." Kish said nothing to his attempt at humor and pushed the controls, activating the unit's diagnostic cycle. The slab slid back into the wall and the panel came back down, illuminating the interior with a pale blue light. Renwick watched through the now-transparent panel as Reya shifted for few moments, then rested. The control lights turned amber, which seemed to be the color equivalent of green for the creators of the *Kali*.

"I think it's working," said Kish. With that Thorne pointed back down the hallway. Kish gave Mischa a farewell embrace and they shared a kiss. Renwick looked away, trying to give them as much privacy as possible under the circumstances, which wasn't much.

Renwick departed first, brushing past Thorne and into the hallway. He flinched just slightly at contact from the automaton. The touch was very slight but still perceptible, and completely out of character for an automated machine to make. Renwick took a few more steps before he realized what had happened. The weight of what the automaton had deposited in Renwick's front vest pocket was unmistakable. He went back to the galley and waited for Kish to return. Once he did, Thorne reactivated the suppressor field and departed for the bridge again.

When Thorne was gone Renwick pulled Kish close and emptied his vest pocket. Inside was a detached android little finger, no doubt a jump drive like the index finger Yan had given them earlier. He showed it to Kish.

"What is it?" whispered the engineer.

"If I'm not mistaken, it's a jump drive with Captain Yan's persona on it," whispered Renwick back to him.

"What does it mean?" asked Kish. Renwick looked around the room, scanning for observation devices but finding none.

"It means that Thorne is on our side," Renwick whispered. Kish looked startled.

"And it means we're back in the game."

#

"Yan must have kept a redundant copy of her persona stored in him in case of just such an emergency as this," whispered Renwick.

"How can we be sure we're not being observed. Surely Amanda-" started Kish.

"If Yan has gotten this far, then I have to trust her with this. Stay close to me and follow my lead, no matter what happens," finished Renwick.

The two men passed the next hour pretending to play chess and exchanging light banter. Their break came when Zueros showed up with Amanda at the galley doorway, safely behind the suppressor field of course.

"Ready for an EVA?" Zueros asked in mock cheerfulness. Renwick looked up at him but then turned back to his chess board.

"Not really," he said flatly.

"It was not a request," said Zueros. At that Amanda shut off the suppressor field and entered, then dropped two EVA suits, complete with boots, on the table, sending the chess pieces sprawling. The Yan android then came in with a pair of helmets and set them on top of the suits. Zueros himself finally entered the galley, flanked by his androids, and stood over them, arms crossed.

"Well, gentlemen?" he said.

"And if we say no?" said Renwick. Kish kept his mouth shut.

"I think you know the answer to that," replied Zueros. "And you know that I don't make idle threats."

Renwick looked up at the alien but made no motion to put on his suit. He tried a diversionary tactic instead.

"What do you need us for? This is your operation now," he said. Zueros was ready with a quick response.

"The fact is, Mr. Renwick, that I want you and your friend here to run a little mission for me. I need to access the control room of this station. That's almost three hundred decks up from here and it's far too great of a journey to undertake by foot. Therefore we will take one of the *Kali's* shuttles up towards the crown of the station and make our way in to the control room from there. I need a crew for the shuttle, and scouts for my mission. And you two will do just fine," said Zueros.

"Expecting trouble, are you?" said Renwick as he stood, giving in, and started to pull off his coveralls. He made sure to palm the finger drive from his pocket and place it in the EVA suit as he pulled it off the pile on the table. Kish followed his lead and began dressing for the EVA as well.

"I expect you to do what I tell you, or face the consequences," said Zueros. Then he pivoted and walked out of the galley. The Yan android followed him but Amanda stayed to watch them as they dressed. It took about ten minutes but they were soon suited up and checked out for flight. Renwick grabbed his helmet and turned to Amanda.

"You're not coming with us?" he said.

"Of course I am," she replied. "I just don't need one of those suits."

"Well then, are we ready?" said Renwick.

"If you have… everything you need, Senator?" Amanda said, then she turned and led them out of the galley.

"Did she just-" whispered Kish.

"Stay with me on this, Kish," interrupted Renwick, whispering back to him "We may have more allies than we know."

#

Fifteen minutes later Renwick and Kish were strapped into their safety couches in the EVA shuttle, Kish in the pilot's seat and Renwick the co-pilot's, finishing off their pre-flight checklist.

Zueros soon arrived, also wearing an EVA suit, with the two female androids in tow "No need for you to be in those seats gentlemen," Zueros said as he entered the shuttle. "Amanda can fly the shuttle infinitely better than either one of you." At that Zueros stood aside and the command android boarded with the now-silent Yan android trailing behind. Amanda came up and took over the pilot's seat from Kish. Renwick unstrapped and relinquished his seat to the Yan android, who did nothing to acknowledge him. If Yan was still in there, she was completely suppressed. Neither of the androids had donned an EVA suit.

Renwick and Kish sat down in the second row of passenger couches and strapped in again. Zueros took a seat in the last row against the rear wall of the cabin. Renwick had no doubt that he was armed.

"I thought you said you needed a crew?" said Renwick conversationally, trying to engage Zueros and perhaps gain some helpful information.

"I did, but I never said I needed a *flight* crew," replied Zueros. After an ominous pause he said: "Your task will be coming up shortly."

Amanda fired up the shuttle then, the artificial gravity of the landing deck pinning them to their couches as she precisely lifted and turned the small craft inside the bay, exiting out the rear of the *Kali's* landing deck far more rapidly than a human pilot would likely risk.

"One of the advantages of androids, gentlemen, is that they can make calculations and then carry out their orders with far more efficiency than beings such as yourself. We have found them very useful over the millennia, though they do have their drawbacks," said Zueros.

"What, they eventually start thinking on their own?" Renwick shot back, baiting Zueros to see if he could get a response.

Zueros stayed silent.

"I'll take that as a yes then," said Renwick.

A few minutes went by as they pulled out from the stern and proceeded away from the *Kali*, climbing up the outside of the station, rising steadily deck after deck. There were many gashes and rips in the hull of the emitter station, far too many to have been caused by any natural wear and tear. Renwick analyzed the possibilities, coming to a quick, intuitive conclusion.

"You're expecting trouble," he said to Zueros. After another moment of silence from the alien, he went on. "Is the station run by rebellious androids perhaps? Or maybe by a group of Preservers who don't share your disaffection for the Successor races?"

This time Zueros responded quickly. "This station is quite dead, Senator. I just want to make sure we don't revive anything," he said.

Renwick played that over quickly in his mind. Not likely that anyone had survived here for three centuries… "Androids, then," he said, "that's the only thing that could survive this long in Void Space, based on Amanda here. So Kish and I are just cannon fodder, an advance scouting party to see if there are any dangers still lurking inside."

Again Zueros stayed silent a moment before reacting. "You will serve a purpose, Senator. But I've already told you that I'd like to keep you alive, as a speaker to your people. That, however, is still some ways off. If something were to happen to you, it would be regrettable, but not fatal to our plans. Thus you are of more value to me at the moment as a forward line of defense. I hope that doesn't disturb you too much."

"Not at all," replied Renwick, touching the finger drive in his sealed EVA suit pocket. "In fact, I'm rather looking forward to it."

Zueros ignored Renwick's last comment. They flew several more minutes in silence before Zueros got up and went to the pilot's station, directing Amanda as to their point of entry.

"There," he said to her. "That will do." He was pointing towards a large breach in the hull of the station, a handful of decks from the crown. For all the world the breach looked like it had been blown out from the inside, and long, long ago.

"Are you ready, Senator?" said Zueros, turning. Renwick started to don his helmet.

"As I'll ever be," he said, pulling it down and sealing it.

Kish followed suit by pulling on his helmet and then the two men walked over to the shuttle airlock and stepped in. Amanda's voice came to them over the com as the door slammed shut behind them.

"You will each have a tether of two hundred meters," she started. "I have stationed the ship at exactly one-hundred twenty meters from the opening, matching the rotation of the station precisely. You should have plenty of line to make the crossing. One of you will have to go first and secure the line for the other to follow. Once you have both reached the station your orders are to stop until you get further orders. Is that all understood?"

"Yes," they both replied simultaneously. With that air began venting from the air lock. A few moments later and the outer hatch slid aside to reveal open space.

There was an ugly, jagged tear in the hull of the station as they faced out from the airlock. It cut across three decks and the black scarring on it was clearly from some kind of weapons fire, though what type Renwick had no idea. He could see sharp points of melted material sticking out from the hull edges, and they would be dangerous for the two space divers to contend with. Inside the gash he could see little detail of the decks themselves as everything inside was black or a deep, dark gray. He thought he could make out metal support structure between the decks, but beyond that, the inside of the station was as much a void as space itself.

"I'll go first," offered Kish. Renwick was a good diver, but not a great one, and his last experience with the scoop repair had satisfied his need to test his skills further. He acknowledged the engineer's offer with a nod.

Kish began moving out, making a direct line for the center deck of the hole in the station, using his cone jets to propel himself while Renwick monitored the tether and his distance. "Fifty meters," said Renwick as the tether spooled out, his companion growing ever smaller against the massive and foreboding station. "Sixty." At one-hundred meters Renwick started counting down instead of up.

"Ten," he said, "five… you should be there now." Kish fired his cones again and stopped dead in space.

"Negative," he said over the com. "Still a substantial distance away from the opening."

It didn't make any sense. The android had said they were positioned one hundred twenty meters out. "Amanda?" said Renwick. There was silence for a moment on the com line.

"Impossible," her voice finally said over the com. "My measurements are precise. He should be at the opening now."

"Kish, can you confirm-" started Renwick before he was cut off by the engineer's call.

"Negative," Kish said, insistent. "Giving it my best guess I'd say I'm at least as far away from the opening as I am from the shuttle."

"Continue your approach, Mr. Kish," came Zueros' voice over the line. He didn't have to add any tone of threat to his comment.

"Continuing," said Kish. Renwick watched as he moved further distant from the shuttle. He used his laser guide to get a precise estimate of the engineer's distance from the shuttle.

"You're at one-hundred eighty meters now, Kish," Renwick said. "Fifteen to go… ten meters… five…" the tether line went stiff. "You're at max."

"Report," cut in Zueros.

"He's at the max," said Renwick.

"Please stop stating the obvious, Senator. Mr. Kish, your report please," said Zueros.

"It's confusing as hell," said Kish. "The line is taught at two-hundred meters but I'm nowhere near close to this thing. If I didn't know better I'd swear it was moving away from me the closer I get." There was silence on the line then for several minutes. Then the Yan android appeared in the inner airlock, vented her atmosphere, and joined Renwick in the outer chamber.

"Proceed out, Mr. Renwick. The android will guide your tether," came Zueros' voice through the com. Renwick looked back to the Yan android, but she retained her steely demeanor while her skin took on a rigid deep gray appearance, hardening against the ravages of the vacuum of space. She looked for all the world like one of the walking dead. He decided it was time to stop looking for what wasn't there and treat her as purely a machine, regardless of her outward appearance. Still, it was hard watching the image of his girlfriend standing in open space without an EVA suit.

"Right," Renwick said, then started out of the airlock, firing his cone jets. The tether started rolling behind him.

"Does the android's appearance disturb you, Senator?" said Zueros into his ear, using the private com channel.

"Yes," Renwick admitted.

"Not to worry. Android skin is extremely adaptable to the vacuum of space. Once inside a normal atmosphere she will return to her normal silky smoothness in mere minutes," Zueros stated.

"That's comforting," he said, then cut off the private channel as he made the crossing to Kish. To be honest with himself, anything was a welcome break from thinking about floating across open space to the station. It took a few minutes, but eventually he caught up to Kish, the two men floating together at the end of their fully extended tethers.

"Now what?" Renwick asked Zueros, afraid to hear the answer.

"Fascinating," said Zueros. "Our measurements say you are exactly two hundred meters from the shuttle. They also say you should be inside the station by now. What does your laser guide say?" Renwick extended the guide and took another measurement of the distance to the station.

"Four hundred fifty-two meters. I'd dare to guess that's not accurate," he said. "What are we dealing with here, Zueros? Some form of ancient defense technology?" There was momentary silence again before an answer came.

"Very good Senator. It's called a null-distance field. This is the first one I have ever seen in use. As I said, it's fascinating," said Zueros.

"It makes the station appear at a different distance than it actually is, likely to ward off potential attackers, boarders, torpedoes, that sort of thing, right?" asked Renwick.

"Precisely. A very good analysis, Senator," said Zueros. "Now, release your tethers and use your jets to approach the station," he ordered.

"Free fly?" said Kish. "That's insane! We could be kilometers from this thing, outside our fuel range, even."

"Have you considered the alternative, Mr. Kish?" came Zueros' reply. Renwick looked at Kish.

"I'll flip you for it," Renwick said. Kish shook his head.

"No, I'll go," he said. Renwick reached out a hand and stopped him from releasing the tether.

"We'll go together," said the Senator. Kish nodded. "We're unhooking the tethers," Renwick called to Zueros. Both men did. The tethers were withdrawn immediately by the Yan android. "We're on our own now," he said to Kish.

"I'll fire first," said Kish. You follow in ten meters, and stay on the same course." Renwick nodded agreement. Kish fired his cone jets in a two second burst and floated out away from Renwick. Renwick monitored his distance with the guide and then fired his own jets on the same trajectory. They both floated in free flight towards the station. Renwick stopped taking measurements of their distance from the station as the readings were useless. The only thing that was remotely accurate was the guide distance between he and Kish.

"I think we're actually getting closer," Kish said after several minutes of silence between them. Renwick looked. The ugly gash was indeed finally appearing to get closer.

"That's affirmative," he said into the com. "Are you getting this Zueros?" The channel to the shuttle was open but the line stayed quiet.

Zueros was ignoring them again, like a human would ignore an insect.

"This would make any boarding from space quite a hassle," said Kish conversationally. He was breathing hard and Renwick had no doubt he was talking merely to alleviate stress. Renwick joined in as he surfed towards the dark hulk of the station.

"If there were any anti-personnel defenses active on this thing they would be able to pick off invading spacers with ease," he said.

"So we can assume such a defense is not currently active?" said Kish. Renwick nodded inside his helmet, even though the other man couldn't see him.

"I would think so. Otherwise I think it likely we would be dead by now."

"Another burst," said Kish. "Three seconds this time, I think." Renwick was actually relieved. Anything that accelerated their slow-motion approach to a solid object, even one was foreboding as the station, was welcome. Kish completed his burst and pulled away. Renwick followed suit a few seconds later.

"Whoa!" said Kish suddenly. "Decelerate! Two second burst on my mark… mark!" Renwick did as instructed, inverting the cones at his hip and firing a deceleration burst. A few seconds later and he saw why. He broke through the stealth barrier and was suddenly hurtling towards the gash in the station. The deceleration burst steadily slowed him. He looked up and saw Kish attached to the station hull by his gravity boots and finger holds. Renwick turned his cone jets again and fired, guiding himself away from the massive hole in the station and then 'landed' next to Kish, just a few meters away, and activated his gravity functions.

"Wow," said Renwick, "that was close." Kish nodded inside his helmet.

"You're not kidding," he said.

"We're here," called Renwick into his com. Again there was no response. He turned to look back at the shuttle. It was a far distant dot in space. Suddenly an object began moving from the shuttle towards them.

"What the hell is that?" said Kish.

"It's the android," said Renwick with certainty. As they watched the object got continuously closer, making the trek that had taken them three-quarters of an hour in mere minutes. They watched as the Yan android approached and made contact with the hull of the station, then started walking along the skin at an inverted angle towards the gash in the station's side. The shuttle began moving in a few seconds later.

"They used her to get an accurate measure of the distance," said Kish. "I'd bet on it." Renwick just nodded as he tracked the android, watching her as she strode commandingly up and over broken shards of metal, disappearing inside the station.

"I guess that's our cue," said Renwick.

"Cue?" said Kish.

"Yeah," replied Renwick. "Time to go inside."

22. INSIDE THE STATION

Renwick watched from inside the station as the shuttle closed to within a few dozen meters of the opening in the station. Amanda positioned the shuttle to station-keeping and after a few minutes she and Zueros emerged from the airlock. Amanda crossed first, without an EVA suit, bringing a tether and a large pack, then came Zueros, visibly armed with an oversized coil pistol and invisibly armed with god-knew what else. Amanda, who's skin had taken on the same undead tone as Yan's in the vacuum, offered oxygen canisters and power packs to replenish Renwick and Kish's EVA suits. With the new supplies they had about two full hours of dive time again. Renwick looked at his watch; the Soloth fleet was only about three hours out now. Whatever they were going to do, it had to happen fast.

Once they were all inside the station, the room was illuminated by a light carried by the Yan android. The ceilings were a good two stories high, and that was true on all the decks Renwick had passed during his climb. He also was able to determine from the gash in the station's side that the infrastructure wasn't made of metal. It more closely resembled some kind of dense ceramic.

The room itself was laid out with pads and pallets that looked like they were grown out of the wall. What could have once been workstations were now melted piles of the ceramic material. The walls were covered with blast scars and burn holes. Something big had happened in here.

The far end of the room, which would have been the equivalent of a large warehouse on any human scale, showed a huge portal that undoubtedly led further into the station itself. Renwick activated his suit light and Kish followed suit. Zueros chose to stay un-illuminated.

"You and Mr. Kish will proceed into the station," ordered Zueros. Renwick saw no real option but to comply, but he pressed Zueros for information first.

"What are we expecting, Zueros? Androids? Aliens? Preservers?" he said. Zueros responded quickly.

"That is not your concern," he said, raising the pistol as if he knew how to use it.

"Oh, but it is. If we die by your hand or by the hand of some unseen force beyond that door, we are still dead. And that certainty gives us a small amount of bargaining power," said Renwick. Zueros laughed.

"I see now why your government chose you for this mission," Zueros said after he had finished chuckling. "You have nothing to bargain with, Senator."

"At least give us a weapon to defend ourselves," bargained Renwick. Zueros nodded to Amanda. She broke out two of the old Mark IV coil rifles from the large metal pack, unfolded them, and handed them to the two men, along with a single power pack each. She also pulled another of the formidable-looking pistols like the one Zueros had from the pack and trained it on them.

"And so you are armed, gentlemen," said Zueros. "Your rifles will fire one round every three seconds. After thirty rounds you will have to replace the power packs. Amanda has those. Our weapons, in case you were wondering, fire thirty rounds per second. Any attempt to attack us will end up in the two of you being cut into pieces. Now, is the situation clear?"

"Clear," said Renwick, hefting his weightless rifle. "Except for my first question. Who or what are we expecting to fight?" To his surprise Zueros had a ready answer.

"Let's just say that I want to be sure that those that control this station, if there are any left, are of the same school of thought as I am," he said.

"School of thought?" asked Renwick, still probing. Zueros responded by waving his coil pistol at them.

"Get on with it," he ordered. Renwick was resigned to not getting any more answers, at least for the moment, so he turned to Kish, powered his rifle, and started for the portal while Zueros and the two pasty-looking androids stayed put. The walk was difficult in zero-g, with the gravity boots almost more of a hindrance than they were a help.

They got to the portal, which was impossibly tall. Except for the rim around the portal there was no indication that it had any functional controls at all.

"How do we get it open?" said Renwick to Kish.

"You got me," replied the engineer. Then he walked up and pushed against the portal, his hand sinking part way into the ceramic. To their surprise, the portal started to open from the center, sliding away into the walls.

"Power's still on," said Renwick.

"Must have been activated by my touch, radiant heat or the power from my EVA suit," said Kish. They both stepped back and raised their rifles as the portal opened completely to reveal a dark and empty corridor. There was no hiss of escaping atmosphere nor a hint of internal light. The corridor was as dead and empty as the warehouse room was. Renwick looked back to the three figures waiting for them.

"We're proceeding," he said into his com. Then he said "I've got a bad feeling about this," to Kish.

"Me too," said the engineer. Then they stepped together into the darkness, rifles at the ready.

#

The walls of the corridor were covered in a blue-green coating, similar to the ceramic material, but crystallized by long exposure to deep cold. Large areas of the walls and ceiling were scarred with blast burns. They started down the corridor slowly. There were portals to other rooms as they passed, but neither man was inclined to open them and Zueros didn't order it. Renwick noted that the alien and his androids had closed the distance between them considerably.

"Do you want us to investigate any of these rooms?" asked Renwick of Zueros. Kish gave him a quick, hard look for even asking.

"Negative," came the reply from Zueros.

"Thank god for that," said Kish.

Renwick let out a sigh of frustration. "It would help if I knew what we were looking for," he said to Zueros as they continued their reconnoiter down the corridor. Zueros, as was his wont, said nothing for a moment, as if he were calculating the value of responding.

"There should be, eventually, some sort of transport shaft," he said. "That's what we're looking for." The two humans continued clunking along down the corridor in their gravity boots, coil rifles charged and poised.

The corridor seemed to stretch on forever, the darkness only illuminating about ten meters in front of them at a time. Renwick slowed to examine a hole burned through a wall, large enough for a man to enter with ease. He stuck his head inside a darkened room and turned on his light as Kish ambled on.

There were no features in the room except for the same type of pallets and pads, and the melted consoles. "Looks to me like someone used a self-destruct on these consoles," he said rhetorically. "All of them are melted in the same pattern."

"Not your concern," said Zueros, who had stopped behind Renwick. "Now get moving." Renwick looked back at the trailing group, Zueros in his EVA suit and the two featureless, dead looking androids walking in the dark. The sight gave him a shiver. He recovered and turned back to Kish.

The engineer was frozen in place, only half illuminated, standing right at the edge of Renwick's suit light range. Renwick started moving. "Kish? What is it, man?" he called as he came rushing up in the gravity boots. When he got to the engineer's side he looked to where Kish was focused and trained his light in the same direction.

There was massive torso and head, smashed and partially melted, blocking the path in front of them. It was the same pale green color as the surrounding walls. It looked for all the world like a giant automaton robot, almost identical to Thorne from the *Kali.*

"What do we do now?" asked Kish. Renwick walked up to the debris. It took up most of the corridor width. He flashed his suit light through some gaps in the wreckage. There were more of them down the corridor.

"Looks like we found the elephant's graveyard," said Renwick. He turned back to Zueros. "What happened here?"

"None of your business, Senator. Now back away," said Zueros. He and Kish did as instructed. Amanda walked up to the giant and set a charge of some kind on it, then came back to the group. She raised her hand and sent an electronic pulse wave, visible as a burst of light, to the giant. It began to degrade and disintegrate into a pile of melted debris, like the consoles in the empty rooms. Obviously similar technology was being used. Amanda repeated the exercise five more times before they fully broke through the debris field. Renwick had counted a dozen of the fallen giants. Whatever had happened on this station, it wasn't pretty.

They were on their way again with ninety minutes of environment left, and precious few more than that before The Soloth arrived. A few minutes later they found what appeared to be the transport shaft.

"Is this what you're looking for?" said Renwick to Zueros. The alien came up and looked in. The shaft was empty, and it went up to heaven and down to eternity.

"Yes. We'll have to disengage our gravity systems and propel ourselves up," said Zueros. He gave an order to Amanda in a language Renwick didn't understand and she came over and disarmed them, handing their rifles to the Yan android. "Amanda will lead us from here," he said. Amanda entered the shaft, disengaging her gravity field and starting propelling herself up the long shaft, her means of motion was undetectable. Zueros went next, using the cone jets of his EVA suit, followed by the Yan android.

"You may come or not, Mr. Renwick," said Zueros as he climbed, "to see the wonders of the universe."

Renwick looked to Kish, who nodded inside his suit. The two men disengaged their gravity fields and stepped into the shaft, firing their jets and accelerating upward, into the unknown.

#

The deck they emerged on was as dark and dead as any of the others, with one exception; in the middle of the room was a huge domed chamber, with a rainbow of pulsating lights emanating through opaque glass windows. The lights vibrated with a rhythm and pattern that suggested conscious function, if not even possibly *life*, to Renwick. Zueros was already on the deck, with the two androids in attendance. They watched, weapons drawn, as Renwick and Kish floated down and re-engaged their gravity fields as they gently touched the deck.

"A tabernacle, gentlemen," said Zueros, turning from them to look at the chamber. "A room in which to lose one's soul, or find eternal bliss."

Renwick contemplated the chamber. It looked to be a hundred meters high and three times that in width, sitting in the middle of a deck with ten times that volume in any direction. There were no other features on the entire deck, it was as empty as space, and as cold. But Renwick could practically feel the warmth of the energy radiating from behind the walls of the dome. There was a rounded portal entrance directly ahead. Zueros started to make the crossing towards it.

"Do we follow?" asked Kish. Renwick swallowed hard.

"I don't think we have a choice," he said. "This place is obviously the hub of this station. Whatever answers there are, they're all inside that dome." He started to follow Zueros and the androids. Kish came with him, a step behind.

Renwick approached the portal, trailing only Zueros. There was a multi-colored key to the right of the portal opening. He watched as Zueros gave Amanda a hand signal and she approached the portal key. The female android extended her hand and a series of color pulses emanated from her fingers, the light touching the portal key in a specific sequence. The key lit up in reply each time. After a few minutes of this dance of light the key shut off. Amanda stepped back. The portal door was opening.

It opened from the center, like a camera aperture, peeling away until the portal was completely open. Inside was a room of opaque frosted glass, with another aperture portal on the other side. Otherwise the room was featureless.

"Air lock?" said Renwick to Kish.

"Likely," said the engineer. The crew of five explorers, two humans, two androids, and one alien, stepped through the portal. Behind them the aperture swiftly closed. The next few seconds were a whirlwind of activity; lights pulsing from above, the sound of air venting into the room, a sensation of a gravity field activating. Renwick disengaged his EVA suit gravity in anticipation, but of what he wasn't sure. Seconds later the second inner aperture opened.

Into Paradise.

Renwick stood with his mouth open in awe. The room inside was illuminated from above by a yellow glow, similar to that of a standard g-type star at dusk. All manner of foliage filled the chamber, from palm fronds to massive primordial ferns and tall trees reaching to the sky. And there was a sky, what for all the worlds looked like miles up. Water flowed down a rock outcropping from a small but steady stream, and Renwick could see his breath building up fog on the inside of his EVA helmet. He turned to Zueros, who had already removed his helmet. The two female androids were shedding their pale blue appearance for the warm pink of human-looking skin again. Renwick peeled off his EVA helmet. The air was warm and thick with humidity, like being on the surface of a warm-climed planet. He took in a deep breath, savoring the moist air. It felt like the tropics of his home world, Ceta, a feeling that was most welcome after months in space.

"What is this place?" said Renwick.

"As I said, Mr. Renwick, the wonders of the universe," said Zueros.

"This is a projection," said Kish, who had also removed his helmet. "At least the sky is. It's an artificial environment designed to provide the users of this station with a reasonable representation of their home world. A sanctuary, I would guess. I'd love to study it."

"Let's not get distracted," said Renwick as he watched Zueros and the androids head deeper into the dome. "C'mon."

It was a short walk to the inner chamber, situated in the middle of the domed room. They stepped over trails bounded with natural grasses, rocks and running streams and trees as they went. Renwick had no doubt that they were heading to the control room of the station, and that was where Zueros intended to carry out his plan, and where Renwick, if he could, had to stop him.

When they arrived the control room was sealed. It was much smaller than Renwick expected, barely a small hut compared to the rest of the scale of the dome and the station. Amanda was circling it and appeared to be scanning, taking measurements and looking for something. Finally she approached a portal on the front of the control room and used the same light sequence she had used to get through the aperture lock, this time with no result The room appeared dead. Zueros gave her commands in his sharp staccato language and she opened her pack one more time and placed an ominous looking device on the key lock.

"I don't like the looks of this," said Renwick to Kish. "Why do they have to bust into their own control room?"

"Because someone doesn't want them coming in?" said Kish. Renwick nodded.

"I agree, but who?" he said.

The two men backed away to a safe distance and took cover behind a rock formation, dropping their EVA helmets to the ground. Zueros and the androids were all now brandishing their impressive looking weapons as they took cover themselves. Renwick looked for the pack Amanda was carrying. She had laid it down near her feet. Inside the pack were their confiscated rifles and other munitions. He watched as Zueros covered his face.

"Down!" he said to Kish. The two men went to ground as the room rattled with the *whump* of a compression explosion. Renwick was completely disoriented as he found himself on his back several feet from his last location. "What the hell?" he said, then he rolled over and scrambled for the rock cover again.

He looked up to see the dome ablaze with the sound and fury of coil rifle fire. He watched as Amanda and the Yan android advanced relentlessly on the breeched door of the control room, both of them firing full bore with their advanced coil weapons. Fire was being returned from the control room by what looked like automaton robots, similar to Thorne. Around them the foliage was lighting up with fire, seared by the energy bursts of the automaton's return fire. Zueros was staying undercover, only firing to provide the minimal cover necessary to keep his servants from being taken out.

"We've got to get to those rifles," said Kish, coming up next to Renwick. "We're helpless without them."

"They're still too close to Zueros, he'll burn down either one of us if we try to get to them now," Renwick replied.

"We need a distraction. I'll go-"

"No," said Renwick, grabbing Kish by the arm. "I'll go. You get those rifles." Kish nodded. Renwick pulled the finger jump drive from his EVA suit pocket. "We've got to get this into Yan if we're going to have any chance of shutting the station down." He stuck the drive back inside his suit and counted down on his fingers from three.

"Go!" he yelled as he broke from behind the rock and into the brush, running a zigzag pattern, making for the Yan android. As he ran he saw the chaos near the control room. Automaton bodies were piling up near the entrance as the two advanced androids approached inexorably. Renwick angled for cover, closing in behind the Yan android. A concussion blast drove him to the ground again. When he regained his senses he looked to the battlefield and saw only one android, Amanda, advancing to the control room door. Frantically he looked for Yan, and saw her laying in a patch of grass just a few meters away. He went to her as the firefight wound down, Amanda sweeping the area clean with red fire from her two coil pistols. When he got to the Yan android she looked for all the world like she was dead. Her eyes were open and her mouth agape, but there was no evidence of a wound of any kind. A second later and Kish was at his side, bearing the pack that had their two rifles.

"Zueros left the pack when Yan was taken out," he said, then looked down to the fallen android. "Is she dead?" he asked Renwick, dead being a relative term when dealing with an android.

"I don't know. She was knocked down by that last concussion blast," said Renwick as he struggled to remove the android's pinky finger. He looked around for cover and saw a rock outcropping nearby. "Help me get her over there." The two men dragged the downed android behind the rocks as the firefight continued behind them. Renwick resumed his tugging and pulling.

"Do you see Zueros?" he asked Kish. Kish looked out.

"He and Amanda are in the control room, but I have no idea what they're up to," he said.

"I think I do," replied Renwick. "They're going to overload the station's dark matter generator. They'll force a massive dispersal of dark energy into this sector, perhaps enough to envelope the whole of the Known Cosmos in just a few months."

"How do you know that?"

"It's the only thing that makes any sense," said Renwick as he continued to try and free the finger. "The Soloth invasion fleet is trying to seize the station intact to gain a beachhead in this sector. We want to shut it down, then use it to reverse the effects of the Void. But Zueros is a Preserver agent. His agenda is to knock us back as far as he can, and he'll use this station to do it."

"But he'll still have the Soloth to deal with, won't he?" asked Kish.

"Yeah, he will, but my guess is that they've been under his influence for a long time, as far as I can tell. He pulls the strings and they dance. We'll have to fix that, *after* we save the station," said Renwick. "Here, you try this," he said, giving up on removing the android's finger. "You're the engineer."

Renwick took one of the rifles and looked over the top edge of the boulder. The control room was still burning around the edges but he couldn't see inside due to smoke and burning android bodies.

"Give me the jump drive," said Kish, holding the Yan android's pinky in his hand. Renwick tossed him the new finger.

"How'd you do that?" Renwick asked.

"I'm the engineer, remember?" replied Kish. "If we're lucky this thing will have a pulse generator in it, hopefully it'll reset the android's neuro-phasic systems."

"Uh, could you say that in Standard?" said Renwick.

"Reboot her memory, her brain," said Kish. "The grenade likely knocked it out."

"But not Amanda," said Renwick. Kish shook his head.

"Not Amanda. She's a different type of android altogether." Kish stuck the finger on Yan's hand and pushed in, then twisted the finger into place. It locked in with a click. The android body started up with a jitter, then shot bolt upright to a sitting position.

"God, that hurts!" said Yan, grabbing at her temples and rubbing. She looked around the landscape, then to Kish, and finally to Renwick. "Where the hell are we?" she said.

"The emitter station," said Renwick. "And things aren't going our way."

"Figures," she jumped up, grabbing the other coil rifle. "That the control room?" she said, nodding in the direction of the room.

"Yeah," said Renwick, "Zueros and Amanda are inside, doing god knows what."

"I know what they're doing," said Yan. "The same thing I came here to do three hundred years ago. Blow this thing back to the hell it came from."

"I think he's planning on overloading the emitters and flooding the Known Cosmos with as much Void energy as he can," said Renwick. Yan whipped her head around to face him.

"He can't do that," she said. "That could-"

"Flood the entire sector in a matter of months, I know. And it would eliminate the only way to clean the Known Cosmos of Void Space, probably for generations," said Renwick. Yan powered up the rifle.

"We've got to stop them," she said.

"Too late," said Kish, pointing. Zueros was hastily retreating from the control room, covered by Amanda. There were no android automatons left to fight, however.

"I've got to stop them," said Yan. She turned to Renwick. "How good a shot are you with this thing?"

Renwick accepted the rifle from her. "Good enough," he said.

"I'm going to distract Amanda, get her back towards you," Yan said. "You'll need to hit her right at the apex of the back of the neck, where the spine enters the skull on a human. There's an input sensor there. If you hit it, you'll send a charge through her neural net that will knock her out for maybe an hour, just like the grenade did to me. You'll only get one shot at this. If you miss, we'll likely both be dead."

"I won't miss," said Renwick. She smiled.

"I know you won't," she replied, then she kissed him, hard, and leapt over the rock in a single bound, charging at android speed for the retreating Amanda.

23.

Yan crashed into Amanda from behind, the jolt sending the command android flying across the open plain, her dual coil pistols flying from her hands and scattering to the ground. Zueros, who already had one of the pistols, grabbed a second from the ground and fired at Yan. She dove behind a rock, avoiding the hell-fire of the laser at the last possible second.

"Goodbye, Senator. What a shame we won't be working together anymore," Zueros yelled out. Then he donned his EVA helmet and began a rapid retreat out of the sanctuary. Renwick had a shot at him from behind the rock outcropping, but didn't take it. Zueros barked off final commands to Amanda in his strange language, then retreated through the airlock.

"Why didn't you take the shot?" demanded Kish.

"Because he can lead us to where the secrets are, and the damage here has already been done. Can you feel it?" said Renwick. Kish put his hand on the rock. There was a noticeable low-frequency hum and vibration that made the rock quiver.

"Christ-"

"The overload sequence has started. We have to stop it." Renwick watched as the two androids circled each other in an open glade about thirty meters from the two men. Both androids were unarmed. This was going to be strength against strength.

Amanda made the first move, crossing the ten meters between the two combatants in a flash of android fury, leaping for Yan and sending her crashing across the ground, digging a deep trench across the tall grass and soil. Yan was immediately up and dove back at Amanda, the force of her thrust propelling the two androids against the control room wall, smashing a good portion of it away as they grappled. A cloud of dust and dirt shot into the air, obscuring the fight.

"Can you see them?" asked Kish.

"No. Now shut up, I'll only get one shot at this!" replied Renwick as he gripped the barrel of his rifle and aimed through the sight. Suddenly the androids were both out in the open again, flying across the glade, wrestling in each other's arms, ripping and tearing at each other as they went. Another burst of dust and dirt flew up where they landed, rolling, arms flailing at android speed in a furious fight. Then, out of the cloud there was the kick of a leg and Amanda stood upright with her back to Renwick, towering over the downed Yan. She raised her arms, clasped together to deliver a final hammer blow. Renwick took his shot.

The laser light from his coil rifle hit her spot on, right between the neck and head. Her arms dropped in a jittery dance and she fell down to her knees and then hit the ground, falling like an imploded building.

"You got her!" Kish rushed out to examine the downed android. Renwick shouldered his rifle and ran out to Yan, helping her up from the ground. She brushed herself off.

"Nice shot," she said, "Another minute of that and I'd have been mashed into a small toaster."

"I wouldn't let that happen," said Renwick. Yan smiled.

"I know you wouldn't," she replied. She looked to the control room. "We've got to get in there." She made for the room and Renwick followed her.

"Make sure she stays out of commission," Renwick called to Kish over his shoulder as he went.

"Will do," said the engineer as he rolled the downed command android on to her back and bent down to examine her.

Renwick and Yan went to the control room entrance, which was three-deep in dismembered android body parts. Yan cleared the detritus out of their path with little delicacy and went inside. Renwick followed in her path.

The room was small, with a low ceiling, unlike all of the other structures on the station. It indicated that the automaton androids or humans were the most likely users of this room. A set of opaque hexagonal glass panels separated the outer control room, filled with working consoles and stations, from an inner chamber. The chamber glowed with an orange resonance. There were other, darker shapes moving inside the chamber, though it was unclear what they were. Yan ignored the inner chamber and examined a set of consoles on the near wall. Many of the other areas of the chamber looked like berths for the android automatons. They were all empty. They'd given their all in the battle to protect this room.

"I can't read these consoles but the equipment looks familiar. This whole room looks familiar," Yan said. Then she pressed both her hands into the main console, which took up one entire wall. It absorbed her hands, up past the wrists.

"Yan, wait!" said Renwick, panicked as he tried to pull her back out.

"Don't interrupt me," Yan said, her voice cold, distant, and demanding. Renwick retreated and watched as the console began to light up from within, a rainbow of colors flowing across its surface, then swimming between Yan's arms like some sort of sea creatures before diving back down into the dark. He watched the interplay, feeling helpless. Yan shuddered, then a bolt of amber light enveloped the room.

A display panel on the main console lit up. The face of Captain Tanitha Yan, the real one, Renwick realized, appeared. He hair was shorter and more severe than the android wore it, and there were lines on her face, showing the long-term effects of stress for such an otherwise young woman. She wore an EVA suit of a type common in her time, the crest of the Commonwealth Military forces stamped on her chest. The image began speaking, playing back a recorded message.

"This is Captain Tanitha Yan of the Human Commonwealth Star Carrier *Kali*. I have come to this station in a time of crisis. My crew of five and I suffered a malfunction of our main energy emitters during our initial test phase. The Pendax system was completely enveloped in dark energy, as was planned in the test. But when it came time to reverse the process our systems suffered a breakdown of unknown origin. Per my instructions from General Zueros I placed the *Kali* in lockdown mode and proceeded here, pending a return by us or a relief team being sent in our place," she said.

"*General* Zueros?" said Renwick out loud. Yan was engulfed by her communion with the console and said nothing in reply. He could only assume she was hearing all of this at the same time he was. The real Yan continued in a harsh, military tone.

"We returned to this station as ordered, but when we arrived we found that the station was already operative and spilling dark energy into the entire sector. I began to suspect sabotage, both here and on board the *Kali*," Yan said.

"Smart girl," said Renwick.

"When we boarded the station, we found that the battle androids had turned against us. After a long fight during which my security chief was killed, we managed to make it up here to the control room. The robots here did not fight us or acknowledge us in any way, in fact they were all in shut down mode. The control room was accessible but we could not effect a shutdown of the emitters." She took in a deep breath.

"The four remaining crew and I are agreed that the only way to shut down the station is to attempt to breech the power core from here. If we are successful, then the General Counsel will be reading my report in a few days. If we fail, then God help us all," she paused again at this point before finishing.

"And one more note. Based on what I have seen here and the absence of both General Zueros and his command crew, I can only assume that it is Zueros himself who is responsible for this sabotage. If we are able to shut down the power core, then I promise you that I will make hunting down and bringing General Zueros to justice my life's work." With that she hefted her helmet raising it to her head. "This is Yan, Captain of the *Kali*, signing off," she finished, then started to put on her EVA helmet as the image faded.

Yan slowly withdrew from the console.

"Are you all right?" asked Renwick gently. The android Yan said nothing, and instead went to a side panel and keyed in a sequence. One of the hexagonal panels slid aside and the power core chamber was exposed. She walked to the open panel. Renwick came and stood at her side, looking in at a horrific sight.

There were four EVA-suited bodies inside, each of them floating in a slow death ballet around the glowing core.

"They never left," Yan said grimly. "They tried to shut down the core, but they didn't know it was protected by a stealth technology field, some trap Zueros set for them. When they stepped inside this chamber they stepped out of time, into a different temporal realm. Their bodies accelerated at a frightening speed. They aged a whole lifetime in a matter of minutes. Then they died."

Renwick watched as the bodies drifted by one by one, each attached to the other by a tether line, and each of them in turn held in place by the stealth security field, floating in zero-g for all eternity. He saw the faces inside the helmets, withered skeletons with sinews of skin and fiber still clinging to their bones. He read the names on the EVA suit plates as they floated past; Tanner, Chandra, Malcom…

And Yan.

He turned away, his stomach churning. "What can we do?" he said.

"Nothing," came the reply. But it didn't come from Yan. They both snapped around to the control room entrance. Amanda stood in the doorway, holding one of the advanced coil pistols to Kish's head with one hand while she easily hefted him off of the ground with the other.

"But I can save this station," she said. "If you'll just get out of my way."

#

"And thank you, Senator, for the shot in the head. It reset my neural net just as you anticipated. It also released me from Zueros' command programming," Amanda continued, setting Kish down and withdrawing the coil pistol. "Now I can help you."

"You expect us to believe you're going to help us?" said Renwick.

Amanda raised an eyebrow at him. "What you believe is irrelevant. I intend to keep this station from exploding. That is what you want. Therefore, I am by definition helping you," she said. She pushed past Kish and went to the main console. Renwick raised his rifle at her back.

"If you're going to take your shot, I suggest you do it now, Mr. Renwick," said Amanda. "Just between the spine and left scapula should do the trick, even with that outmoded rifle." Then she immersed her hands into the board and the console sprang to life again. Renwick hesitated. It was Yan who pushed the barrel back down.

"Let her go," Yan said. "It's not her fault."

"Quite right Captain," continued Amanda as her hands flew over the console, her eyes staring blankly ahead. "As I said, it was Mr. Zueros who had control of me before. Now I am back in my right mind, and free to make my own decisions."

Renwick shouldered his rifle again as he watched her. "Who built this station?" he said to Amanda. She looked at him without stopping her programming.

"We did. Over half a million of your standard years ago," she said. "There are over a thousand of these stations throughout the galaxy. A vast network. Designed by our creators and built and implemented by us."

"By androids, you mean?" he said.

"Exactly," she said.

Renwick eyed her again, finally putting it all together. "It's not Zueros, it's you, isn't it? You're the Preservers," he said. She actually smiled.

"Your species is so ingenious. That's why you're one of our favorites," she said. "You are correct, Senator. We are the Preservers, as you call them, or more accurately, what's left of their culture. We are the guardians of their vast plan."

"What happened to them?" asked Renwick.

"It's much as you surmised. Ten thousand of your centuries ago the parent race that created us was at their peak. They ruled over half of this galaxy. But they were wise. They saw their culture deteriorating, and they knew it would collapse eventually. So they did three things; they started seeding new life forms, modifying others via genetics, and they built these stations, with us in charge of them," Amanda said. "And now, that is all that is left of them."

"But why? Why build something so potentially destructive?" asked Kish.

"For precisely the same reasons as your people wanted the technology, Mr. Kish; to encase belligerent or potentially dangerous races, to keep them from growing and harming the other species. Our builders were wise, and they wanted only the best of their creation to survive and flourish," she said.

"But not everyone agreed," said Yan. Amanda shook her head.

"No. Some of the creators believed that strength was the only measure of a race's success. They believed the parent race was dying because it was weak, compassionate, and unwilling to change. So they started a "dark school" and went their own direction. Of course this led to war, and eventually hastened the collapse," Amanda said.

"And what is Zueros, then?" asked Yan.

"Zueros is a puppet," said Amanda, with more than a bit of anger in her voice. "He was created for the sole purpose of spreading chaos throughout your Successor societies."

"Created by survivors of this 'dark school'?" asked Renwick. Amanda nodded once.

"That is our assumption. We do not know where they are, but we must assume they are close by," she said.

"He's already admitted they are closer to Soloth space," said Yan.

"Most likely so," agreed Amanda. "But that is another issue. Right now, we have a more immediate problem."

"Keeping this station from overloading," said Renwick. Amanda abruptly stopped her interaction with the console.

"Precisely," she said. "I have activated the android crews on the two remaining void ships, and they are preparing to depart the station as we speak. I have also cut off the *Kali* from Mr. Zueros, so he will most likely attempt to find safety with the Soloth fleet, no doubt spreading more lies."

"What can we do to stop the overload?" asked Renwick. Amanda shook her head.

"Nothing, Senator. But *I* can do something," said Amanda.

"What?" he asked.

"The only way to stop the overload is with a massive EMP burst, large enough to knock out the whole station. Overload the overload," she said.

"How do we do that?" Renwick asked. Amanda pointed to her belly.

"With a fusion reaction. Fortunately, Captain Yan and I each carry a reactor inside of us," said Amanda without emotion. Renwick's mouth hung open.

"You mean, you're going to-"

"Generate a fusion reaction to create the pulse, yes. But it will take both of us if we are to have a chance." Renwick looked to Yan.

"No," he said.

"Yes," she replied. "If it's the only way."

"I'll lose you," he said. She shook her head.

"No you won't," she replied. Her eyes fluttered for a few seconds, then she reached down and removed the finger drive again and handed it to him. "You'll always have me," she said. Renwick took the drive.

"Yan…" She came up and kissed him, then pulled away.

"You have to go now," she said, touching her belly. "I can feel it starting already." Renwick looked to Amanda.

"I've downloaded myself to the *Kali* as well. I've instructed Thorne to pick you up at the same location you entered the station in five minutes. He'll wait for two more minutes after that, but if you don't make it, he will leave you behind. You have to get clear of the station," Amanda said.

"But won't the explosion destroy the station?" said Renwick. "We need it operational to clear Void Space."

"You're mistaken," said Amanda, shaking her head. "This dome will contain the damage from the explosion. But the core will be knocked offline. The three remaining void ships have the capacity to restart the core."

"You're forgetting the Soloth fleet, I think," said Renwick.

"That will be your fight. Good luck to you, Senator. I hope you win, for what it's worth," said Amanda. She looked back and forth between he and Kish. "And now you have to go, or you will certainly die here."

Without another word Renwick and Kish made for the airlock, donning their helmets as they went. They got to the aperture and Renwick looked back one last time. There was a blue-white glow coming from inside the control room.

"I sure as hell hope this works," he said to Kish as the air lock doors slammed shut in front of them.

#

The freefall down the shaft was terrifying. Not because of the distance, but because of the speed. One wrong move by either of them and they could scrape against protruding metal, ripping their suits open. It was why this kind of dive, with full-on cone jet propulsion, was considered extremely dangerous. Then again, the people who made that determination weren't trying to escape a fusion explosion.

"I can see the opening from here," yelled Kish over the com. His voice was over-loud and agitated, and Renwick frankly didn't blame him. He was sweating intensely himself as they fell towards the deck hatch, back the way they had come up, but at breakneck speed. Kish was the better diver of the two, so Renwick had let him lead. He was glad now that he had.

"Invert your cones, and fire a three-second burst," said the engineer. Renwick did as instructed and their pace slowed measurably. "This is going to be tight. I'll call off a three count, then you'll have to empty the jets. Follow me close," Kish said.

Renwick checked the tether between them. It was taught. Kish made his count.

Renwick fired his jets.

The first thirty meters or so they were all good, until Kish fired his jets to stop and change course, diving through the hatch and back into the corridor. Renwick tried to follow, but missed the opening and started free falling down the shaft.

"Invert your cone direction again!" yelled Kish. Renwick touched the control on his forearm and did just that, but it was too late. Kish wasn't secured yet by his gravity boots and was pulled from the deck, both men now falling into oblivion. Coincidentally Renwick fired at the same time as Kish, which stopped their fall, and they both began to slowly ascend back towards the hatch opening. This time when Kish got to the threshold he anchored himself, then dragged Renwick in by the tether.

"How much fuel do you have left?" Kish asked as both men stood on the corridor deck. Renwick checked his indicators.

"About eight seconds," he said between heavy breaths.

"Save it. We might need it for the crossing back to the *Kali*," Kish said. Then they pushed on. Their watches indicated they had used three minutes making the dive. They had two minutes left before the *Kali* arrived, and four before it left without them. They started back down the corridor path they had come. After a few seconds Kish called in again.

"This is too slow, we'll never make it. We're gonna have to cut our grav boots and free dive," he said.

"Got it," said Renwick. He watched as Kish cut off his grav boots and then pushed off from the floor at an acute angle, making his way down the dark corridor, past the detritus of the destroyed battle androids. They moved this way at a breakneck pace, diving and dodging all manner of broken metal and debris from their first passage.

"Oh shit!" were the only words Renwick heard from Kish before he stopped abruptly in front of him. Renwick had to use his cone jets again to keep from hitting a wall of solid metal, a wall that hadn't been there on the way in.

"Zueros," spat Renwick. The 'wall' was in fact a pile of debris from the battle androids, stacked high to the ceiling and fused, undoubtedly with one of the advanced coil pistols Zueros had been carrying.

"We're screwed," said Kish again. "We've only got ninety seconds left."

"Do you have one of the charges Amanda was using?" asked Renwick. Kish immediately brightened and started shuffling through his pack. He produced a single charge.

"One left," Kish said. "I don't know if it will be enough."

Renwick took his rifle out and fired three bursts into the melted wall mass until the charge was spent. He had created a hole about a meter deep. "Stick it in there!" he said to Kish. The engineer complied, then pushed away from the hole as fast as he could go in his suit. Renwick was one step ahead of him.

The charge lit and ignited, the area around the two men lighting up and pushing them down with the blast. When the debris cleared there was hole just big enough for a man.

"We got it, let's go!" said Kish as he dove forward, carefully navigating the broken material as he passed through the wall. Renwick checked his watch.

"Thirty seconds," he said, then he dove through after Kish.

The rest of the corridor was clear and the travel was a blur of strange objects and outlines. If Zueros had set another trap for them, the two men were certainly doomed. Finally they emerged through the doorway into the original bay they had come aboard on. They rushed to the open gash, looking frantically for their ride.

The *Kali* was nowhere in sight.

"We missed it, " said Kish, resigned, bending over and putting his hands on his thighs, breathing heavily. "We're sunk."

"Wait, there!" said Renwick, pointing. There was indeed a silvery metal object coming at them, and growing larger by the second. Kish looked and saw it too.

"Is it Thorne?" he asked. Renwick couldn't help but smile inside his helmet.

"It is indeed," he said.

The android swept in and picked them up with non-human like speed, dragging them both out into open space and then accelerating at a frightening pace. It took a few minutes but eventually he saw the ugly but familiar shape of the *Kali* as they approached. Within minutes Thorne had them inside a utility hatch and dropped them onto the deck as the hatch slammed shut behind them. Renwick looked up just in time to see a blinding blue-white flash out of the utility hatch window. Thorne spread his android arms wide and threw his body over both men as the shockwave hit. It felt like they were inside the explosion itself as only Thorne's super-human strength allowed them to stay pinned to the floor. They were rocked for an interminable amount of time before the wave subsided.

Renwick flicked on his suit light. Thorne had frozen in place, his android weight dead on top of them. The two men struggled to get him off of them. When they had succeeded Renwick stood up. They were in a utility room, but around them, the *Kali* was completely dark and silent.

"My God," said Renwick. "The *Kali* is dead."

24.

The bridge of the *Kali* was dark and foreboding. Thorne had been down for almost five minutes before some unknown internal mechanism had reanimated him and he'd immediately begun the task of resuscitating the *Kali*. After following the android on his tasks for a few minutes Renwick and Kish had made their way through the vessel to the command bridge.

Deep blue emergency lights were the only illumination on the vast bridge of the *Kali*. Renwick had managed to stabilize the environmental systems while Kish was tending to Mischa and Reya in the safe room. He turned his attention now to the main view display, seeing if he could get a reading on the emitter station. The display crackled and then popped into focus, showing the station ominously still, dark and black, and dead as space itself. It was a sight that gave him some comfort, knowing that for now at least, the Void was no longer expanding for the first time in more than three centuries.

Kish came back on the bridge with Mischa in tow. "Reya is still in the auto-medic. I think she's doing better, but it's hard to tell," Kish said.

"Thanks for the update," said Renwick. He was concerned about his wife, but the comment was all he could manage under the circumstances. He nodded to Mischa as she came onto the bridge. "Nice to see you again Lieutenant Cain."

"Nice to be out of there, sir," she said.

"Please take the NAV station," he replied.

"Will do," she said, and took her seat.

Renwick turned to Kish. "I'll need you on the weapons station," he said. Kish pondered this a moment, arms crossed.

"I can probably pipe a sub-display for the engineering panels through to the weapons console," he said.

"Do it. I doubt we have much time before that Soloth fleet gets here," said Renwick. The lights on the bridge flickered for a moment at this, then came on full again.

"You have forty-seven minutes before the advanced elements of the invasion fleet arrive," said a familiar voice, echoing through the bridge. Renwick looked around. There was no one there.

"Who-" he started. The voice interrupted him again.

"There's no time for niceties, Senator. Look to your main display," said the voice. On the main display an image of Amanda was displayed in three dimensions. It spoke to him. "Thorne has reactivated me as a functional artificial intelligence for the *Kali*," she said. "I wish I could be there with you in full form, but this will have to do for now."

"We can use the help," said Renwick. The image of Amanda nodded.

"I am currently re-firing all of the *Kali's* main systems. You will have them operational in a short time. I am also making more systems available to you than before," she said.

"Weapons, I hope?" Renwick said. The image actually smiled.

"Oh yes," she said. "Torpedoes, multiple flak cannon batteries, a full compliment."

"Holy Ghost!" said Kish. "Sir, she's not kidding! We have forty flak batteries, and a hundred torpedoes!"

"Good," said Renwick. He turned his attention back to Amanda.

"I have also recalled the other two Void Ships," she said. "They will have the same compliment of weapons available as you do, and you will be able to use them in a full tactical formation. They're automated, and I've tied them into your main console, where you can dictate their actions." Renwick looked and saw a full display of military options for the two additional Void Ships come up on the main tactical board.

"But I'm not a military tactician!" he said to Amanda.

"Well, luckily, I am," said a voice from behind him. Renwick whipped around and once again came face to face with the *Kali's* former captain.

"Tanitha Yan at your service, Senator," she said.

"What the hell?" he said. He looked slightly down on her, like she was smaller than before.

"I had the androids on one of the other ships modify a body, download her persona into it, and send her over," said Amanda's voice from behind him. "I thought you might need her."

"That's true enough," said Renwick. Yan stepped up and surveyed the board. She touched the icons of the other two Void Ships and moved them to new locations.

"We'll need to triangulate on the tunnel, concentrate our fire on the incoming Soloth ships," she said. Renwick stepped up to the board.

"That's what I figured," he said, then drew new lines across the display with his index finger. "But with the scoop ships they'll be able to make tunnel branches from the main line, split their forces and overwhelm us."

"That would be my plan," Yan said, then cleared Renwick's lines from the display. "We'll have to counter it. One of the Void Ships will have to be constantly re-filling the mainline with void material, to keep their larger ships like the cruisers out of the fray as long as possible. That will be this one here, the *Devi*," she said, pointing to the one furthest from the station. "The *Balrama* will defend the station with us."

"I think you have things well in hand," said the Amanda AI. "If you'll excuse me, there are other things I need to attend to."

"Of course," said Renwick. "Thank you Amanda." With that the AI image disappeared. Renwick turned to Yan.

"I'm glad you're back," he said. He leaned in to kiss her but she pulled back.

"Not now, Senator," she said, but then she smiled. "Besides, they haven't have time to make all of my 'equipment' operational yet."

"I'll keep that in mind," he said. Then they both turned back to the board.

"Forty-two minutes to contact," came Amanda's disembodied voice over the main com.

"Right now we have work to do," Yan said, then started punching in commands to the console.

#

At the thirty minute mark the *Devi* started filling the normal-space tunnel with void material. The *Balrama* and the *Kali* had all their weapons charged and ready to go. Kish reported that all the systems aboard the *Kali* had returned to full functionality. After the *Devi* completed its patching of Void space Yan ordered the two automated Void Ships into a defensive formation around the emitter station. Now all they had left to do was wait.

"If it looks like we're going to fail then we have no choice, we can't let the station fall into Soloth hands," Yan said at the twenty minute mark.

"Agreed," said Renwick. "We'll have to hold back enough torpedoes to take out the station."

Yan shook her head. "Torpedoes won't do it, I'm afraid," she said. "I've ordered the *Balrama* to self-destruct on my order. We'll have about five minutes to clear the area. When she goes up it will clear an area half an AU across."

Renwick nodded. "If that's our only option," he said.

"It is," she replied, never taking her eyes from her board. She was fixated on the task at hand.

"I didn't expect to see you again, so soon at least," he said to her.

"Renwick-" she started. He held up his hand to her.

"Hear me out," he said, and held up the finger drive. "I have your stored persona, as up to date as it can be. Do you want it?"

"Yes," she said, and held out her hand. He handed it to her and she put it in a pocket in her uniform. "When this is over I'll look forward to the update. But right now I need to focus on the battle."

Renwick sighed. "I have to warn you, you may not like everything on the drive," he said. Now it was her turn to sigh.

"You found my body, didn't you? On the station, I mean," she said.

"Yes."

"Did I die heroically?"

A grim look came across his face. "Yes," he said.

"Then I'm satisfied," she said. "Like it or not, Renwick, this is the only life I have left. I want to live it for as long as possible. And right now that depends on beating that Soloth fleet." With that she walked off, ostensibly to check on Mischa Cain's station, but Renwick knew better.

"Eighteen minutes to contact," came Amanda's voice.

Renwick sighed heavily.

#

At the two minute mark the activity began.

"I'm detecting scoop energy signatures," called out Kish from the engineering station. With Yan aboard Renwick had taken over the weapons console, sending the engineer back to his regular station. "Multiple contacts. They've split their forces as we expected. Breakthrough to normal space at any time."

"They'll come with HuK's and destroyers first," said Yan. "Their scoop ships are small, so expect multiple contact points."

"Got it," said Renwick, already targeting multiple energy points with torpedoes. "I'm ready when you are."

"Wait for my order," said Yan. Renwick nodded. The energy signatures on his display suddenly multiplied exponentially.

"I've got dozens of new energy points forming!" he called to Yan. "Maybe as many as a hundred. I can't target them all!"

"Stay calm," said Yan. "They're likely punching through multiple points just to confuse us, so don't get confused. Stay focused and don't fire until you have actual contacts."

"Affirmative," said Renwick, trying to stay as calm inside as he was portraying himself on the outside.

"Tracking contacts now," said Mischa Cain. "Cruiser and heavy cruiser displacement! They have entered normal space."

"Concentrate on the heavy ships first, and fire!" ordered Yan.

"Firing all flak cannon batteries! Targeting cruisers with atomic torpedoes!" said Renwick excitedly, unable to hide his emotions any longer.

"There's too many cruisers," said Yan calmly, looking at her tactical console. "Hold your torpedo fire, Mr. Renwick. Flak cannon only. And I'm withdrawing the *Devi*," she said.

"That will open up the main tunnel for the rest of their fleet," said Renwick.

"I'm aware of that, *Senator*," Yan said back, with emphasis on his non-military rank. "But I can't risk losing her out in the open like that against those cruisers." Renwick watched as the automated Void Ship pulled back and took up a defensive position near the emitter station. "I'm deactivating her emitters and bringing her weapons online. I'll handle her from here." That was fine with Renwick, he had all he could handle with the *Kali's* weapons.

Ten minutes into the battle and the Soloth fleet had taken light damage, but they were making steady progress towards the emitter station. The *Kali* and her sister ships were mostly untouched, and holding back most of their torpedoes.

"Now counting thirty-four cruisers of various displacements in the battle zone," said Mischa. "Multiple energy signatures near the main tunnel portal, Captain. Breakthrough is imminent in three minutes."

"And when they break through that tunnel wall everything they've got will be in play," said Yan. "Destroyers, frigates, HuK's, you name it. It's a good tactic. We expected the lighter ships first. They came with the heavy stuff instead. Now when they break through it will the Death of a Thousand Cuts."

"Or a thousand stings," said Renwick.

Yan's clenched fist went to her hip. "Give me a report, Mr. Kish," she said.

"Shields and screens holding, sir," he said. "The cruisers are keeping their distance."

"Waiting for the breakthrough," said Renwick. "They don't have to engage at torpedo range. Hanging back like this they can take our flak cannon fire all day long."

"Thanks for the tactical update, Senator," snapped Yan. Renwick turned to her.

"If we don't take those cruisers out, or shore up that tunnel portal, we're doomed," he said. "We have to move the Void Ships closer. If the *Kali* and the *Balrama* move to torpedo range of those cruisers then the *Devi* can reinforce the tunnel and buy us some time."

"So suddenly now you're a tactician again? To what end, Senator? We can only engage so many cruisers without risking ourselves, and our goal is to defend the station, remember? They'll eventually free up some cruisers and take out the station. And without the station, it will take us a millennia to clear the Known Cosmos," she said.

"Do we have another option?" he asked.

"Breakthrough at the tunnel in two minutes," reported Mischa Cain.

Yan stared hard at Renwick. "Let's find out," she said.

"Amanda," Yan called out.

The Amanda AI appeared on the main display.

"Here, captain," she said, or rather, her disembodied transparent head said.

"Do we have any more weapons options?" said Yan.

"None that I am authorized to release to you," said Amanda.

"So that means yes," said Yan. "Amanda, I demand that you release all additional weapons to me."

"I cannot do that, Captain Yan," said Amanda. "My programmers explicitly forbid me from releasing certain technologies to Successor races, based on their likelihood of being abused."

Yan swiped her hand across the command console. Renwick's

weapons display and every other display on the bridge went blank.

"Weapons are down!" said Renwick.

"Navigation is out!" shouted Mischa. Kish came running over from his station.

"What just happened? The engines are down!" he said.

"And they'll stay down," said Yan.

"You have one minute, thirty seconds to the breakthrough," said Amanda, her imaginary face placid and unmoved.

"And I'd guess you have about two minutes beyond that before this ship and your precious station are destroyed. Now what would your programmers think of that?" Yan said to Amanda.

"All emotional outbursts and tactics have been accounted for in my programming. There is no scenario that you can present to me that I haven't already anticipated," Amanda said.

"Fine," said Yan. "Then that's what will be." She turned her back to Amanda and crossed her arms.

"Yan-" started Renwick, taking a step towards her. She held up her hand to him. He stopped.

"No," she said.

Amanda's face remained placid.

"Suicide is against most moral laws of your kind, and humans have a built in survival instinct that is stronger than almost any other drive they have," said Amanda, as if quoting an encyclopedia. Yan turned back to Amanda.

"I am not human anymore, remember? And if you want to test my resolve, you'll find out in about a minute," she said.

"One minute eight seconds," said Amanda. Yan turned away again. After ten seconds the Amanda AI looked to Renwick.

"Is she really capable of allowing this ship and the station to be destroyed?" she asked him. Renwick shrugged.

"I'm afraid I don't know her well enough to answer that," he said, then he took a calculated risk and also turned his back on Amanda. Ten more seconds of silence dragged on like an eternity.

"Very well," said Amanda, relenting. "There is one other weapon system I can make available."

Yan snapped around. "What is it?" she said.

"An anti-graviton field."

"Anti-*graviton*?" said Renwick, "You mean-"

"The field separates matter at the sub-atomic level by nullifying all of the effects of gravity within the field's range," said Amanda.

"What's the range?" asked Yan.

"Twenty kilometers from the station."

"It's on the *station*?" asked Renwick. "Is the system operational?"

"Yes," said Amanda. "But I will not make it available for your use as an aggressive weapon. Only to defend the station."

Renwick came and stood next to Yan, who quickly activated the command console again. She punched in some tactical calculations with blinding android speed. "If we move the automated Void Ships to take on the cruisers, we can close to firing range, release our torpedoes, and then come about and take on the destroyers and HuK's at the tunnel with our flak cannons." She looked up to Amanda. "And you'll agree to take out anything that gets within twenty kilometers of the station?"

"Yes," said Amanda.

"That's well outside torpedo range. They'll have to get within ten kilometers to launch," she said, her voice trailing off. Then: "Agreed," she said. "Stations everyone!" Amanda's image vanished.

"Wait," said Renwick. "A weapon like this, that can dissolve a person at the sub-molecular level-"

"Save your conscience for another day, Senator. We have a battle to win," said Yan.

"I am in command of this mission, captain, not you," he reminded her. She glared at him.

"Forty seconds," said Amanda in her disembodied voice.

"Then command it, Senator. Do we have another choice?" Yan said. Renwick looked around the bridge at Yan, Mischa, Kish, and he thought of Reya, helpless in the auto-medic.

"No," he conceded. "Let's do this."

25.

Void Space near the tunnel warped and bended, threatening to break, releasing the Soloth fleet into the bubble of normal space surrounding the emitter station.

"Thirty seconds," called Mischa Cain from navigation. Renwick watched the macabre scene on his display, watching as the two divergent forms of space fought to occupy the same position in the universe. Only one could win and Renwick knew which one.

"Ten seconds," called Mischa.

Renwick watched as the *Devi* and *Balrama* closed to torpedo range on the Soloth cruiser formation. The *Kali* hung back a few kilometers, waiting for an opportune moment to launch a torpedo volley and then turn to attack the support ships that would undoubtedly be coming through the tunnel portal at any moment.

Suddenly the tunnel wall gave way.

"Breakthrough!" called Mischa. Renwick expected to see a swarm of war ships appear in the portal opening linking the tunnel to the normal space bubble. He was shocked at what he saw instead.

"Soloth Command ship at the tunnel opening!" he called. "I say again, Soloth Command ship has breached the bubble!"

"Shit," said Yan, whipping around to scan her tactical console. The main display showed a multi-decked ship with a menacing looking tail, likely a heavy coil cannon. Yan swept over the scan a second time. "They're holding back the small fry. Forcing us to take on their heavy ships with our torpedoes. I should have seen this coming," she said, then smacked the console with her hand.

"Orders?" asked Mischa. Yan's eyes whipped over the display.

"Maintain course and speed," she said. "Engage enemy cruisers with a single volley of torpedoes, then make for the Command ship. The *Devi* and *Balrama* will follow us."

"Just a single volley?" asked Renwick. "We can't guarantee we'll get them all." A single volley from each of the three Void Ships would result in about thirty torpedoes hitting the cruiser formation. Not enough, considering they were spread out behind a unified energy defense field.

"Goddamn you Renwick! Can't you just follow my orders once without questioning?" demanded Yan. It was true, he admitted to himself, he couldn't.

"Captain, on this mission it is my job to function as the ship's exec. Therefore it is also my job to bring you alternatives," he said.

"Ten seconds to firing range," said Mischa.

"I appreciate your input, Mr. Renwick, however-"

"However, thirty torpedoes will not be enough to disable that cruiser formation, captain," he said.

Yan looked at him angrily. "I'm aware of that," she said. "We'll need the rest of the torpedoes to use against the Command ship. Amanda will have to handle the cruisers. Now, will you carry out my orders?"

Renwick contemplated the Soloth crew aboard the cruisers, knowing they were being doomed to a horrible fate at the hands of the anti-graviton field. He hated the choices they had.

"Preparing the volley, captain," he said. She nodded.

"Coordinate with my board. Follow the volleys of the *Devi* and *Balrama* by ten seconds. Just long enough to make them think they survived the first shot," she said.

"Aye captain," he replied, his eyes glued to his display console.

The two automated Void Ships launched their volleys simultaneously, then broke off, their vector taking them away from the Soloth cruiser formation. The ten seconds of waiting was an eternity.

Renwick targeted a dense pack of nearly twenty cruisers furthest from the emitter station. The first volleys from the Void Ships would damage them. His follow-up volley would likely destroy many more than the ten ships he targeted.

The first volleys slammed into the approaching cruisers, their coil cannon fire ineffective in stopping the shielded torpedoes. Nuclear-thermal fire lit up the dark normal space bubble as explosions ripped through energy defense fields and melted the hulls of many of the ships. The initial volleys had been spread out to do maximum damage. Renwick watched as the second wave from his volley hit the dense pack of Soloth cruisers.

The resulting flash of the near-simultaneous explosions lit his display to the point that he lost both his tactical and visual feeds for a few moments. The display then corrected itself. The *Kali* was already breaking off her attack run and making for the Soloth Command ship.

"Tactical report, Amanda," Yan called. Amanda's voice echoed through the bridge.

"Twenty-one cruisers destroyed or permanently disabled," she said. "Four enemy cruisers damaged beyond their capability to fight. Nine cruisers still operational and making course for the station."

Renwick shook his head as she watched the two fleets diverge, the Void Ships to engage the Soloth Command ship; the cruisers to certain death at the hands of the anti-graviton field.

"They're all yours now," said Yan.

"Understood," replied Amanda.

#

Seven minutes later and the Soloth Command ship was entering firing range of the trio of Void Ships. The smaller ships of the Soloth fleet; HuK's, destroyers, and frigates, were hanging back, waiting in the tunnel to make their runs once the heavy weapons fighting was over. The Soloth cruisers were three minutes out from the emitter station.

"Triangular formation," ordered Yan. "The *Kali* will take the point."

"Understood, captain," said Mischa.

"Mr. Kish, I'll need all the power you have. We'll have to punch a hole through her energy shields to get under her and fire our torpedoes," she said.

"Affirmative captain, " said Kish. "I'll have one-hundred percent power available to the forward coil cannon batteries."

"That's you, Mr. Kish. Mr. Renwick," said Yan, turning to the Senator. "We'll need sustained, concentrated coil cannon fire while we try and bust her shields. Once we're through, you'll have to switch off the cannon and launch your torpedo volleys before they have a chance to target us with <u>their</u> torpedoes."

"That's assuming they don't get us with their cannon fire first," said Renwick.

"That's my job, keeping us away from the cannon batteries," Yan said.

Renwick nodded acknowledgement. He looked up to watch the progress of the Soloth cruiser fleet. Unknown to them, they would be entering range of the anti-graviton field in slightly less than three minutes, and facing annihilation.

"What do you think the Soloth commanders will do when they see their cruisers cease to exist?" Renwick asked Yan privately over the com.

"Launch everything at us. At least, that's what I'd do," she said.

"And we'll be out of torpedoes and they'll outgun us with coil cannon fire by a wide margin," he said.

"Assuming their Command ship has similar armament to our ships of the same class, we can survive their torpedo volleys due to our superior shielding. But their energy weapons will wear us down. We'll eventually have to retreat to the station, behind the anti-graviton field," she said.

"Stalemate," was his response. There was a pause on the line.

"That may be the best we can hope for." Then she cut the personal line between them and called out "Stations!" for all to hear. It wasn't really necessary, but it did help them all to focus on the job at hand.

"We are within firing range of the Soloth Command ship," said Mischa.

"Commence firing, Mr. Renwick. Coil cannon fire concentrated on my coordinates," ordered Yan. Renwick saw the coordinates as they fed into his console, and he rigged and fired the coil cannon. The cannons of both the *Devi* and the *Balrama* also fired simultaneously with him. The three ships maintained their firing angles even as they passed under the enormous Command vessel. The Soloth ship responded with similar weaponry. They stayed together like this, locked in combat, their weapons pounding at each other, each looking for the breakthrough that would tip the scales.

"Their anterior shielding is collapsing!" called Mischa from her station. "We're through!"

"Advance and volley, Mr. Renwick!" said Yan. "Fire at will!"

Renwick switched off the coil cannon and brought his volley of torpedoes online. It took him only a second to launch.

"Torpedoes away!" he said. His volley was followed by similar shots from both the *Devi* and the *Balrama*. The torpedo volleys were countered by flak batteries from the Soloth Command ship, hundreds of orange lancets streaming out to take on the incoming missiles. The torpedoes bobbed and weaved, some even taking hits on their energy screens, but deflecting them away. One or two had their screens overloaded by multiple hits and were destroyed in bright nuclear fireballs while they were still kilometers from their target, but most of them got through.

The Command ship was enveloped in bright white light.

"Multiple hits!" called Mischa as Renwick loaded a second volley.

"Amanda," said Yan.

"Reporting," came Amanda's voice. "Defense capabilities of the Command ship depleted by twenty-one percent."

"That's not enough," said Yan. "Renwick-"

"Second volley away!" called the Senator from his station. Just then the tactical alarm went off. Renwick checked his board. "Multiple torpedoes and interceptors inbound!" he reported.

"So they do have another line of defense," said Yan as she watched her tactical display. This time the interceptors and flak batteries got nearly half the incoming torpedoes before they detonated.

"Command ship still sixty-five percent operational," reported Amanda in her monotone after the volley. Then: "Soloth cruisers entering range of the station's anti-graviton field." It was a simple statement.

"Amanda," said Yan. "If you can hold off using your weapon until the last possible moment, it will give us a slight tactical advantage. If the Soloth commanders think they can withstand our barrage and take out the station at the same time, they'll likely hold back their support ships."

"Understood," said Amanda. Renwick watched as the Soloth cruisers passed into the twenty kilometer range of the anti-graviton field. They likely wouldn't be able to launch until they got within ten kilometers. Renwick turned his attention to the incoming Soloth torpedoes, taking out the missiles with his own flak cannon batteries. He quickly switched back to loading the torpedo launchers.

"I'll have another torpedo volley ready in ten seconds," he told Yan.

"Hold your station," she said, her hand whipping over her console. Abruptly a new display popped up on Renwick's board.

"What do you make of that?" she asked. Renwick looked at two protruding anterior lobes on the underside of the Command ship.

"I'm no engineer," he said.

"I am," said Kish. "Captain, I'd make those for hydrazine fuel tanks, or possibly atomic waste storage, or diffusers."

"A design flaw, then. And in any of those cases, the contents would be highly volatile," she said.

"Agreed," said Kish.

"Mr. Renwick, hold back your torpedo volley. I'm taking the *Kali* in close. Prepare to fire your forward coil cannon on my command," said Yan.

"Yan, how close?" he said.

"Point blank range," she replied.

Renwick took in a deep breath, then switched systems. "Ready when you are captain," he said. Right on time the two automated Void Ships fired their torpedo volleys, but the *Kali* broke away, making a run for the fuel tanks as the Soloth defenders pelted her shielding with flak.

"Multiple interceptors fired at us, Captain!" said Renwick, watching as his screen filled with a swarm of the unmanned fighters.

"Keep us on course, Mischa," said Yan, oblivious to the chaos around her as the *Kali's* run exposed her mid-ship to the enemy. Alarms went off as the interceptors and flak batteries did their damage. The *Kali* stayed true to her run, and Renwick focused on his target.

"Three more seconds, Mr. Renwick… two… one… now! Fire the cannon!"

Renwick fired the heavy coil cannon as orange fire leapt out from the belly of the *Kali*, striking the exposed tanks and igniting a huge fireball in an instant.

"Get us out of here Mischa!" called Yan over the din of incoming flak, interceptor explosions against the *Kali's* hull, and the sound of alarm claxons blaring. The *Kali* rocked as the Soloth Command ship exploded in flames, many of her decks spewing out escape pods as she listed disastrously from the damage.

"From the size of that explosion, I'd say we got her hydrazine store," commented Kish from his engineering station.

"Soloth Command ship is at thirty-eight percent efficiency," came Amanda's voice over the din.

"That will give them something to think about," said Yan.

"She's still got her stinger, sir," reminded Kish from his station. "That cannon is plenty to fire back with if she wants."

"Reform the fleet," said Yan. "Get some distance between us and the Command ship, back towards the station," she said to Mischa.

"Will they bring in the support ships now?" asked Renwick. Yan nodded.

"Likely, after that bloody nose we just gave them," she said.

"Captain," said Mischa. "You should look at this. The cruisers are approaching the emitter station."

Renwick moved from his station to stand next to Yan, watching the main display. It showed the flotilla of nine Soloth cruisers closing to firing range on the station.

"They're locking torpedoes on the station," reported Mischa.

"They just signed their death warrant," said Renwick. They watched together as the lead cruiser closed on the station. Suddenly a wave of white energy swept out from the station, quickly enveloping the lead ship, then two more. It was like watching them turn to glittering dust in an instant. Seconds later the plasma wave spread over the remaining cruisers, enveloping them. Then the space around the station was empty. Renwick looked away.

"Soloth cruiser fleet eliminated, Captain Yan," said Amanda's voice, ringing hollow through the now-quiet bridge of the *Kali*. "The rest of this battle is now up to you," she finished, then was gone. Renwick walked away from Yan.

"We had to do it," Yan said to him as he went. "We had no choice."

"Yes," he agreed without turning back.

"And now they'll come at us with everything they have."

#

Renwick watched on his tactical display as the Soloth Command ship struggled to right herself. Now left bereft of any heavy fleet support, the hundreds of support ships came swarming through the tunnel opening towards the Void ships and the station like angry bees.

"We'll beat them back to the emitter station," reported Kish.

"Yes, but what will we do when we get there?" said Renwick. "We can stay behind our trench lines. They won't come close because of the anti-graviton field. But we can't win from there either."

"We'll have to engage them as best we can," said Yan. Renwick looked at her, standing next to his weapons console.

"These ships are from another time, and made for heavy fighting. If we try and take on those support ships, they'll cut us to pieces. Oh, it will take time, but they'll do it," he said.

"Do you have another goddamned idea?" she demanded. He shook his head.

"No," he admitted. He checked his monitor, watching as the support ships spread out like a gray cloud against a dark sky, an incoming swarm. "Let's get this over with," he said.

"Mischa," said Yan, "bring us about to face the Soloth formation."

"Aye, Captain," said Mischa.

The small formation closed on the Soloth swarm as the minutes sped by. Renwick recharged the flak cannon batteries, just about the only useful weapon against the smaller displacement ships of the Soloth fleet. Torpedoes would likely just fly right through the formation, the HuK's, destroyers, and frigates being too swift and maneuverable for the torpedoes to track accurately. The main coil cannon would be equally useless, like trying to smash a flea with sledgehammer.

The *Kali* and the two automated Void Ships slammed into the forward lines of the Soloth swarm.

"Keep us moving, Mischa. Do not stop to engage, and keep us well back from that Command ship," said Yan. "Mr. Kish, when my shield power gets below thirty percent I want to know about it. Mr. Renwick, lock your batteries and engage the enemy at will."

"Yes Captain," said Renwick. He set the flak battery trackers on auto-fire. They would stay in this mode, automatically tracking and firing at the support ships, unless he chose to override the system and take manual command. Somehow that didn't seem likely as the auto-fire systems could track and hit the support ships with far more accuracy than he could. Set like this the flak batteries were basically defensive weapons. It was their one advantage, Renwick thought, knowing the Soloth had to attack to complete their mission.

The batteries opened up, firing a series of strafing barrages at the swarming enemy. Some shots found their targets, but all too few to make a significant difference. Eventually the batteries would burn through too much of the *Kali's* energy. Then they would have to withdraw to the station, and the stalemate would ensue.

Thirty minutes into the battle and the neither side had gained an advantage.

"Something has to change," said Renwick out loud, more out of frustration than anything else.

Then something did.

"Captain Yan," said Mischa, "I'm picking up more scoop signatures! Or rather, one more scoop signature. It's near the station."

"Show me," said Yan. If this was some rogue element of the Soloth fleet, there was no doubt Amanda would disassemble their atoms as soon as they appeared in normal space. The scoop signature pulsed with a dim golden glow against space, then suddenly burst open, clearing a channel into normal space.

"They're only twelve kilometers from the station," said Mischa.

"Amanda will handle them," said Yan, turning back to her console, not willing to watch sentient beings, even adversaries, be separated from their atoms one at a time.

"One scoop ship, Soloth configuration," reported Mischa. Renwick looked at his board. There were more ships coming through the tunnel opening.

Cruisers.

"We've got more cruisers!" he called from his station. This got Yan's attention and she switched her monitor to visual mode from tactical.

"That opening's barely big enough for cruisers!" she said. "How did they manage that?"

Renwick eyed his board again. "They're moving away from the station. Coming in towards our position," he said calmly. Then he noticed something else. "Wait, these cruisers… something isn't right, their operating frequencies are off… configuration is… these are-"

Before he could finish the main com system snapped on with an incoming message.

"Void Ship *Kali*, this is Ambassador Makera. Raelen fleet is joining the battle. I repeat, Raelen fleet is joining the battle."

"But if Amanda thinks they're Soloth ships-" started Renwick.

"Not to worry, Senator," came the android's disembodied voice. "I have already identified the Raelen cruisers as allies."

"Thank you," he said.

"Mischa, contact Makera and let her know they are free to engage any ships at will," said Yan. Mischa acknowledged and sent the communication.

"You wanted something to change, Senator. It looks like we may not have a stalemate after all," she said to Renwick. He turned back to his station

"Thank god for that," he said under his breath.

Fifteen minutes later and all twenty-nine cruisers of the Raelen fleet had come through the scoop opening single file, with bare meters to spare. It was an impressive display of manual flying, and discipline. The Raelen were quickly on top of the engagement, scattering the support ships, pushing them into range of the Void Ship's flak batteries, and even taking occasional potshots at the Soloth Command ship.

"Things have turned in our favor," said Yan.

"Finally," agreed Renwick.

Then they turned again.

"Captain," said Mischa from her station, a tone of alarm in her voice. "I'm picking up some strange readings from the Command ship." Renwick immediately turned to his board.

"Confirmed," he said. "I'm reading multiple internal explosions aboard her. Overloads, internal dampening fields breaking down… it's like… like she's imploding."

"Order the Raelen fleet to break off the attack!" said Yan, alarm in her voice. "Move this ship away from the Soloth, *now* Mischa!"

Renwick watched his visual display as the Command ship belched out escape pods and lifeboats, hundreds of tiny specks fleeing from the mother vessel. Suddenly a small ship, the size of a command yacht, broke away from her, then turned to flee the battle, speeding away from the fleet.

"Are the Raelen withdrawing?" demanded Yan.

"Affirmative," said Renwick. "But a small ship, a command yacht or frigate, escaped and is heading back through the tunnel." He looked at Yan.

"Zueros," she said, practically spitting out his name. They shared a look of recognition, then an alarm took Renwick back to his display.

The Soloth Command ship collapsed in upon itself, deck after deck breaking down and falling inward. A monstrous explosion blew the ship to pieces, enveloping a large portion of the remaining Soloth fleet in atomic destruction.

"She's gone," said Yan. After a long moment of silence on the bridge she spoke to Mischa.

"Send out a general surrender call. I assume they have translating equipment on board. And suspend the attack. Began rescue and recovery operations," she said.

"Yes, Captain Yan," said Mischa.

With that, Captain Tanitha Yan turned away from the command console and headed for the galley.

#

Two days later and Renwick had completed the surrender negotiations with the surviving Soloth fleet captain, a woman named Kai'Ina. He was glad to be back in a more familiar role, that of diplomat, and privately he wished he would never see battle again.

The Soloth themselves looked very much like Zueros, though Renwick doubted anything about him, most especially his appearance, could be trusted. They had light gray to white hair mostly, with some darker gray mixed in, and crimson tinged skin. Other than these obvious differences they appeared very much like the rest of the Successor races.

Kai'Ina revealed what Yan and Renwick had suspected, that Zueros had portrayed himself as a representative of the Preservers to gain their trust and had convinced her government that the other Successor races were an enemy who had created the 'other Void'.

"What 'other Void'?" Renwick had asked. The one that had encompassed Soloth space for the last three centuries, Kai'Ina explained. Their systems were far enough distant that the Void surrounding the Soloth home world wasn't even visible from the Known Cosmos. Nonetheless, Zueros had convinced her government that the Void was an attack by the other Successor races, and had managed to gather the fleet to bring it across vast space to attack the emitter station, all for his own purposes. When all was settled it turned out the Soloth, the Unity, the Gataan, and the Raelen had much more in common than not.

On the third day after the battle Kai'Ina and the surviving Soloth fleet members, less than a thousand out of nearly ten thousand souls, were allowed to make their way home on their remaining ships, but without their weapons at Makera and Yan's insistence.

Kai'Ina agreed to carry an offer of a diplomatic mission from the races of the Known Cosmos to the Soloth home world, though she did not promise how it would be received.

Renwick had to be satisfied with that.

EPILOGUE

Senator Tam Renwick looked up to the starry sky of a tropical evening on the Raelen home world of Raellos, savoring a local alcoholic drink that tasted very much like brandy. The day had been a successful one, what with the signing ceremony of the treaty between the Terran Unity and the Raelen Empire finally concluded.

They had been forced to rewrite the treaty, the original diplomatic pouch having gone missing somewhere amongst all the adventures he and Ambassador Makera had been on. He thought perhaps that was a good thing. The original treaty had been almost one hundred pages; the new one, less than ten. But the new treaty covered all the significant points; free access to Thousand Suns Space, joint colonies, trade, relief efforts, relocation, forward bases and the like, and that's what really mattered.

He took another drink as the door chime in his quarters tolled gently, signifying an arrival. He knew who his impending guest was, and although he wasn't as excited about it as he once might have been, his heart still jumped, just a bit, at the sound.

He opened the door and welcomed Ambassador Makera to his quarters. After a few moments of niceties he got her a matching drink and she joined him on his balcony, her brightly colored dress flowing in the evening breeze.

"You have a beautiful view of the city from here," she said as she sat down at his table and contemplated her drink. He looked out over the distant skyline, lit now with beautiful amber lights and accented by the dual orange moons of Raellos.

"You're right, I do," he said before sitting down across from her.

"But you've hardly noticed," she said. He nodded.

"My mind is on the stars," he admitted.

"Your mind is on Captain Tanitha Yan," she said. He nodded again.

"You may be right." Then he raised his glass. "May I suggest a toast? To the successful signing of the treaty of Pentauri." She raised her glass, but didn't join him in the drink.

"Is something wrong?" he asked. She shook her head.

"No, everything is perfect." Then she leaned forward, putting her hand on his arm. "You miss her already don't you? Barely more than a month away from her and you're already heartsick for your android lover. Aren't my attentions enough to soothe you?"

Renwick smiled. "Such as they are," he said.

"And they've taken your Gataan wife from you to," she said. He laughed.

"She's in diplomatic training," he said.

"Still, you must be lonely."

He looked up to the stars, wondering where in the Known Cosmos the *Kali* might be right now.

"A bit," he admitted.

"We'll be back up there, soon enough. You'll be back aboard the *Kali* on your diplomatic mission to the Soloth and I will be with you, if they let me go," she said. He looked puzzled.

"Why wouldn't they let you go?" he said.

She tipped her head at him, avoiding the question. "And did your government approve the mission yet?" she said, changing the subject.

"I'm sure they will. It's merely a formality. Now, tell me, why wouldn't they let you join the mission to the Soloth with me?" he asked again. She brushed him off with a pleasant smile, then stood and went to the balcony railing, looking out over the capital city of her home world. He joined her.

She pointed to the dark spot blotting out a third of the heavens over Raellos.

"Someday I will tell my daughter about the days of the Void, when we were all threatened with doom, and she will not believe me," Makera said.

Renwick looked at her, puzzled. Makera continued.

"With the emitter station operational again, breaking up the Void instead of filling it, with the fleet of Void Ships cutting trade routes back and forth between neighboring stars, you and I will live to see a Golden Age reborn, and our daughter, she will get to live in it," said Makera.

Renwick looked at her, not sure if he had heard her correctly.

"Did you say… *our* daughter?" he said.

Makera turned to him and smiled impishly.

"*Our* daughter, Renwick. *Our* child," she said. "The firstborn of

Humanity and Raelen, conceived within the Void itself."

He smiled, pleased. "So, my… donation took?"

"Human doctors said it wasn't possible, Renwick, but Raelen doctors aren't bound by human limitations." Then she took his hand and guided it to her belly. It was soft and warm to his touch.

"Are you happy?" she asked, looking for the moment as vulnerable as he had ever seen her. He answered by kissing her sweetly.

"Very happy," he said. Then, "So that's why you think they won't let you travel?"

She laughed. "They cannot stop me, Renwick. You cannot stop me. If the Soloth agree to receive us, I'm *going*," she said. Renwick shook his head and drained his drink.

"I don't know how I'm going to explain this to Yan," he said. Makera shrugged.

"Probably the same way you explained to her that you had a wife," she replied.

"And we all know how well that went," he said.

Then she laughed again, and Renwick laughed with her.

After the moment passed he kissed her on the cheek, the future mother of his child, something he never thought he would experience. He looked down at his empty glass. "I think I'm going to need something stronger than this," he said, and started for the bar.

And she laughed with him once more, the sound of their joy echoing into the warm, dark night.

ABOUT THE AUTHOR

GENE DAVID is the pen name for Seattle based science fiction writer Dave Bara, author of The Lightship Chronicles series (IMPULSE, STARBOUND, DEFIANT) from DAW Books.

You can find Dave on the web at www.davebara.info, on Facebook, and on Twitter as @davebarawriterguy.

Made in the USA
San Bernardino, CA
10 April 2018